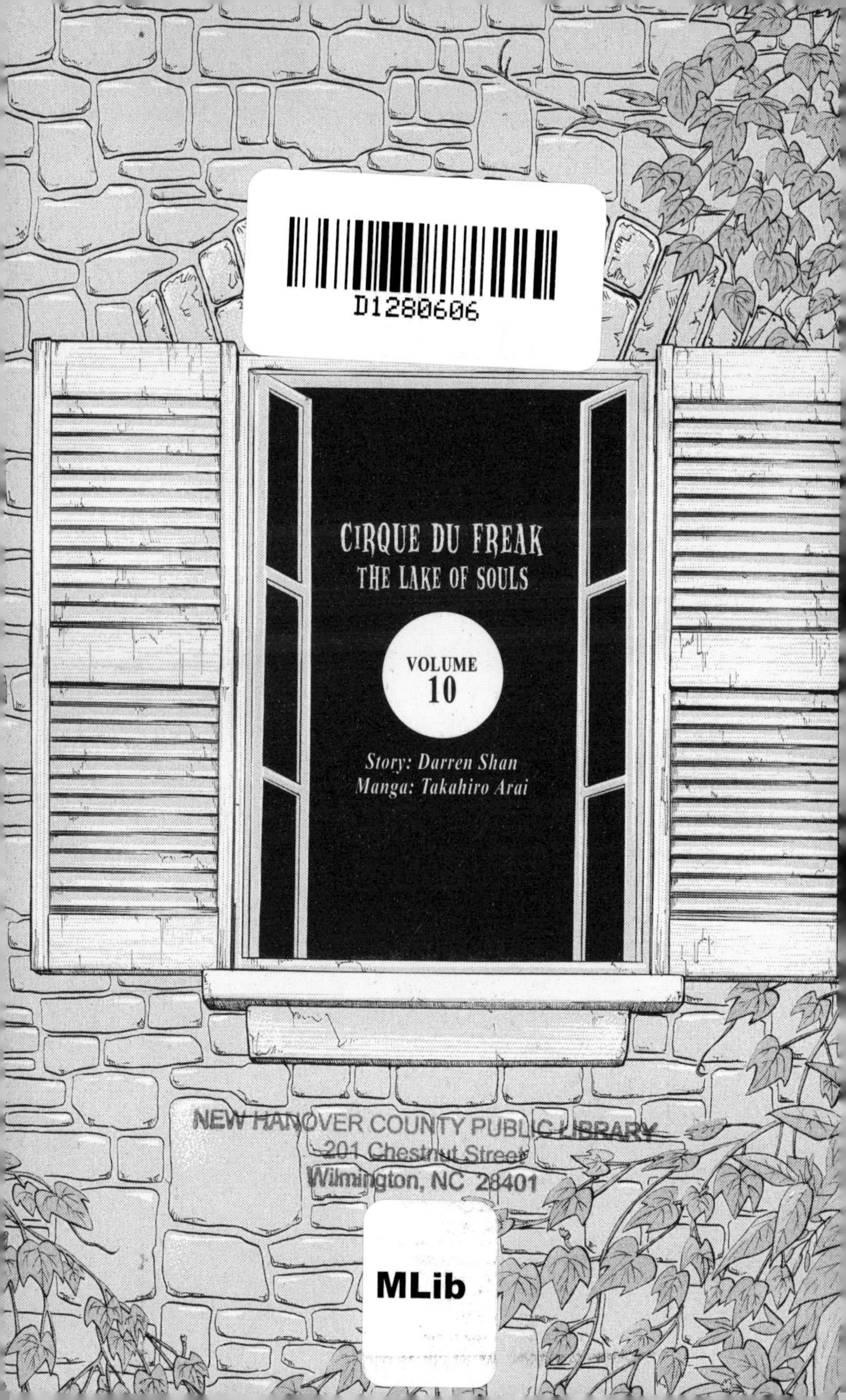
CIRQUE DU FREAK
THE LAKE OF SOULS
VOLUME
10
Story: Darren Shan
Manga: Takahiro Arai

A SUMMARY OF *KILLERS OF THE DAWN*:

DESPITE BEING PREOCCUPIED BY THE SCHEMES OF HIS OLD FRIEND STEVE (NOW HALF-VAMPANEZE), DARREN PREPARES FOR THE BATTLE WITH HIS ULTIMATE FOE, THE LORD OF THE VAMPANEZE. WHEN THE TIME ARRIVES, MR. CREPSLEY ENTERS COMBAT WITH THE ENEMY AND SUCCEEDS DESPITE THE TERRIBLE ODDS. IN ORDER TO SAVE THE LIVES OF HIS FRIENDS, THE VAMPIRE CHOOSES HIS OWN DEATH. REELING WITH THE SHOCK OF LOSING HIS FRIEND AND TEACHER, DARREN UNCOVERS THE TERRIBLE TRUTH: THE REAL VAMPANEZE LORD IS NONE OTHER THAN STEVE*!!* HOW WILL DARREN RESPOND TO THESE OVERLAPPING NIGHTMARES...?

CIRQUE DU FREAK 10
CONTENTS

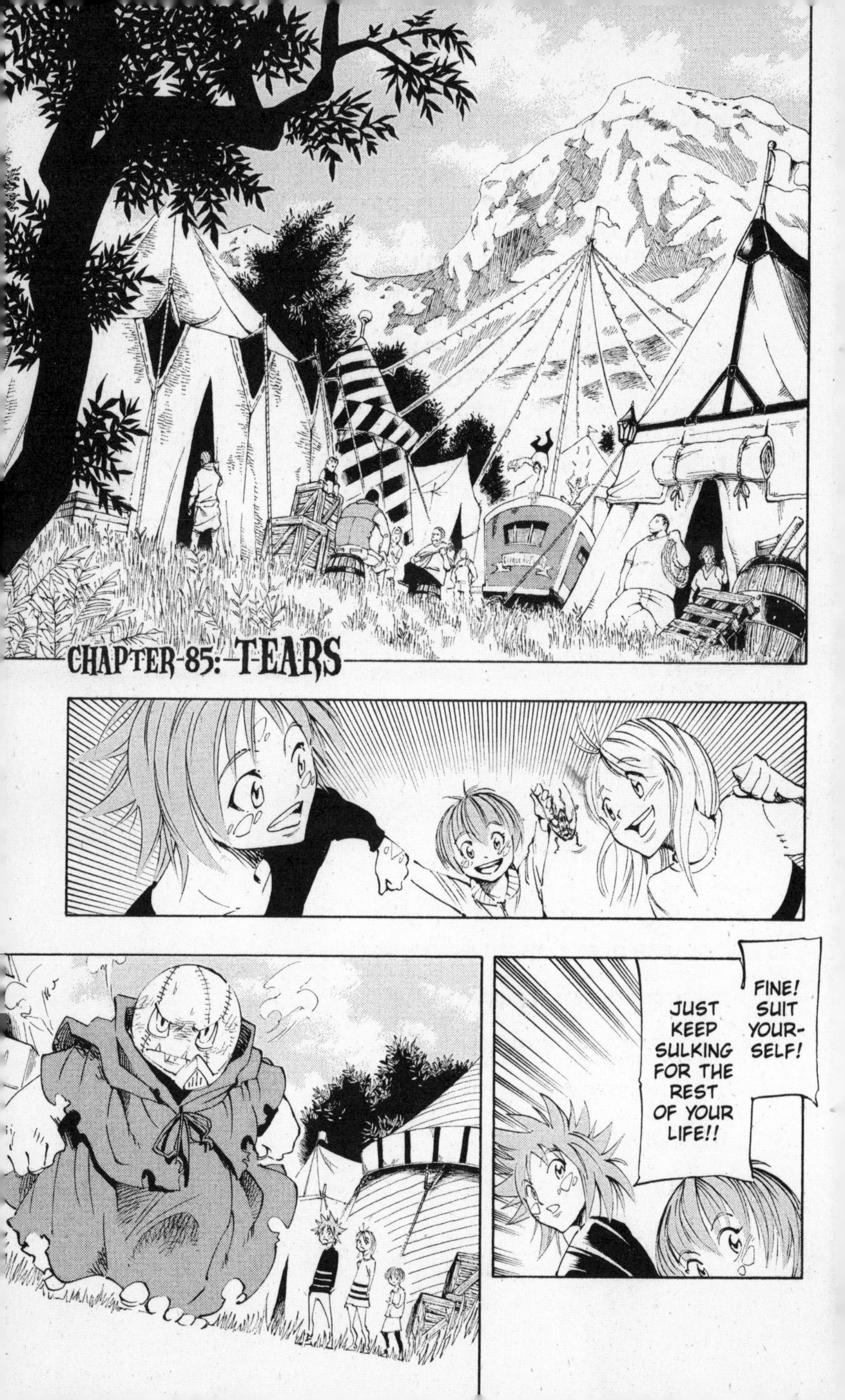
CHAPTER 85: TEARS
FINE! SUIT YOURSELF! JUST KEEP SULKING FOR THE REST OF YOUR LIFE!!

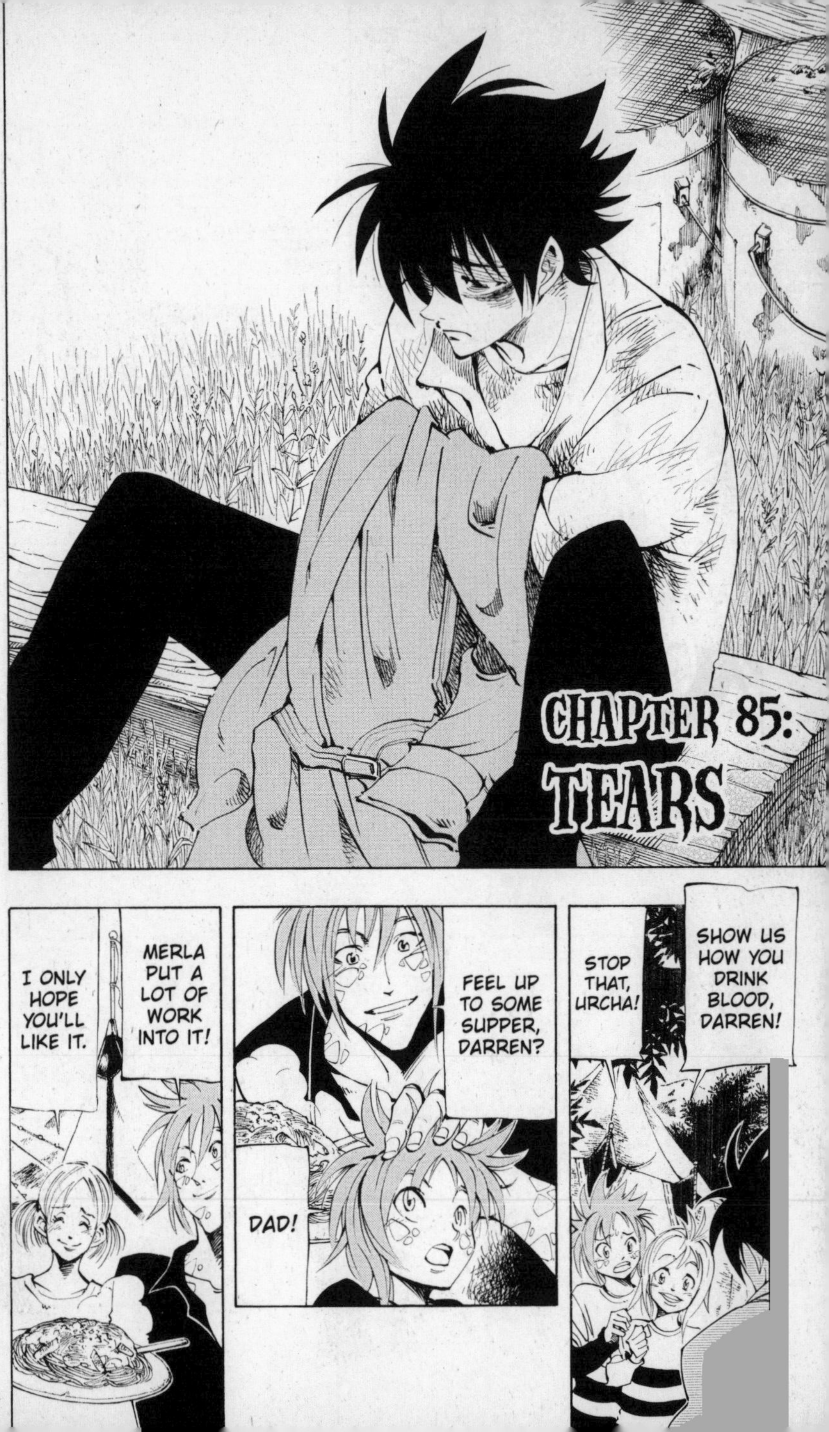
CHAPTER 85: TEARS
SHOW US HOW YOU DRINK BLOOD, DARREN!
STOP THAT, URCHA!
FEEL UP TO SOME SUPPER, DARREN?
DAD!
MERLA PUT A LOT OF WORK INTO IT!
I ONLY HOPE YOU'LL LIKE IT.

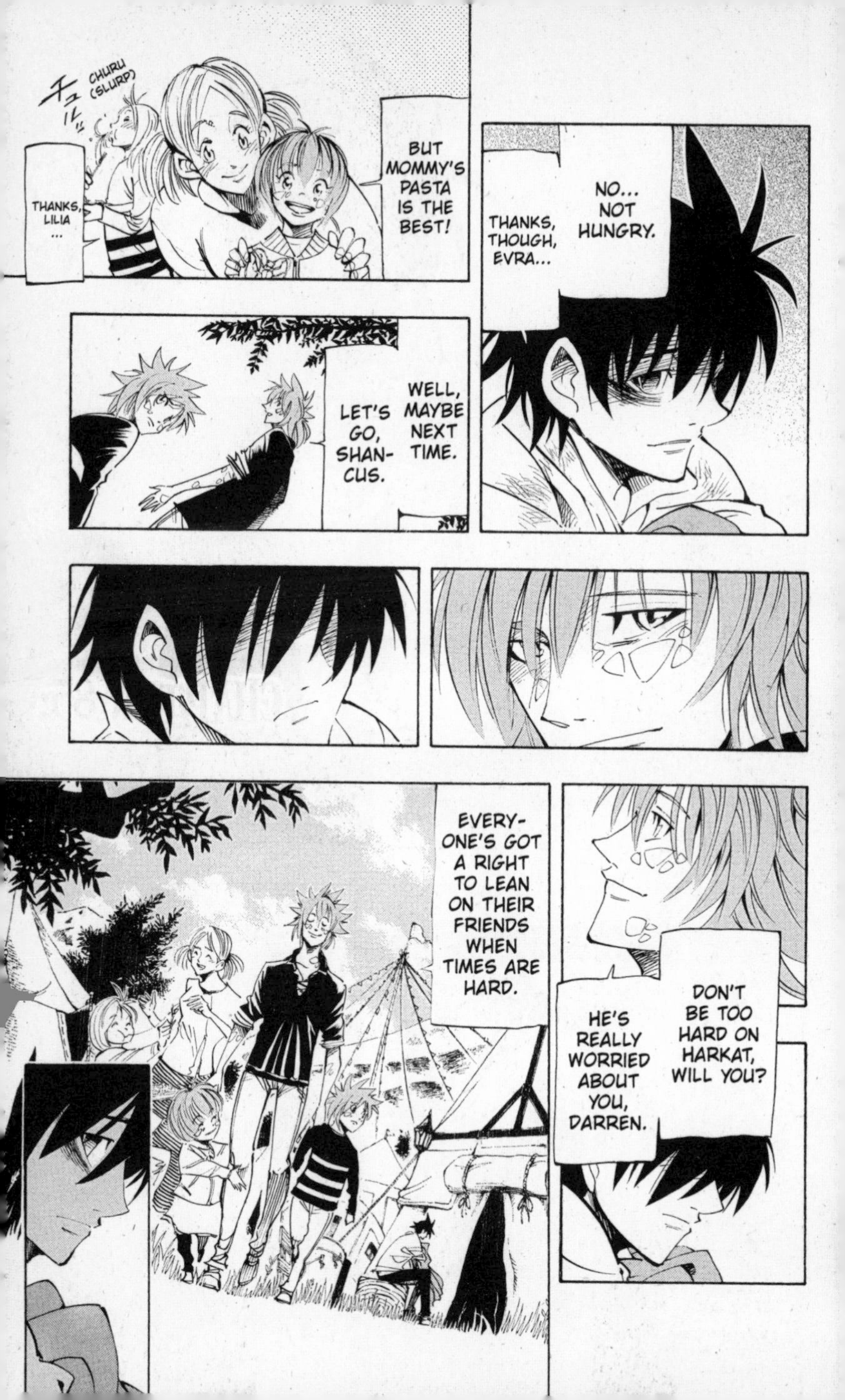
BUT MOMMY'S PASTA IS THE BEST!
CHURU (SLURP)
THANKS, LILIA ...
NO... NOT HUNGRY.
THANKS, THOUGH, EVRA...
WELL, MAYBE NEXT TIME.
LET'S GO, SHAN-CUS.
DON'T BE TOO HARD ON HARKAT, WILL YOU?
HE'S REALLY WORRIED ABOUT YOU, DARREN.
EVERY-ONE'S GOT A RIGHT TO LEAN ON THEIR FRIENDS WHEN TIMES ARE HARD.

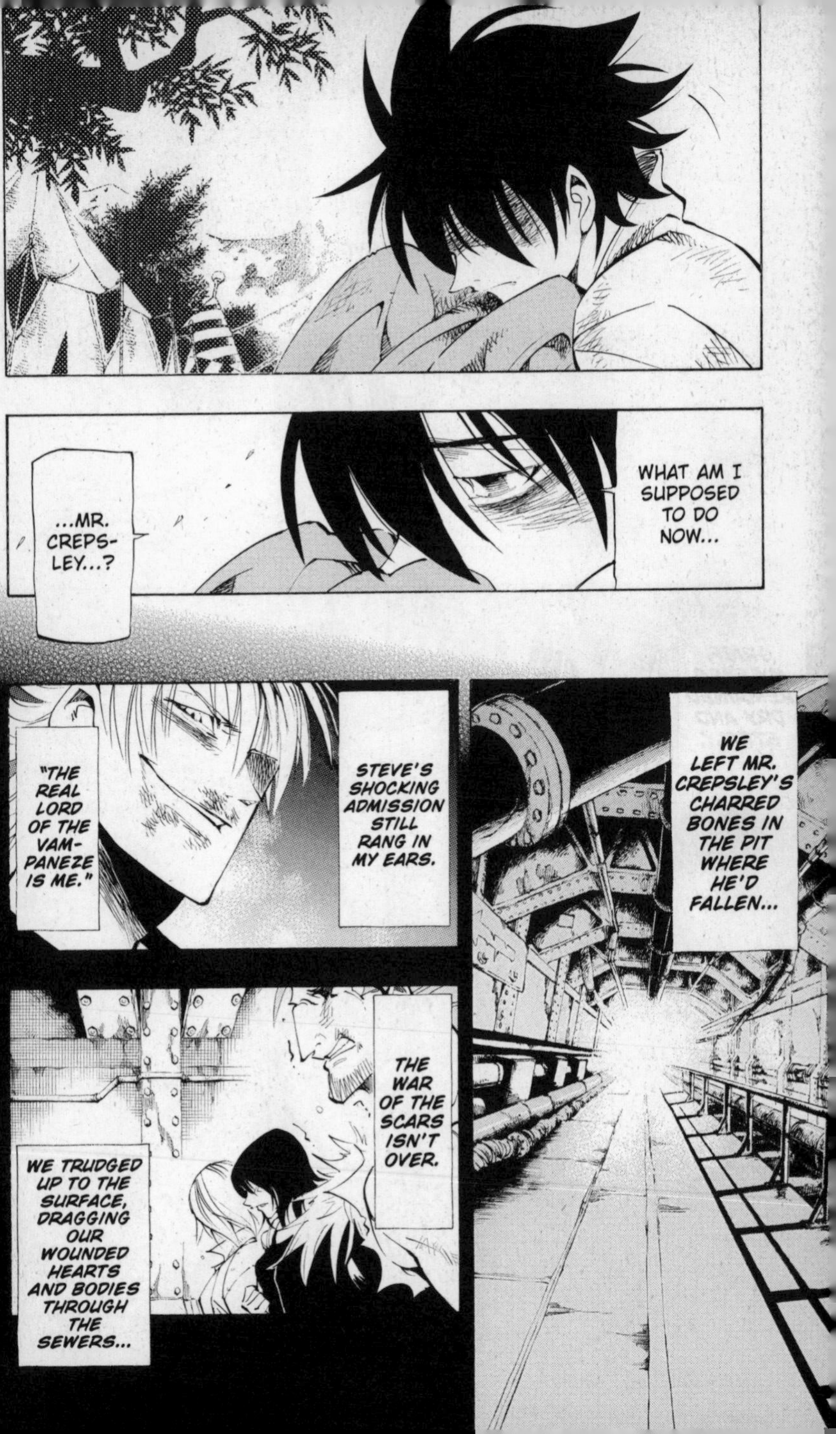
WHAT AM I SUPPOSED TO DO NOW...
...MR. CREPSLEY...?
WE LEFT MR. CREPSLEY'S CHARRED BONES IN THE PIT WHERE HE'D FALLEN...
STEVE'S SHOCKING ADMISSION STILL RANG IN MY EARS.
"THE REAL LORD OF THE VAMPANEZE IS ME."
THE WAR OF THE SCARS ISN'T OVER.
WE TRUDGED UP TO THE SURFACE, DRAGGING OUR WOUNDED HEARTS AND BODIES THROUGH THE SEWERS...

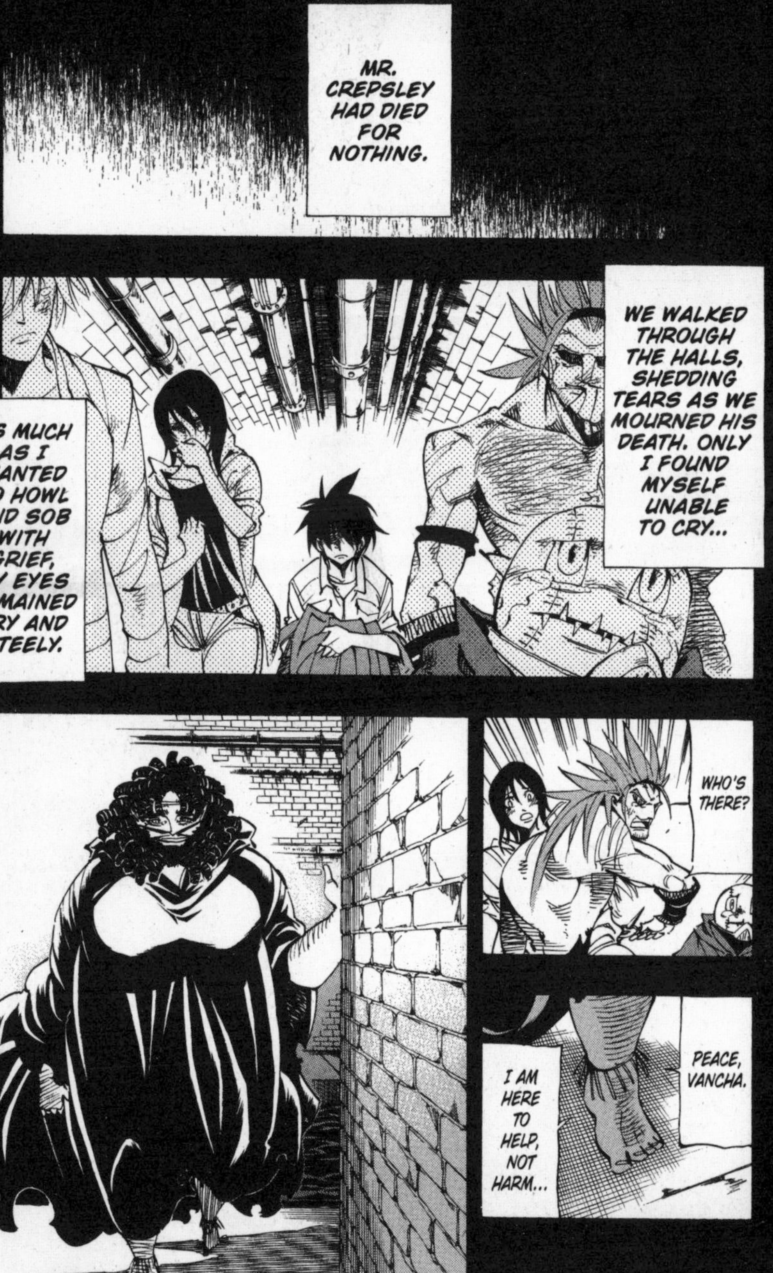
MR. CREPSLEY HAD DIED FOR NOTHING.
WE WALKED THROUGH THE HALLS, SHEDDING TEARS AS WE MOURNED HIS DEATH. ONLY I FOUND MYSELF UNABLE TO CRY...
AS MUCH AS I WANTED TO HOWL AND SOB WITH GRIEF, MY EYES REMAINED DRY AND STEELY.
WHO'S THERE?
PEACE, VANCHA.
I AM HERE TO HELP, NOT HARM...

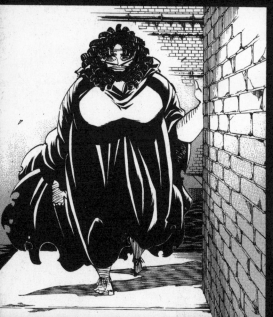

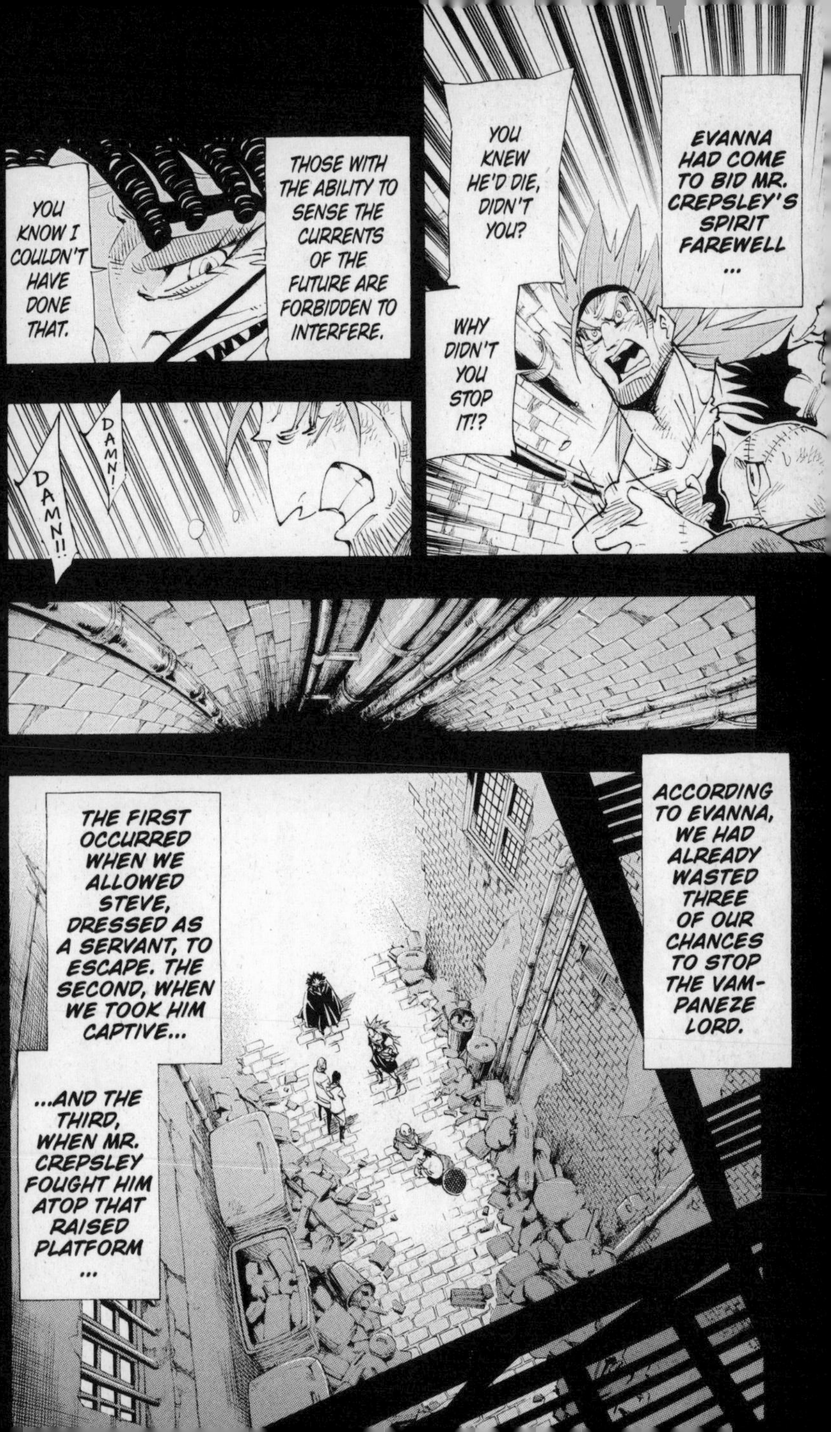
EVANNA HAD COME TO BID MR. CREPSLEY'S SPIRIT FAREWELL...
YOU KNEW HE'D DIE, DIDN'T YOU?
WHY DIDN'T YOU STOP IT!?
THOSE WITH THE ABILITY TO SENSE THE CURRENTS OF THE FUTURE ARE FORBIDDEN TO INTERFERE.
YOU KNOW I COULDN'T HAVE DONE THAT.
DAMN!
DAMN!!
ACCORDING TO EVANNA, WE HAD ALREADY WASTED THREE OF OUR CHANCES TO STOP THE VAMPANEZE LORD.
THE FIRST OCCURRED WHEN WE ALLOWED STEVE, DRESSED AS A SERVANT, TO ESCAPE. THE SECOND, WHEN WE TOOK HIM CAPTIVE...
...AND THE THIRD, WHEN MR. CREPSLEY FOUGHT HIM ATOP THAT RAISED PLATFORM...

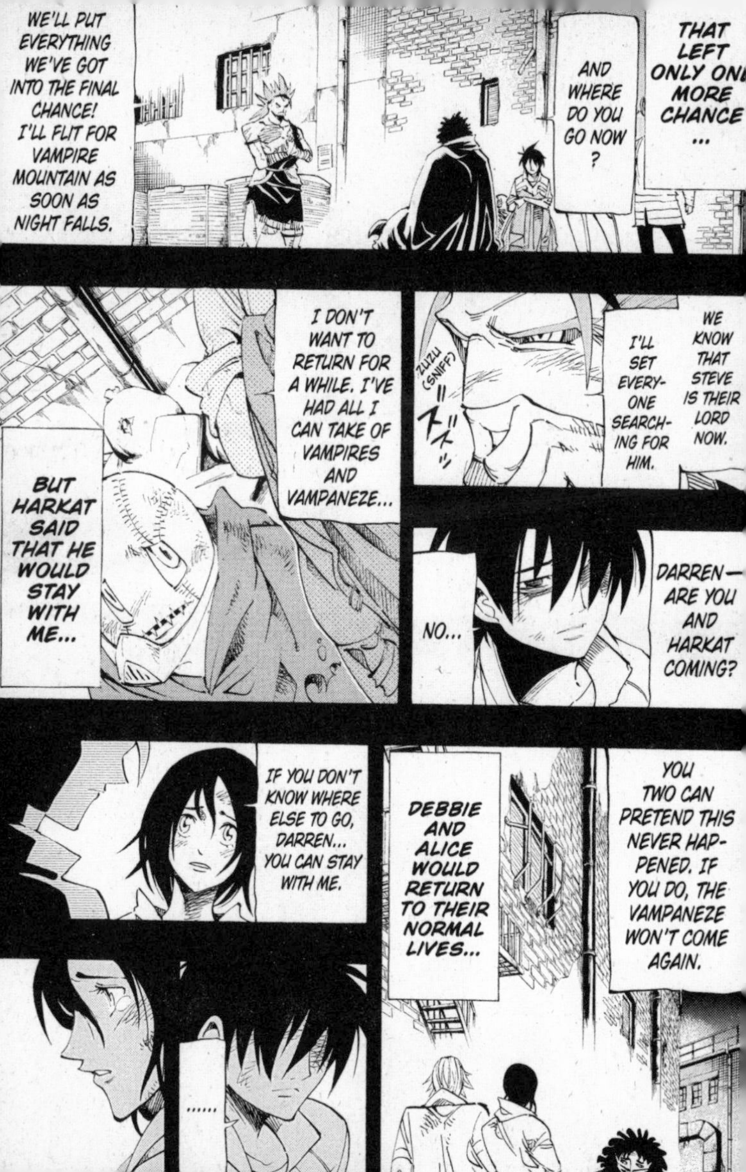
THAT LEFT ONLY ON MORE CHANCE ...
AND WHERE DO YOU GO NOW ?
WE'LL PUT EVERYTHING WE'VE GOT INTO THE FINAL CHANCE! I'LL FLIT FOR VAMPIRE MOUNTAIN AS SOON AS NIGHT FALLS.
WE KNOW THAT STEVE IS THEIR LORD NOW.
I'LL SET EVERY-ONE SEARCH-ING FOR HIM.
ZUZU (SNIFF)
DARREN— ARE YOU AND HARKAT COMING?
NO...
I DON'T WANT TO RETURN FOR A WHILE. I'VE HAD ALL I CAN TAKE OF VAMPIRES AND VAMPANEZE...
BUT HARKAT SAID THAT HE WOULD STAY WITH ME...
YOU TWO CAN PRETEND THIS NEVER HAP-PENED. IF YOU DO, THE VAMPANEZE WON'T COME AGAIN.
DEBBIE AND ALICE WOULD RETURN TO THEIR NORMAL LIVES...
IF YOU DON'T KNOW WHERE ELSE TO GO, DARREN... YOU CAN STAY WITH ME.
......

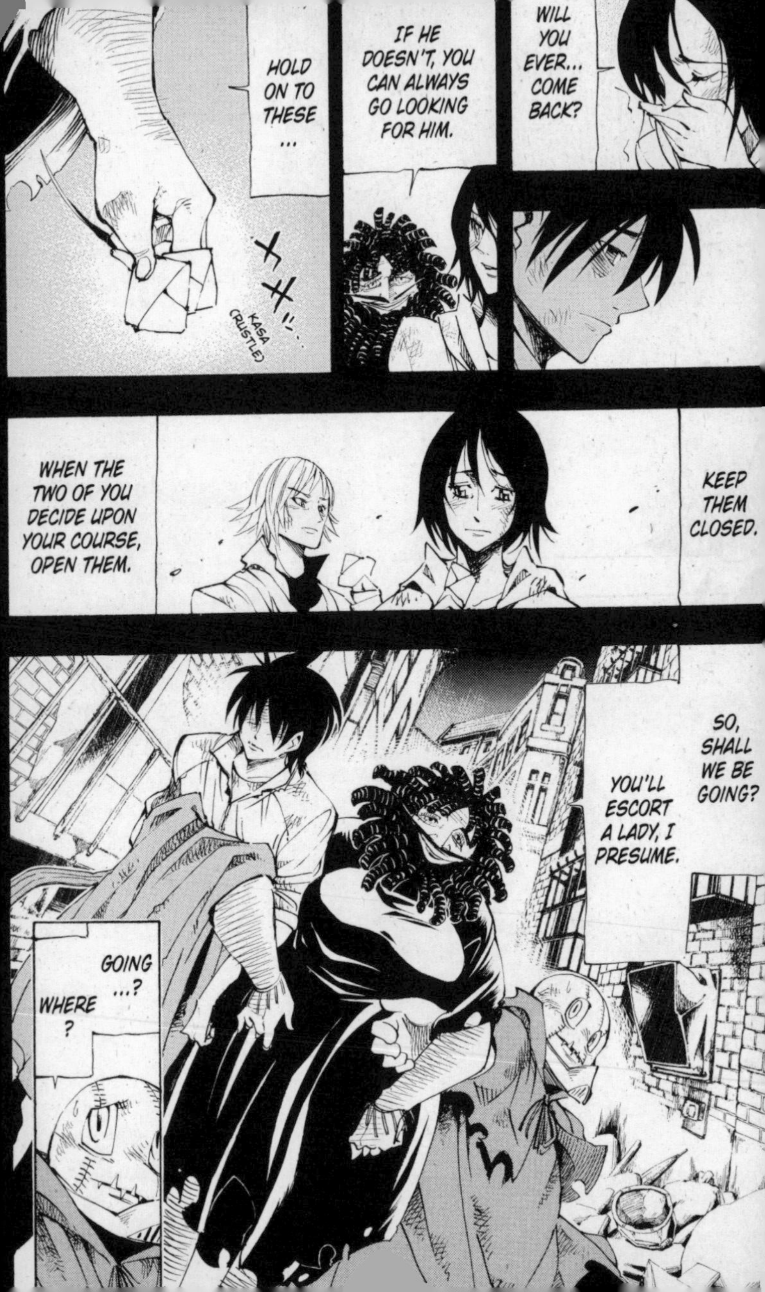
WILL YOU EVER... COME BACK?
IF HE DOESN'T, YOU CAN ALWAYS GO LOOKING FOR HIM.
HOLD ON TO THESE ...
KASA (RUSTLE)
KEEP THEM CLOSED.
WHEN THE TWO OF YOU DECIDE UPON YOUR COURSE, OPEN THEM.
SO, SHALL WE BE GOING?
YOU'LL ESCORT A LADY, I PRESUME.
GOING ...?
WHERE ?

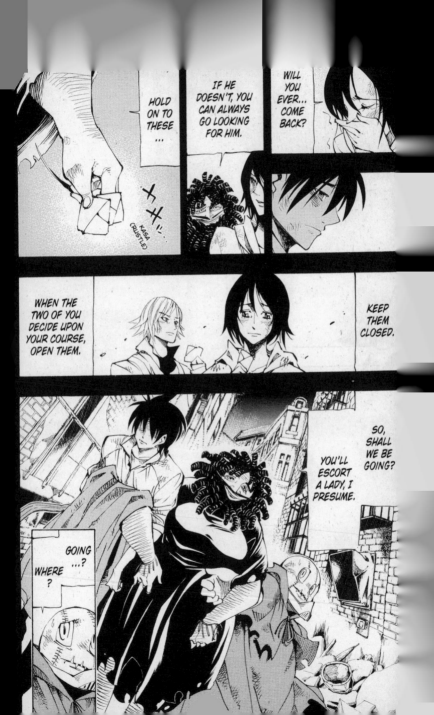

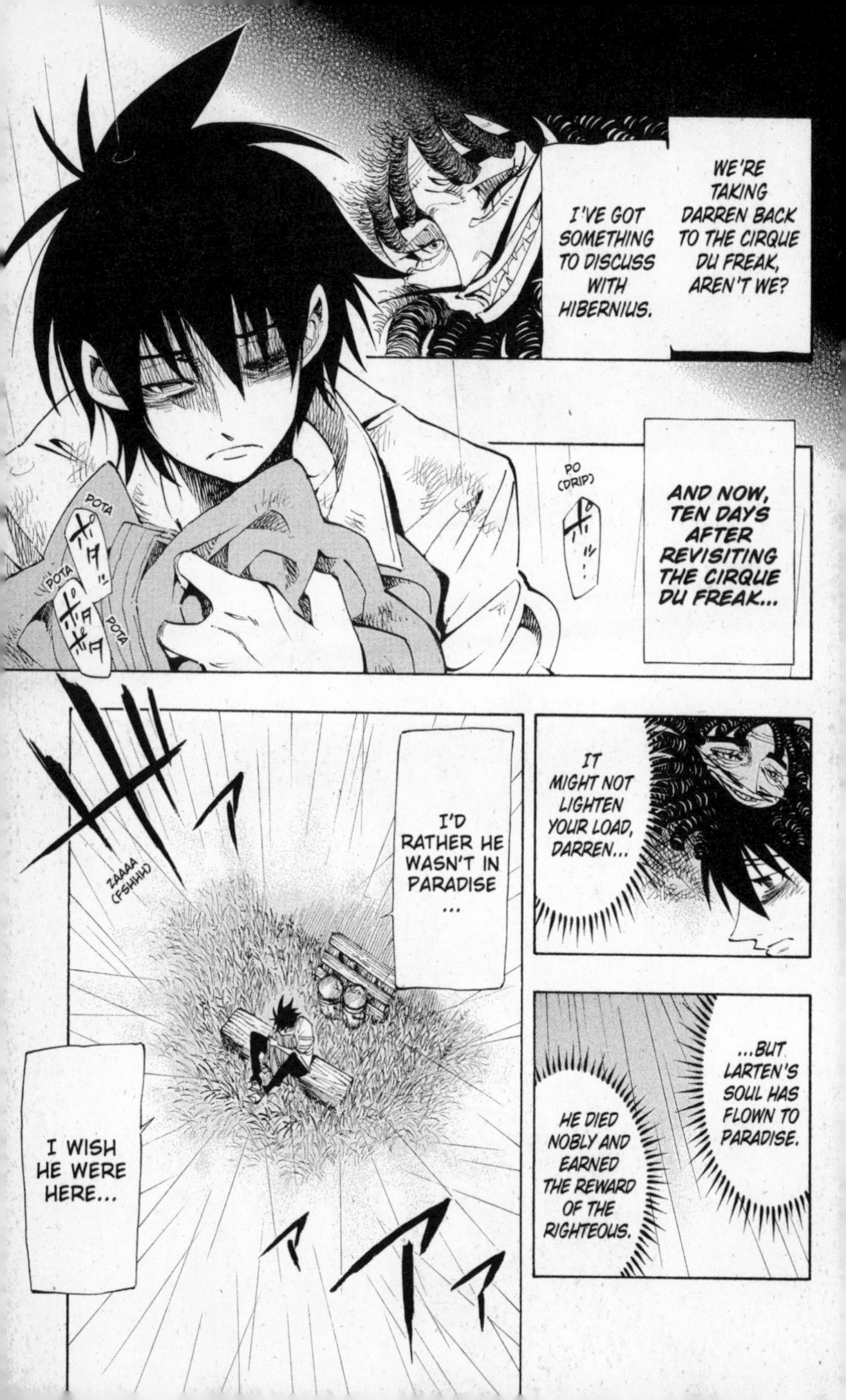
WE'RE TAKING DARREN BACK TO THE CIRQUE DU FREAK, AREN'T WE?
I'VE GOT SOMETHING TO DISCUSS WITH HIBERNIUS.
AND NOW, TEN DAYS AFTER REVISITING THE CIRQUE DU FREAK...
PO (DRIP)
POTA
POTA
POTA
IT MIGHT NOT LIGHTEN YOUR LOAD, DARREN...
...BUT LARTEN'S SOUL HAS FLOWN TO PARADISE.
HE DIED NOBLY AND EARNED THE REWARD OF THE RIGHTEOUS.
I'D RATHER HE WASN'T IN PARADISE...
ZAAAA (FSHHH)
I WISH HE WERE HERE...

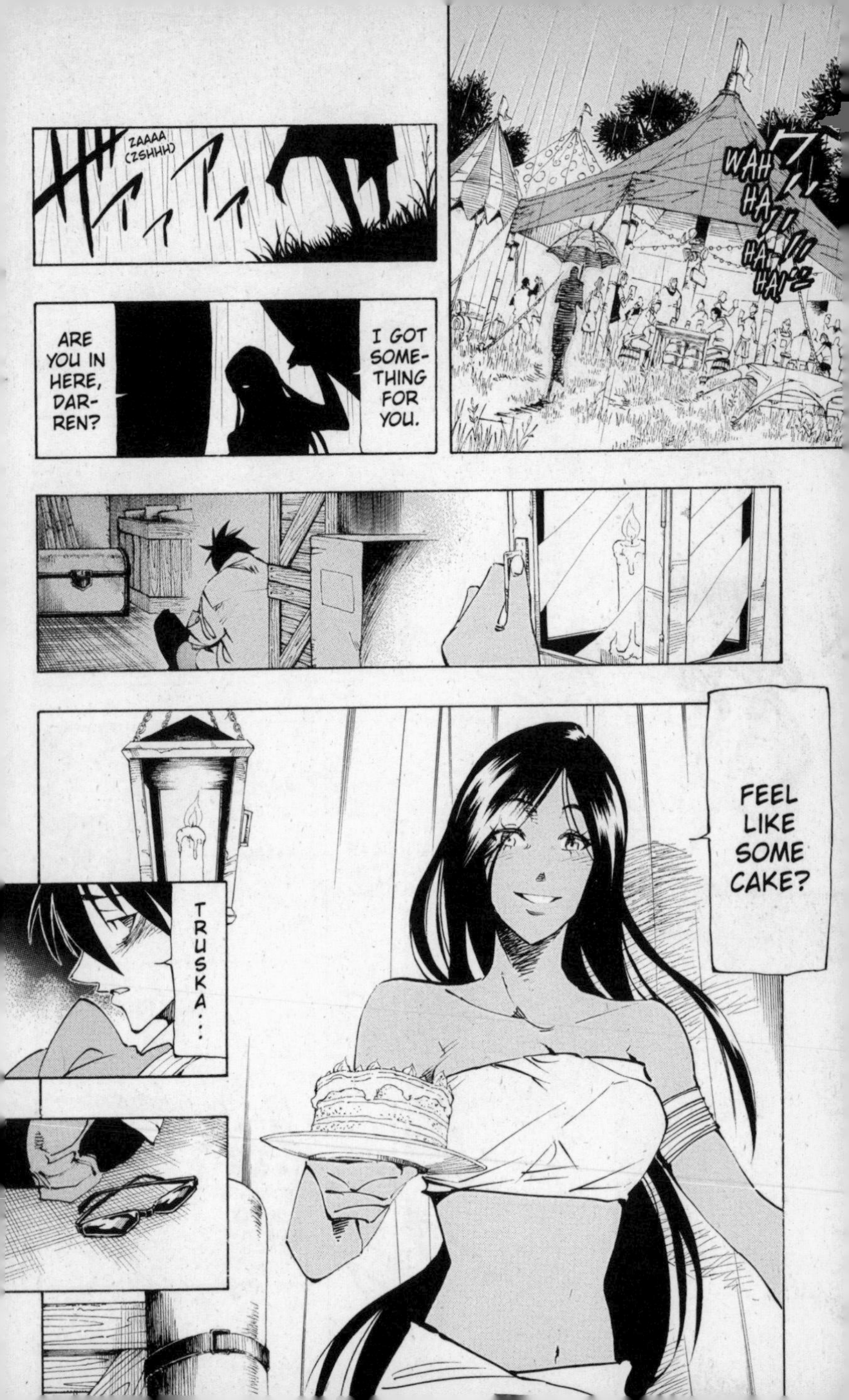
WAH HA HA HA!
ZAAAA (ZSHHH)
I GOT SOME-THING FOR YOU.
ARE YOU IN HERE, DAR-REN?
FEEL LIKE SOME CAKE?
TRUSKA...

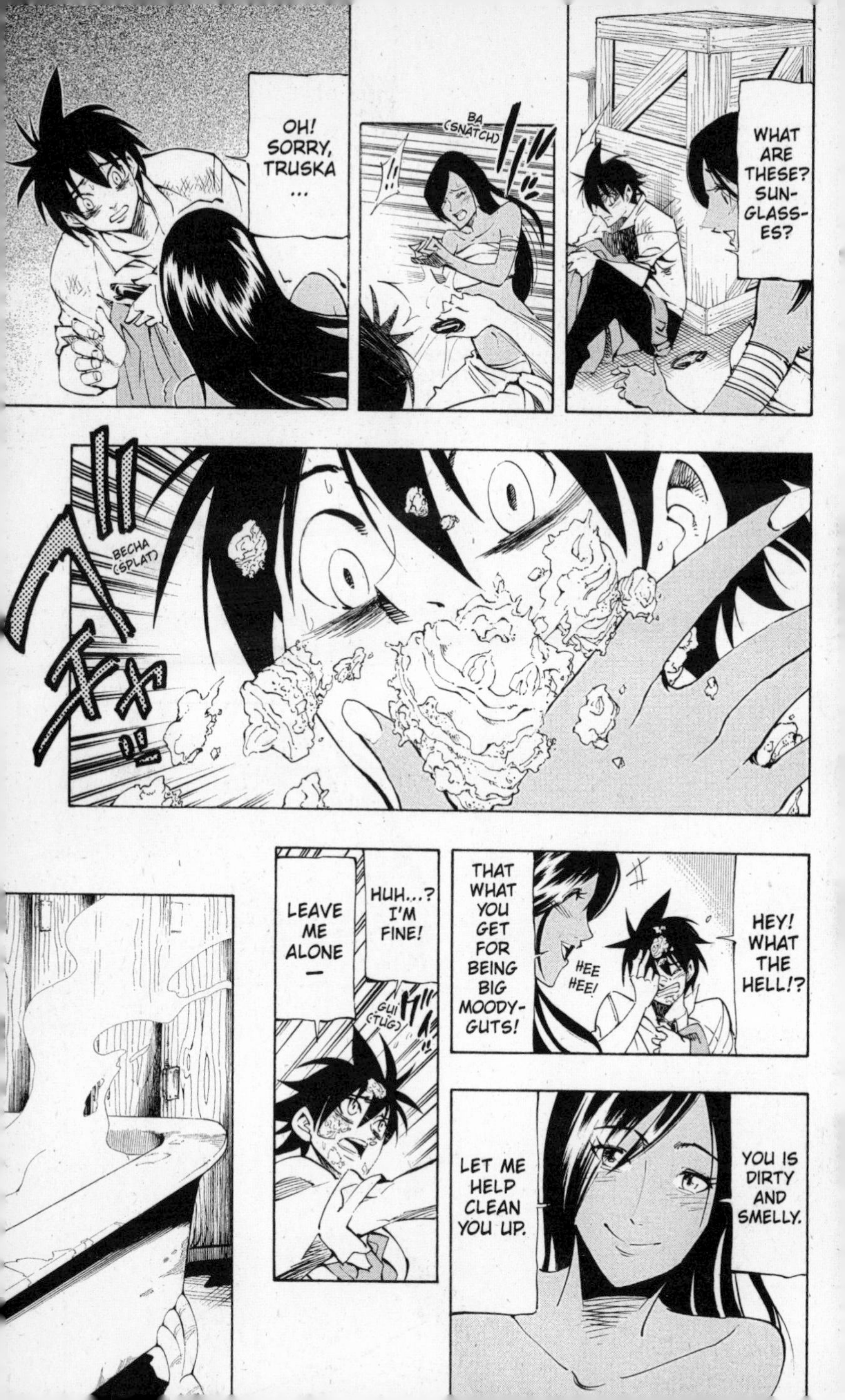
WHAT ARE THESE? SUN-GLASS-ES?
BA (SNATCH)
OH! SORRY, TRUSKA ...
BECHA (SPLAT)
HEY! WHAT THE HELL!?
THAT WHAT YOU GET FOR BEING BIG MOODY-GUTS!
HEE HEE!
YOU IS DIRTY AND SMELLY.
LET ME HELP CLEAN YOU UP.
HUH...? I'M FINE!
LEAVE ME ALONE —
GUI (TUG)

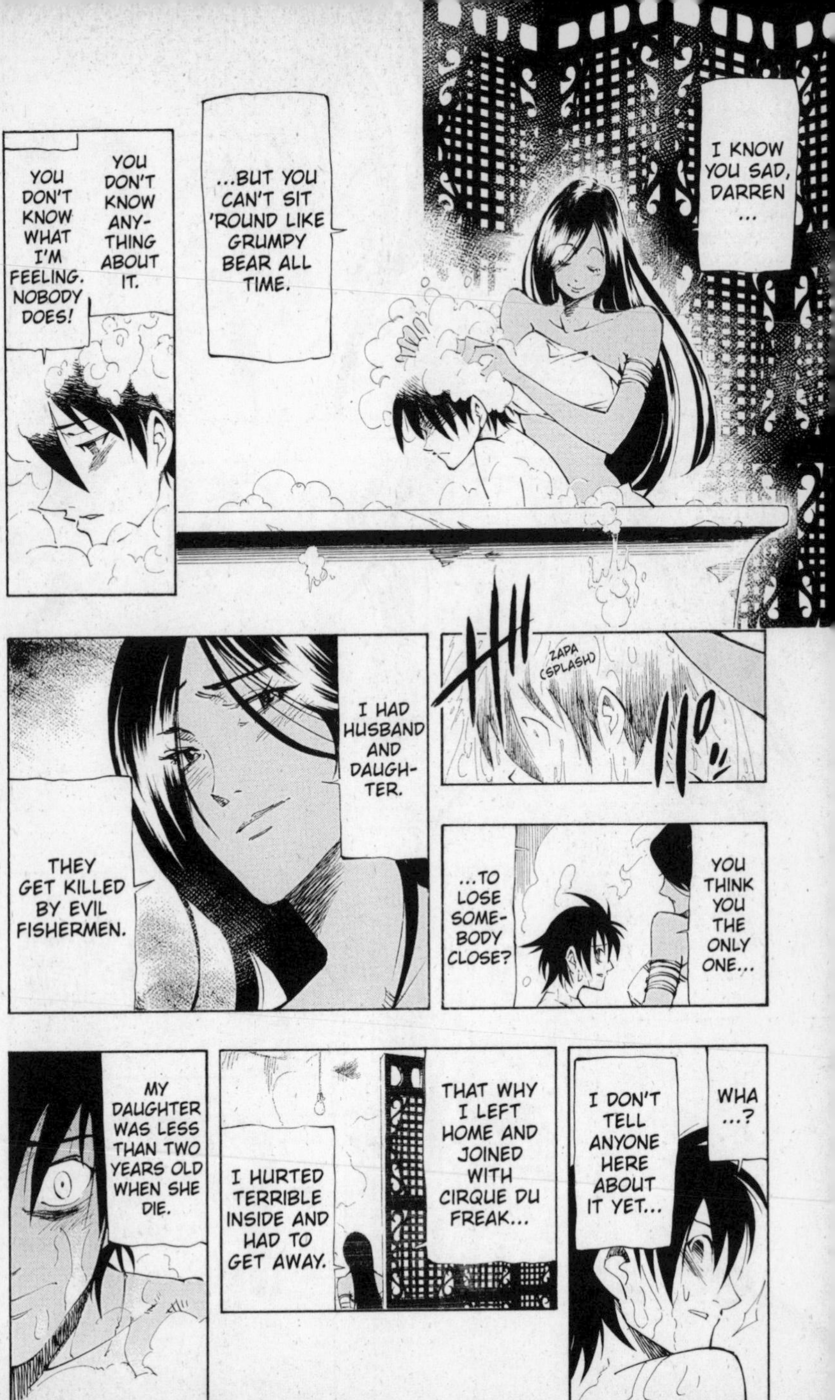
I KNOW YOU SAD, DARREN...
...BUT YOU CAN'T SIT 'ROUND LIKE GRUMPY BEAR ALL TIME.
YOU DON'T KNOW ANYTHING ABOUT IT.
YOU DON'T KNOW WHAT I'M FEELING. NOBODY DOES!
ZAPA (SPLASH)
YOU THINK YOU THE ONLY ONE...
...TO LOSE SOMEBODY CLOSE?
I HAD HUSBAND AND DAUGHTER.
THEY GET KILLED BY EVIL FISHERMEN.
WHA...?
I DON'T TELL ANYONE HERE ABOUT IT YET...
THAT WHY I LEFT HOME AND JOINED WITH CIRQUE DU FREAK...
I HURTED TERRIBLE INSIDE AND HAD TO GET AWAY.
MY DAUGHTER WAS LESS THAN TWO YEARS OLD WHEN SHE DIE.

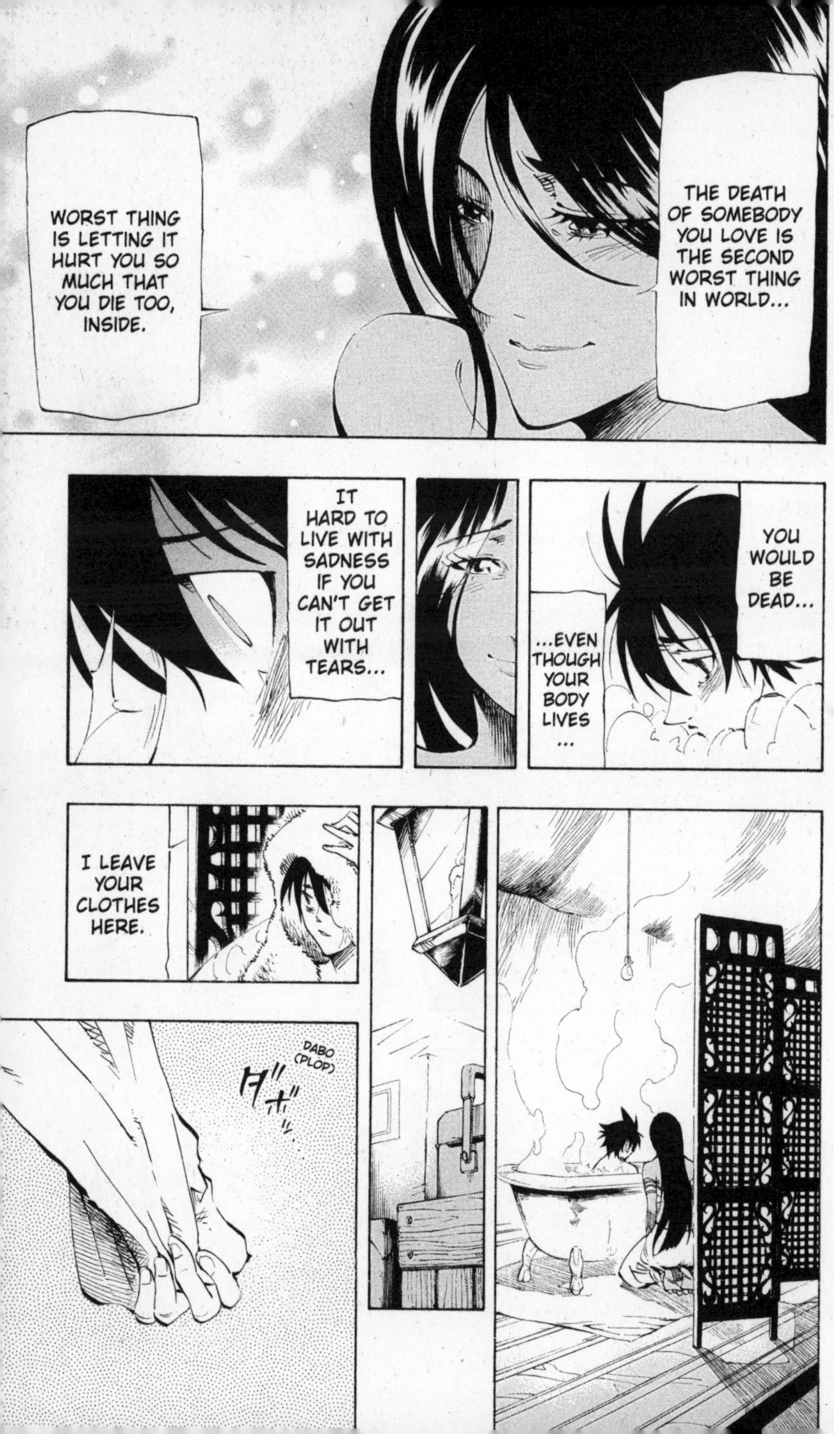
THE DEATH OF SOMEBODY YOU LOVE IS THE SECOND WORST THING IN WORLD...
WORST THING IS LETTING IT HURT YOU SO MUCH THAT YOU DIE TOO, INSIDE.
YOU WOULD BE DEAD...
...EVEN THOUGH YOUR BODY LIVES ...
IT HARD TO LIVE WITH SADNESS IF YOU CAN'T GET IT OUT WITH TEARS...
I LEAVE YOUR CLOTHES HERE.
ダボ
DABO (PLOP)

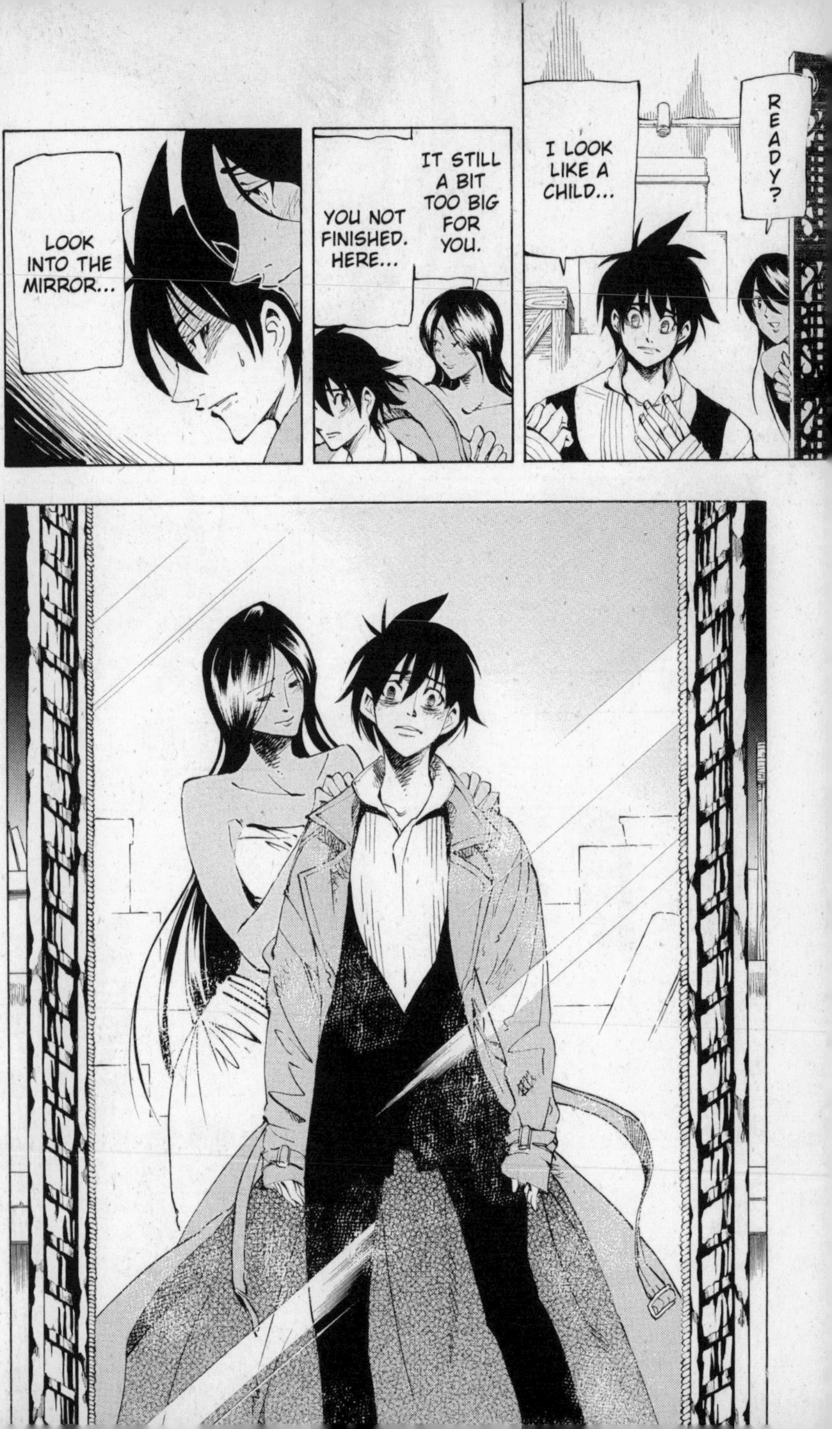
READY?
I LOOK LIKE A CHILD...
IT STILL A BIT TOO BIG FOR YOU.
YOU NOT FINISHED. HERE...
LOOK INTO THE MIRROR...

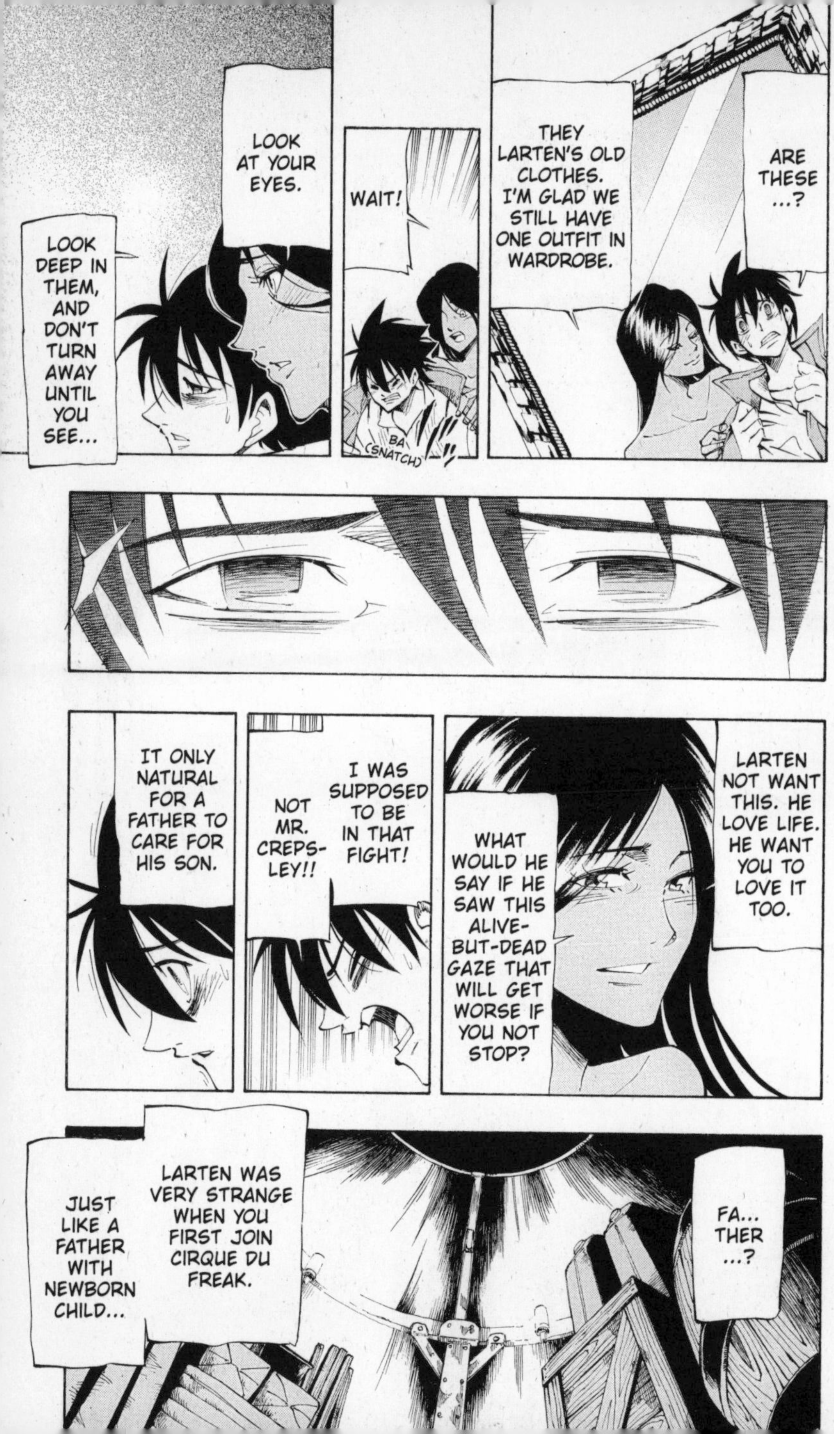
ARE THESE ...?
THEY LARTEN'S OLD CLOTHES. I'M GLAD WE STILL HAVE ONE OUTFIT IN WARDROBE.
WAIT!
BA (SNATCH)
LOOK AT YOUR EYES.
LOOK DEEP IN THEM, AND DON'T TURN AWAY UNTIL YOU SEE...
LARTEN NOT WANT THIS. HE LOVE LIFE. HE WANT YOU TO LOVE IT TOO.
WHAT WOULD HE SAY IF HE SAW THIS ALIVE-BUT-DEAD GAZE THAT WILL GET WORSE IF YOU NOT STOP?
I WAS SUPPOSED TO BE IN THAT FIGHT!
NOT MR. CREPS-LEY!!
IT ONLY NATURAL FOR A FATHER TO CARE FOR HIS SON.
FA... THER ...?
LARTEN WAS VERY STRANGE WHEN YOU FIRST JOIN CIRQUE DU FREAK.
JUST LIKE A FATHER WITH NEWBORN CHILD...

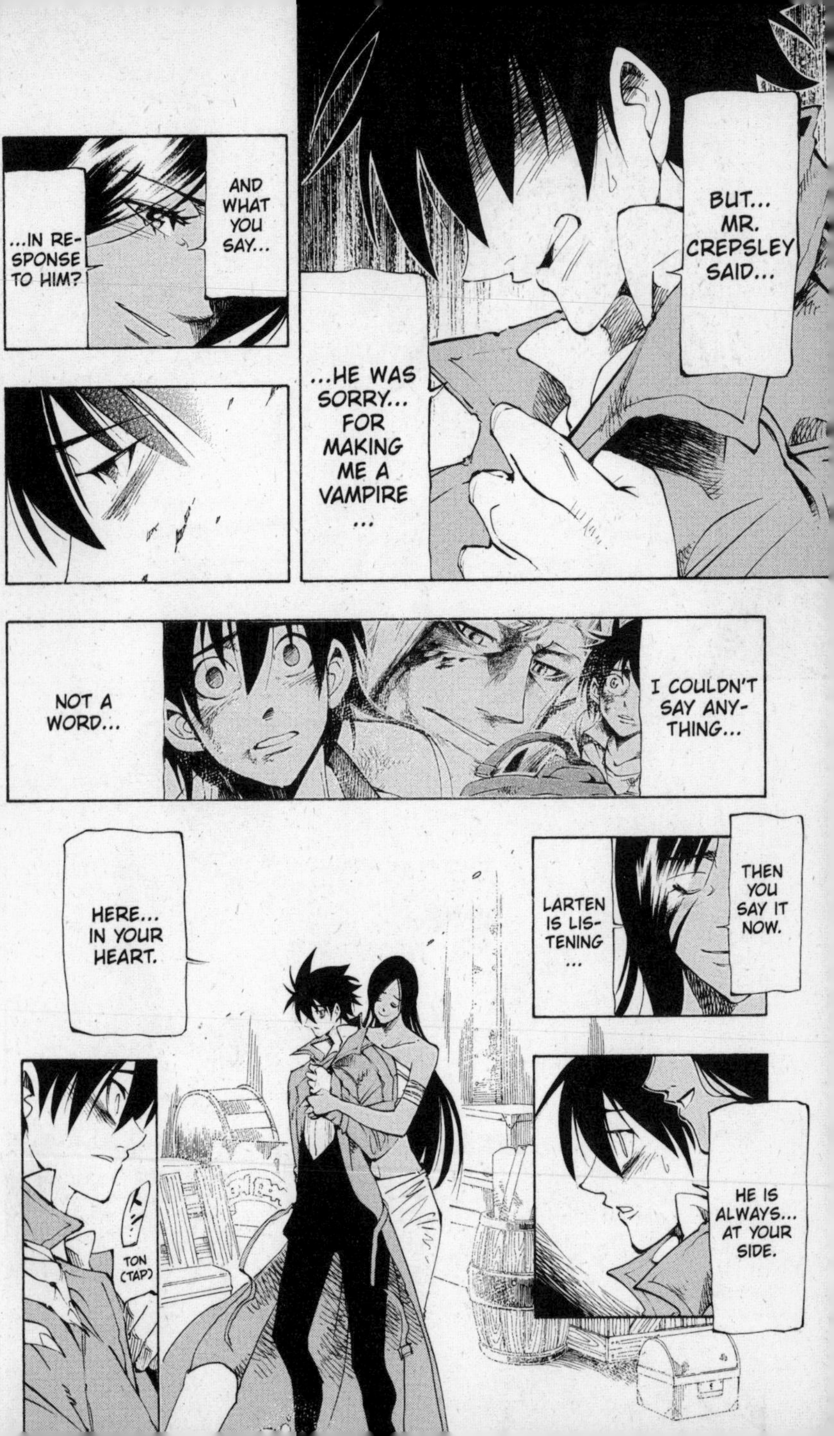

BUT... MR. CREPSLEY SAID...
...HE WAS SORRY... FOR MAKING ME A VAMPIRE...
AND WHAT YOU SAY...
...IN RESPONSE TO HIM?
I COULDN'T SAY ANYTHING...
NOT A WORD...
THEN YOU SAY IT NOW.
LARTEN IS LISTENING...
HE IS ALWAYS... AT YOUR SIDE.
HERE... IN YOUR HEART.
TON (TAP)

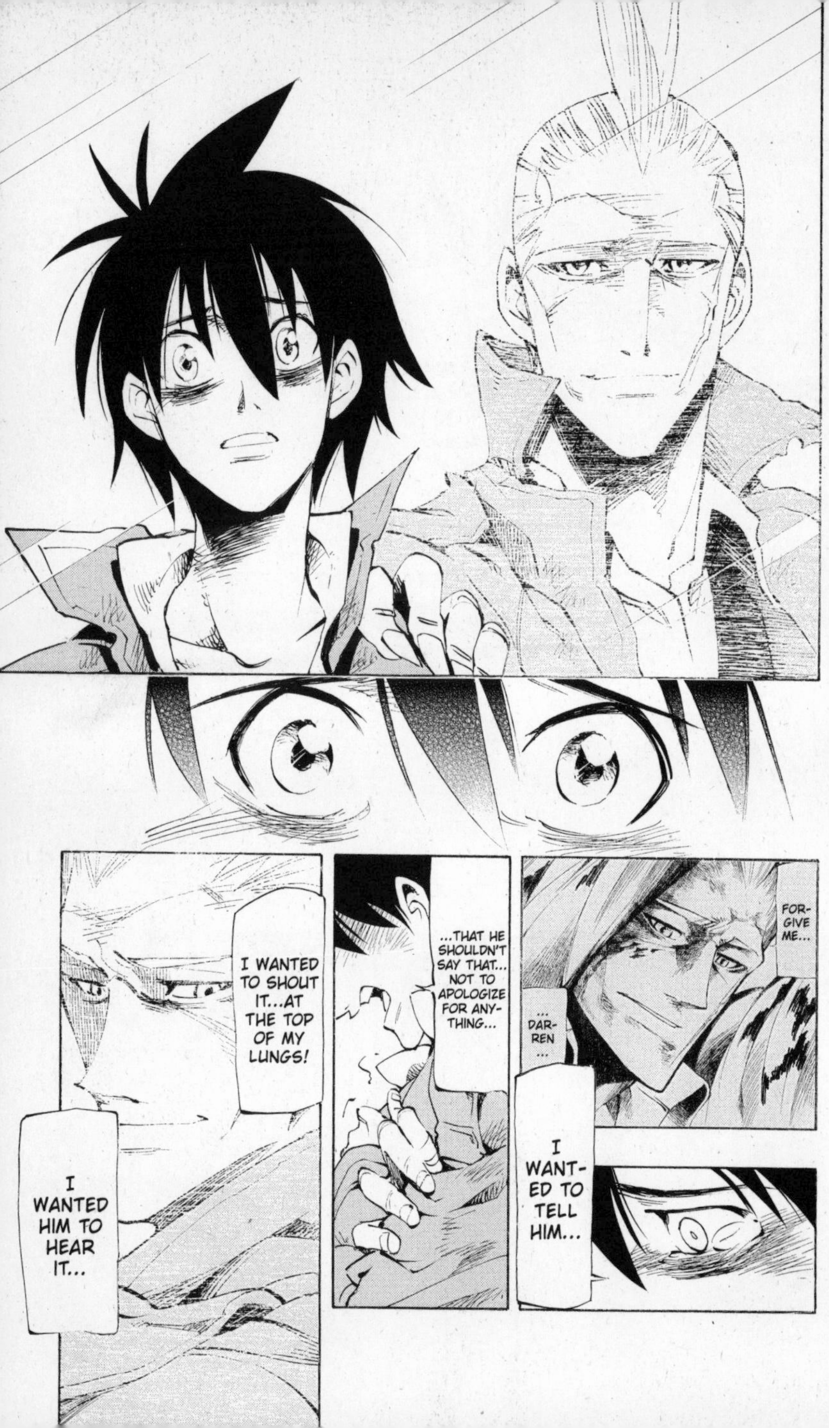
FORGIVE ME...
...DARREN...
I WANTED TO TELL HIM...
...THAT HE SHOULDN'T SAY THAT... NOT TO APOLOGIZE FOR ANYTHING...
I WANTED TO SHOUT IT...AT THE TOP OF MY LUNGS!
I WANTED HIM TO HEAR IT...

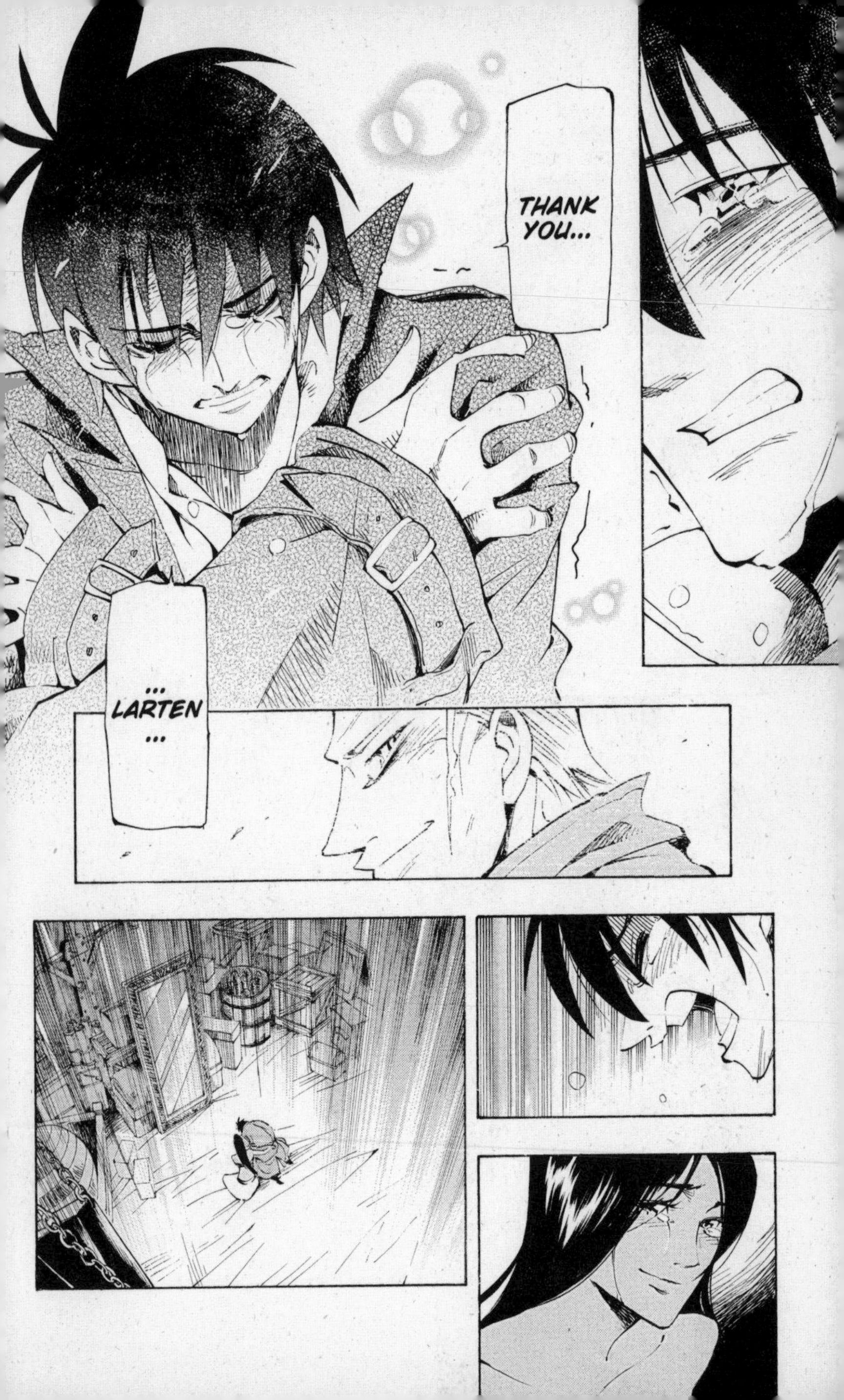
THANK YOU...
...LARTEN...

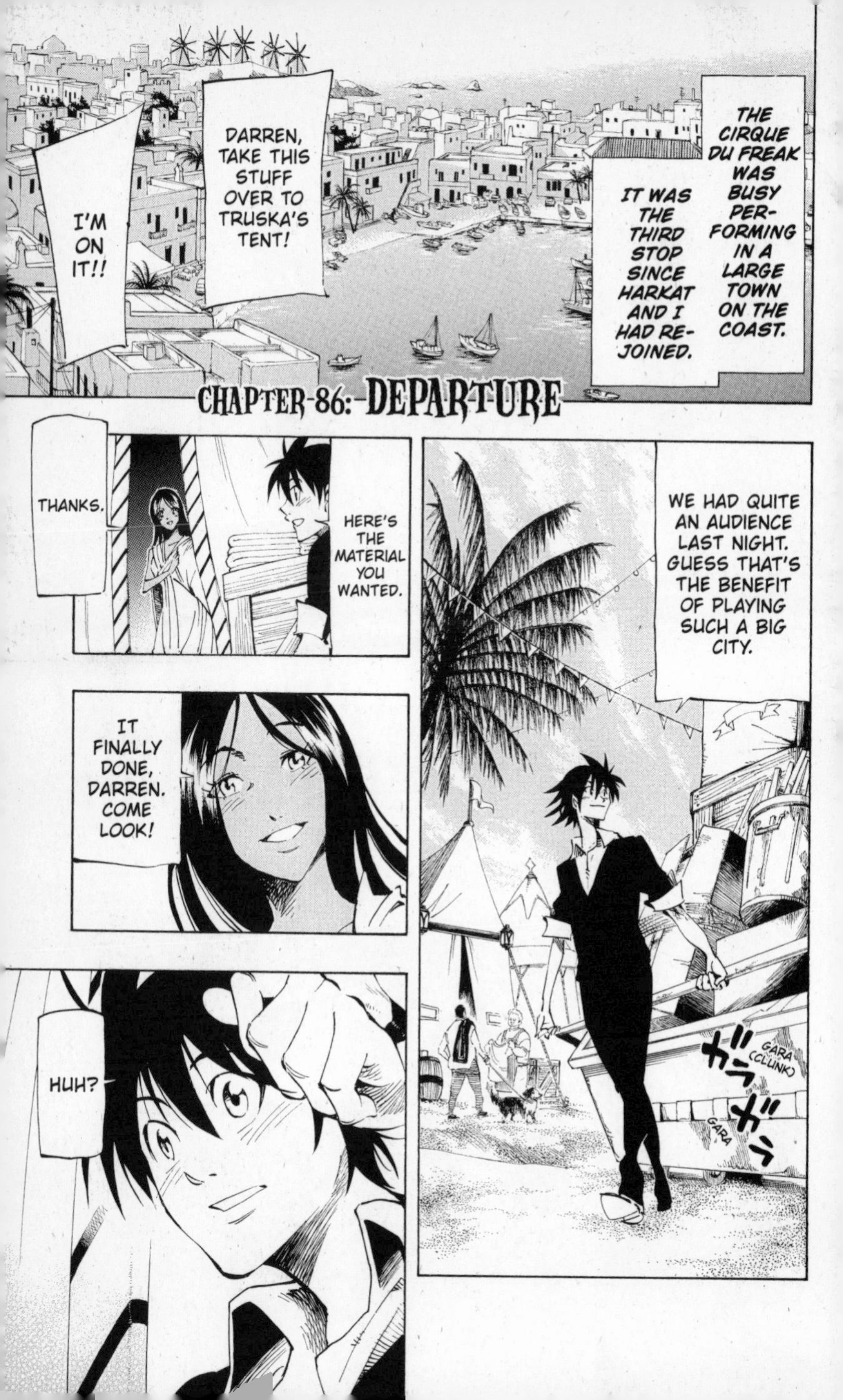
THE CIRQUE DU FREAK WAS BUSY PER-FORMING IN A LARGE TOWN ON THE COAST.
IT WAS THE THIRD STOP SINCE HARKAT AND I HAD RE-JOINED.
DARREN, TAKE THIS STUFF OVER TO TRUSKA'S TENT!
I'M ON IT!!
CHAPTER 86: DEPARTURE
WE HAD QUITE AN AUDIENCE LAST NIGHT. GUESS THAT'S THE BENEFIT OF PLAYING SUCH A BIG CITY.
GARA (CLUNK)
GARA
HERE'S THE MATERIAL YOU WANTED.
THANKS.
IT FINALLY DONE, DARREN. COME LOOK!
HUH?

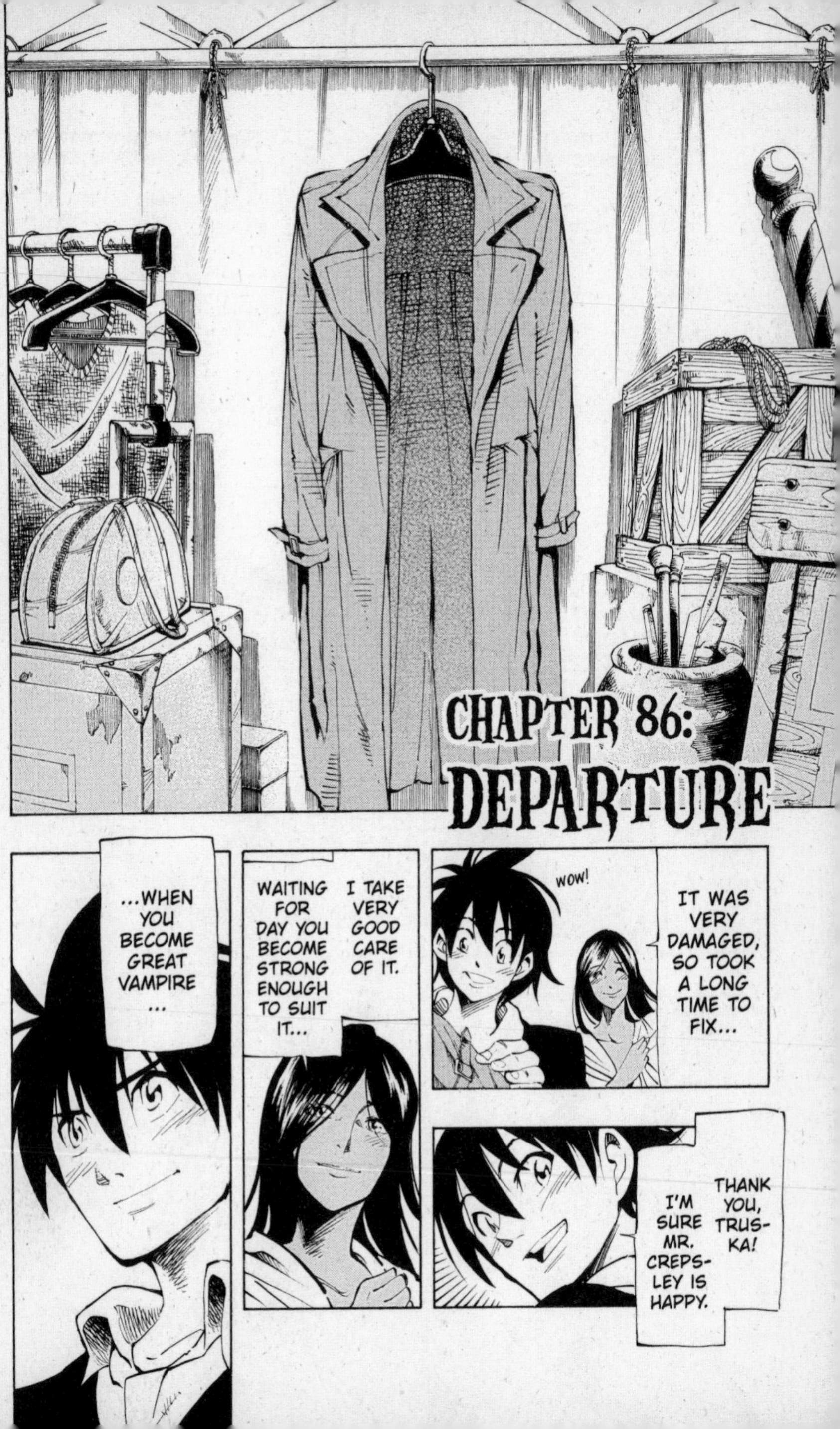
CHAPTER 86:
DEPARTURE
WOW!
IT WAS VERY DAMAGED, SO TOOK A LONG TIME TO FIX...
THANK YOU, TRUS-KA!
I'M SURE MR. CREPS-LEY IS HAPPY.
I TAKE VERY GOOD CARE OF IT.
WAITING FOR DAY YOU BECOME STRONG ENOUGH TO SUIT IT...
...WHEN YOU BECOME GREAT VAMPIRE ...

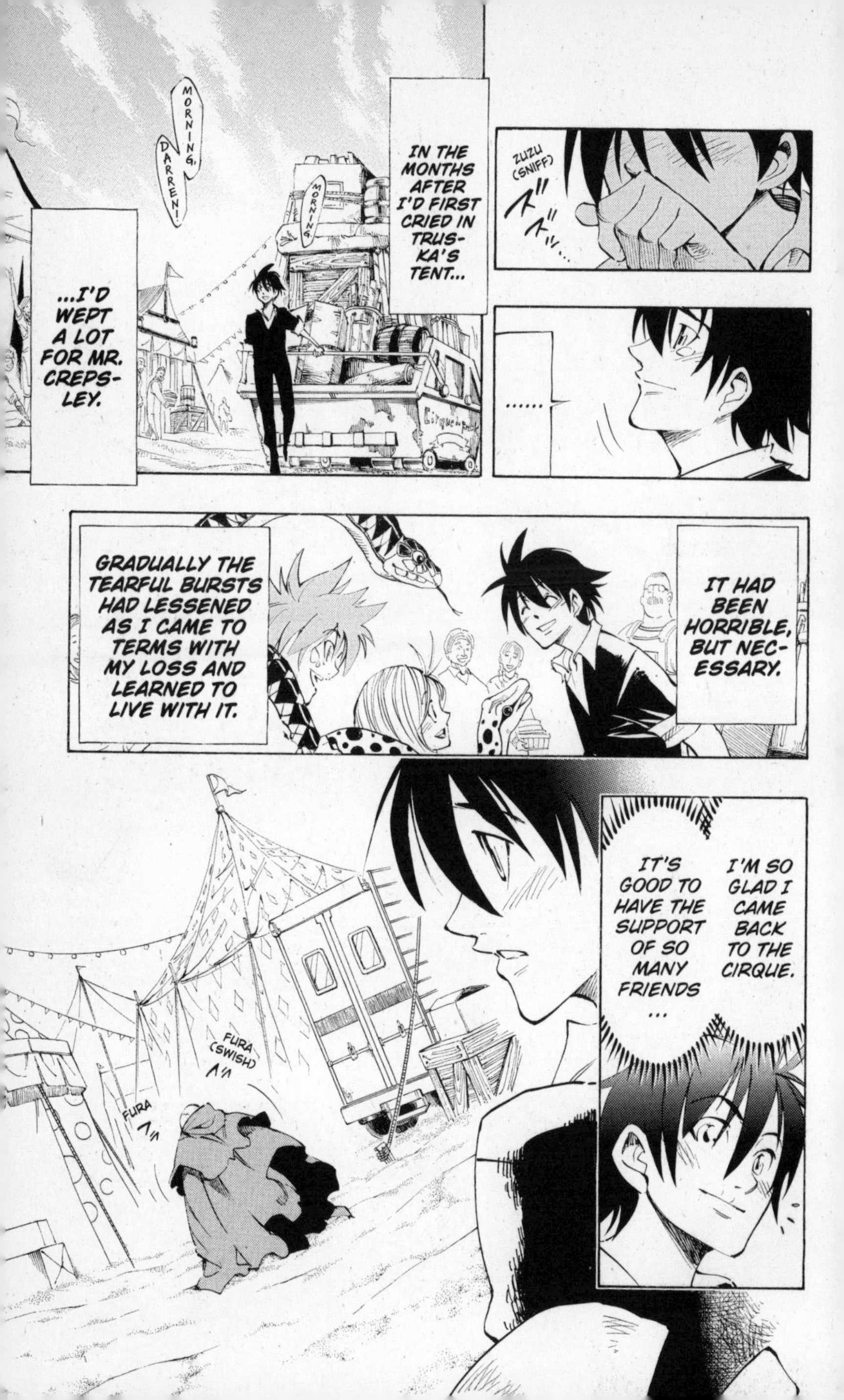
ZUZU (SNIFF)
......
MORNING, DARREN!
MORNING
IN THE MONTHS AFTER I'D FIRST CRIED IN TRUSKA'S TENT...
...I'D WEPT A LOT FOR MR. CREPSLEY.
IT HAD BEEN HORRIBLE, BUT NECESSARY.
GRADUALLY THE TEARFUL BURSTS HAD LESSENED AS I CAME TO TERMS WITH MY LOSS AND LEARNED TO LIVE WITH IT.
I'M SO GLAD I CAME BACK TO THE CIRQUE.
IT'S GOOD TO HAVE THE SUPPORT OF SO MANY FRIENDS...
FURA (SWISH)
FURA

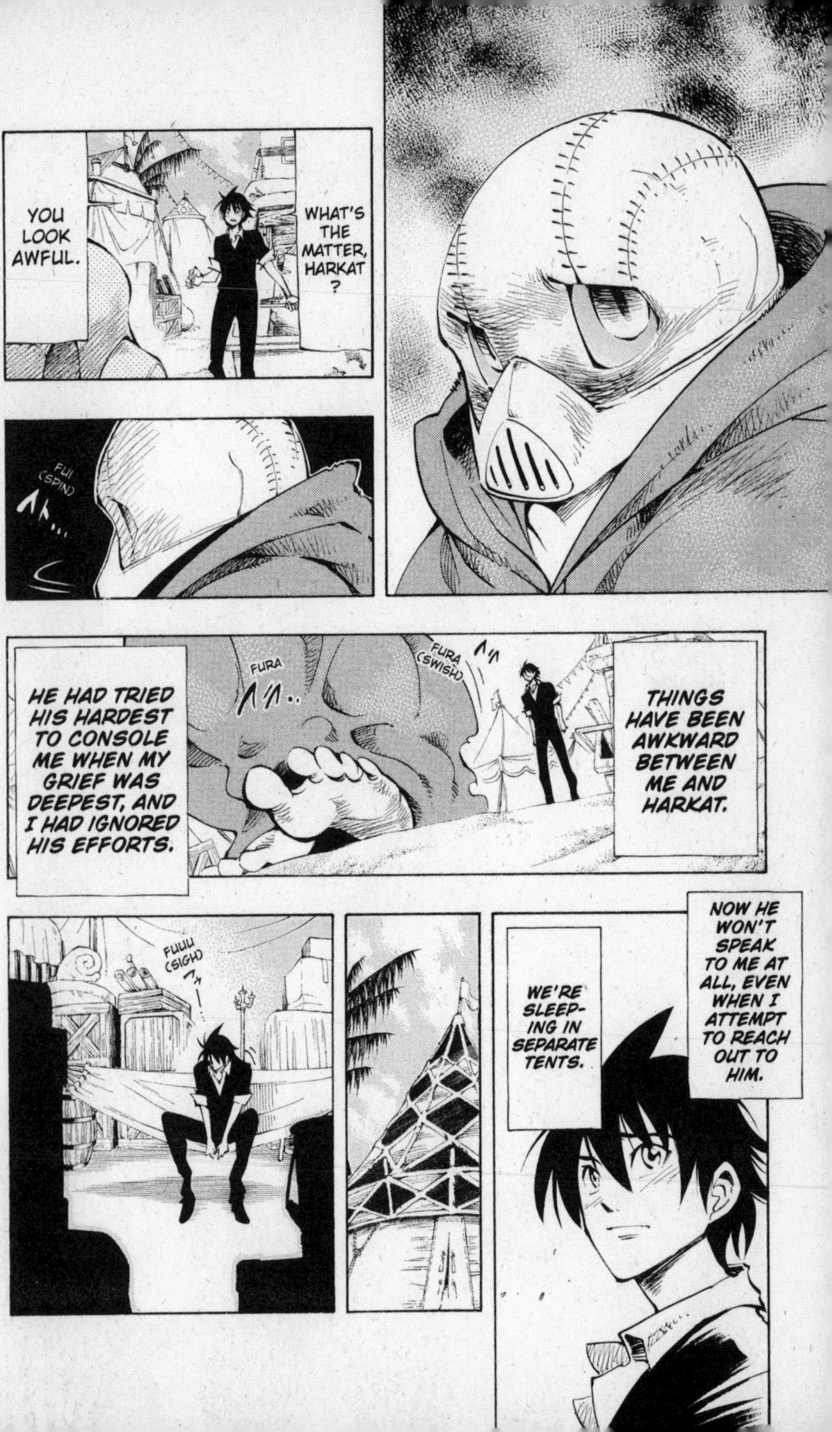
WHAT'S THE MATTER, HARKAT?
YOU LOOK AWFUL.
FUI (SPIN)
THINGS HAVE BEEN AWKWARD BETWEEN ME AND HARKAT.
FURA (SWISH)
FURA
HE HAD TRIED HIS HARDEST TO CONSOLE ME WHEN MY GRIEF WAS DEEPEST, AND I HAD IGNORED HIS EFFORTS.
NOW HE WON'T SPEAK TO ME AT ALL, EVEN WHEN I ATTEMPT TO REACH OUT TO HIM.
WE'RE SLEEPING IN SEPARATE TENTS.
FUUU (SIGH)

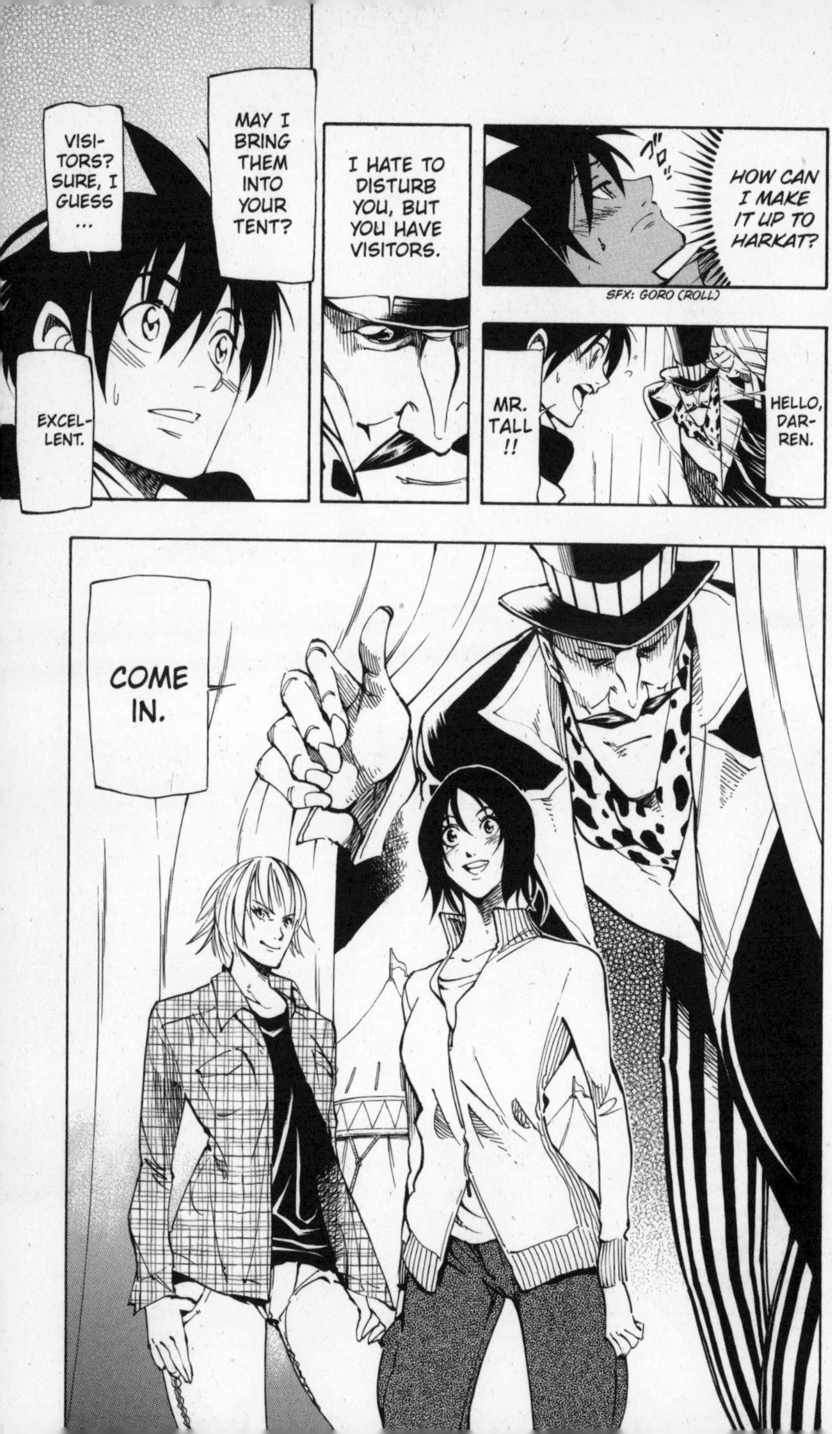
HOW CAN I MAKE IT UP TO HARKAT?
SFX: GORO (ROLL)
HELLO, DAR-REN.
MR. TALL !!
I HATE TO DISTURB YOU, BUT YOU HAVE VISITORS.
MAY I BRING THEM INTO YOUR TENT?
VISI-TORS? SURE, I GUESS ...
EXCEL-LENT.
COME IN.

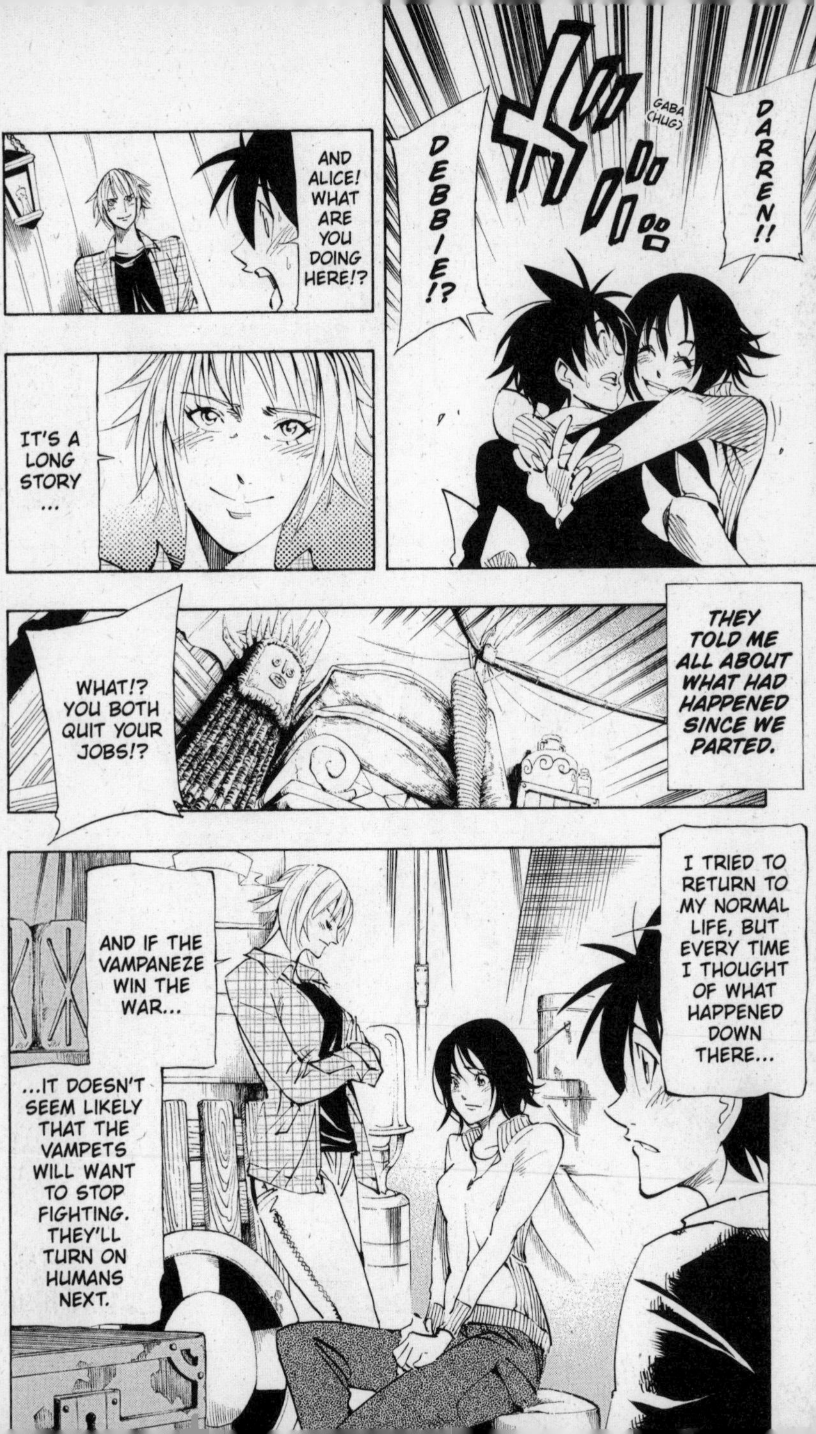
DARREN!!
GABA (HUG)
DEBBIE!?
AND ALICE! WHAT ARE YOU DOING HERE!?
IT'S A LONG STORY...
THEY TOLD ME ALL ABOUT WHAT HAD HAPPENED SINCE WE PARTED.
WHAT!? YOU BOTH QUIT YOUR JOBS!?
I TRIED TO RETURN TO MY NORMAL LIFE, BUT EVERY TIME I THOUGHT OF WHAT HAPPENED DOWN THERE...
AND IF THE VAMPANEZE WIN THE WAR...
...IT DOESN'T SEEM LIKELY THAT THE VAMPETS WILL WANT TO STOP FIGHTING. THEY'LL TURN ON HUMANS NEXT.

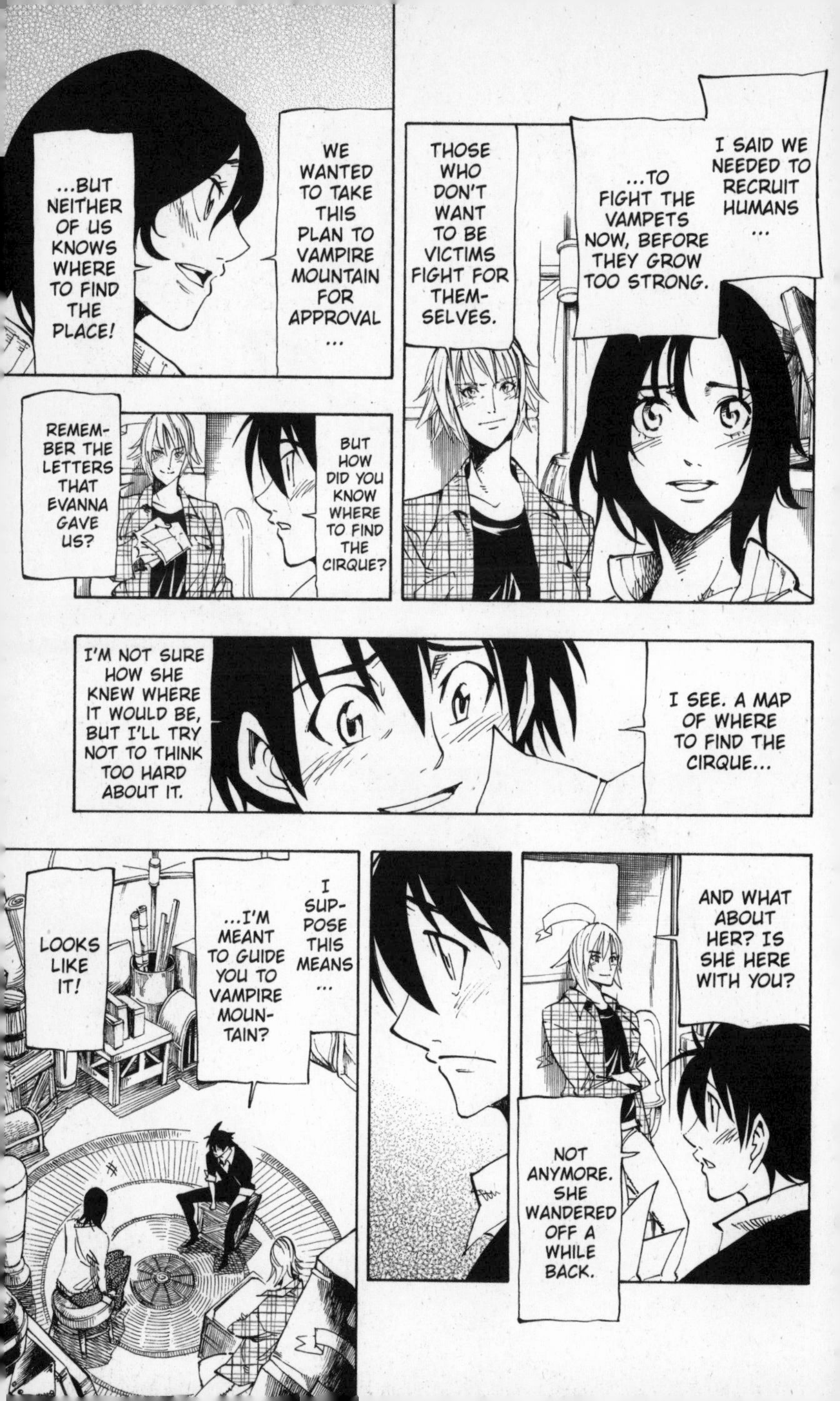
I SAID WE NEEDED TO RECRUIT HUMANS...
...TO FIGHT THE VAMPETS NOW, BEFORE THEY GROW TOO STRONG.
THOSE WHO DON'T WANT TO BE VICTIMS FIGHT FOR THEMSELVES.
WE WANTED TO TAKE THIS PLAN TO VAMPIRE MOUNTAIN FOR APPROVAL...
...BUT NEITHER OF US KNOWS WHERE TO FIND THE PLACE!
BUT HOW DID YOU KNOW WHERE TO FIND THE CIRQUE?
REMEMBER THE LETTERS THAT EVANNA GAVE US?
I SEE. A MAP OF WHERE TO FIND THE CIRQUE...
I'M NOT SURE HOW SHE KNEW WHERE IT WOULD BE, BUT I'LL TRY NOT TO THINK TOO HARD ABOUT IT.
AND WHAT ABOUT HER? IS SHE HERE WITH YOU?
NOT ANYMORE. SHE WANDERED OFF A WHILE BACK.
I SUPPOSE THIS MEANS...
...I'M MEANT TO GUIDE YOU TO VAMPIRE MOUNTAIN?
LOOKS LIKE IT!

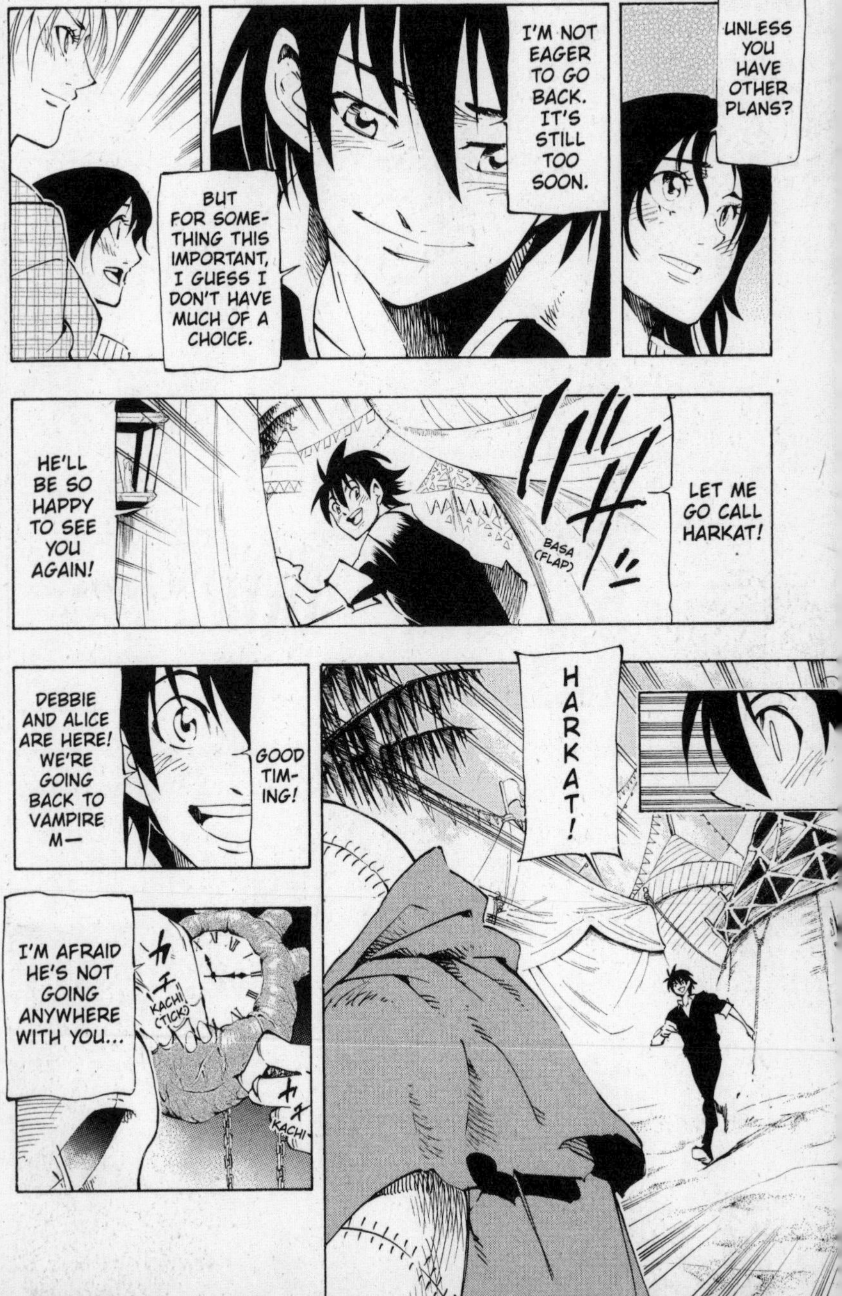
UNLESS YOU HAVE OTHER PLANS?
I'M NOT EAGER TO GO BACK. IT'S STILL TOO SOON.
BUT FOR SOME-THING THIS IMPORTANT, I GUESS I DON'T HAVE MUCH OF A CHOICE.
LET ME GO CALL HARKAT!
BASA (FLAP)
HE'LL BE SO HAPPY TO SEE YOU AGAIN!
HARKAT!
GOOD TIM-ING!
DEBBIE AND ALICE ARE HERE! WE'RE GOING BACK TO VAMPIRE M—
KACHI (TICK)
KACHI
I'M AFRAID HE'S NOT GOING ANYWHERE WITH YOU...

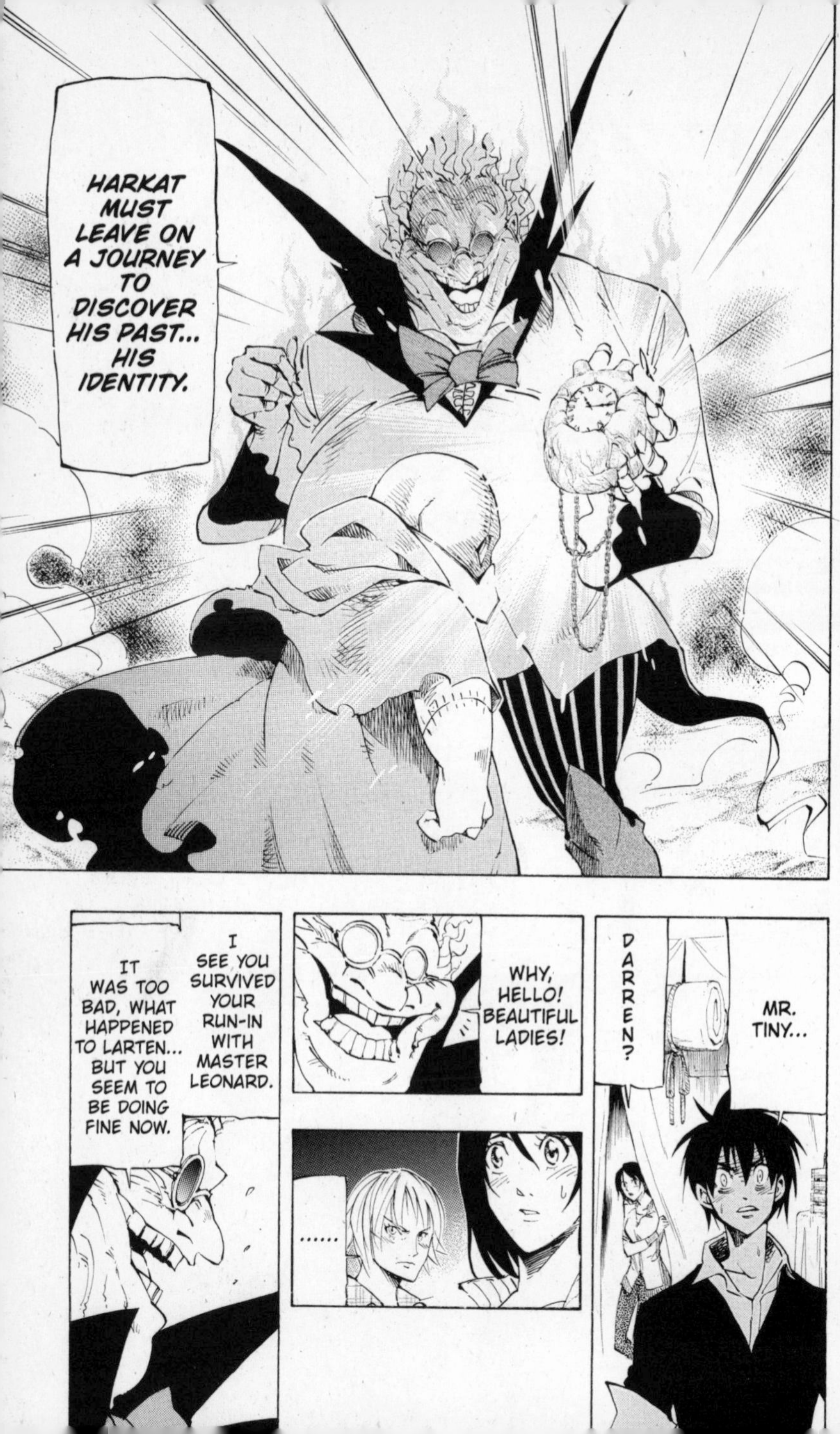
HARKAT MUST LEAVE ON A JOURNEY TO DISCOVER HIS PAST... HIS IDENTITY.
MR. TINY...
DARREN?
WHY, HELLO! BEAUTIFUL LADIES!
......
I SEE YOU SURVIVED YOUR RUN-IN WITH MASTER LEONARD.
IT WAS TOO BAD, WHAT HAPPENED TO LARTEN... BUT YOU SEEM TO BE DOING FINE NOW.

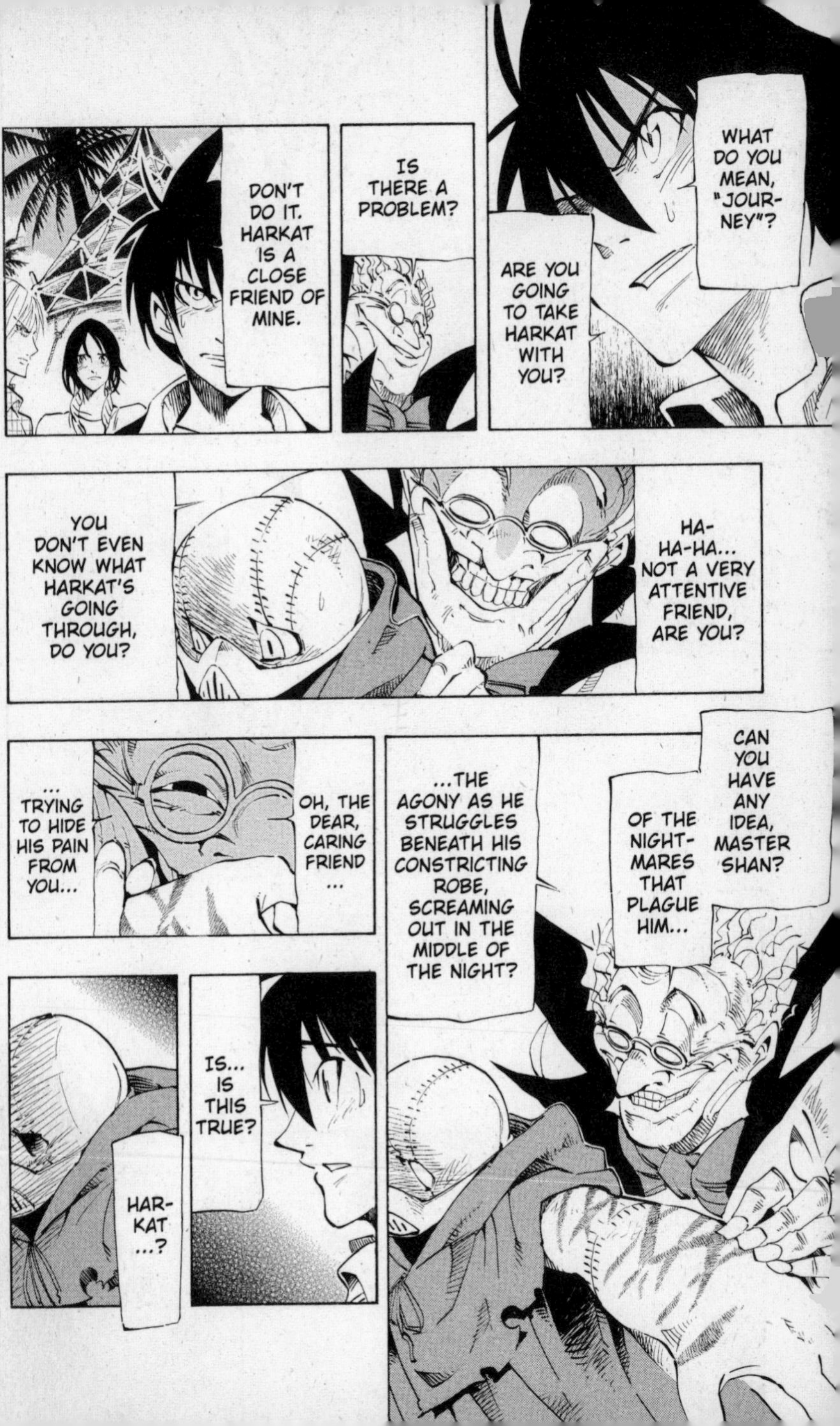
WHAT DO YOU MEAN, "JOURNEY"?
ARE YOU GOING TO TAKE HARKAT WITH YOU?
IS THERE A PROBLEM?
DON'T DO IT. HARKAT IS A CLOSE FRIEND OF MINE.
HA-HA-HA... NOT A VERY ATTENTIVE FRIEND, ARE YOU?
YOU DON'T EVEN KNOW WHAT HARKAT'S GOING THROUGH, DO YOU?
CAN YOU HAVE ANY IDEA, MASTER SHAN?
OF THE NIGHTMARES THAT PLAGUE HIM...
...THE AGONY AS HE STRUGGLES BENEATH HIS CONSTRICTING ROBE, SCREAMING OUT IN THE MIDDLE OF THE NIGHT?
OH, THE DEAR, CARING FRIEND...
...TRYING TO HIDE HIS PAIN FROM YOU...
IS... IS THIS TRUE?
HARKAT...?

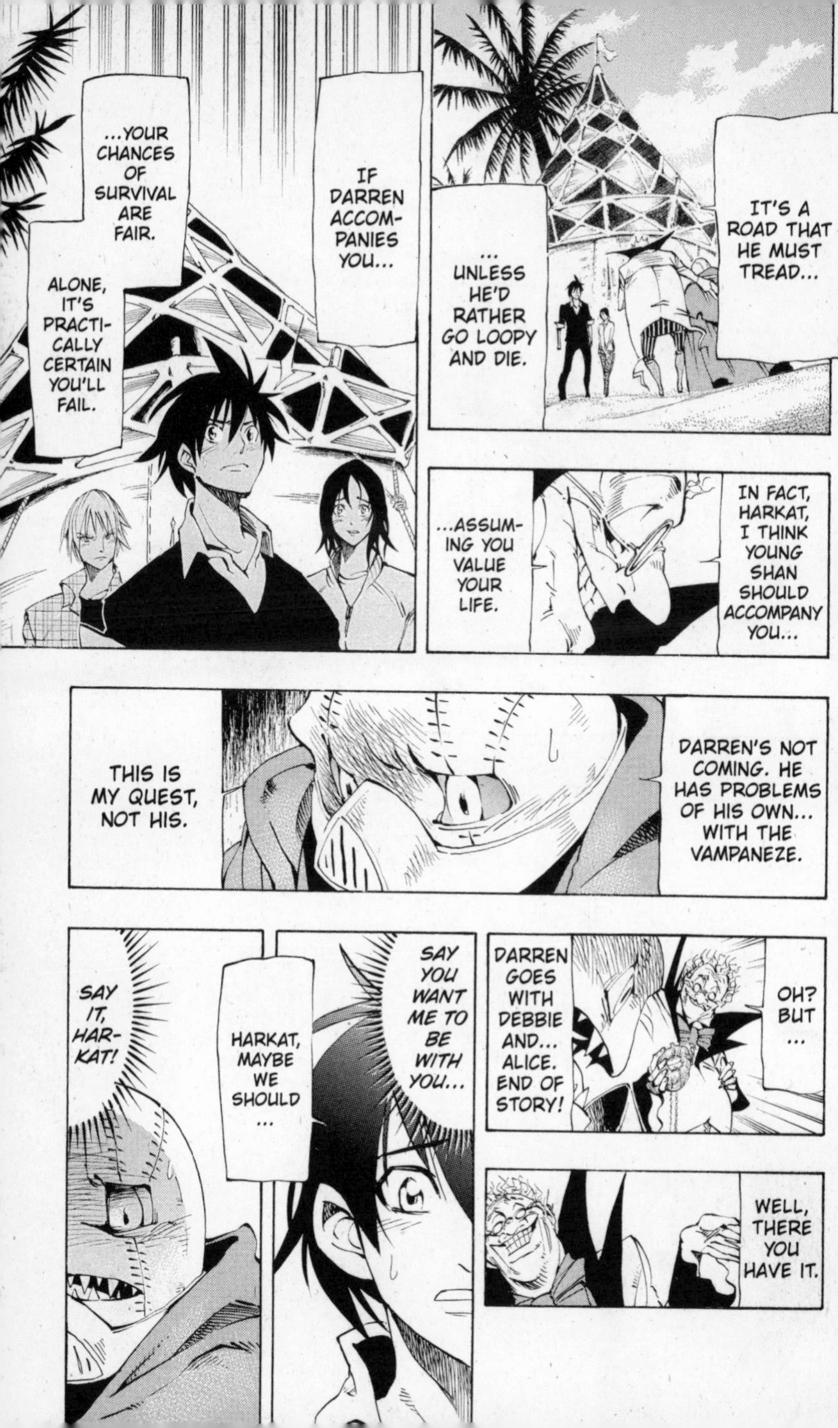
IT'S A ROAD THAT HE MUST TREAD...
... UNLESS HE'D RATHER GO LOOPY AND DIE.
IN FACT, HARKAT, I THINK YOUNG SHAN SHOULD ACCOMPANY YOU...
...ASSUMING YOU VALUE YOUR LIFE.
IF DARREN ACCOMPANIES YOU...
...YOUR CHANCES OF SURVIVAL ARE FAIR.
ALONE, IT'S PRACTICALLY CERTAIN YOU'LL FAIL.
DARREN'S NOT COMING. HE HAS PROBLEMS OF HIS OWN... WITH THE VAMPANEZE.
THIS IS MY QUEST, NOT HIS.
OH? BUT...
DARREN GOES WITH DEBBIE AND... ALICE. END OF STORY!
WELL, THERE YOU HAVE IT.
SAY YOU WANT ME TO BE WITH YOU...
HARKAT, MAYBE WE SHOULD...
SAY IT, HARKAT!

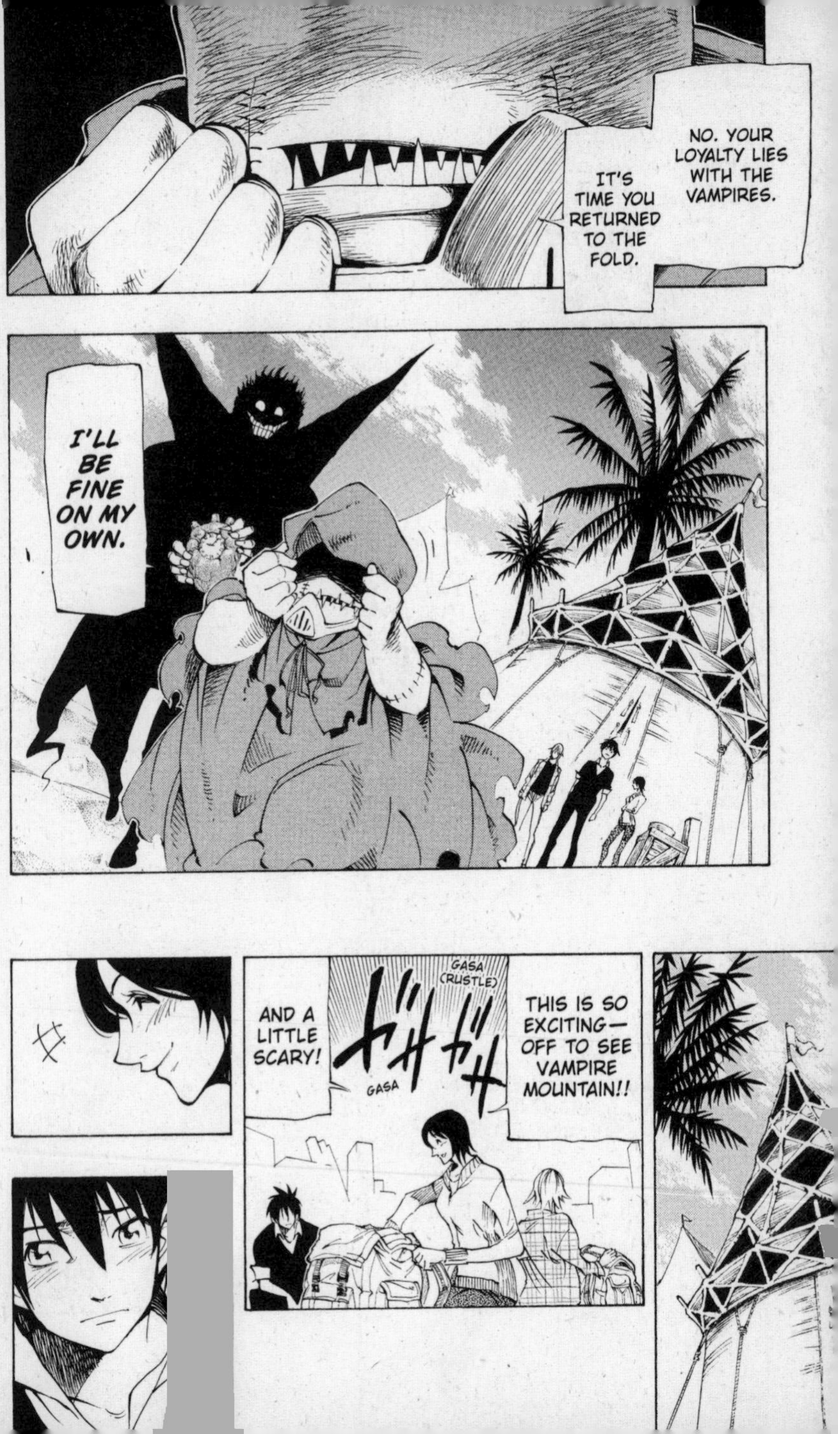
NO. YOUR LOYALTY LIES WITH THE VAMPIRES.
IT'S TIME YOU RETURNED TO THE FOLD.
I'LL BE FINE ON MY OWN.
THIS IS SO EXCITING— OFF TO SEE VAMPIRE MOUNTAIN!!
GASA (RUSTLE)
GASA
AND A LITTLE SCARY!

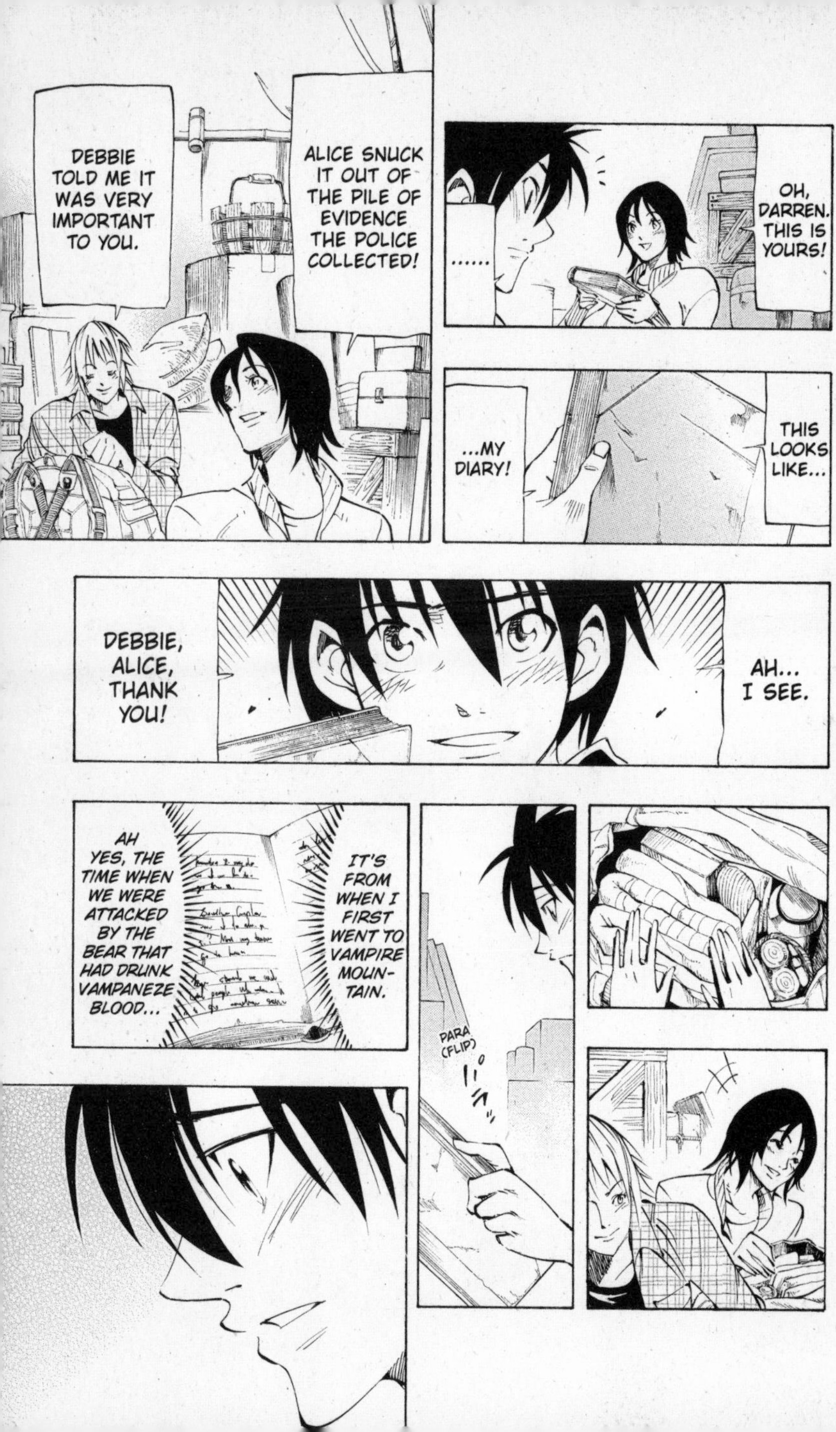
OH, DARREN. THIS IS YOURS!
......
THIS LOOKS LIKE...
...MY DIARY!
ALICE SNUCK IT OUT OF THE PILE OF EVIDENCE THE POLICE COLLECTED!
DEBBIE TOLD ME IT WAS VERY IMPORTANT TO YOU.
AH... I SEE.
DEBBIE, ALICE, THANK YOU!
PARA (FLIP)
IT'S FROM WHEN I FIRST WENT TO VAMPIRE MOUNTAIN.
AH YES, THE TIME WHEN WE WERE ATTACKED BY THE BEAR THAT HAD DRUNK VAMPANEZE BLOOD...

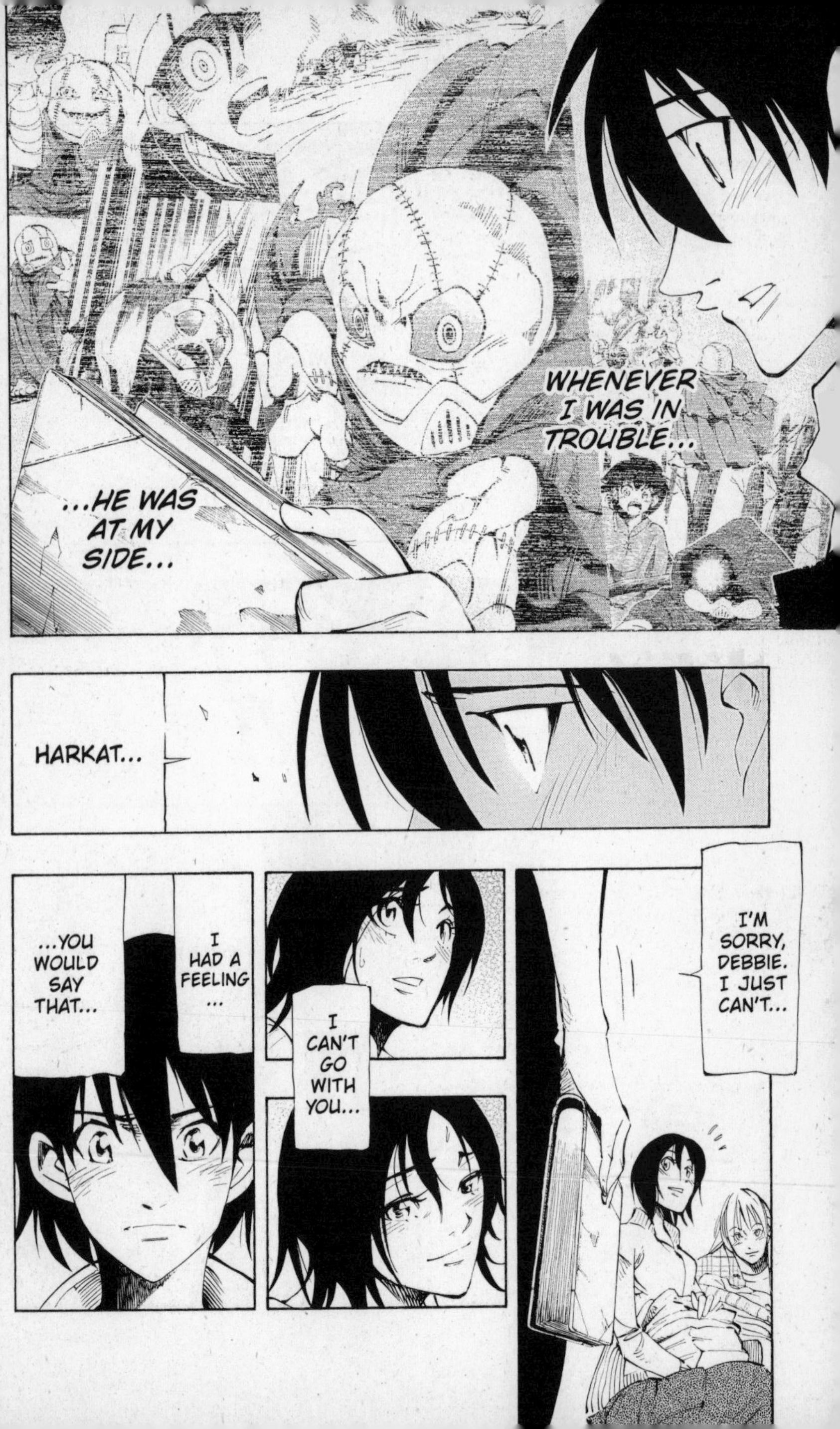
WHENEVER I WAS IN TROUBLE...
...HE WAS AT MY SIDE...
HARKAT...
I'M SORRY, DEBBIE. I JUST CAN'T...
I CAN'T GO WITH YOU...
I HAD A FEELING...
...YOU WOULD SAY THAT...

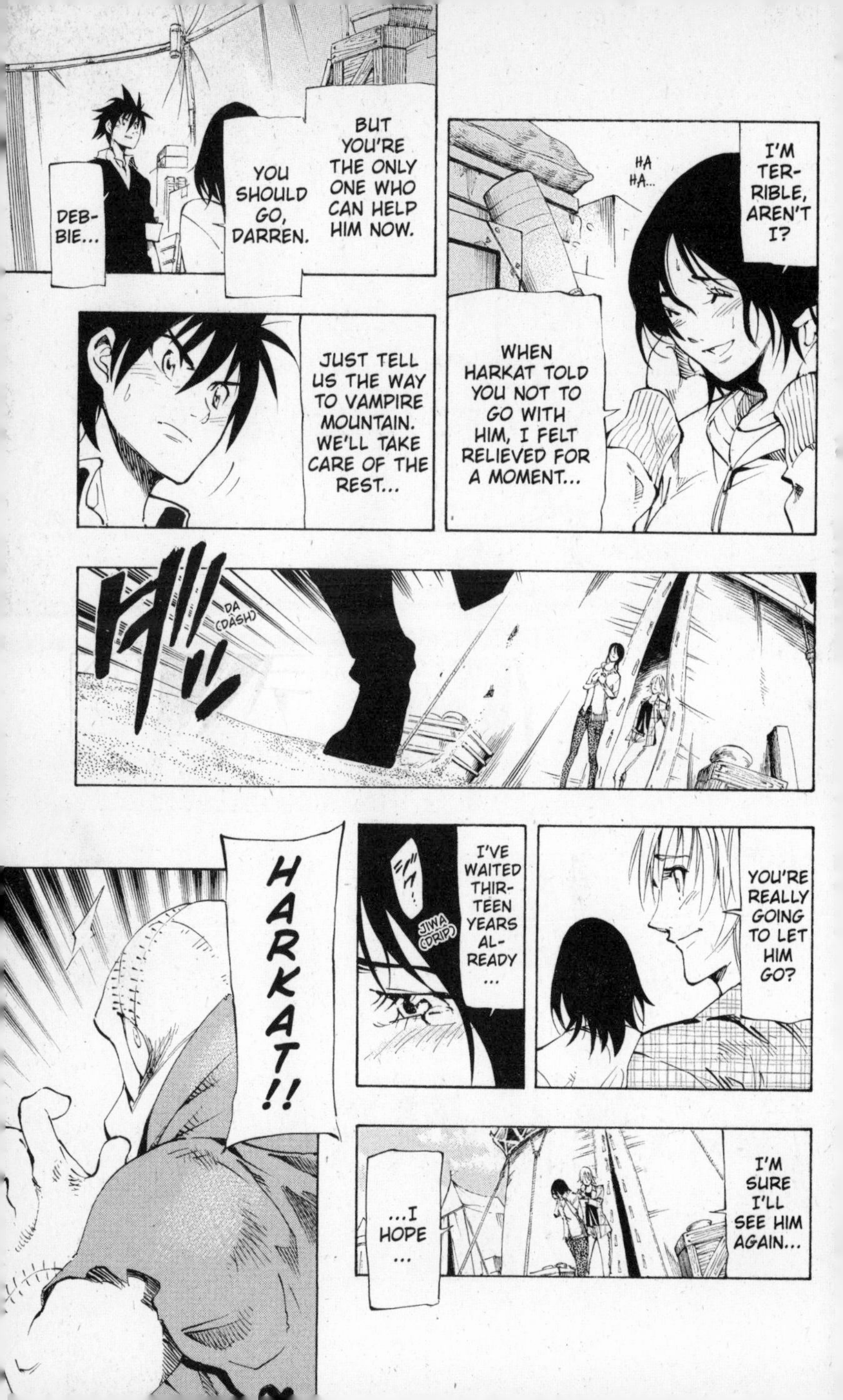
HA HA...
I'M TER-RIBLE, AREN'T I?
WHEN HARKAT TOLD YOU NOT TO GO WITH HIM, I FELT RELIEVED FOR A MOMENT...
BUT YOU'RE THE ONLY ONE WHO CAN HELP HIM NOW.
YOU SHOULD GO, DARREN.
DEB-BIE...
JUST TELL US THE WAY TO VAMPIRE MOUNTAIN. WE'LL TAKE CARE OF THE REST...
DA (DASH)
YOU'RE REALLY GOING TO LET HIM GO?
I'VE WAITED THIR-TEEN YEARS AL-READY...
JIWA (DRIP)
I'M SURE I'LL SEE HIM AGAIN...
...I HOPE...
HARKAT!!

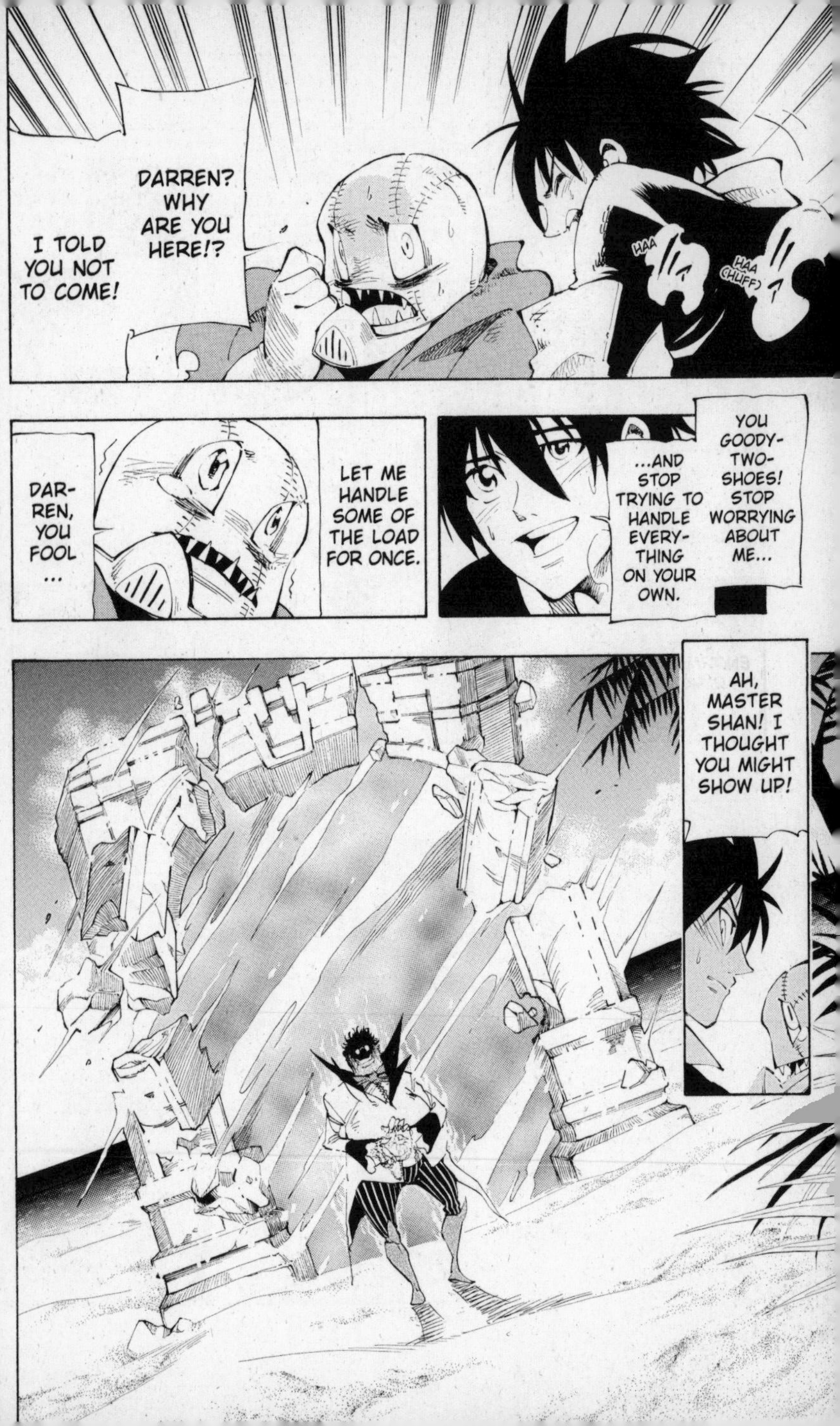
HAA
HAA (HUFF)
DARREN? WHY ARE YOU HERE!?
I TOLD YOU NOT TO COME!
YOU GOODY-TWO-SHOES! STOP WORRYING ABOUT ME...
...AND STOP TRYING TO HANDLE EVERYTHING ON YOUR OWN.
LET ME HANDLE SOME OF THE LOAD FOR ONCE.
DARREN, YOU FOOL...
AH, MASTER SHAN! I THOUGHT YOU MIGHT SHOW UP!

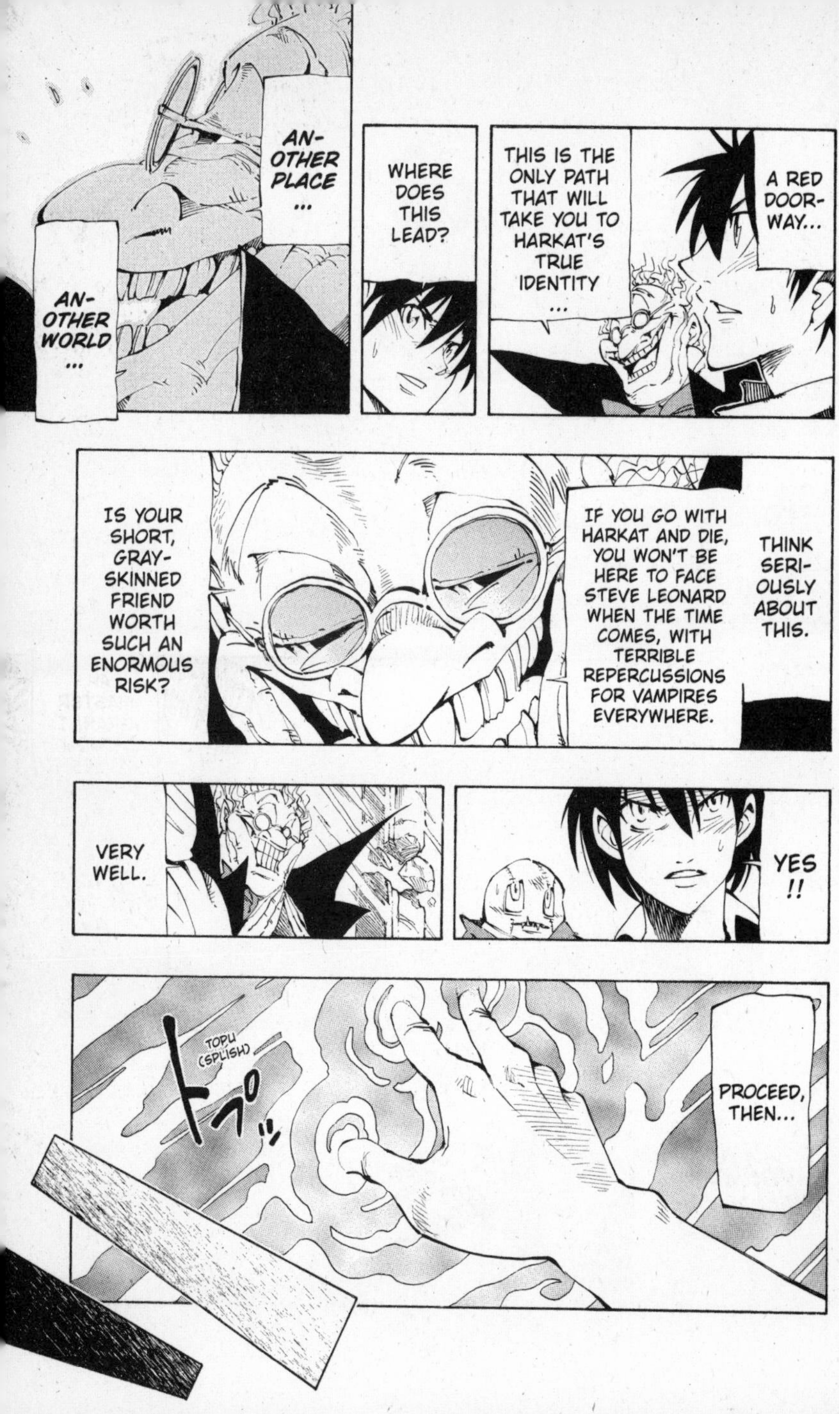
A RED DOOR-WAY...
THIS IS THE ONLY PATH THAT WILL TAKE YOU TO HARKAT'S TRUE IDENTITY...
WHERE DOES THIS LEAD?
AN-OTHER PLACE...
AN-OTHER WORLD...
THINK SERI-OUSLY ABOUT THIS.
IF YOU GO WITH HARKAT AND DIE, YOU WON'T BE HERE TO FACE STEVE LEONARD WHEN THE TIME COMES, WITH TERRIBLE REPERCUSSIONS FOR VAMPIRES EVERYWHERE.
IS YOUR SHORT, GRAY-SKINNED FRIEND WORTH SUCH AN ENORMOUS RISK?
YES!!
VERY WELL.
PROCEED, THEN...
TOPU (SPLISH)

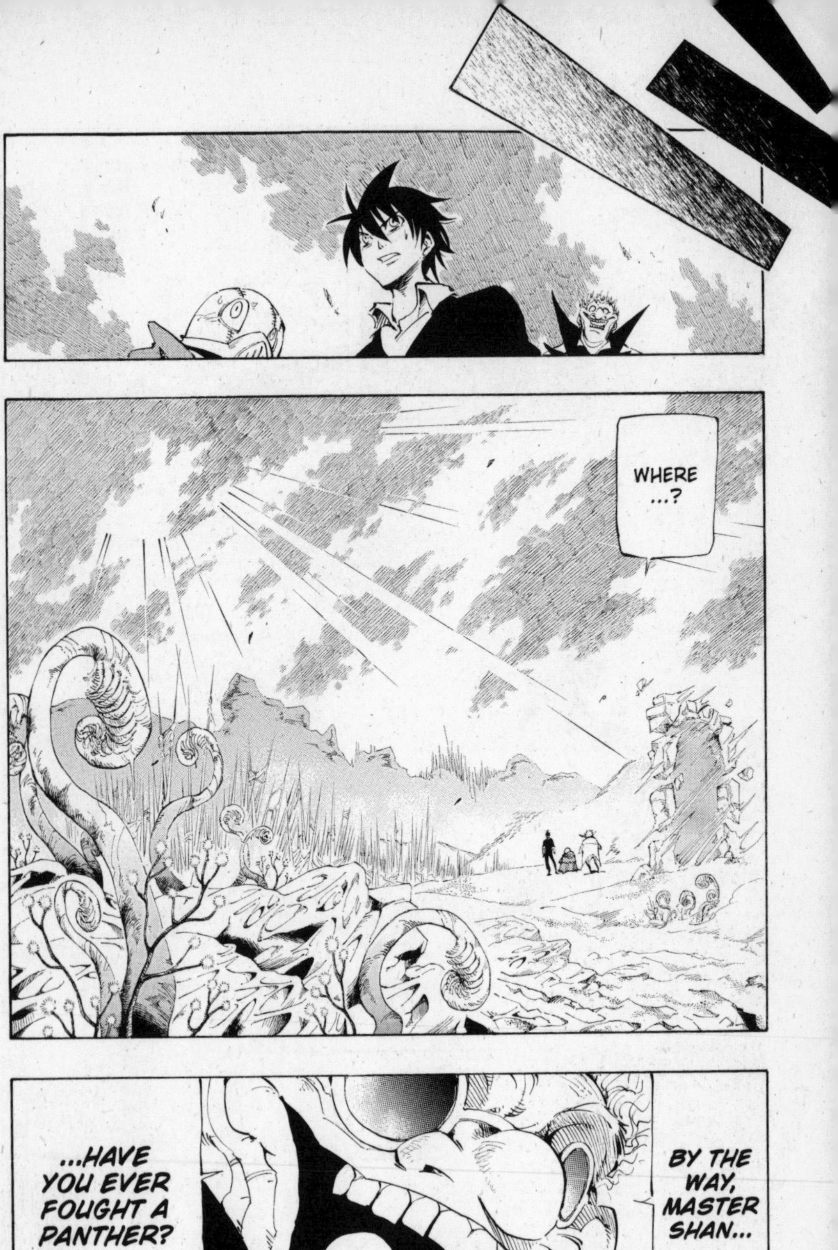
WHERE ...?
BY THE WAY, MASTER SHAN...
...HAVE YOU EVER FOUGHT A PANTHER?

CHAPTER 87: THE PIT

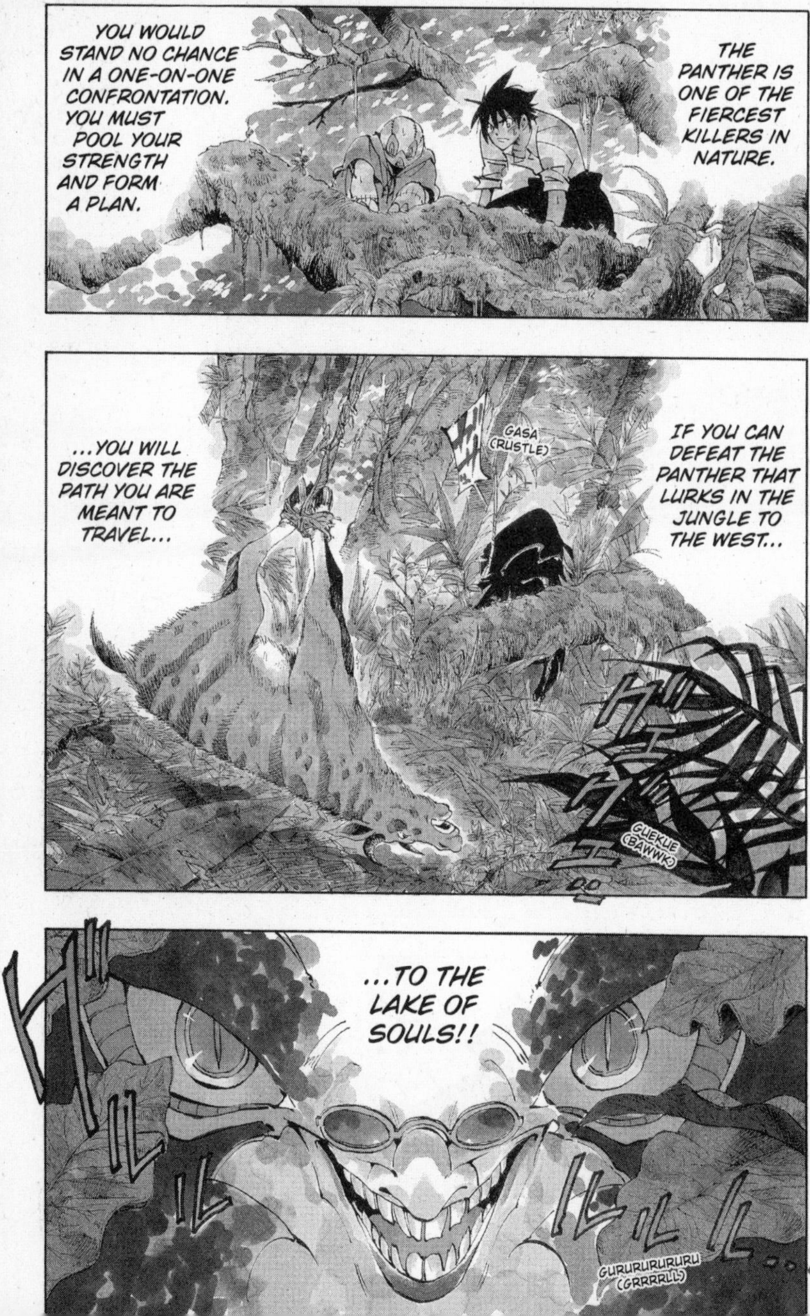
THE PANTHER IS ONE OF THE FIERCEST KILLERS IN NATURE.
YOU WOULD STAND NO CHANCE IN A ONE-ON-ONE CONFRONTATION. YOU MUST POOL YOUR STRENGTH AND FORM A PLAN.
IF YOU CAN DEFEAT THE PANTHER THAT LURKS IN THE JUNGLE TO THE WEST...
GASA (RUSTLE)
...YOU WILL DISCOVER THE PATH YOU ARE MEANT TO TRAVEL...
GUEKUE (BAWWK)
...TO THE LAKE OF SOULS!!
GURURURURURU (GRRRRLL)

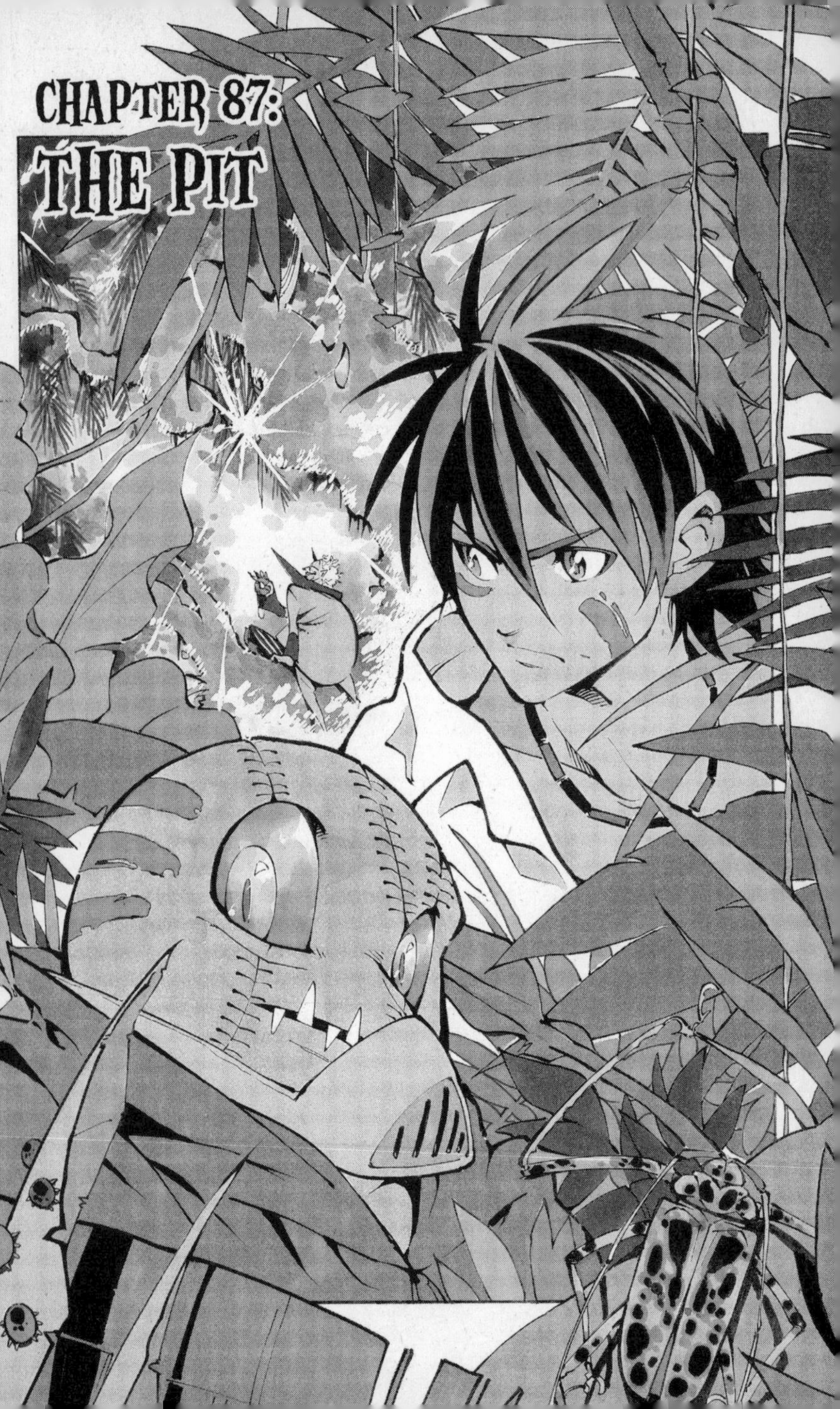
CHAPTER 87:
THE PIT

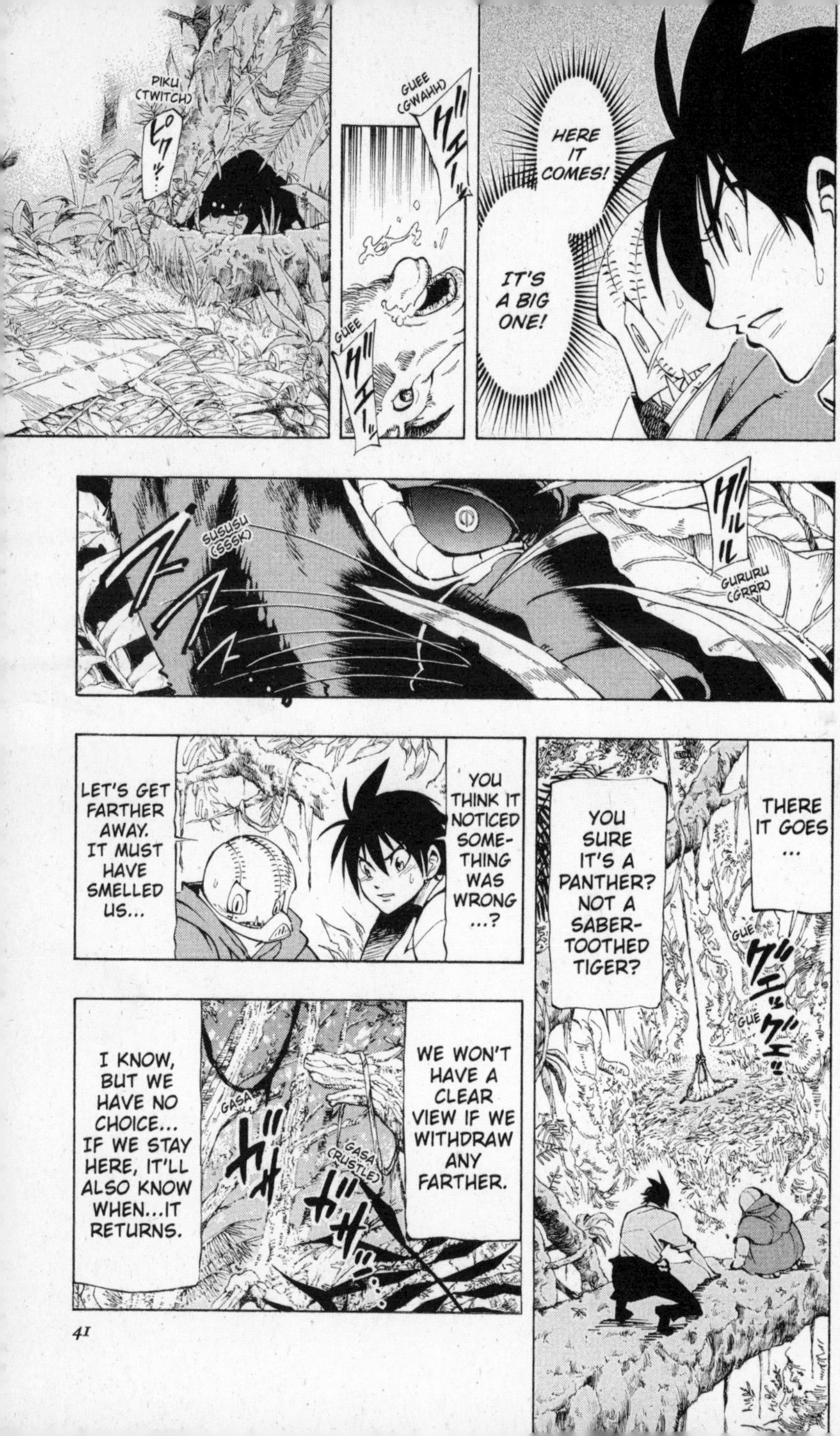
HERE IT COMES!
IT'S A BIG ONE!
GUEE (GWAHH)
GUEE
PIKU (TWITCH)
GURURU (GRRR)
SUSUSU (SSSK)
THERE IT GOES ...
YOU SURE IT'S A PANTHER? NOT A SABER-TOOTHED TIGER?
GUE
GUE
YOU THINK IT NOTICED SOME-THING WAS WRONG ...?
LET'S GET FARTHER AWAY. IT MUST HAVE SMELLED US...
WE WON'T HAVE A CLEAR VIEW IF WE WITHDRAW ANY FARTHER.
GASA (RUSTLE)
GASA
I KNOW, BUT WE HAVE NO CHOICE... IF WE STAY HERE, IT'LL ALSO KNOW WHEN...IT RETURNS.

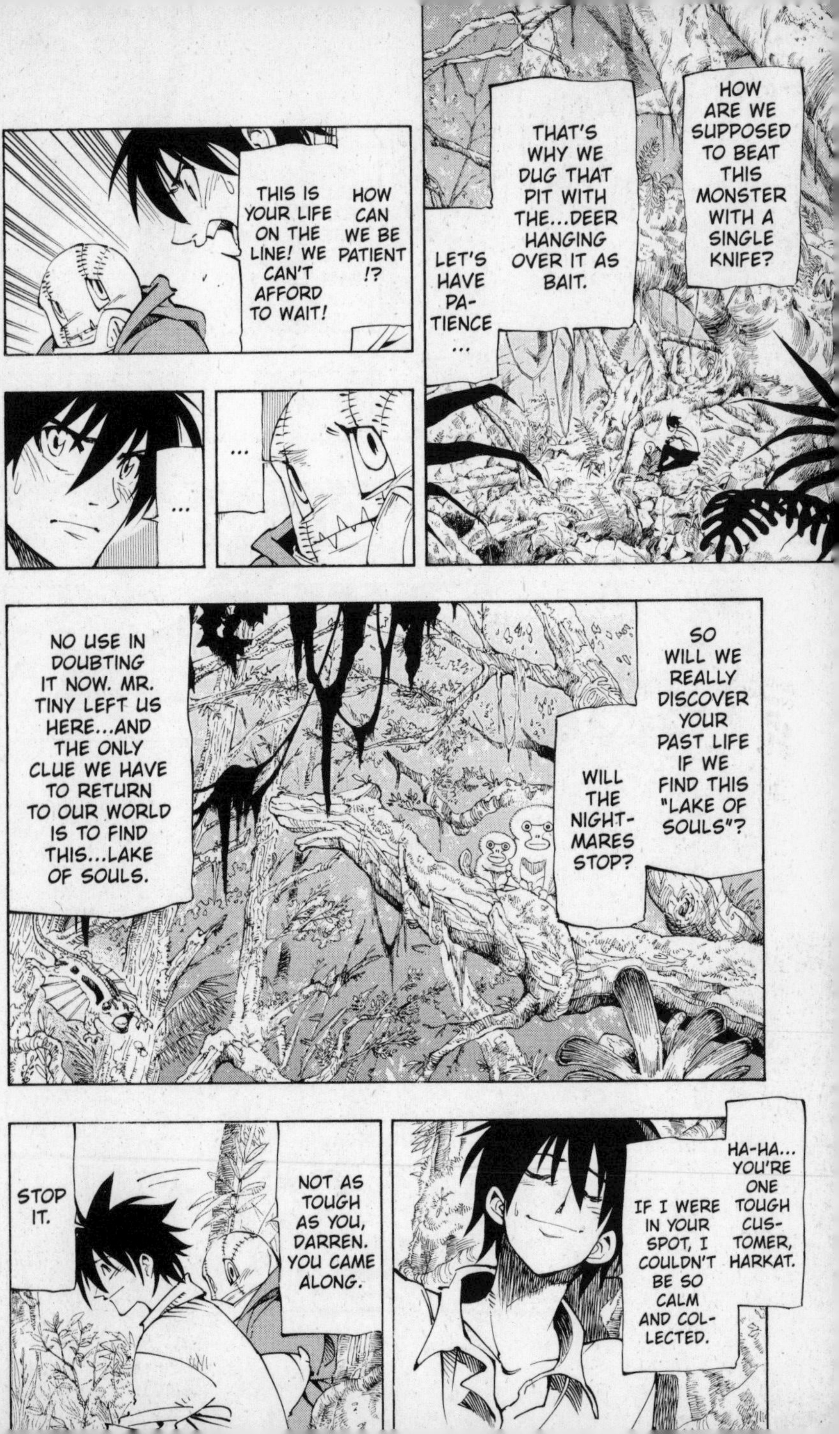

HOW ARE WE SUPPOSED TO BEAT THIS MONSTER WITH A SINGLE KNIFE?
THAT'S WHY WE DUG THAT PIT WITH THE...DEER HANGING OVER IT AS BAIT.
LET'S HAVE PATIENCE...
HOW CAN WE BE PATIENT!?
THIS IS YOUR LIFE ON THE LINE! WE CAN'T AFFORD TO WAIT!
...
...
SO WILL WE REALLY DISCOVER YOUR PAST LIFE IF WE FIND THIS "LAKE OF SOULS"?
WILL THE NIGHTMARES STOP?
NO USE IN DOUBTING IT NOW. MR. TINY LEFT US HERE...AND THE ONLY CLUE WE HAVE TO RETURN TO OUR WORLD IS TO FIND THIS...LAKE OF SOULS.
HA-HA... YOU'RE ONE TOUGH CUSTOMER, HARKAT.
IF I WERE IN YOUR SPOT, I COULDN'T BE SO CALM AND COLLECTED.
NOT AS TOUGH AS YOU, DARREN. YOU CAME ALONG.
STOP IT.

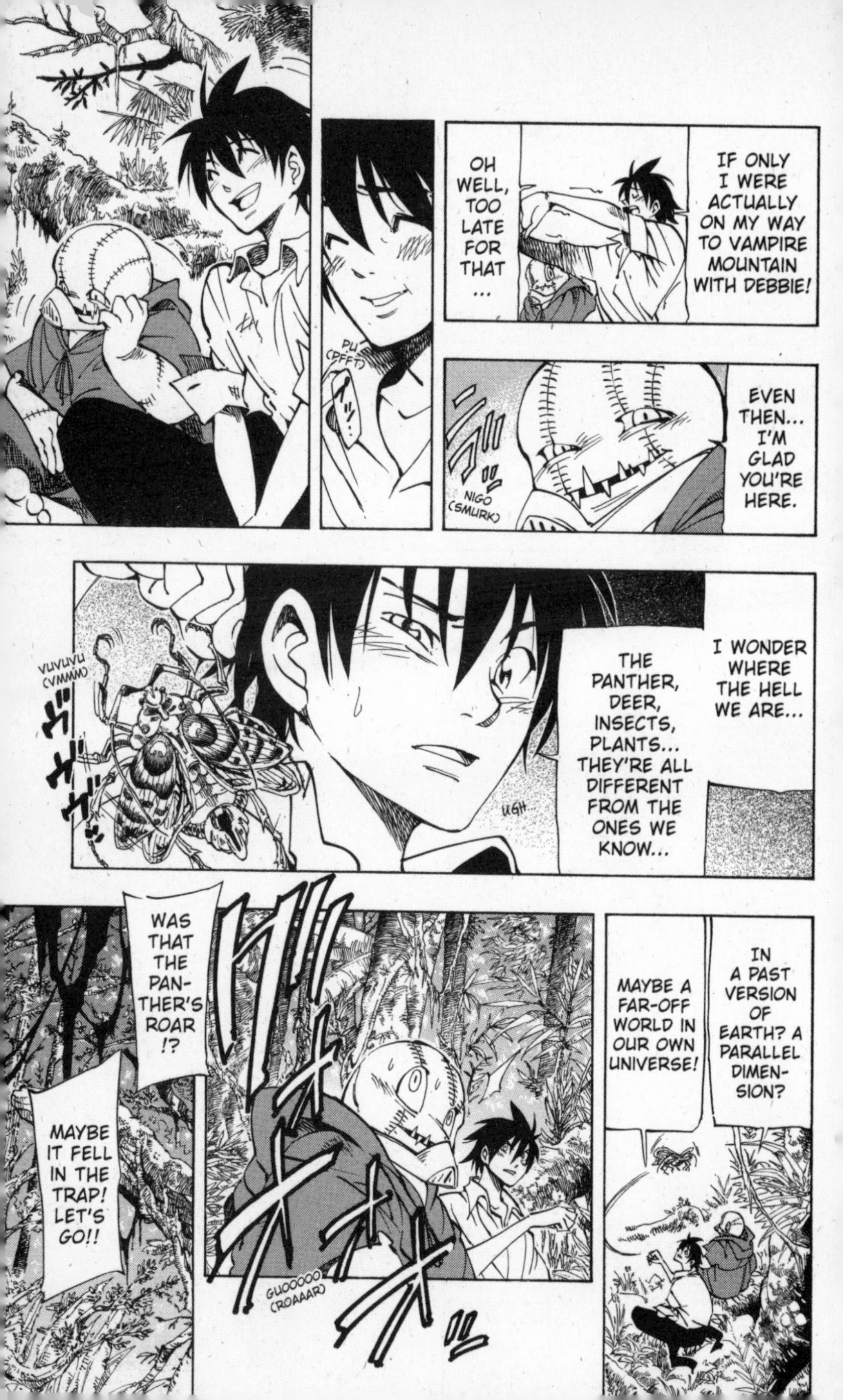
IF ONLY I WERE ACTUALLY ON MY WAY TO VAMPIRE MOUNTAIN WITH DEBBIE!
OH WELL, TOO LATE FOR THAT ...
EVEN THEN... I'M GLAD YOU'RE HERE.
NIGO (SMURK)
PU (PFFT)
I WONDER WHERE THE HELL WE ARE...
THE PANTHER, DEER, INSECTS, PLANTS... THEY'RE ALL DIFFERENT FROM THE ONES WE KNOW...
UGH
VUVUVU (VMMM)
IN A PAST VERSION OF EARTH? A PARALLEL DIMEN-SION?
MAYBE A FAR-OFF WORLD IN OUR OWN UNIVERSE!
GUOOOOO (ROAAAR)
WAS THAT THE PAN-THER'S ROAR !?
MAYBE IT FELL IN THE TRAP! LET'S GO!!

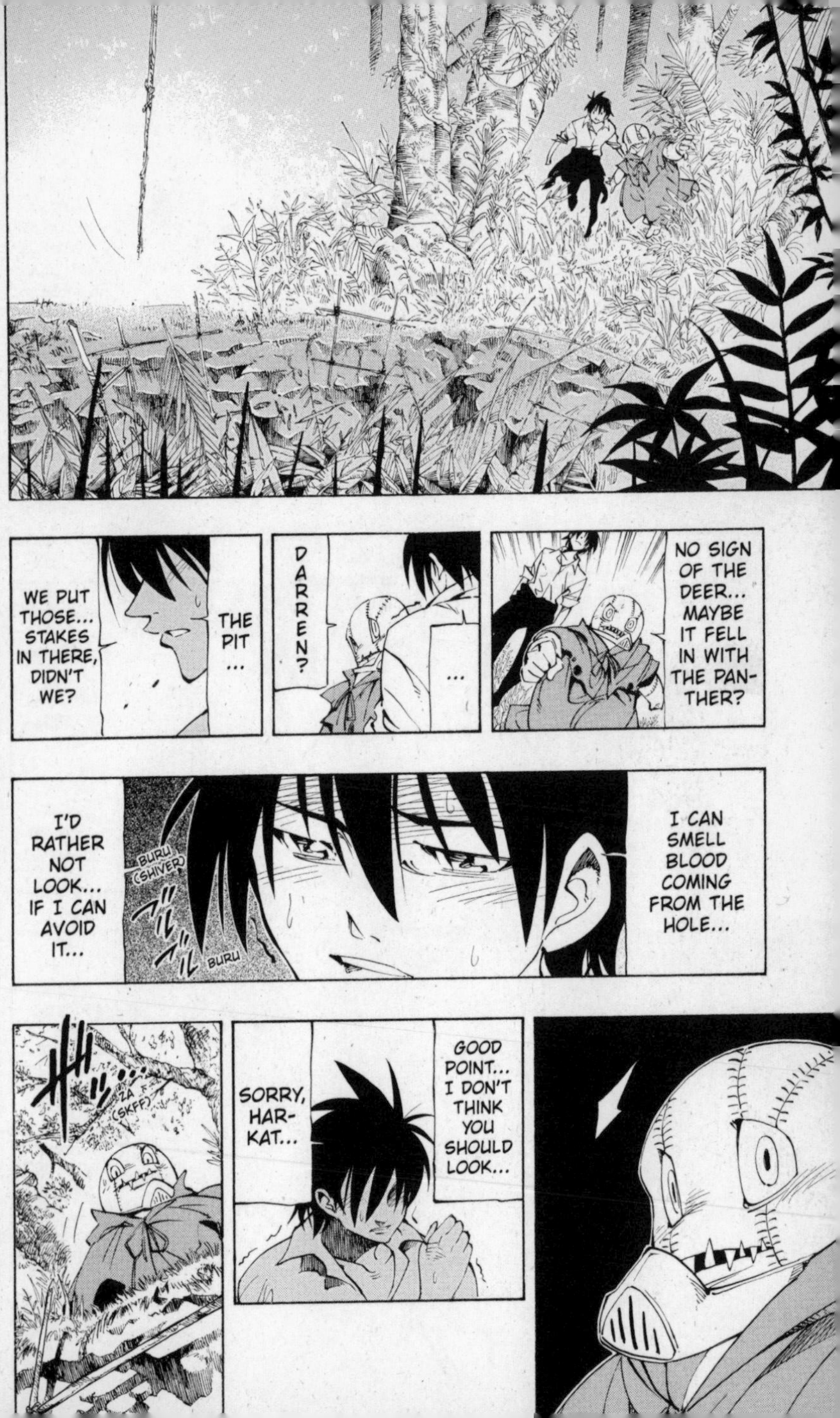
NO SIGN OF THE DEER... MAYBE IT FELL IN WITH THE PANTHER?
...
DARREN?
THE PIT...
WE PUT THOSE... STAKES IN THERE, DIDN'T WE?
I CAN SMELL BLOOD COMING FROM THE HOLE...
BURU (SHIVER)
BURU
I'D RATHER NOT LOOK... IF I CAN AVOID IT...
GOOD POINT... I DON'T THINK YOU SHOULD LOOK...
SORRY, HAR-KAT...
ZA (SKFF)

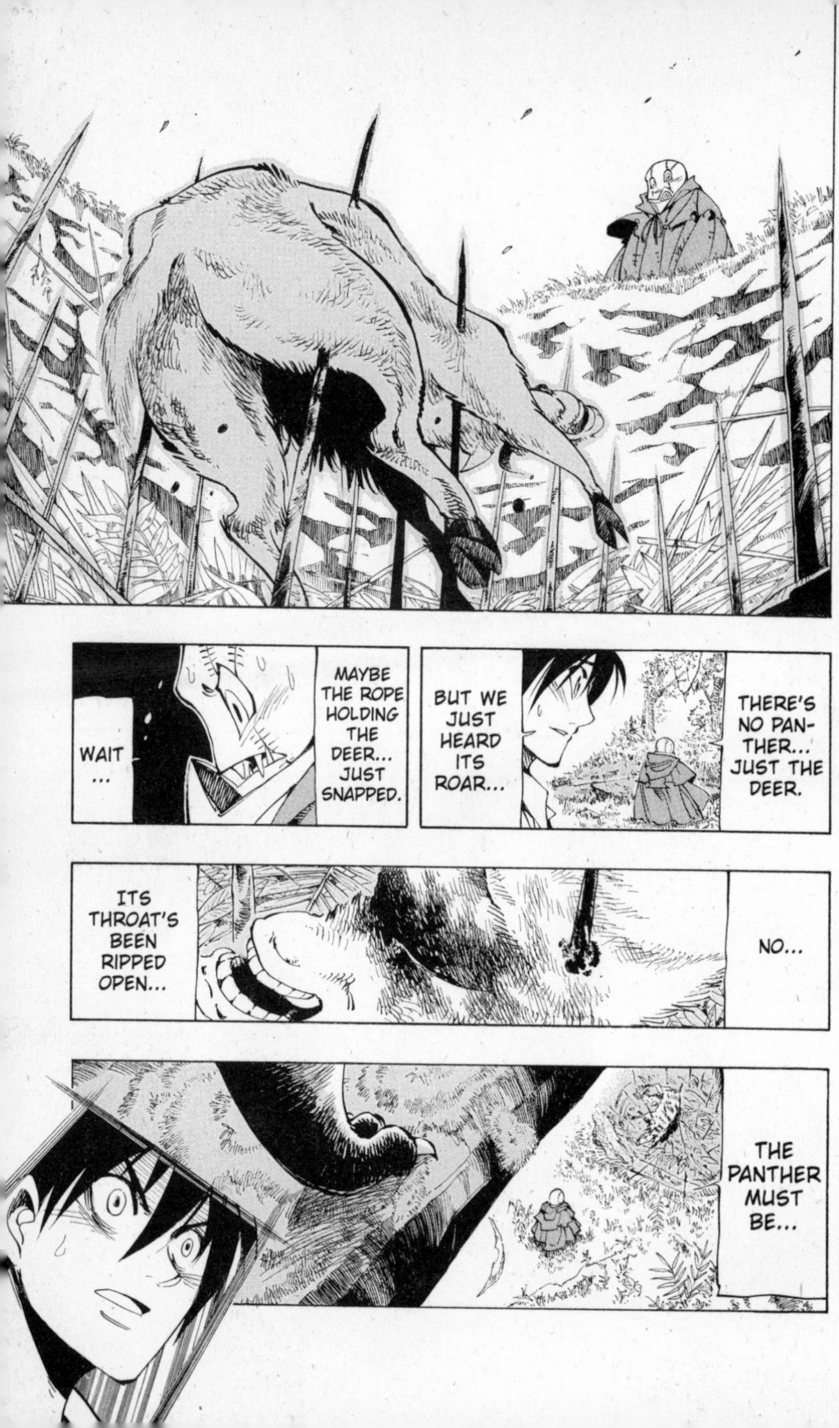
THERE'S NO PAN-THER... JUST THE DEER.
BUT WE JUST HEARD ITS ROAR...
MAYBE THE ROPE HOLDING THE DEER... JUST SNAPPED.
WAIT...
NO...
ITS THROAT'S BEEN RIPPED OPEN...
THE PANTHER MUST BE...

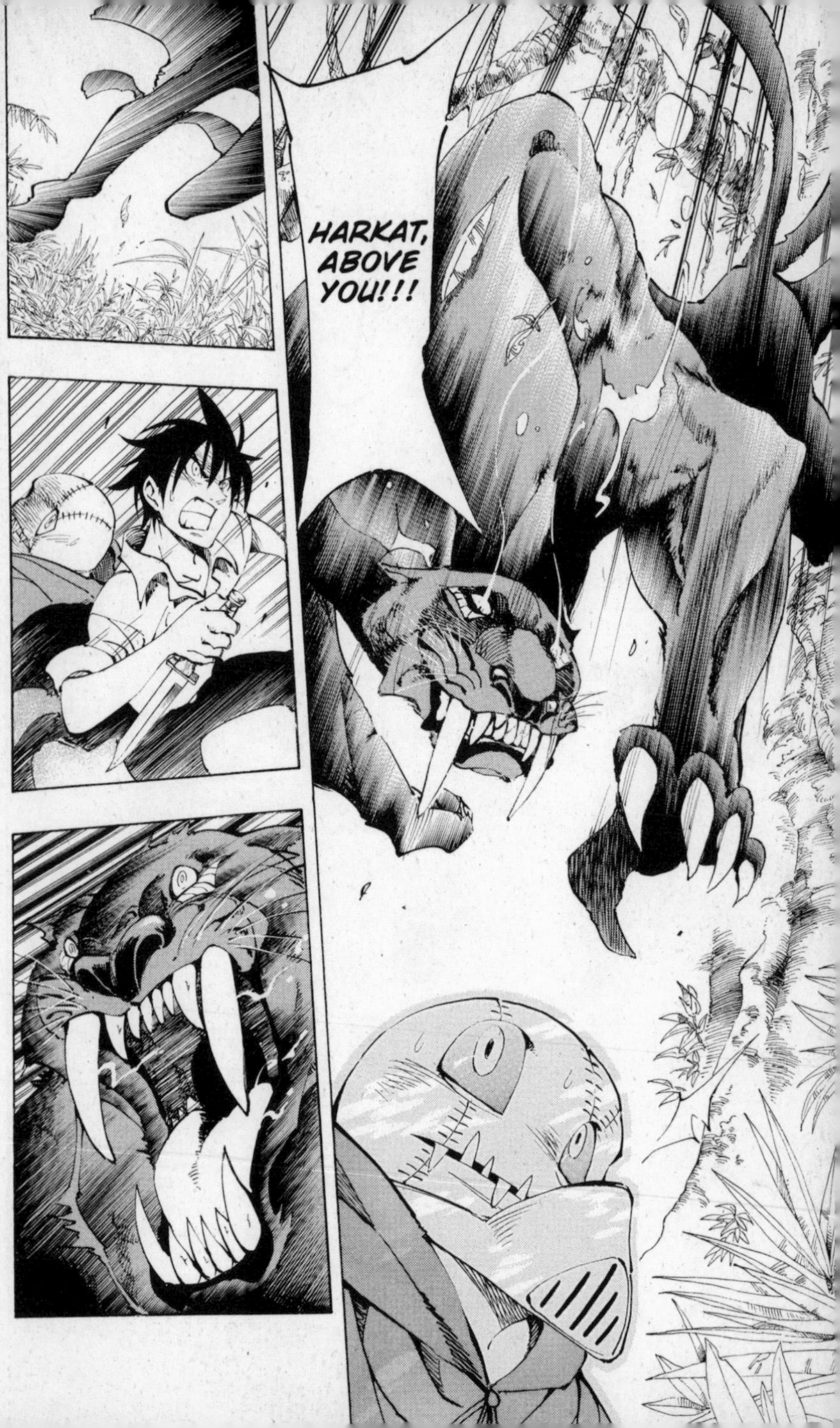
HARKAT, ABOVE YOU!!!

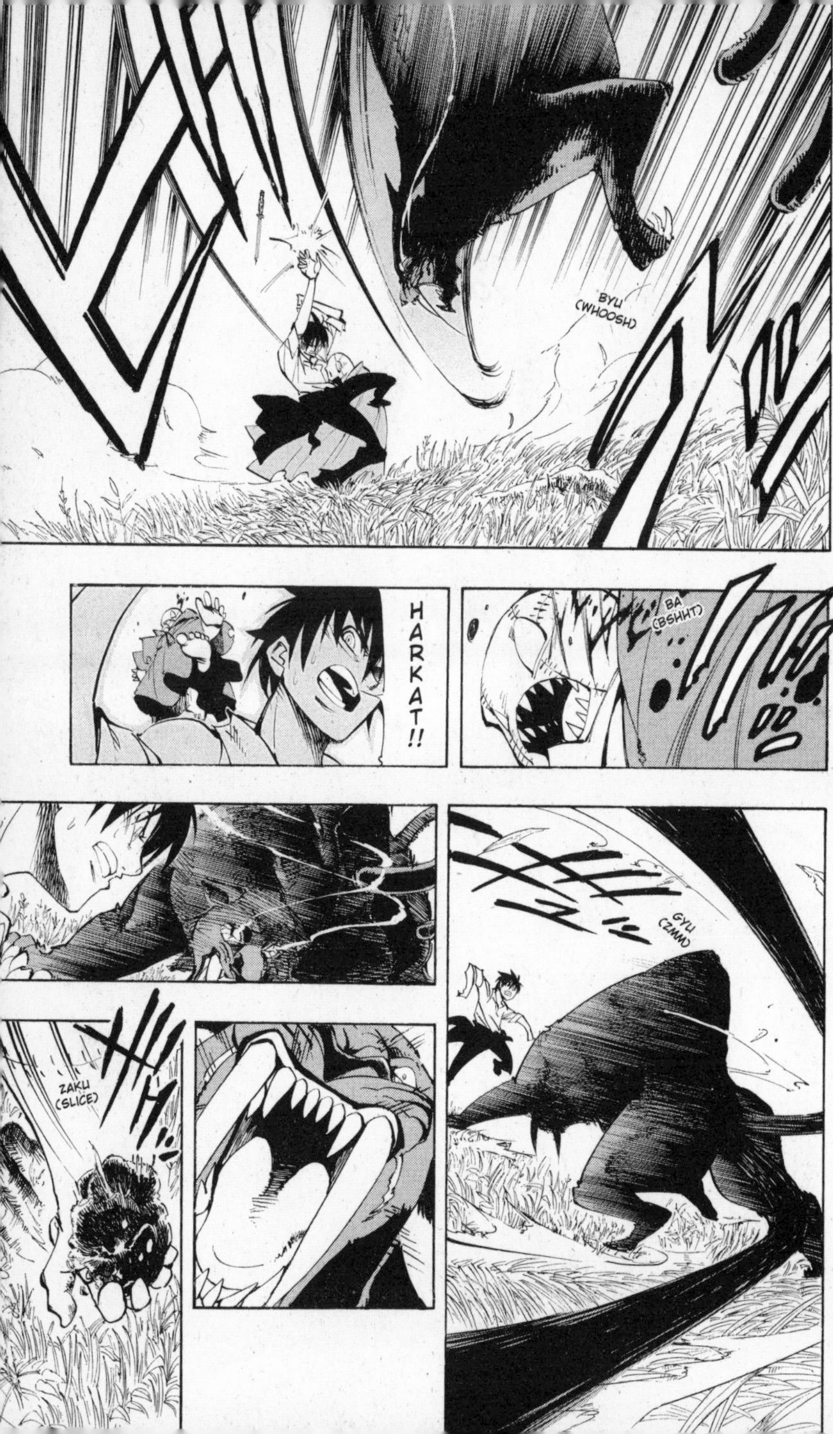
BYU (WHOOSH)
BA (BSHHT)
HARKAT!!
GYU (ZMM)
ZAKU (SLICE)

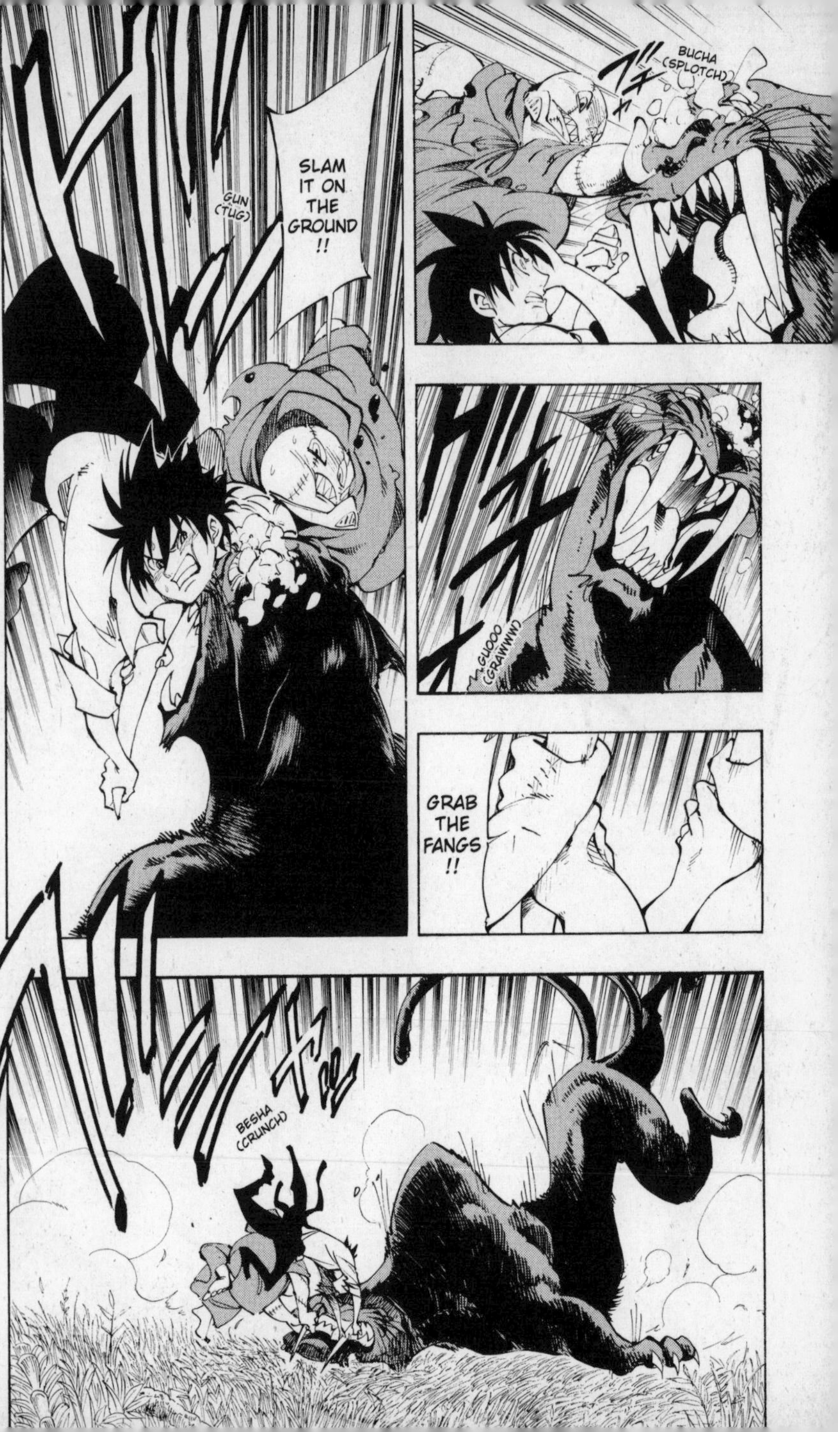
BUCHA (SPLOTCH)
GUOOO (GRAWWW)
GRAB THE FANGS !!
SLAM IT ON THE GROUND !!
GUN (TUG)
BESHA (CRUNCH)

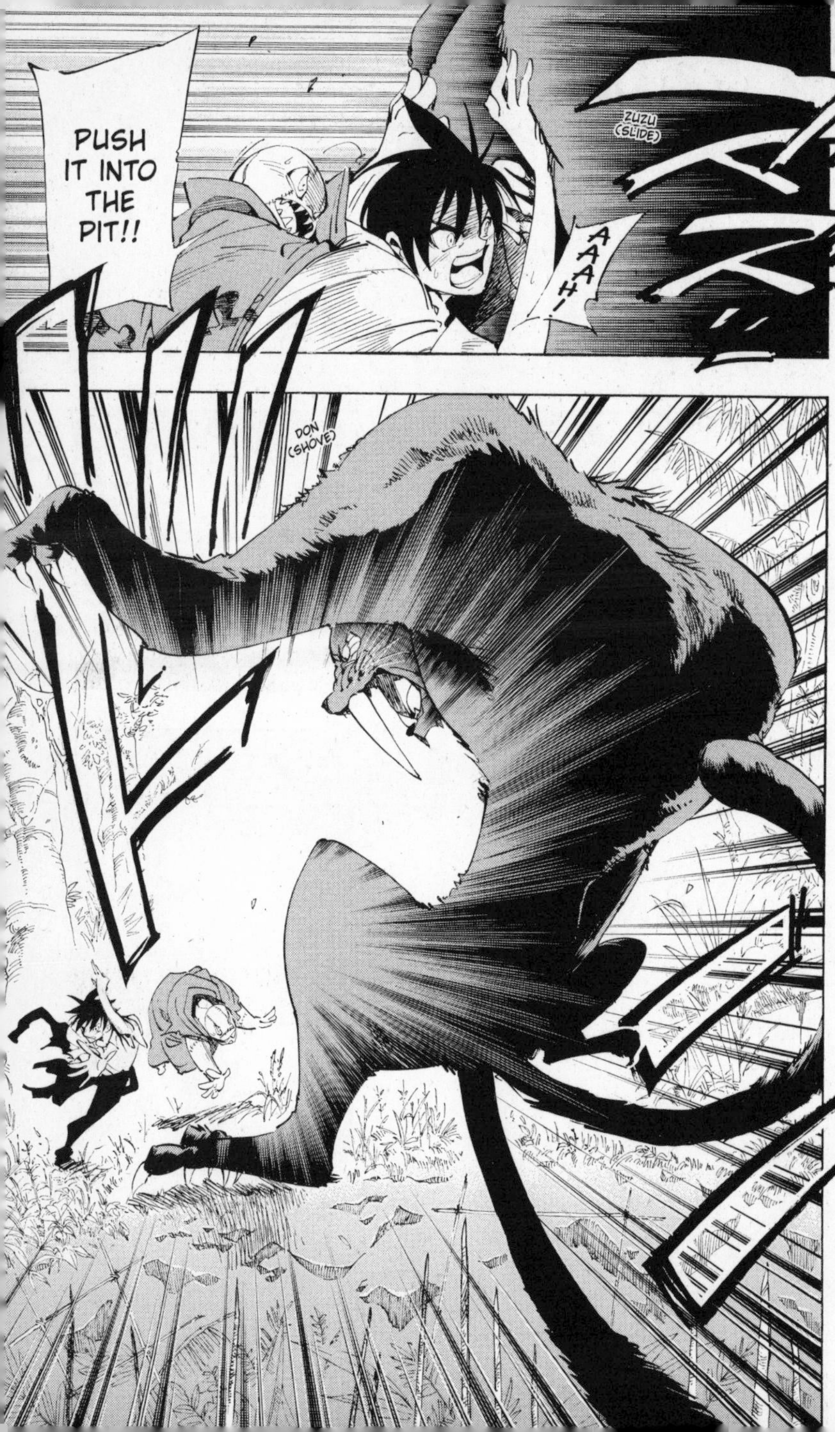
ZUZU (SLIDE)
AAAH!
PUSH IT INTO THE PIT!!
DON (SHOVE)

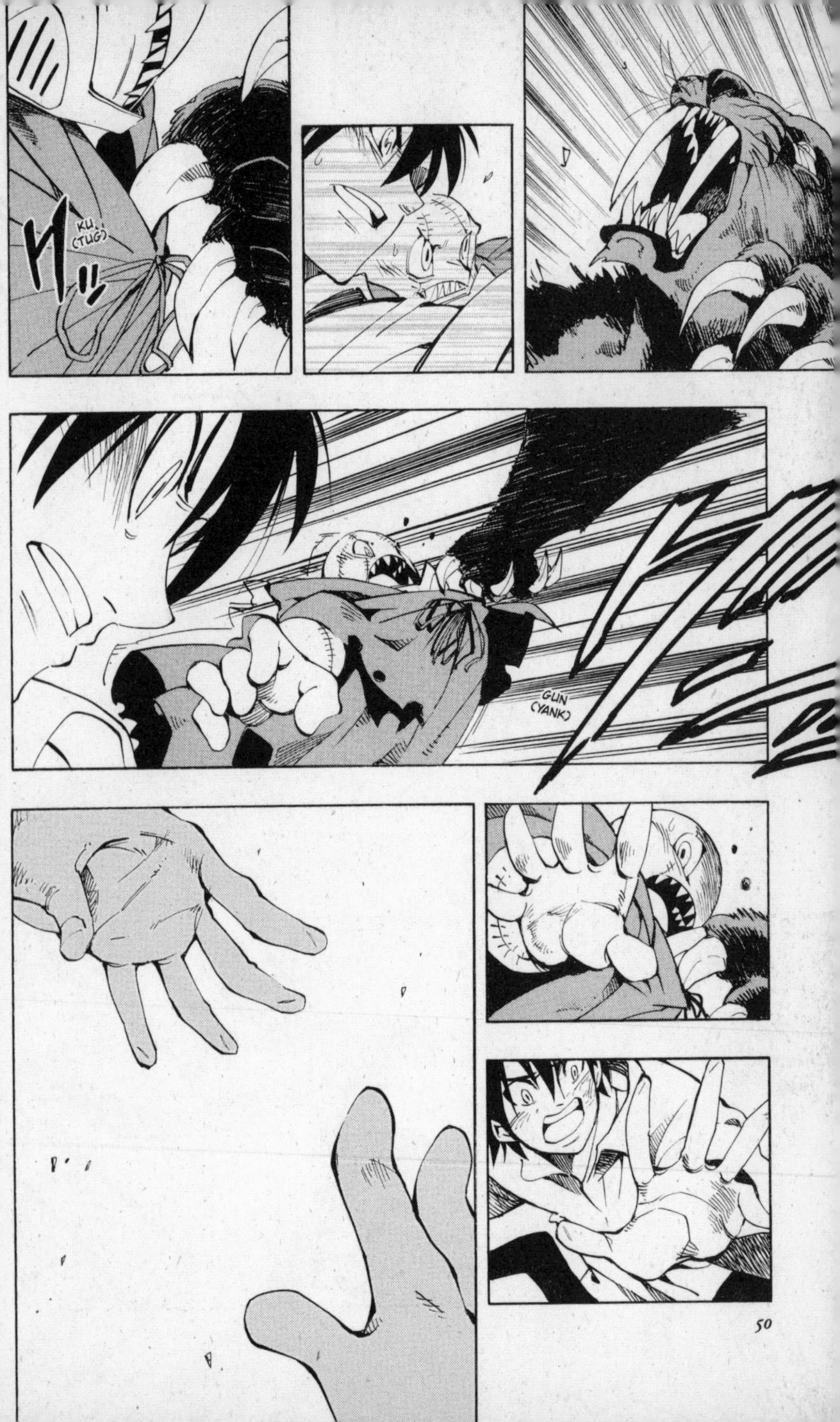
KU (TUG)
GUN (YANK)

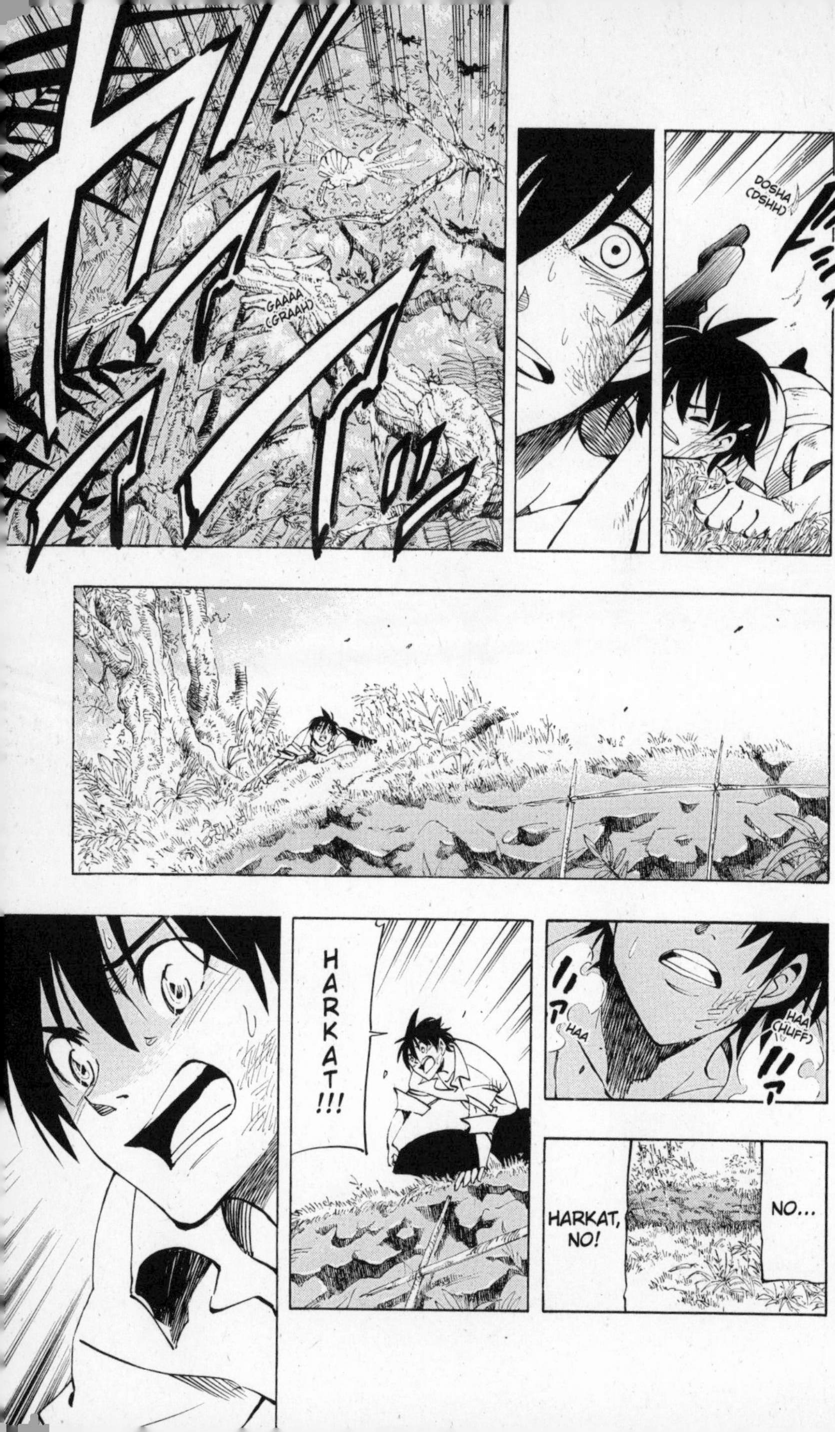
DOSHA (DSHH)
GAAAA (GRAAH)
HAA (HUFF)
HAA
NO…
HARKAT, NO!
HARKAT!!!

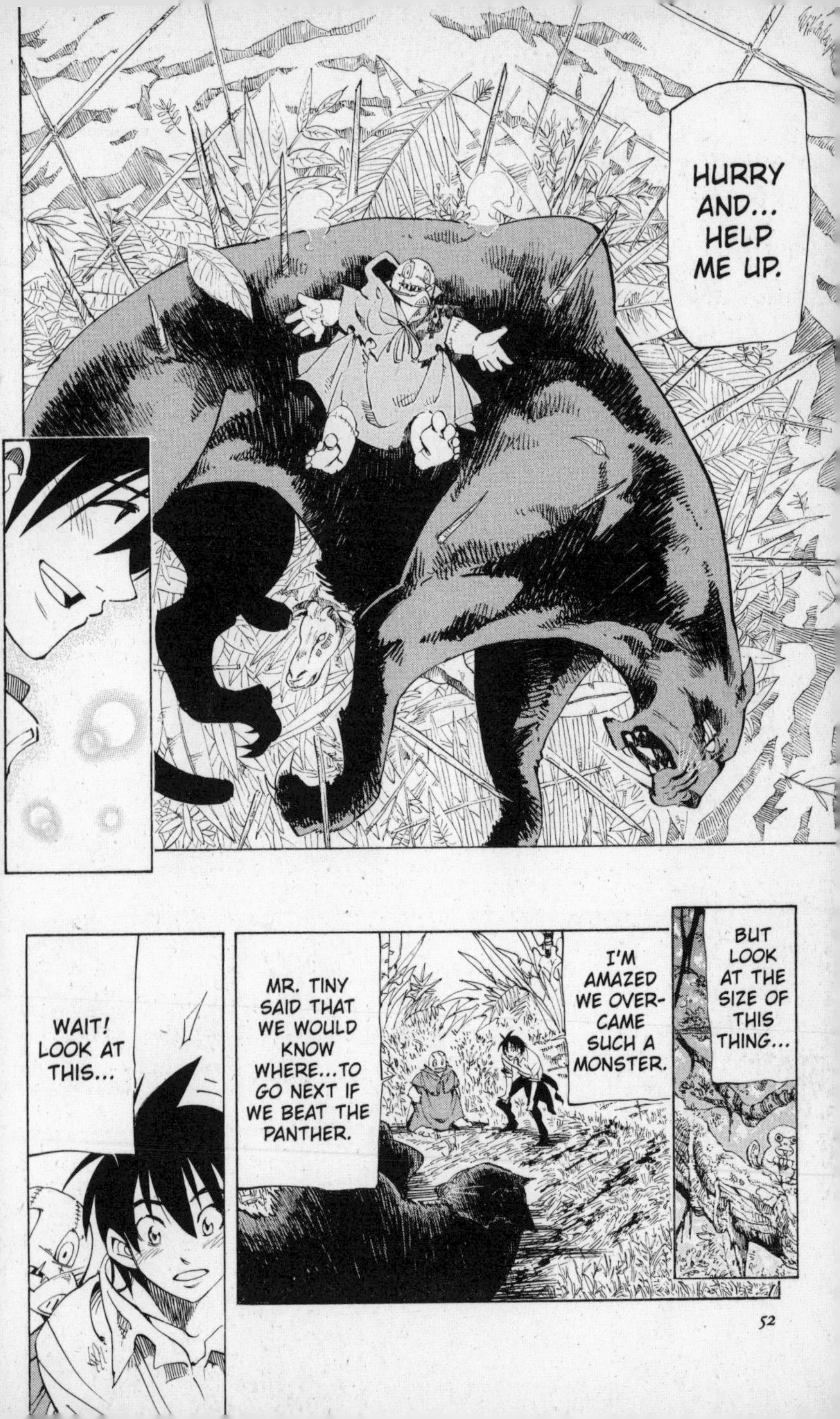
HURRY AND... HELP ME UP.
BUT LOOK AT THE SIZE OF THIS THING...
I'M AMAZED WE OVER-CAME SUCH A MONSTER.
MR. TINY SAID THAT WE WOULD KNOW WHERE...TO GO NEXT IF WE BEAT THE PANTHER.
WAIT! LOOK AT THIS...

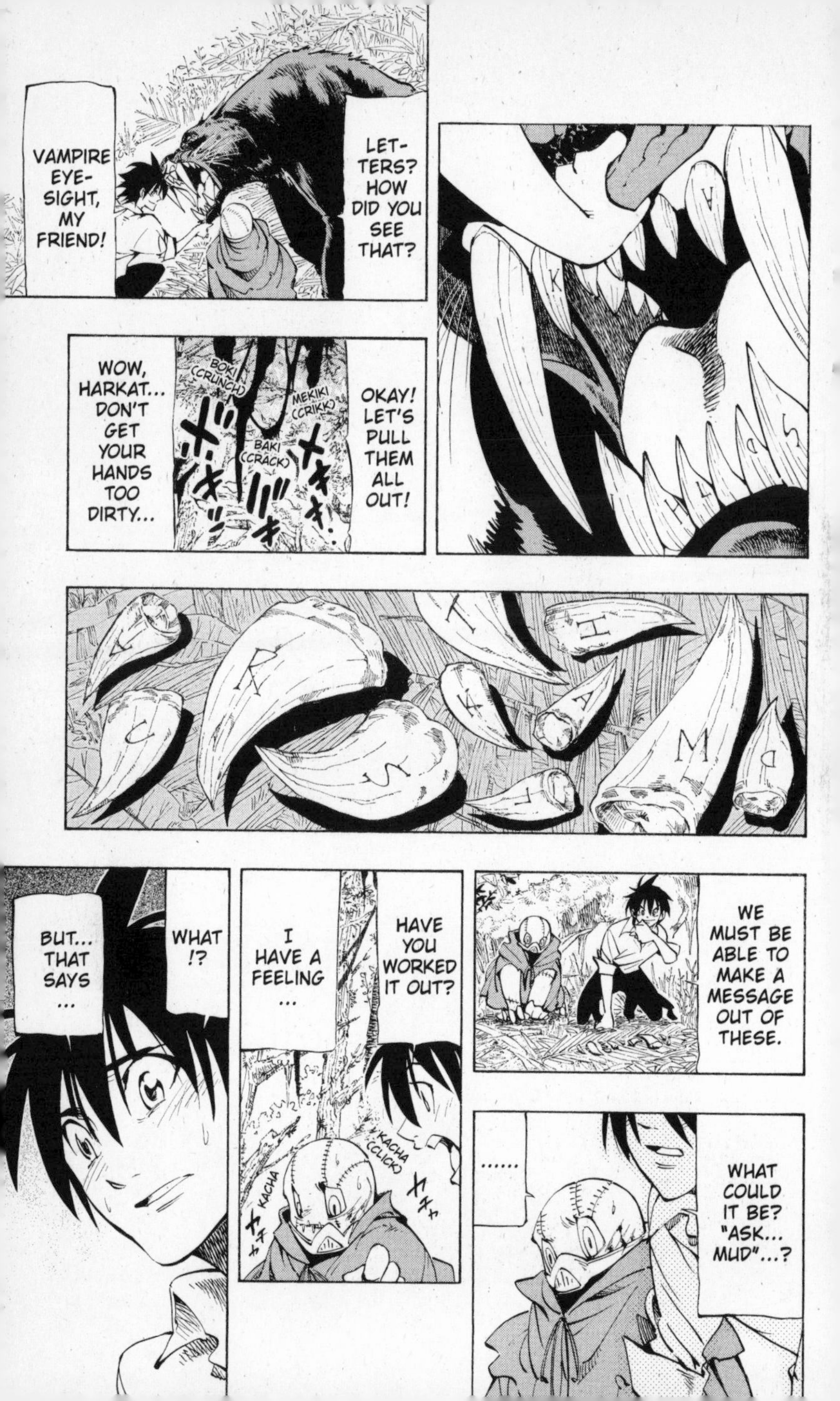
LET-TERS? HOW DID YOU SEE THAT?
VAMPIRE EYE-SIGHT, MY FRIEND!
OKAY! LET'S PULL THEM ALL OUT!
MEKIKI (CRIKK)
BAKI (CRACK)
BOKI (CRUNCH)
WOW, HARKAT... DON'T GET YOUR HANDS TOO DIRTY...
WE MUST BE ABLE TO MAKE A MESSAGE OUT OF THESE.
WHAT COULD IT BE? "ASK... MUD"...?
......
HAVE YOU WORKED IT OUT?
I HAVE A FEELING ...
KACHA (CLICK)
KACHA
WHAT !?
BUT... THAT SAYS ...

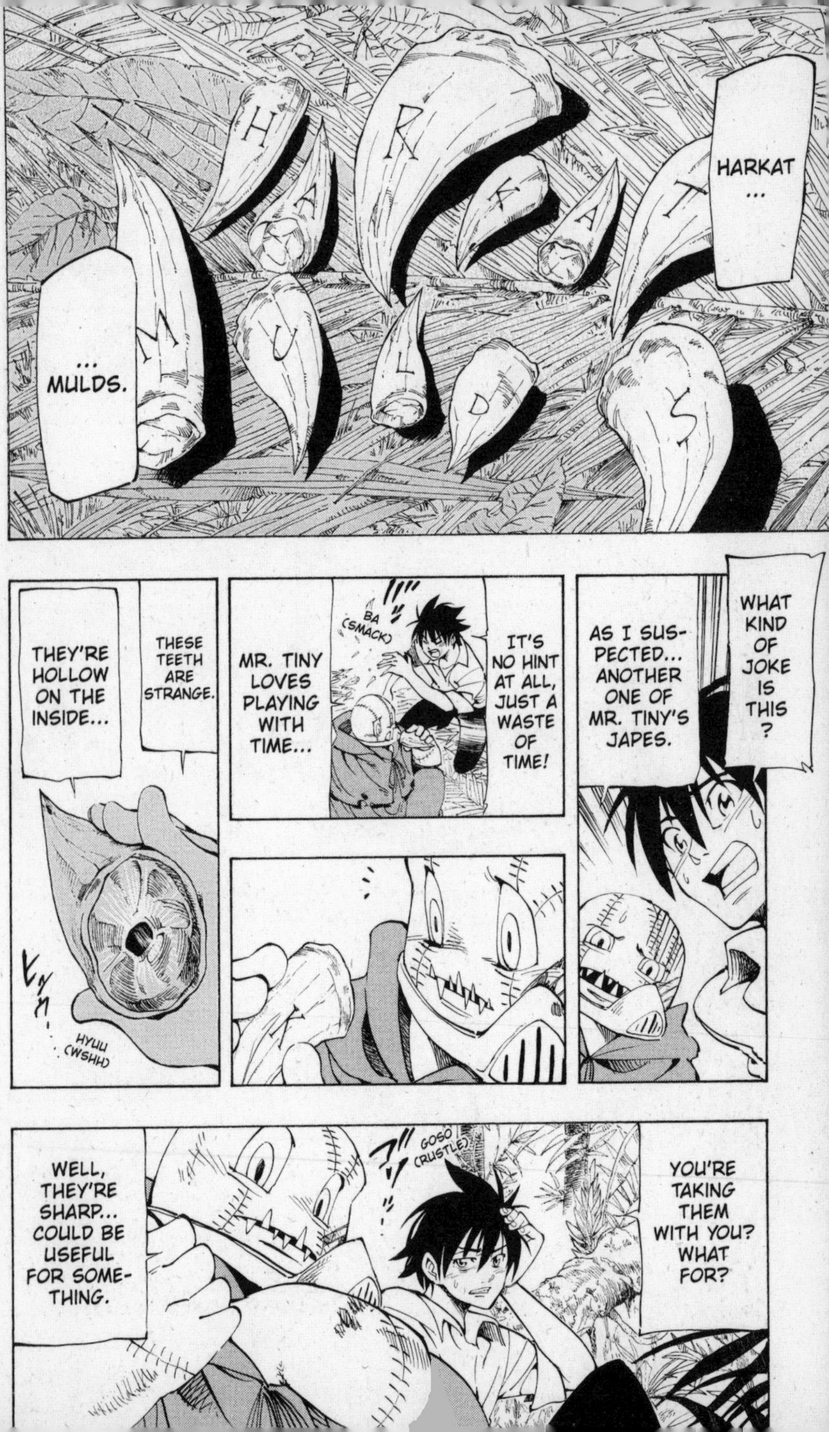
HARKAT ...
... MULDS.
WHAT KIND OF JOKE IS THIS ?
AS I SUSPECTED... ANOTHER ONE OF MR. TINY'S JAPES.
IT'S NO HINT AT ALL, JUST A WASTE OF TIME!
BA (SMACK)
MR. TINY LOVES PLAYING WITH TIME...
THESE TEETH ARE STRANGE.
THEY'RE HOLLOW ON THE INSIDE...
HYUU (WSHH)
YOU'RE TAKING THEM WITH YOU? WHAT FOR?
GOSO (RUSTLE)
WELL, THEY'RE SHARP... COULD BE USEFUL FOR SOME-THING.

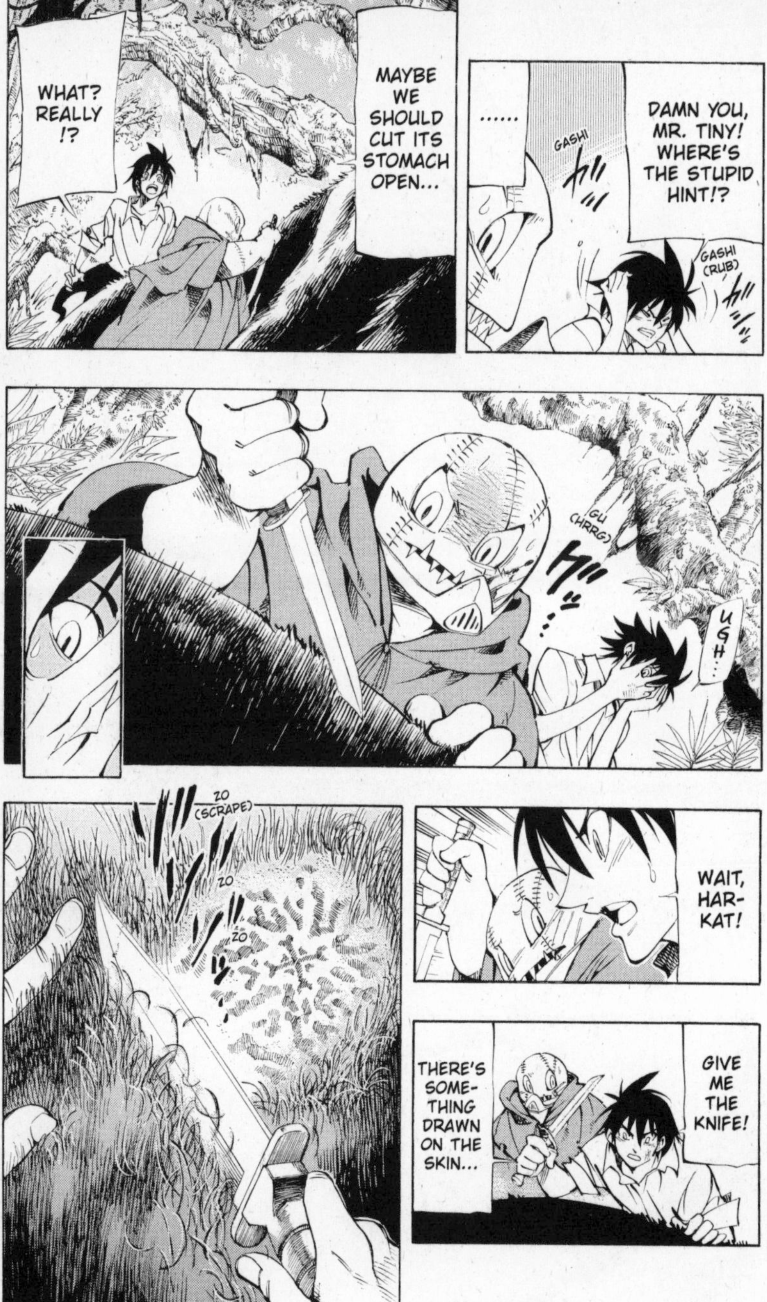

......
DAMN YOU, MR. TINY! WHERE'S THE STUPID HINT!?
GASHI
GASHI (RUB)
MAYBE WE SHOULD CUT ITS STOMACH OPEN...
WHAT? REALLY!?
GU (HRRG)
UGH...
WAIT, HAR-KAT!
GIVE ME THE KNIFE!
THERE'S SOME-THING DRAWN ON THE SKIN...
ZO (SCRAPE)
ZO
ZO

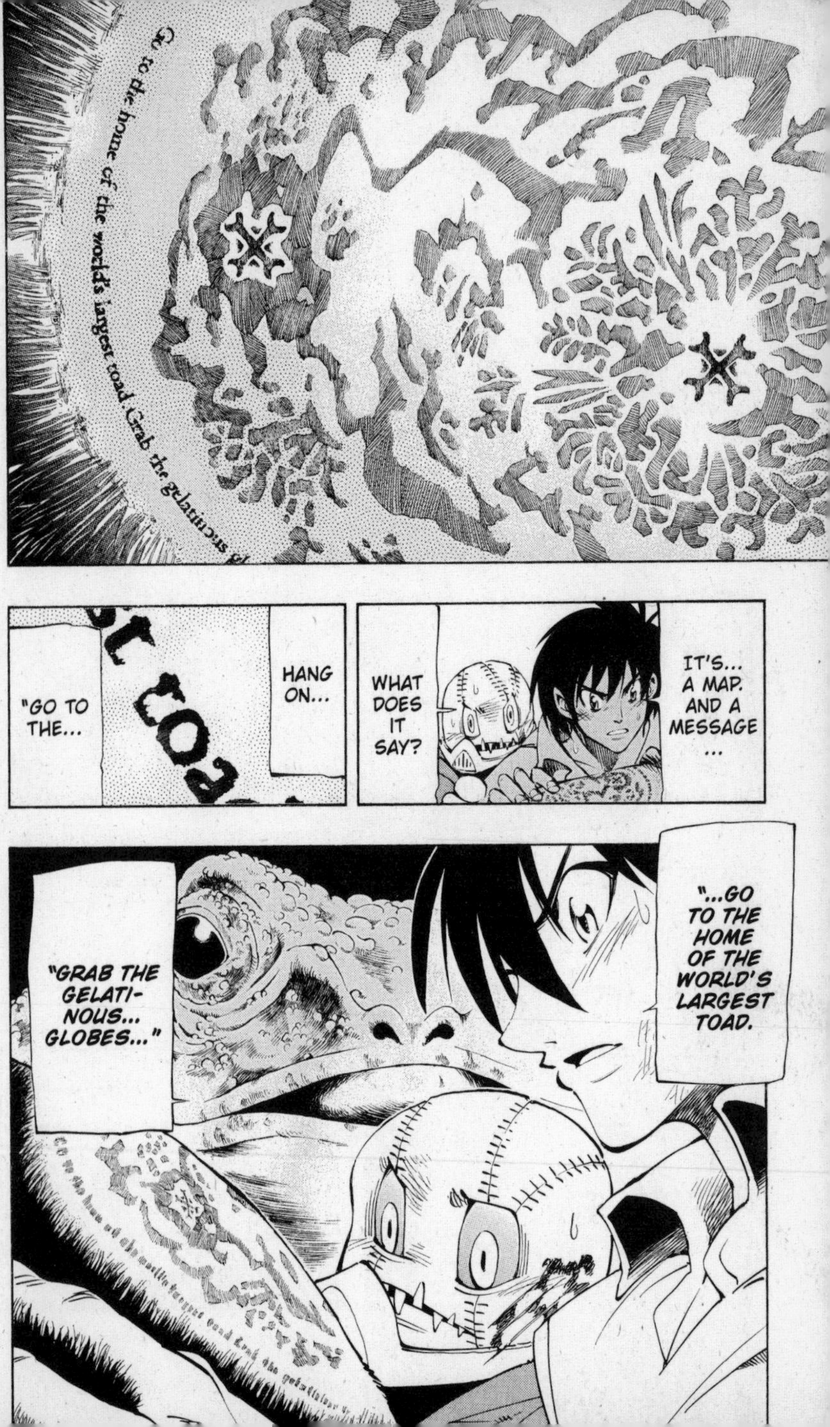
Go to the home of the world's largest toad Grab the gelatinous
IT'S... A MAP. AND A MESSAGE ...
WHAT DOES IT SAY?
HANG ON...
"GO TO THE...
"...GO TO THE HOME OF THE WORLD'S LARGEST TOAD.
"GRAB THE GELATI- NOUS... GLOBES..."

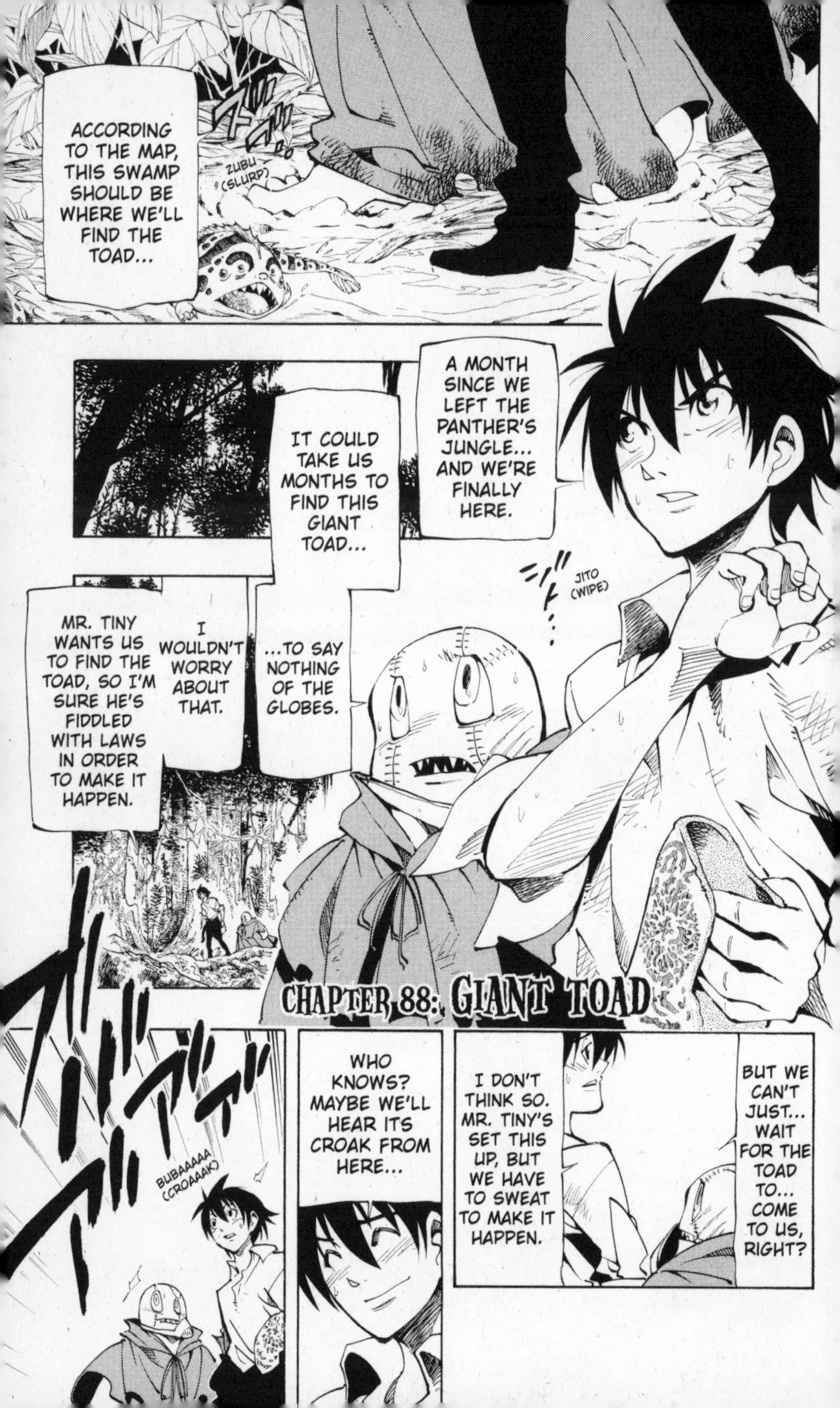
ACCORDING TO THE MAP, THIS SWAMP SHOULD BE WHERE WE'LL FIND THE TOAD...
ZUBU (SLURP)
A MONTH SINCE WE LEFT THE PANTHER'S JUNGLE... AND WE'RE FINALLY HERE.
JITO (WIPE)
IT COULD TAKE US MONTHS TO FIND THIS GIANT TOAD...
...TO SAY NOTHING OF THE GLOBES.
I WOULDN'T WORRY ABOUT THAT.
MR. TINY WANTS US TO FIND THE TOAD, SO I'M SURE HE'S FIDDLED WITH LAWS IN ORDER TO MAKE IT HAPPEN.
CHAPTER 88: GIANT TOAD
BUT WE CAN'T JUST... WAIT FOR THE TOAD TO... COME TO US, RIGHT?
I DON'T THINK SO. MR. TINY'S SET THIS UP, BUT WE HAVE TO SWEAT TO MAKE IT HAPPEN.
WHO KNOWS? MAYBE WE'LL HEAR ITS CROAK FROM HERE...
BUBAAAAA (CROAAAK)

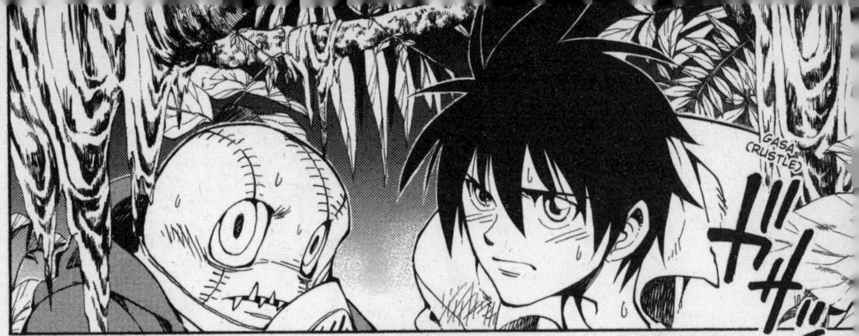
GASA
(RUSTLE)

CHAPTER 88: GIANT TOAD

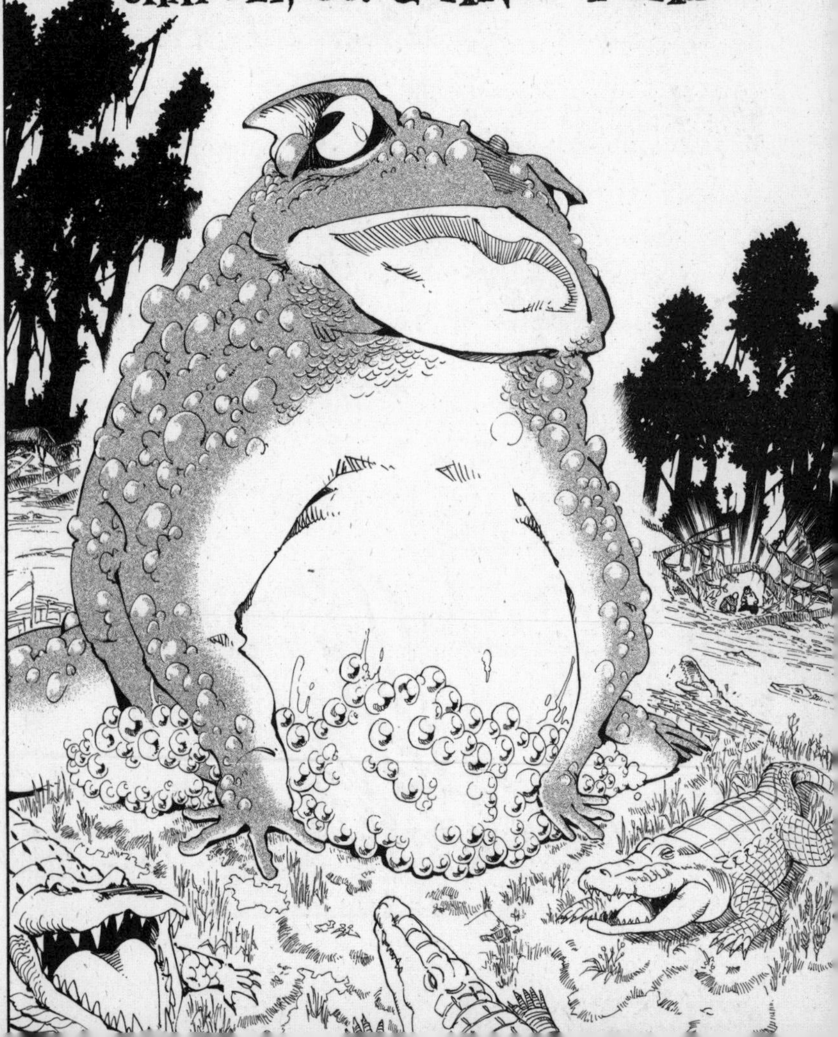

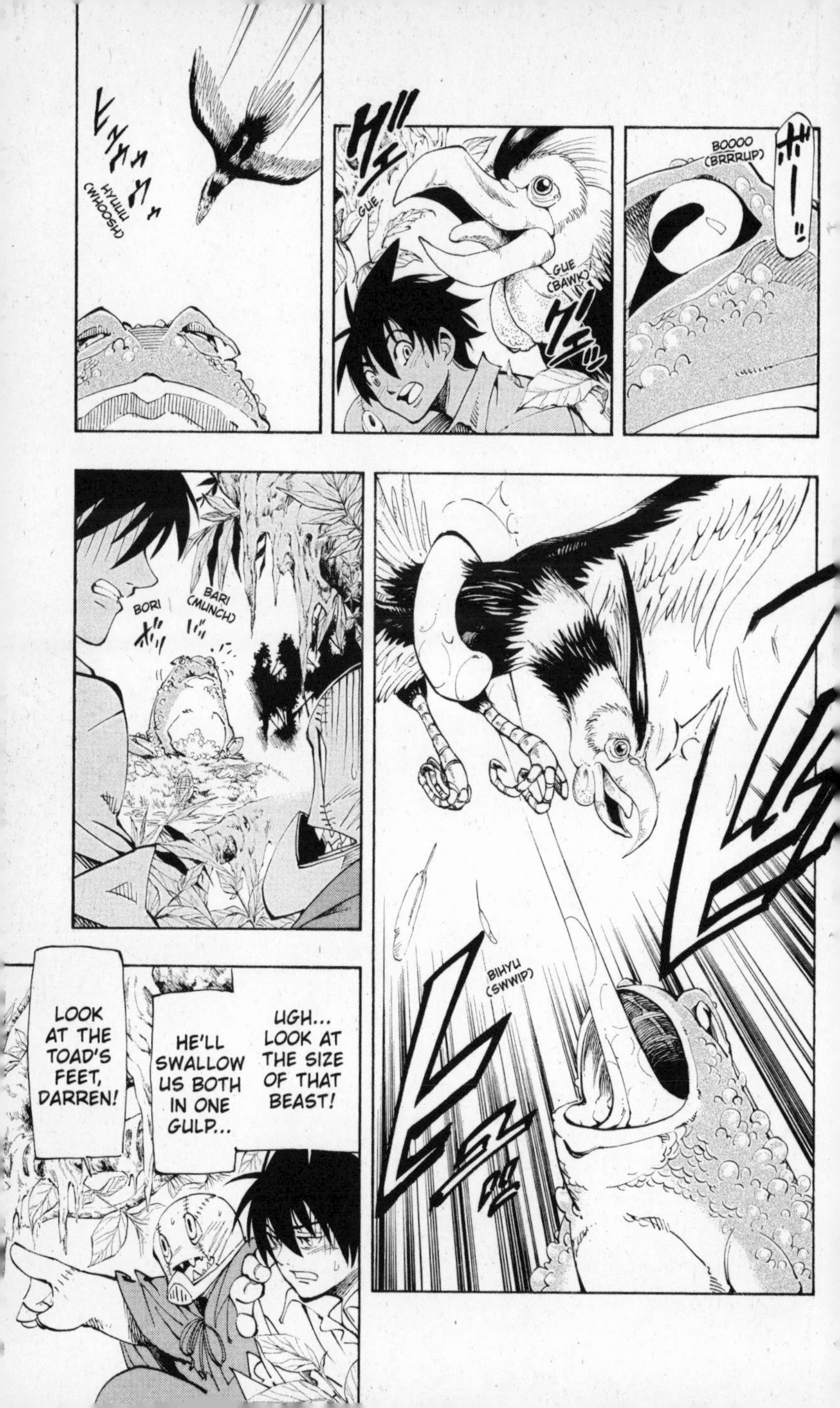
BOOOO (BRRRUP)
GUE
GUE (BAWK)
HYUUU (WHOOSH)
BIHYU (SWWIP)
BORI
BARI (MUNCH)
UGH... LOOK AT THE SIZE OF THAT BEAST!
HE'LL SWALLOW US BOTH IN ONE GULP...
LOOK AT THE TOAD'S FEET, DARREN!

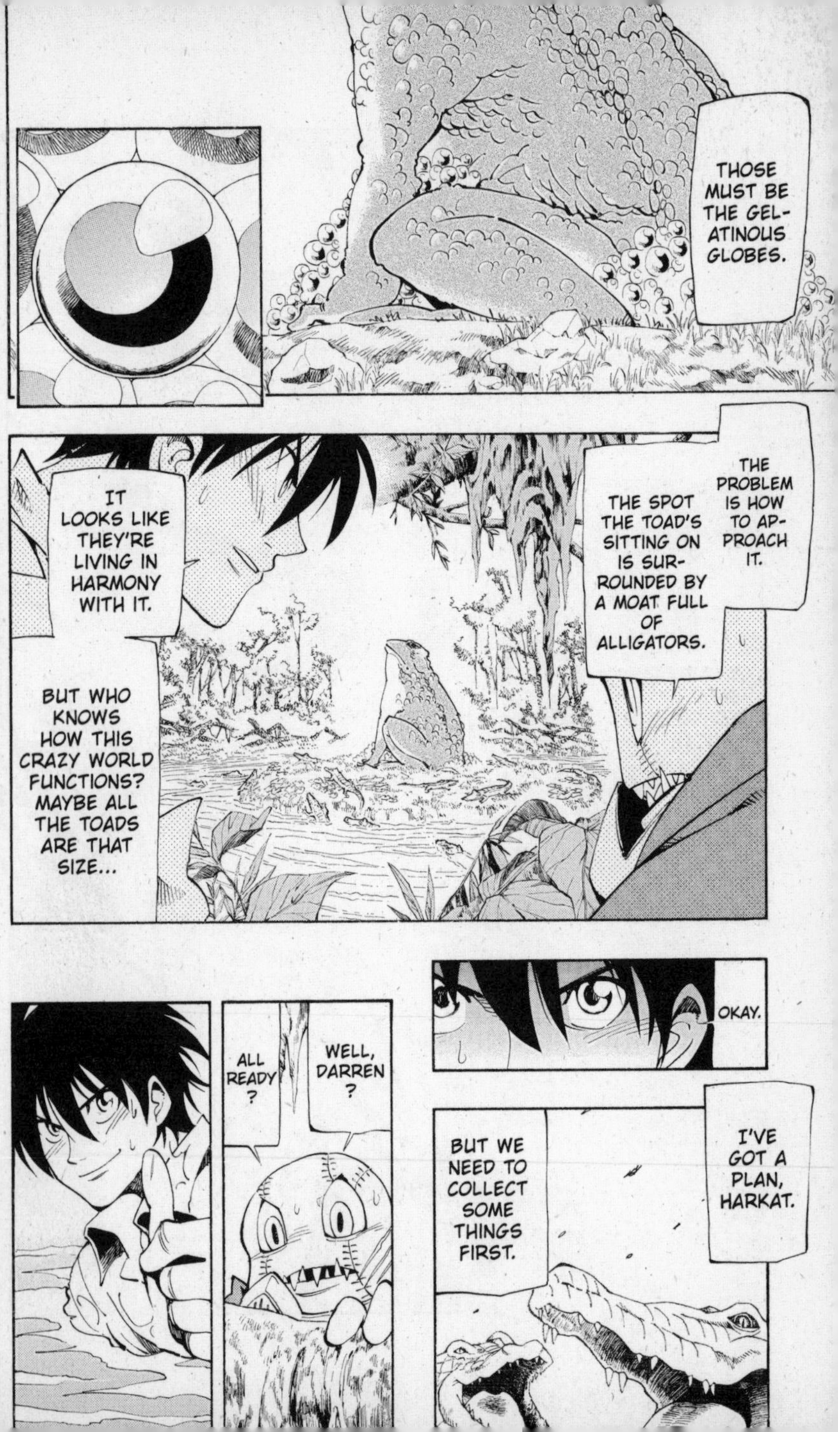
THOSE MUST BE THE GEL-ATINOUS GLOBES.
THE PROBLEM IS HOW TO AP-PROACH IT.
THE SPOT THE TOAD'S SITTING ON IS SUR-ROUNDED BY A MOAT FULL OF ALLIGATORS.
IT LOOKS LIKE THEY'RE LIVING IN HARMONY WITH IT.
BUT WHO KNOWS HOW THIS CRAZY WORLD FUNCTIONS? MAYBE ALL THE TOADS ARE THAT SIZE...
OKAY.
I'VE GOT A PLAN, HARKAT.
BUT WE NEED TO COLLECT SOME THINGS FIRST.
WELL, DARREN?
ALL READY?

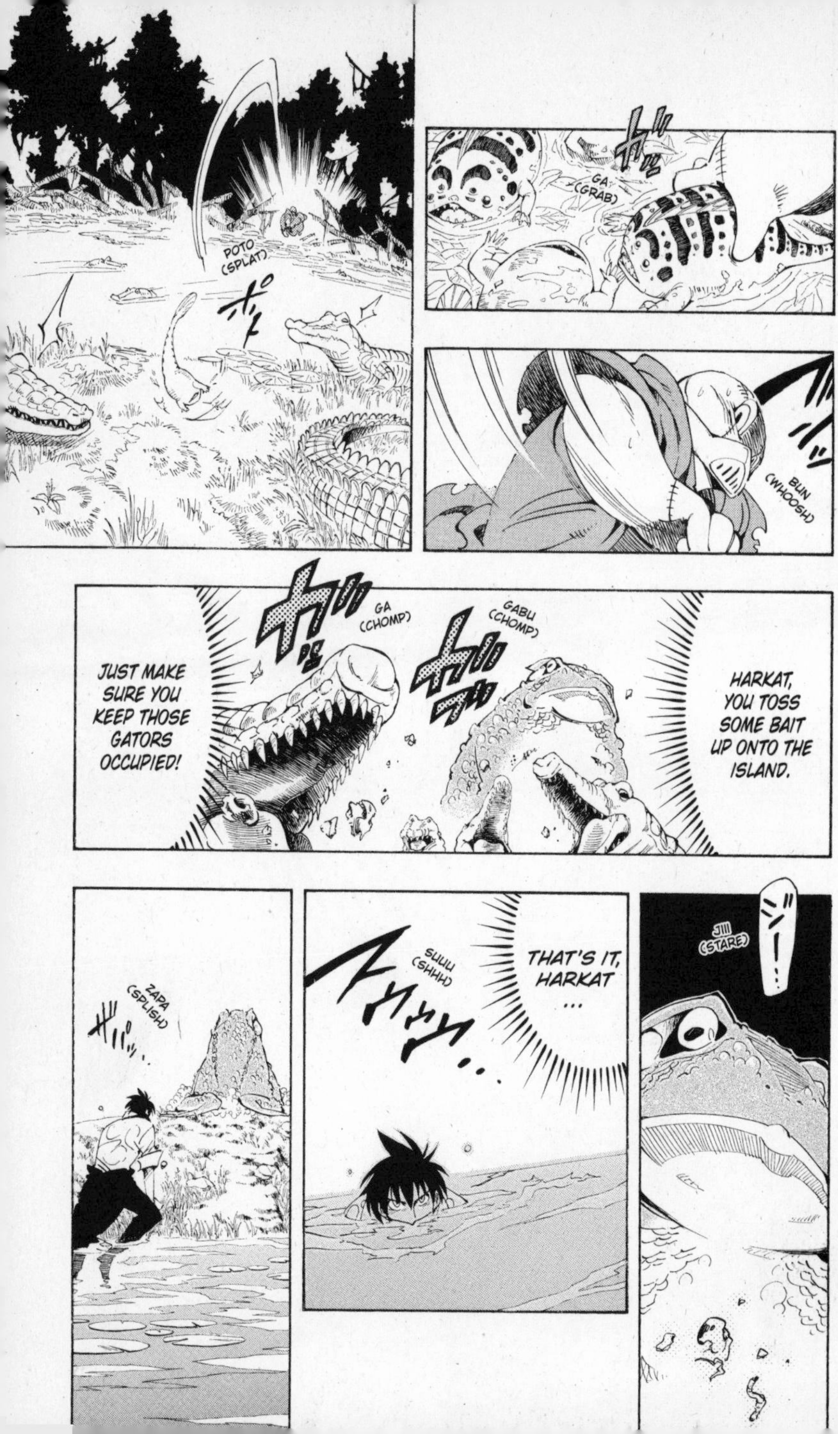
GA
(GRAB)
BUN
(WHOOSH)
POTO
(SPLAT)
HARKAT, YOU TOSS SOME BAIT UP ONTO THE ISLAND.
GABU
(CHOMP)
GA
(CHOMP)
JUST MAKE SURE YOU KEEP THOSE GATORS OCCUPIED!
JIII
(STARE)
THAT'S IT, HARKAT ...
SUUU
(SHHH)
ZAPA
(SPLISH)

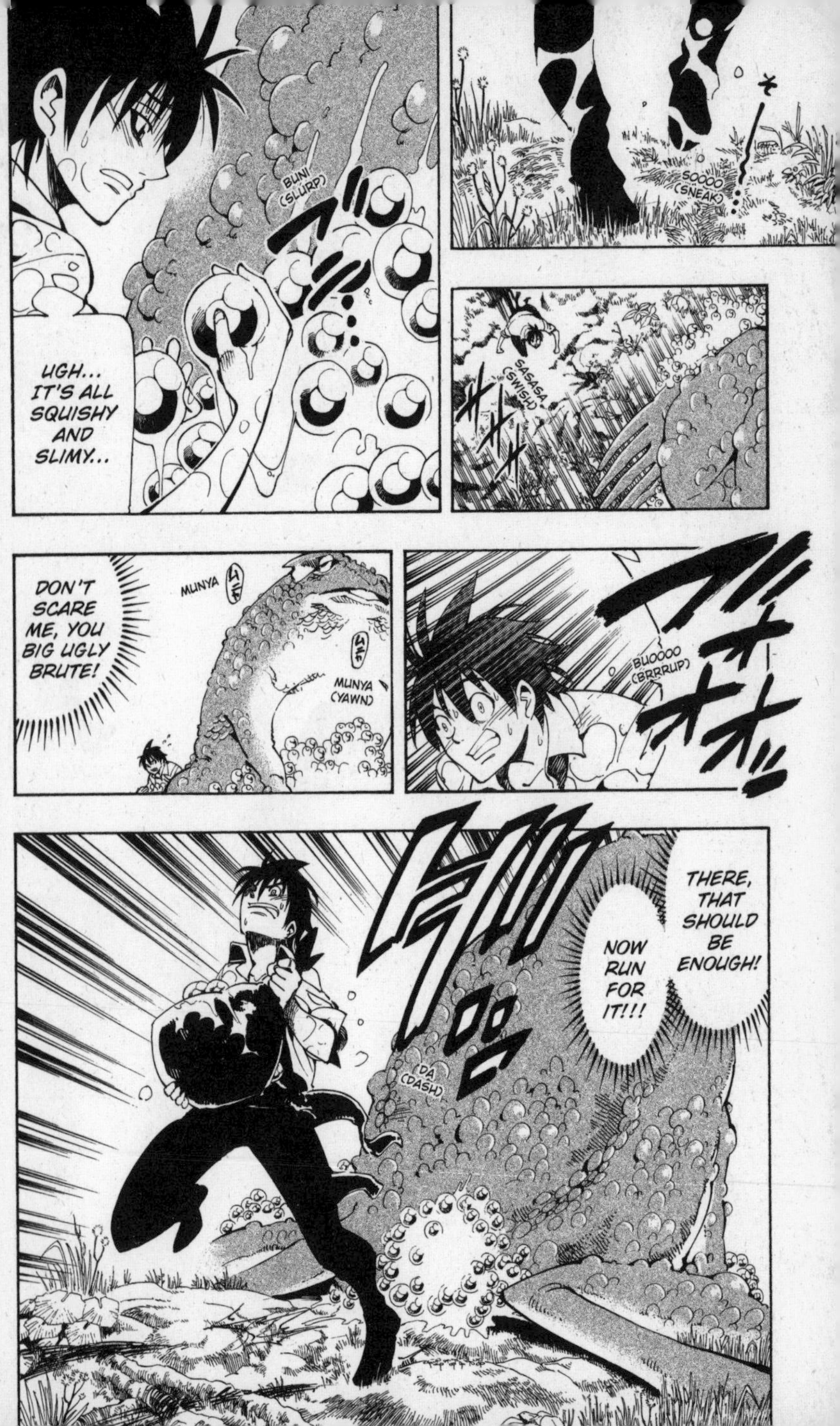
SOOOO (SNEAK)
BUNI (SLURP)
UGH... IT'S ALL SQUISHY AND SLIMY...
SASASA (SWISH)
BUOOOO (BRRRUP)
MUNYA
MUNYA (YAWN)
DON'T SCARE ME, YOU BIG UGLY BRUTE!
THERE, THAT SHOULD BE ENOUGH!
NOW RUN FOR IT!!!
DA (DASH)

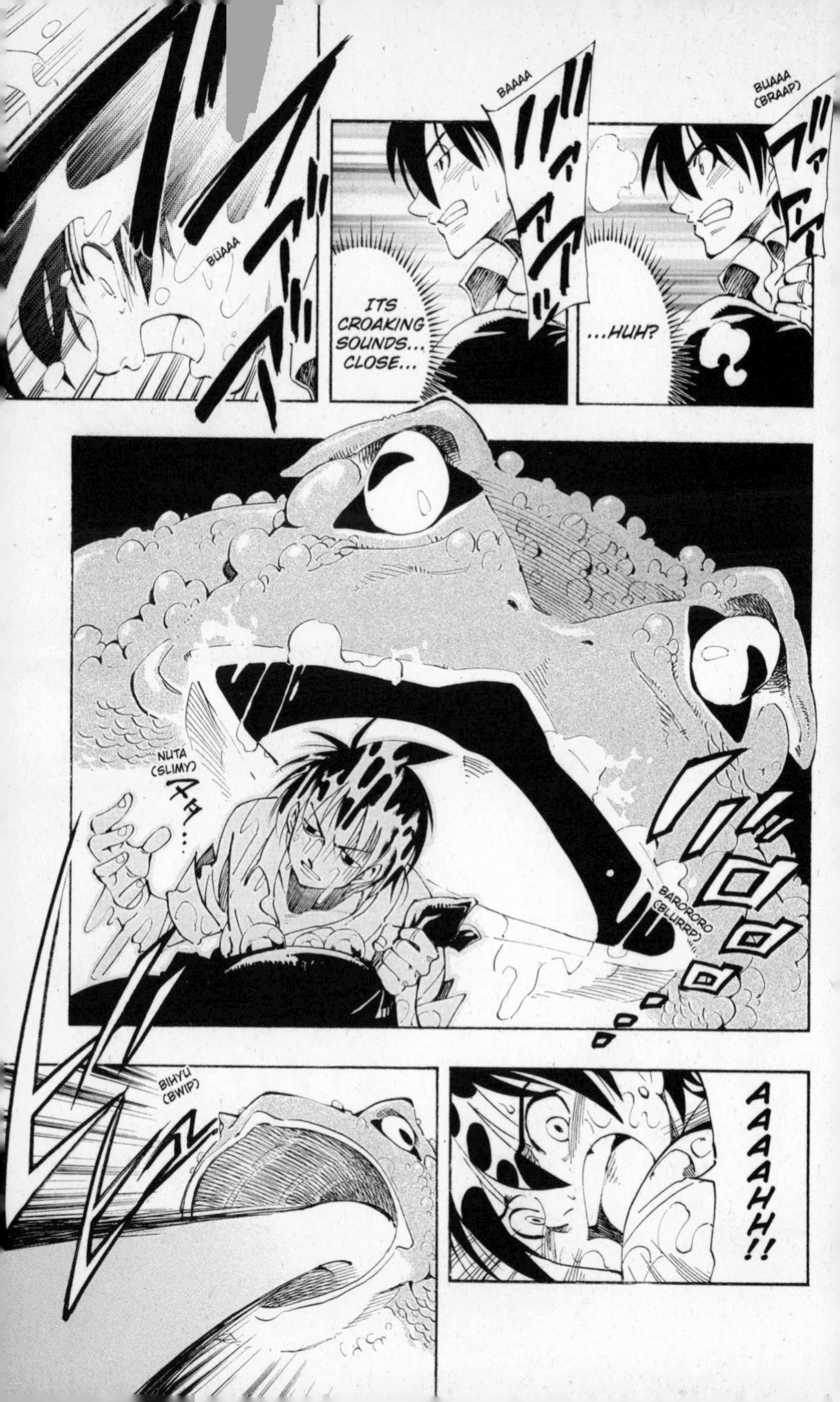
BUAAA (BRAAP)
...HUH?
BAAAA
ITS CROAKING SOUNDS... CLOSE...
BUAAA
NUTA (SLIMY)
BARORORO (BLURRP)
AAAAAHH!!
BIHYU (BWIP)

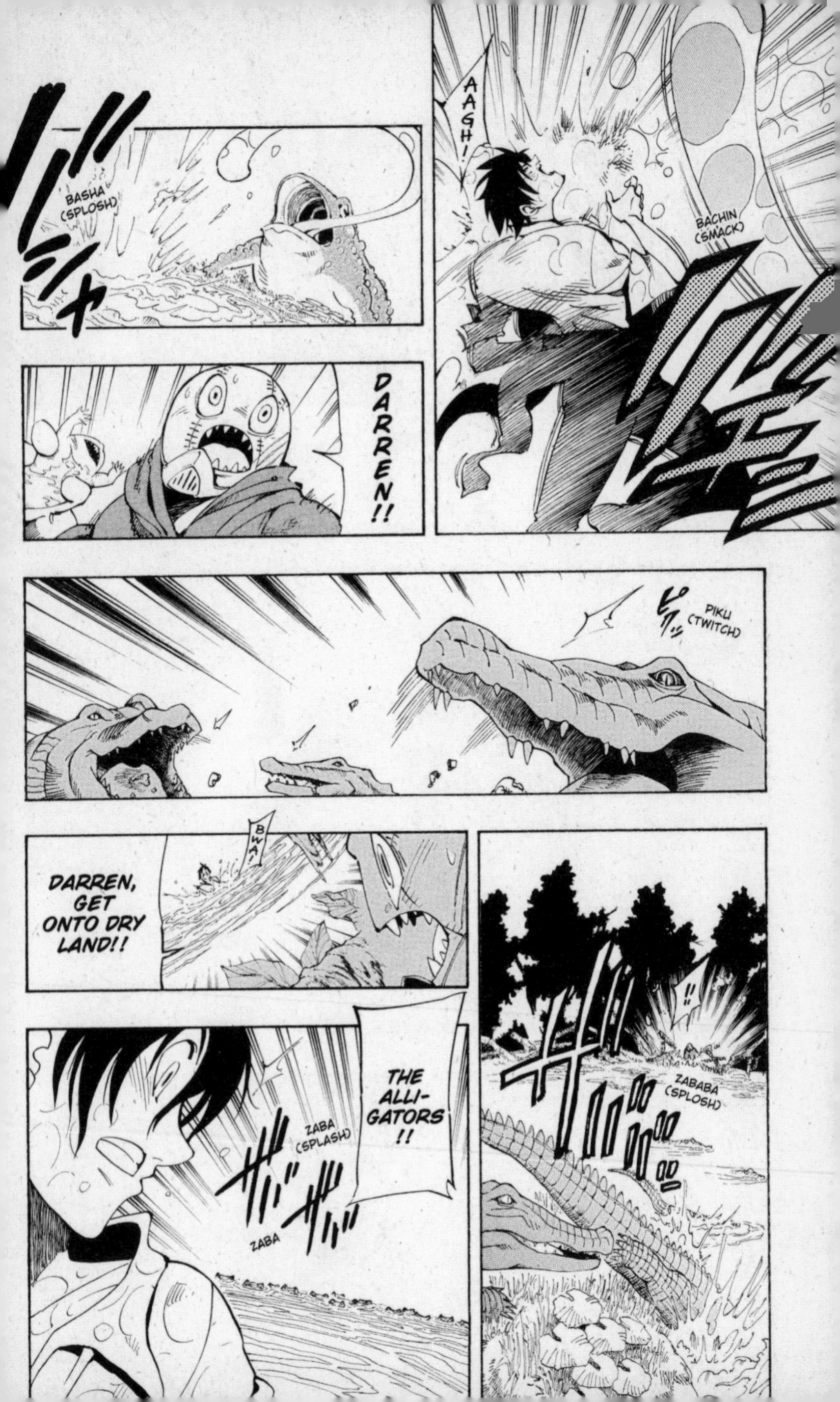
AAGH!
BACHIN (SMACK)
BASHA (SPLOSH)
DARREN!!
PIKU (TWITCH)
!!
ZABABA (SPLOSH)
BWA!
DARREN, GET ONTO DRY LAND!!
THE ALLIGATORS!!
ZABA (SPLASH)
ZABA

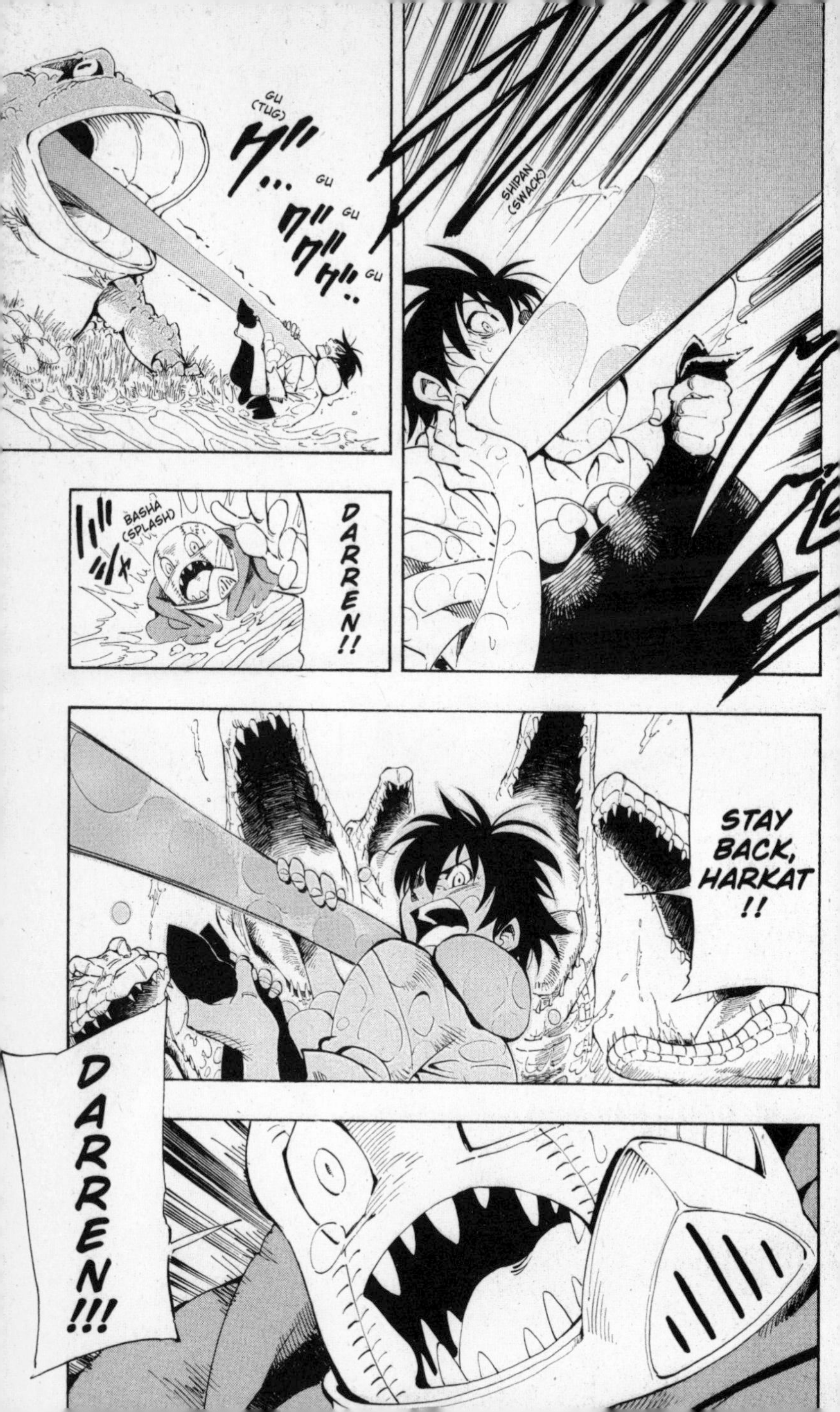
SHIPAN (SWACK)
GU (TUG)
GU
GU
GU
DARREN!!
BASHA (SPLASH)
STAY BACK, HARKAT!!
DARREN!!!

GAKAAA
(FLASH)

GUIEEE
ゲエ・・
エ・・

GOEE
(GRAAK)
ゴエ・・
エ・・

KURA
(CRAZE)
クラ

KURA

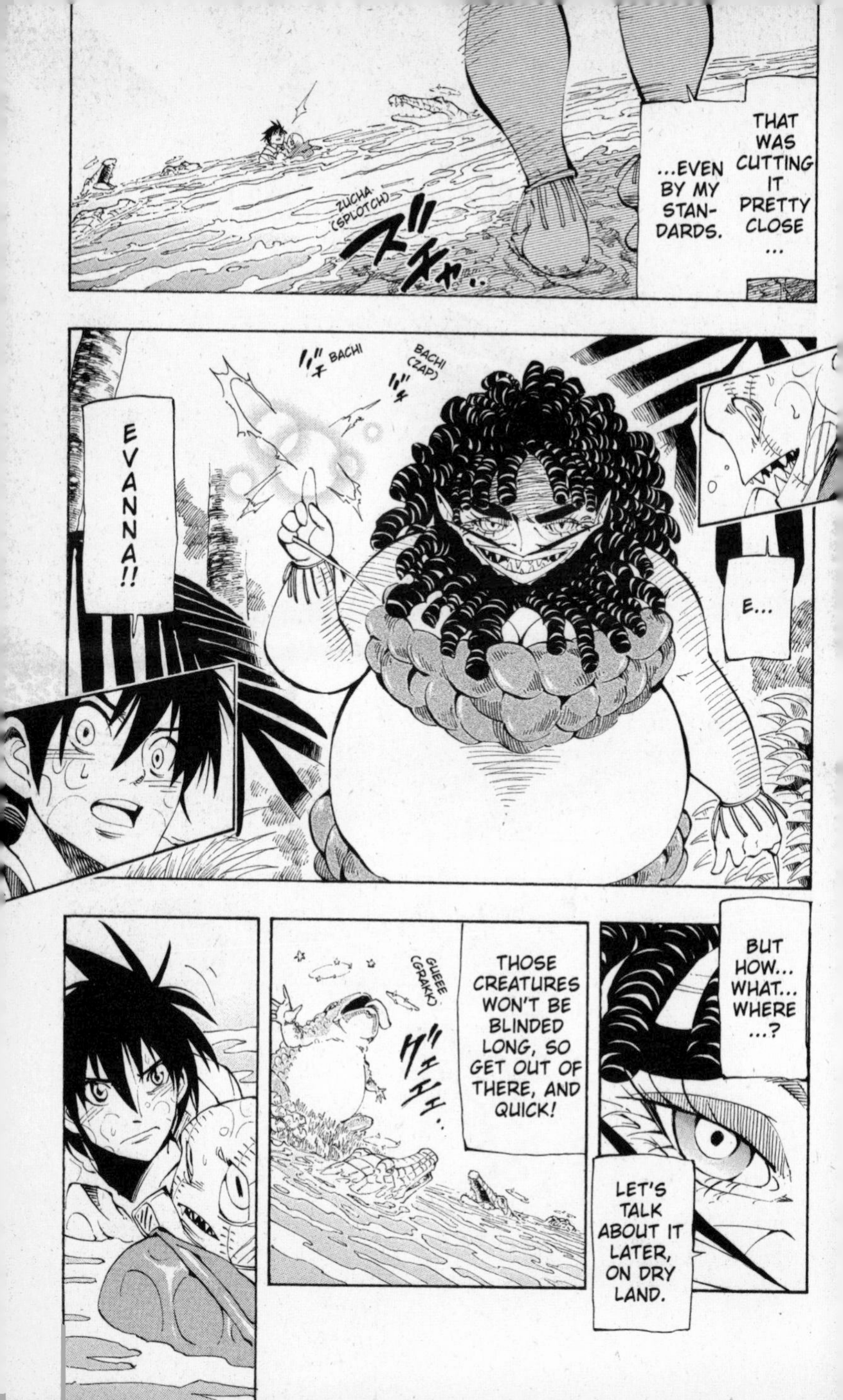
THAT WAS CUTTING IT PRETTY CLOSE...
...EVEN BY MY STANDARDS.
ZUCHA (SPLOTCH)
E...
BACHI (ZAP)
BACHI
EVANNA!!
BUT HOW... WHAT... WHERE...?
LET'S TALK ABOUT IT LATER, ON DRY LAND.
THOSE CREATURES WON'T BE BLINDED LONG, SO GET OUT OF THERE, AND QUICK!
GUEEE (GRAKK)

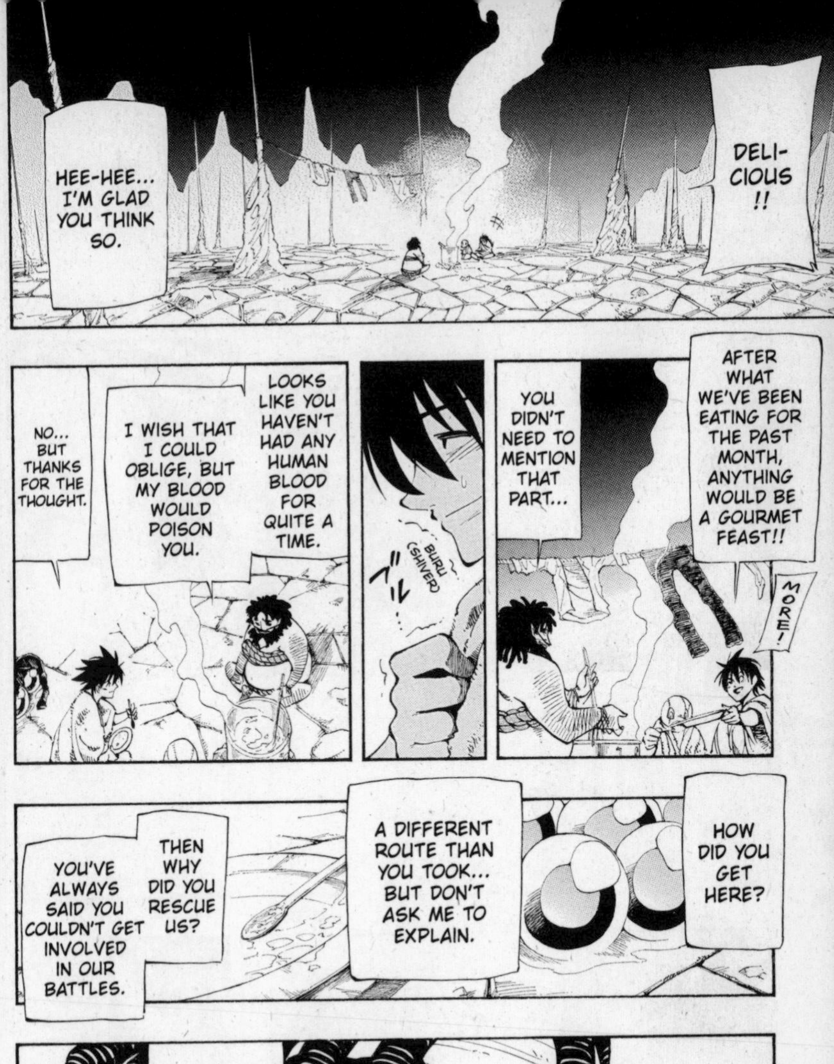
DELI-CIOUS!!
HEE-HEE... I'M GLAD YOU THINK SO.
AFTER WHAT WE'VE BEEN EATING FOR THE PAST MONTH, ANYTHING WOULD BE A GOURMET FEAST!!
MORE!
YOU DIDN'T NEED TO MENTION THAT PART...
BURU (SHIVER)
LOOKS LIKE YOU HAVEN'T HAD ANY HUMAN BLOOD FOR QUITE A TIME.
I WISH THAT I COULD OBLIGE, BUT MY BLOOD WOULD POISON YOU.
NO... BUT THANKS FOR THE THOUGHT.
HOW DID YOU GET HERE?
A DIFFERENT ROUTE THAN YOU TOOK... BUT DON'T ASK ME TO EXPLAIN.
THEN WHY DID YOU RESCUE US?
YOU'VE ALWAYS SAID YOU COULDN'T GET INVOLVED IN OUR BATTLES.
NOT IN YOUR FIGHT WITH THE VAMPANEZE. WHEN IT COMES TO ALLIGATORS AND TOADS, I HAVE A FREE HAND.
I'M HERE TO ACT AS YOUR GUIDE ON THE NEXT STRETCH OF YOUR ADVENTURE.
THAT'S WHY I INTERVENED. AS PART OF YOUR QUEST, I CAN PLAY AN ACTIVE ROLE IN IT, AT LEAST FOR A WHILE.

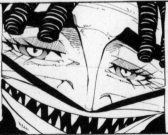

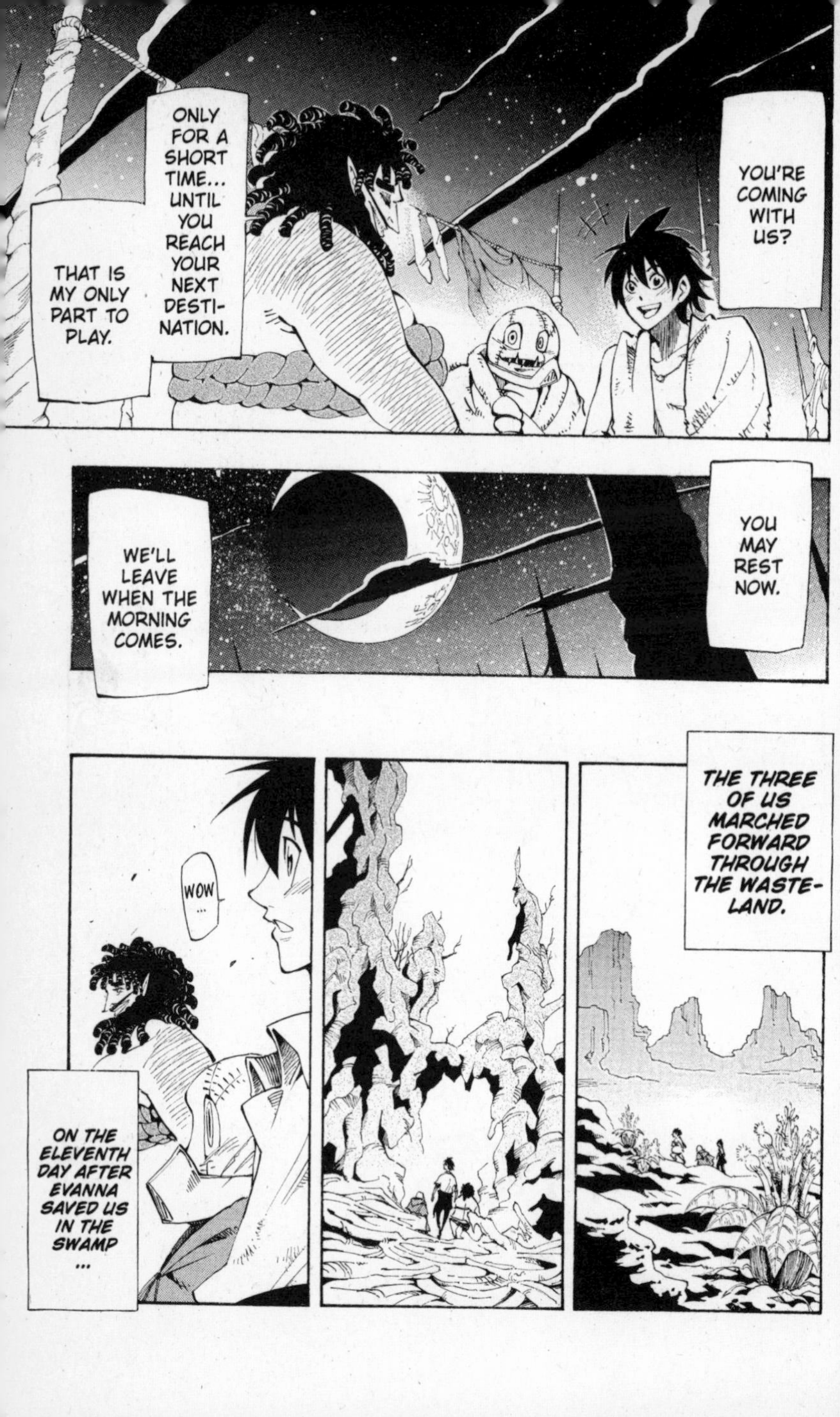

YOU'RE COMING WITH US?
ONLY FOR A SHORT TIME... UNTIL YOU REACH YOUR NEXT DESTINATION.
THAT IS MY ONLY PART TO PLAY.
YOU MAY REST NOW.
WE'LL LEAVE WHEN THE MORNING COMES.
THE THREE OF US MARCHED FORWARD THROUGH THE WASTELAND.
WOW...
ON THE ELEVENTH DAY AFTER EVANNA SAVED US IN THE SWAMP...

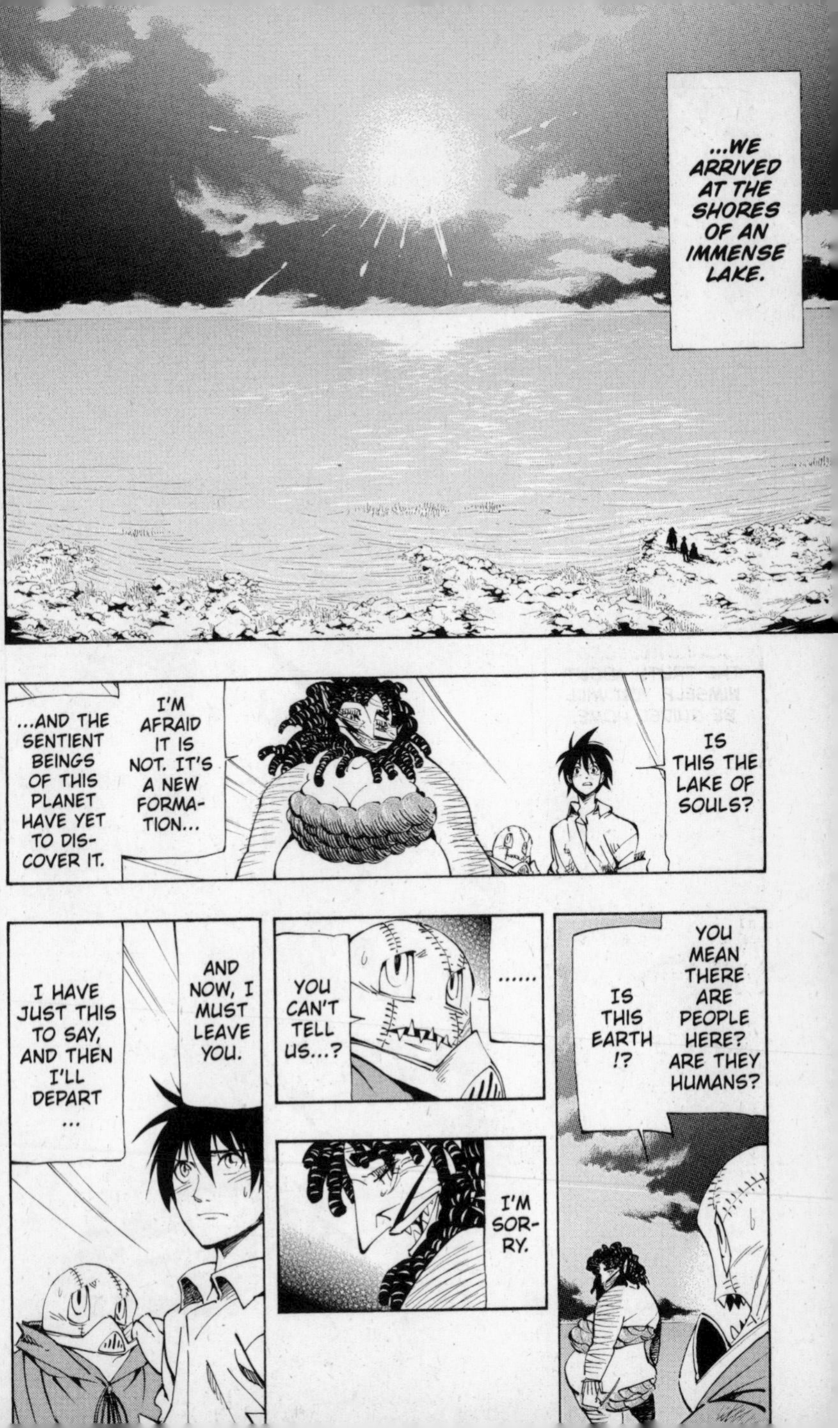
...WE ARRIVED AT THE SHORES OF AN IMMENSE LAKE.
IS THIS THE LAKE OF SOULS?
I'M AFRAID IT IS NOT. IT'S A NEW FORMATION...
...AND THE SENTIENT BEINGS OF THIS PLANET HAVE YET TO DISCOVER IT.
YOU MEAN THERE ARE PEOPLE HERE? ARE THEY HUMANS?
IS THIS EARTH !?
......
YOU CAN'T TELL US...?
I'M SORRY.
AND NOW, I MUST LEAVE YOU.
I HAVE JUST THIS TO SAY, AND THEN I'LL DEPART ...

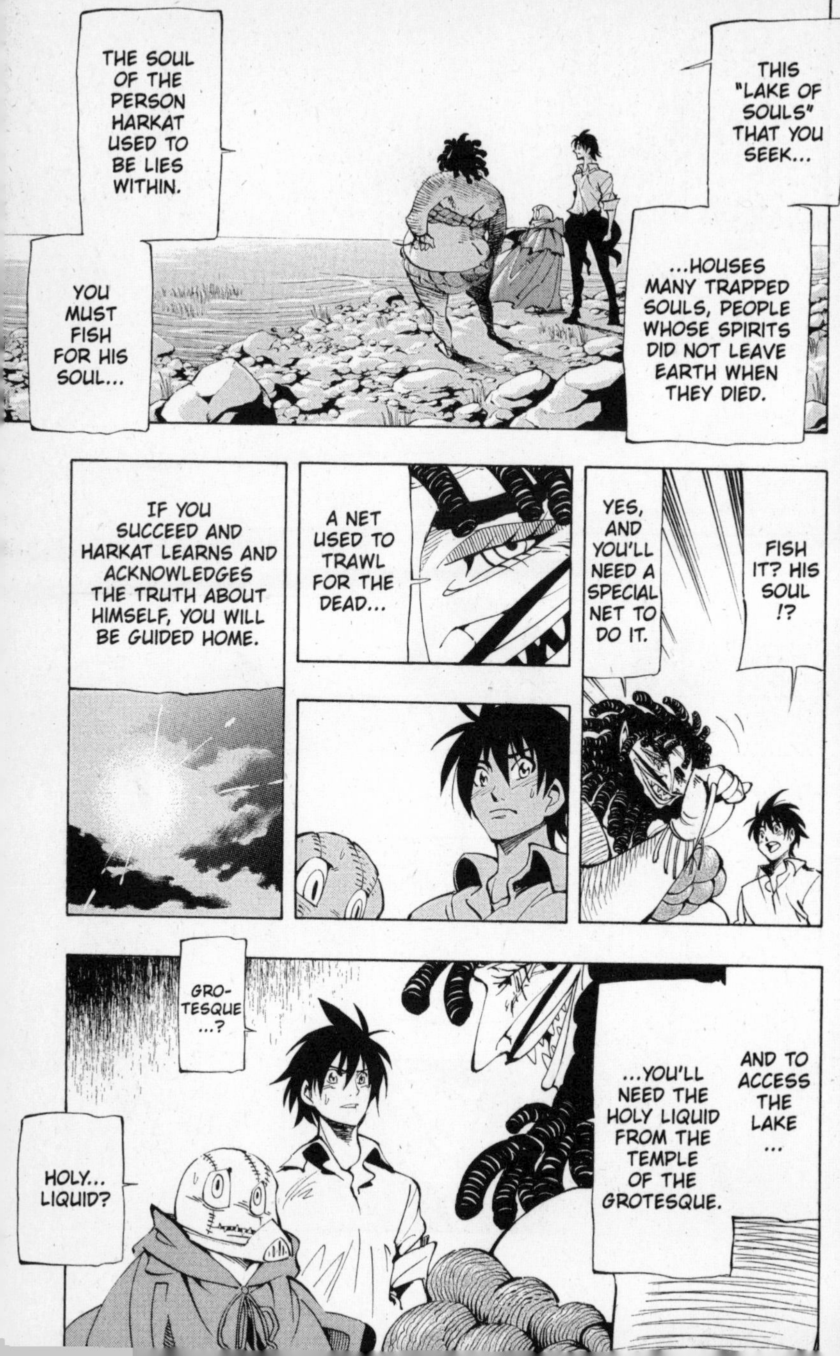
THIS "LAKE OF SOULS" THAT YOU SEEK...
...HOUSES MANY TRAPPED SOULS, PEOPLE WHOSE SPIRITS DID NOT LEAVE EARTH WHEN THEY DIED.
THE SOUL OF THE PERSON HARKAT USED TO BE LIES WITHIN.
YOU MUST FISH FOR HIS SOUL...
FISH IT? HIS SOUL !?
YES, AND YOU'LL NEED A SPECIAL NET TO DO IT.
A NET USED TO TRAWL FOR THE DEAD...
IF YOU SUCCEED AND HARKAT LEARNS AND ACKNOWLEDGES THE TRUTH ABOUT HIMSELF, YOU WILL BE GUIDED HOME.
AND TO ACCESS THE LAKE ...
...YOU'LL NEED THE HOLY LIQUID FROM THE TEMPLE OF THE GROTESQUE.
GRO-TESQUE ...?
HOLY... LIQUID?

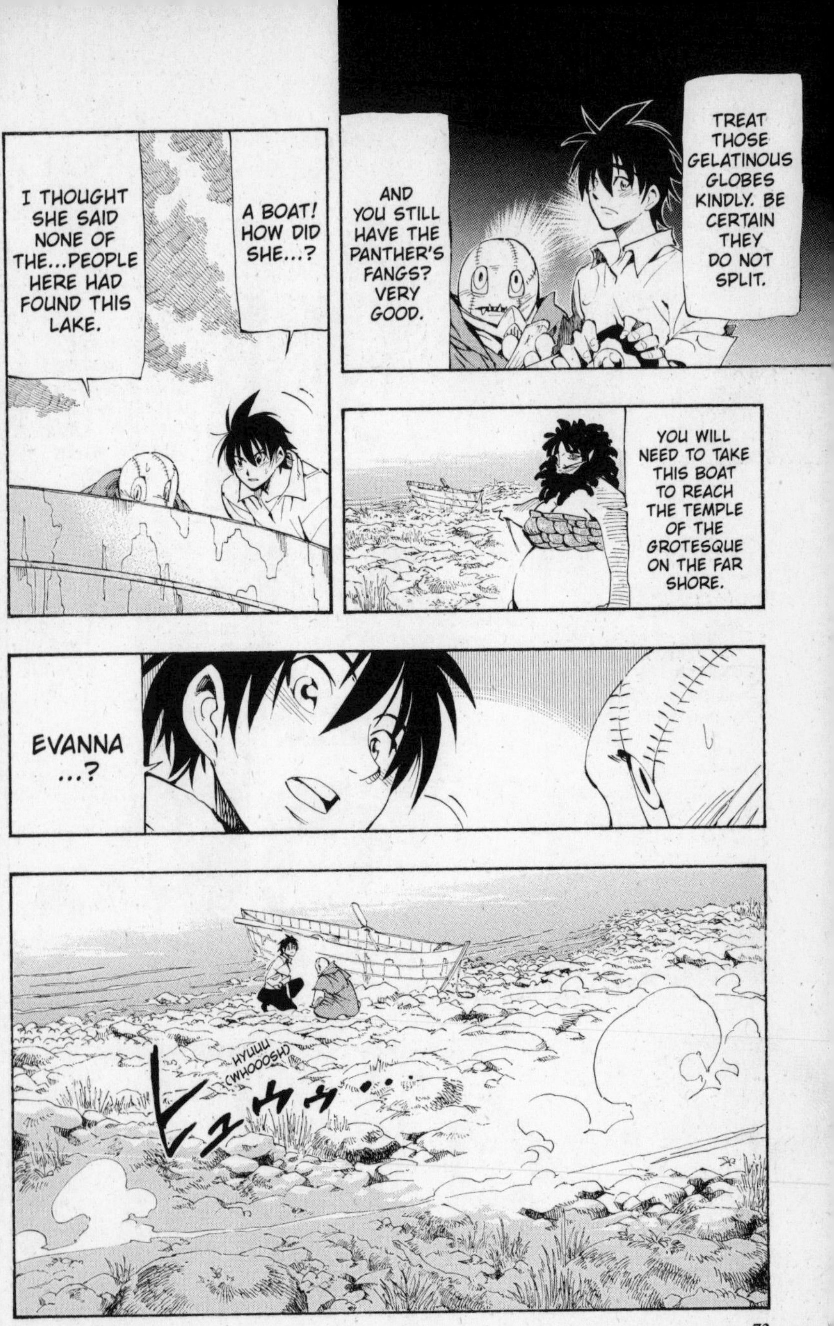
TREAT THOSE GELATINOUS GLOBES KINDLY. BE CERTAIN THEY DO NOT SPLIT.
AND YOU STILL HAVE THE PANTHER'S FANGS? VERY GOOD.
YOU WILL NEED TO TAKE THIS BOAT TO REACH THE TEMPLE OF THE GROTESQUE ON THE FAR SHORE.
A BOAT! HOW DID SHE...?
I THOUGHT SHE SAID NONE OF THE...PEOPLE HERE HAD FOUND THIS LAKE.
EVANNA ...?
HYUUU (WHOOOSH)
ヒュウゥ…

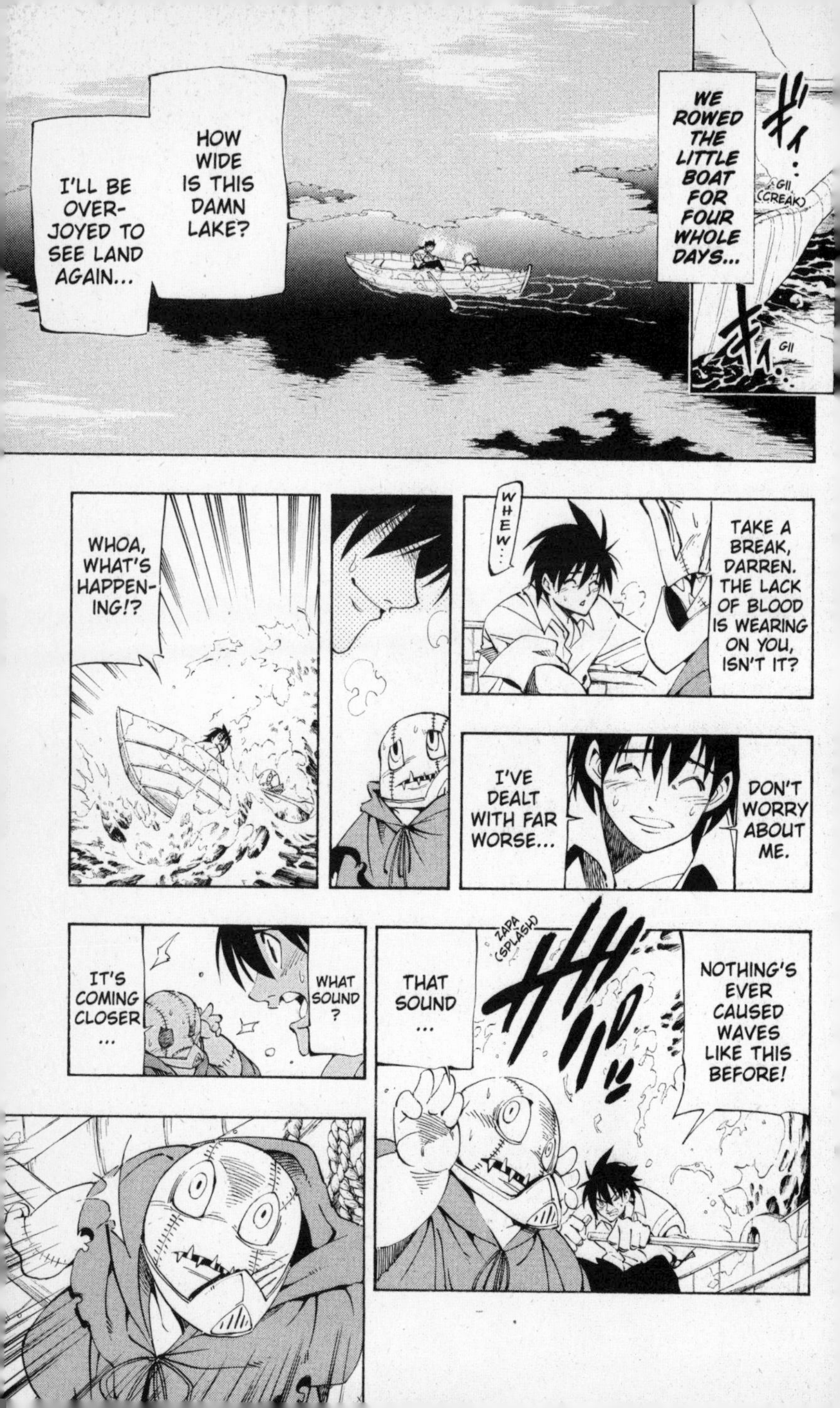
WE ROWED THE LITTLE BOAT FOR FOUR WHOLE DAYS...
GII (CREAK)
GII
HOW WIDE IS THIS DAMN LAKE?
I'LL BE OVER-JOYED TO SEE LAND AGAIN...
WHEW...
TAKE A BREAK, DARREN. THE LACK OF BLOOD IS WEARING ON YOU, ISN'T IT?
DON'T WORRY ABOUT ME.
I'VE DEALT WITH FAR WORSE...
WHOA, WHAT'S HAPPENING!?
NOTHING'S EVER CAUSED WAVES LIKE THIS BEFORE!
ZAPA (SPLASH)
THAT SOUND ...
WHAT SOUND ?
IT'S COMING CLOSER ...

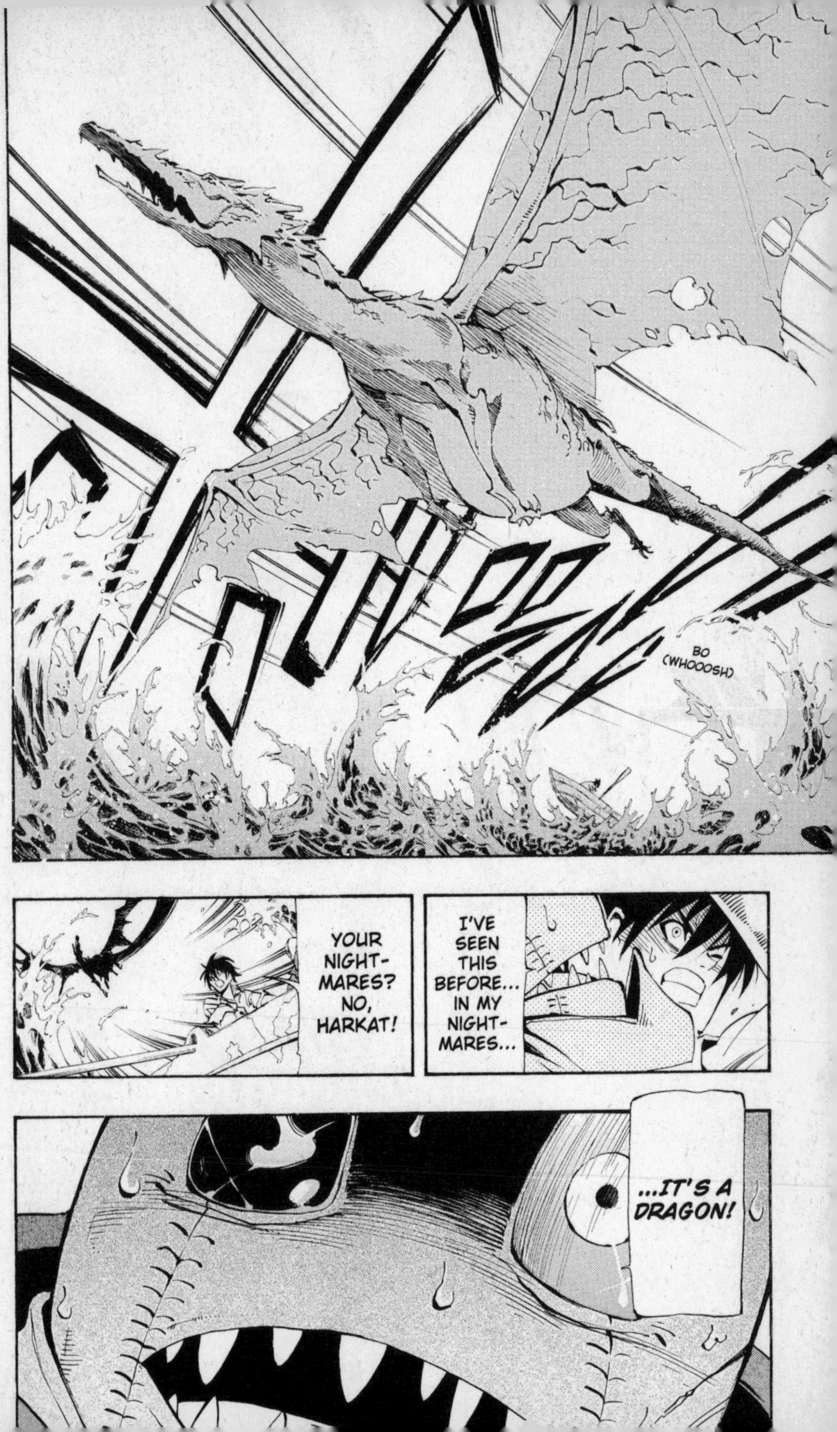
BO (WHOOOSH)
I'VE SEEN THIS BEFORE... IN MY NIGHT-MARES...
YOUR NIGHT-MARES? NO, HARKAT!
...IT'S A DRAGON!

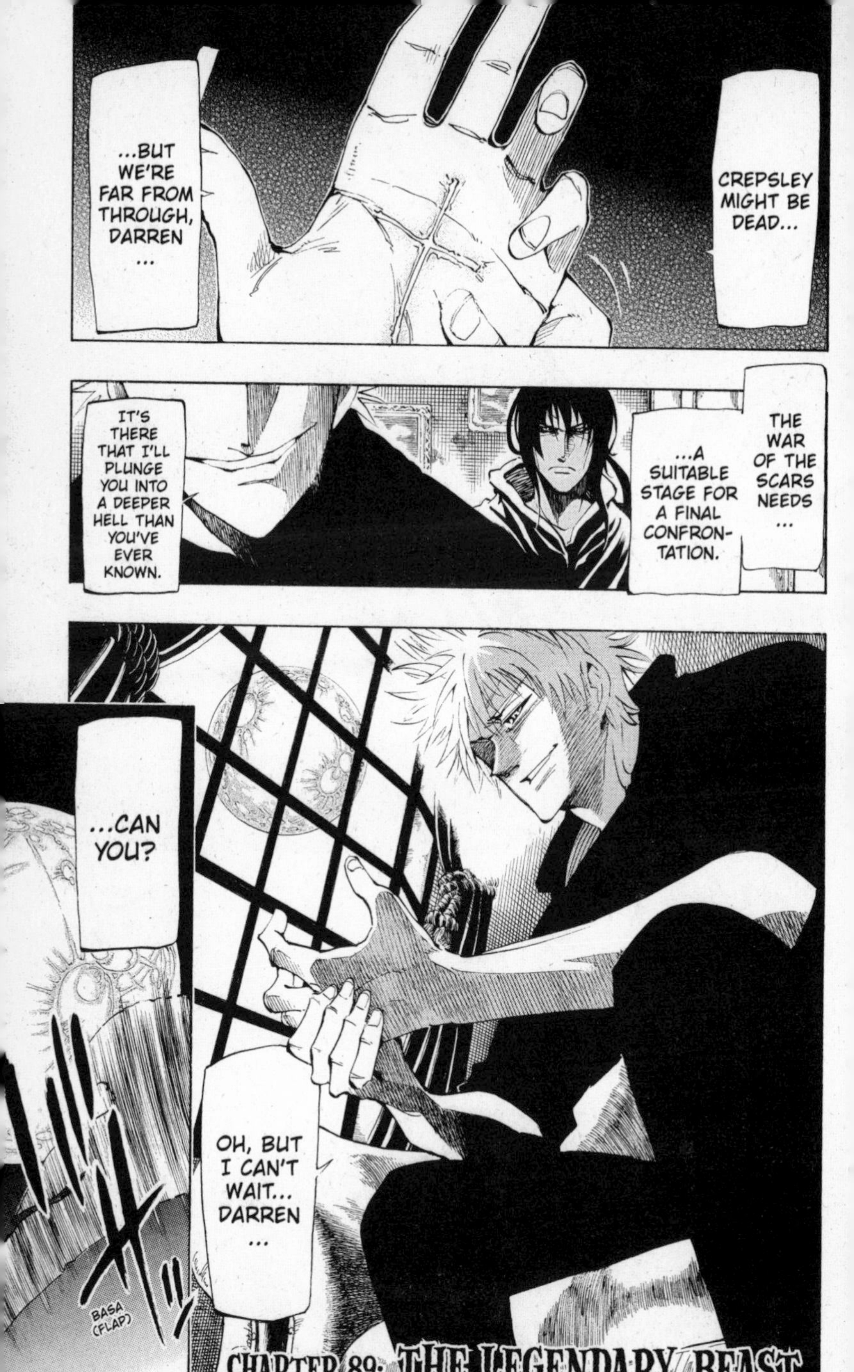
CREPSLEY MIGHT BE DEAD...
...BUT WE'RE FAR FROM THROUGH, DARREN ...
THE WAR OF THE SCARS NEEDS ...
...A SUITABLE STAGE FOR A FINAL CONFRONTATION.
IT'S THERE THAT I'LL PLUNGE YOU INTO A DEEPER HELL THAN YOU'VE EVER KNOWN.
...CAN YOU?
OH, BUT I CAN'T WAIT... DARREN ...
BASA (FLAP)

CHAPTER 89: THE LEGENDARY BEAST

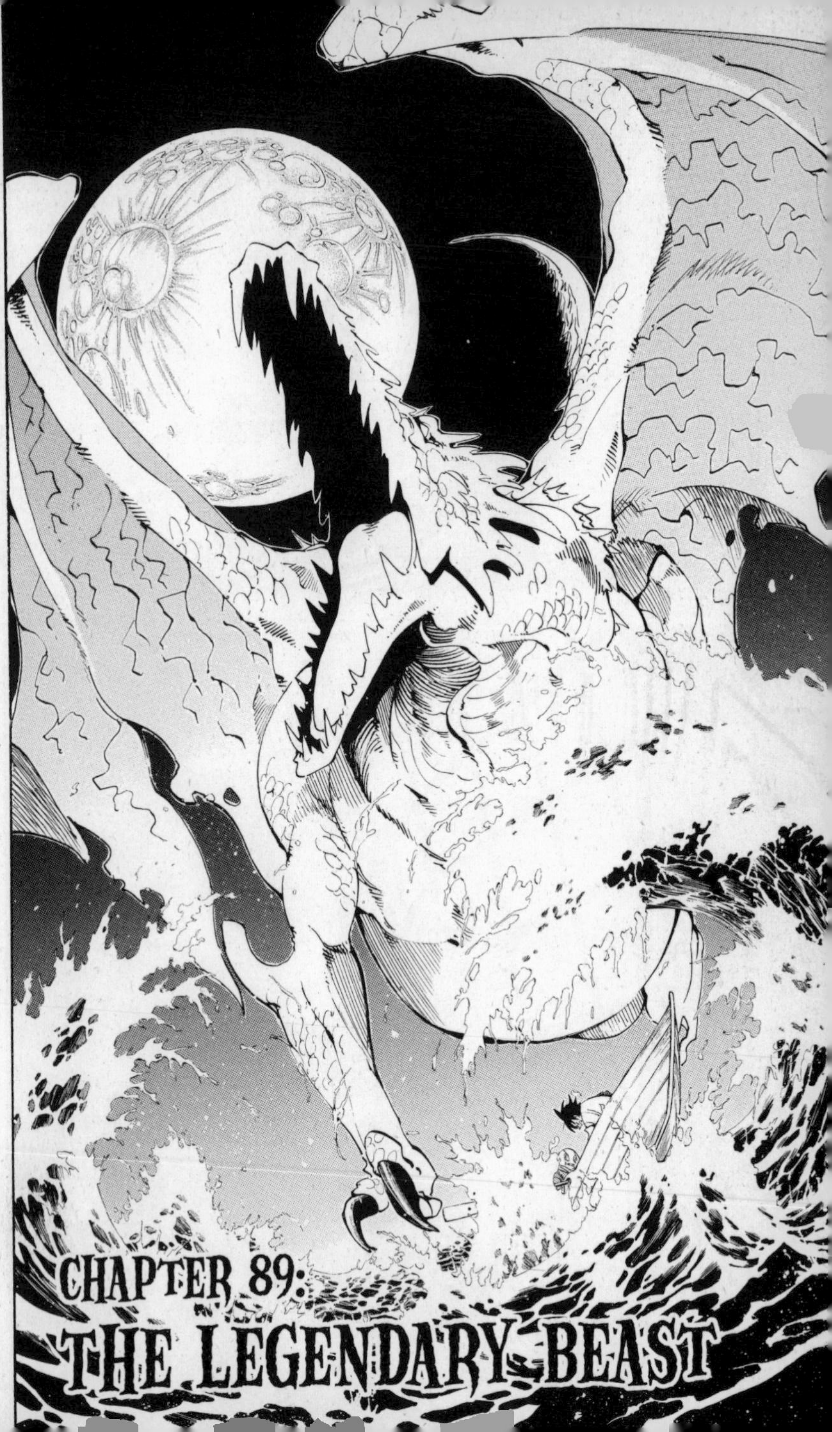
CHAPTER 89:
THE LEGENDARY BEAST

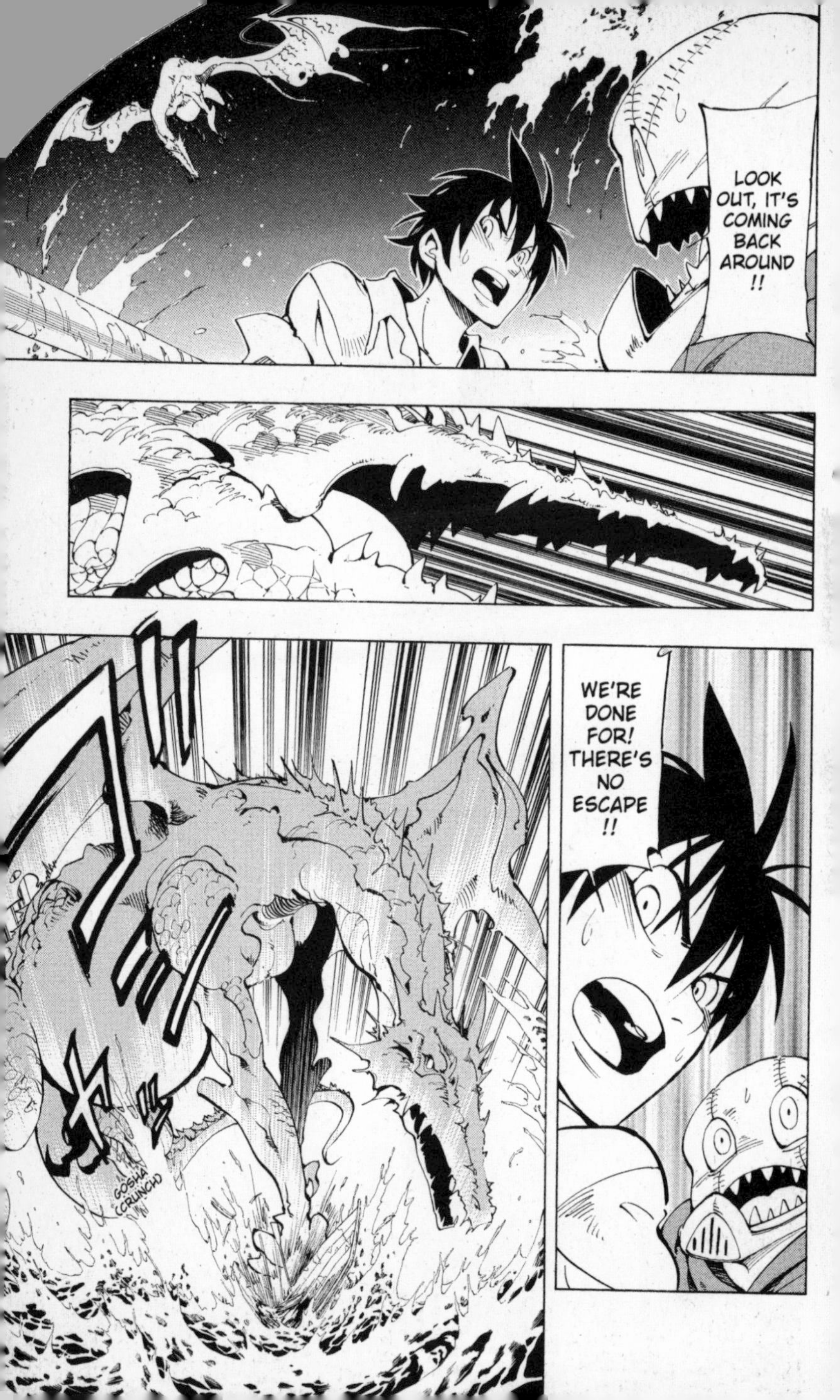
LOOK OUT, IT'S COMING BACK AROUND !!
WE'RE DONE FOR! THERE'S NO ESCAPE !!
GOSHA (CRUNCH)

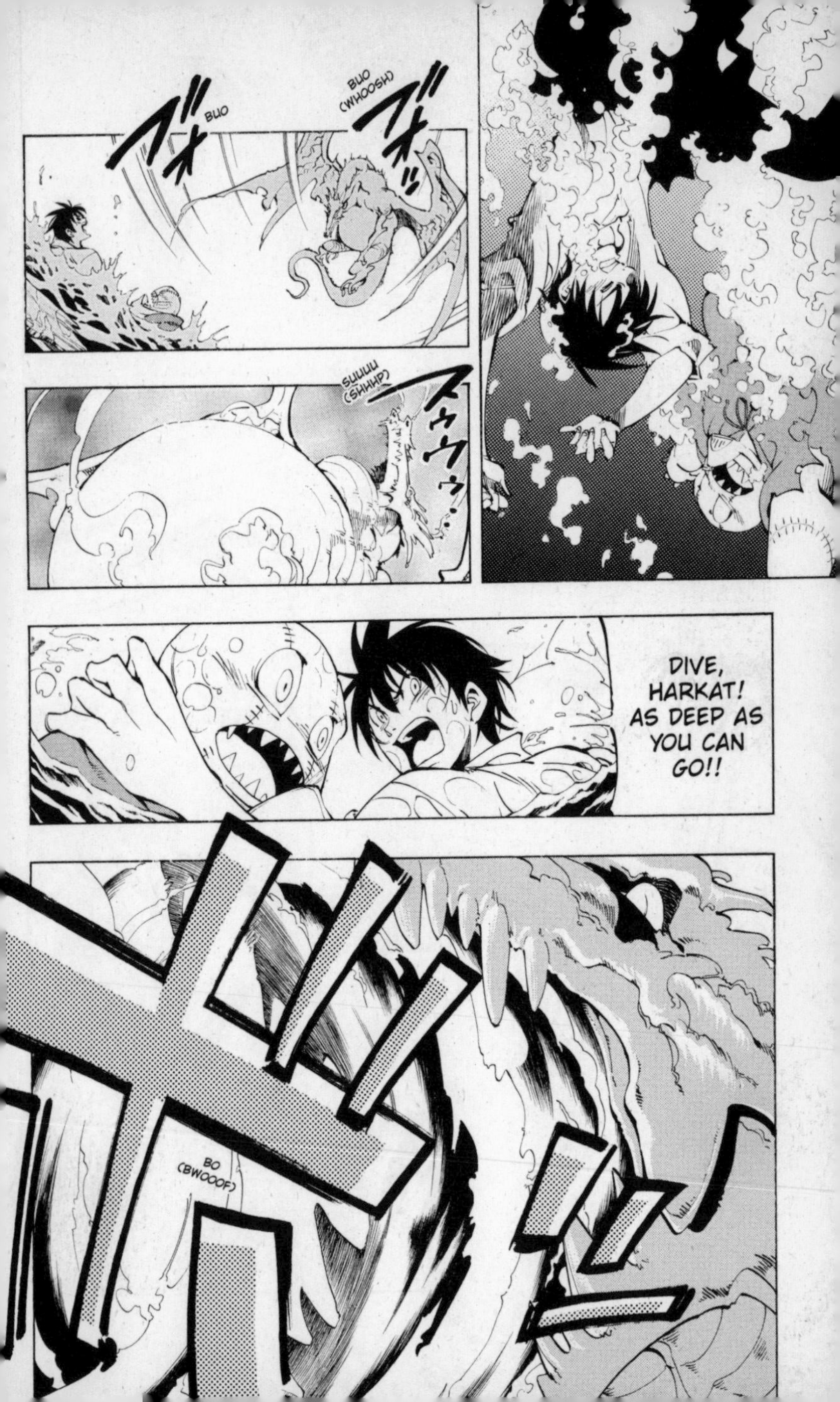
BUO (WHOOSH)
BUO
SUUUU (SHHHP)
DIVE, HARKAT! AS DEEP AS YOU CAN GO!!
BO (BWOOOF)

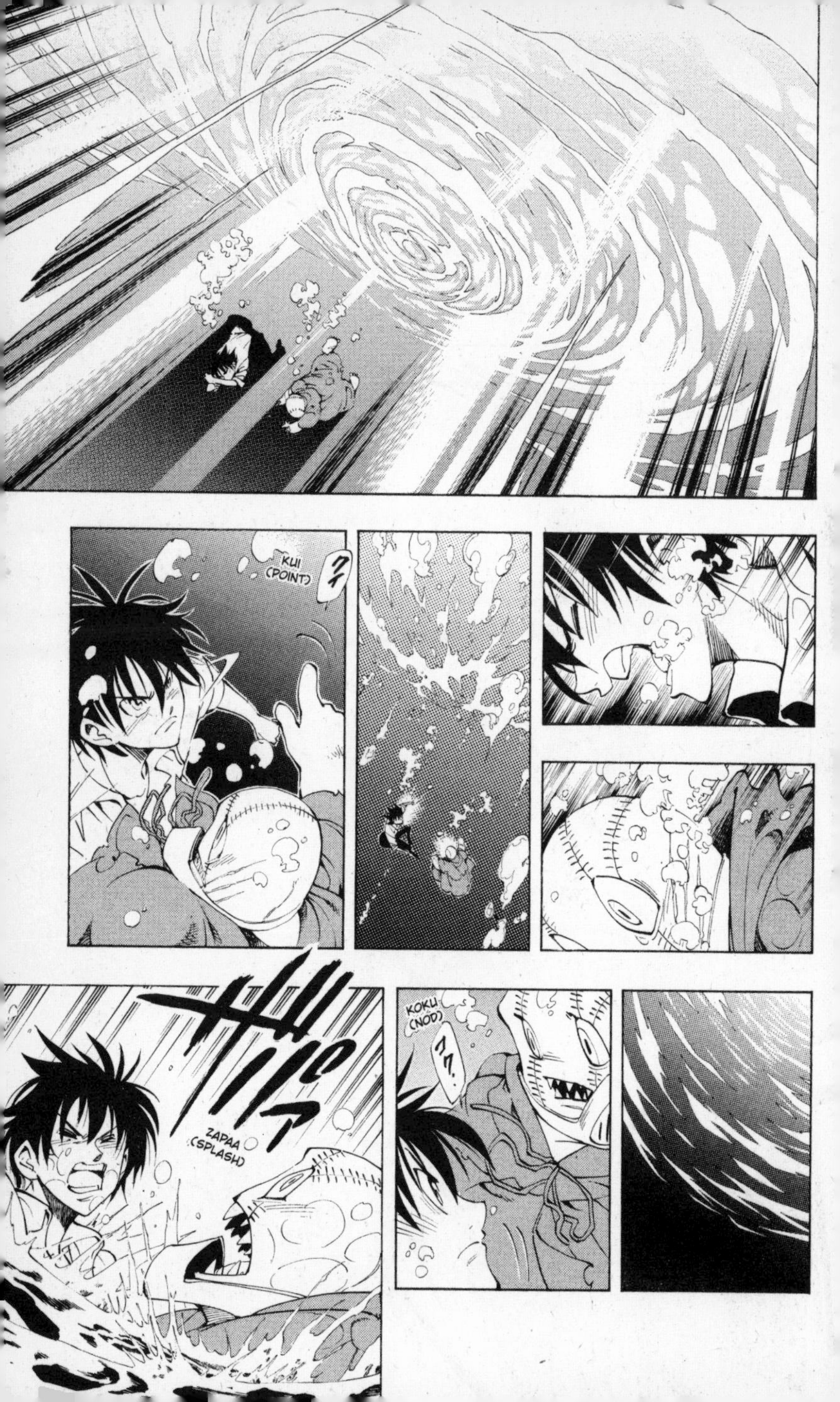
KUI (POINT)
KOKU (NOD)
ZAPAA (SPLASH)

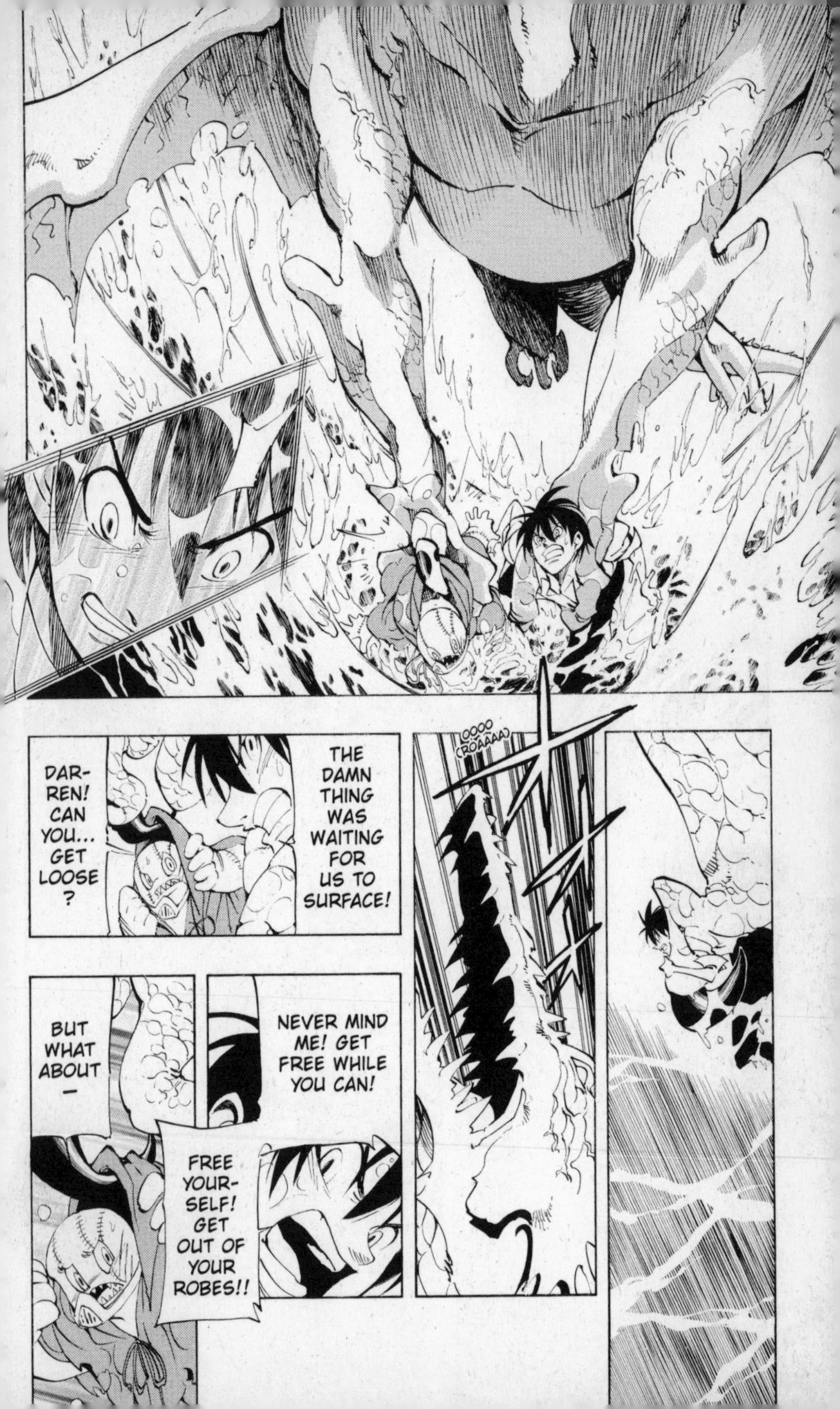
LOOOO
(ROAAAA)
THE DAMN THING WAS WAITING FOR US TO SURFACE!
DARREN! CAN YOU... GET LOOSE?
NEVER MIND ME! GET FREE WHILE YOU CAN!
BUT WHAT ABOUT—
FREE YOURSELF! GET OUT OF YOUR ROBES!!

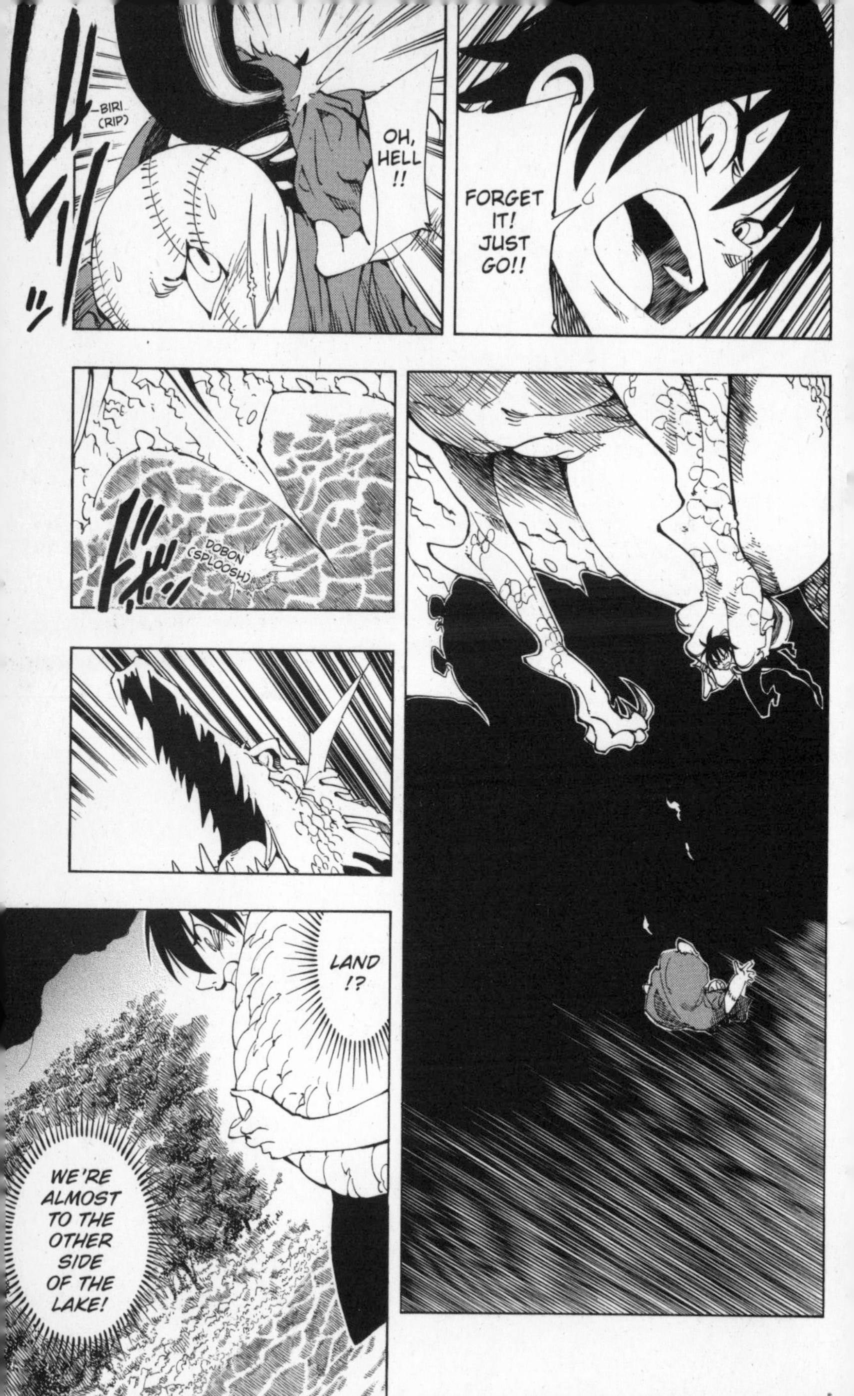

FORGET IT! JUST GO!!
OH, HELL!!
BIRI (RIP)
DOBON (SPLOOSH)
LAND!?
WE'RE ALMOST TO THE OTHER SIDE OF THE LAKE!

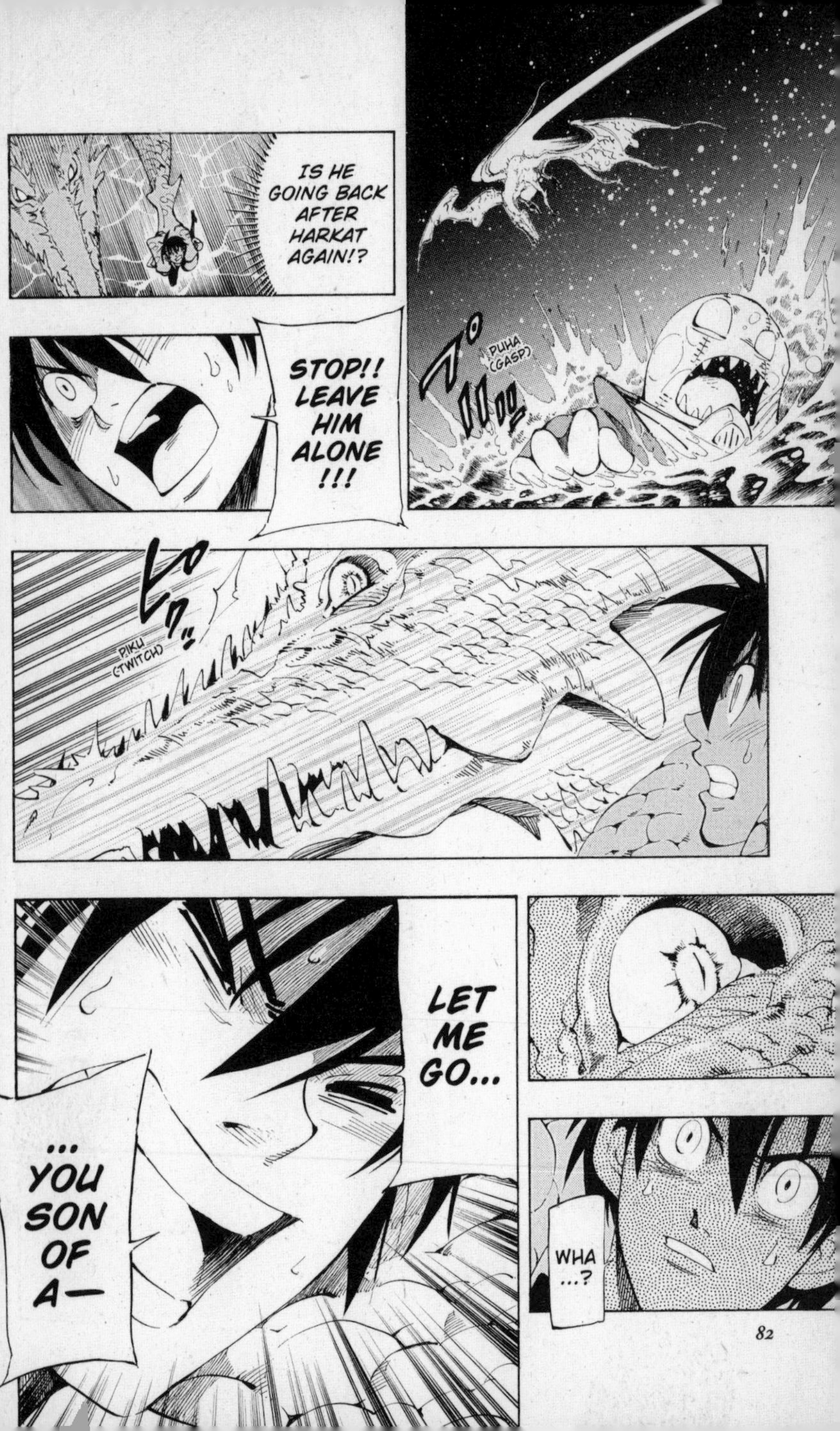
PUHA (GASP)
IS HE GOING BACK AFTER HARKAT AGAIN!?
STOP!! LEAVE HIM ALONE!!!
PIKU (TWITCH)
WHA ...?
LET ME GO...
... YOU SON OF A—

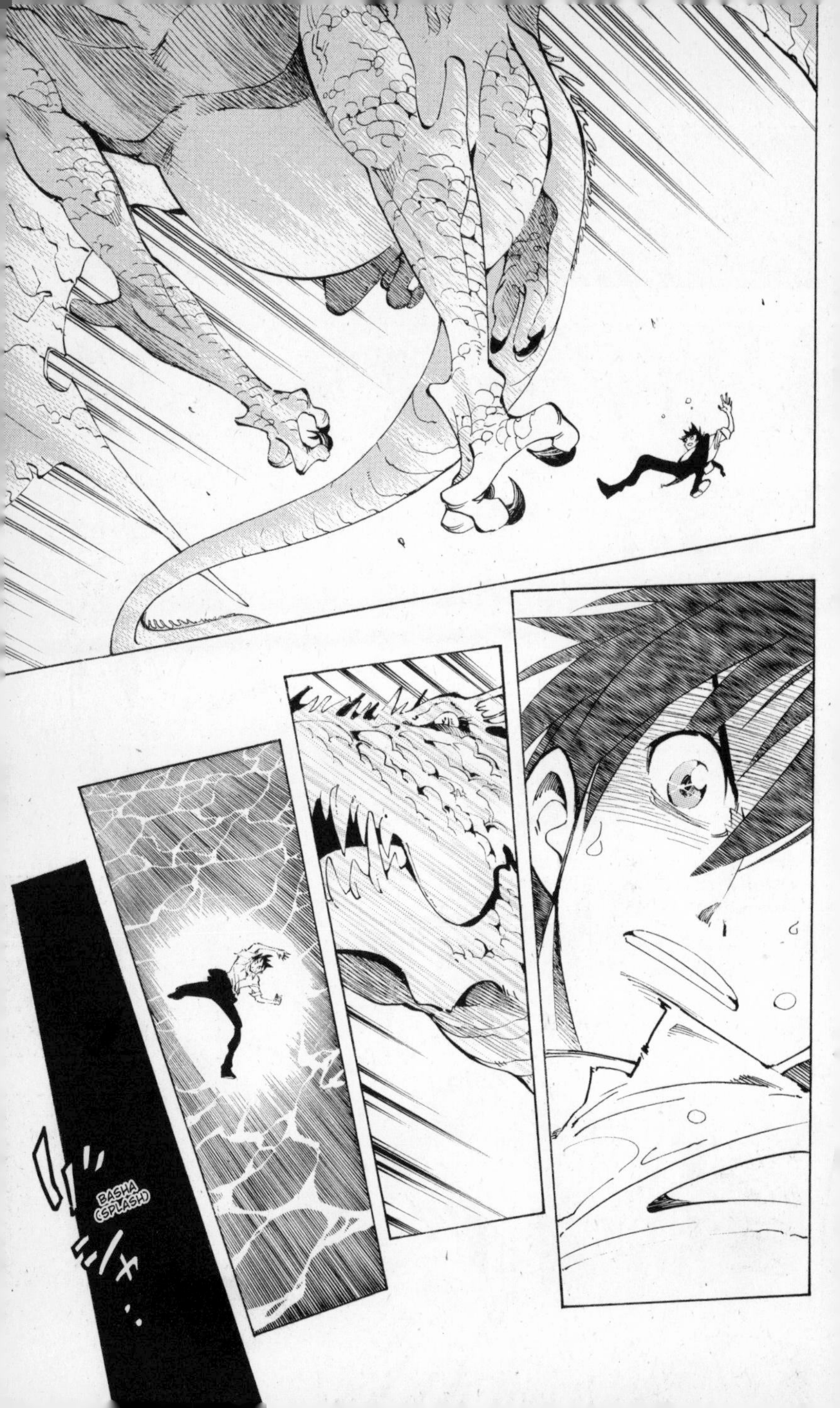
BASHA
(SPLASH)

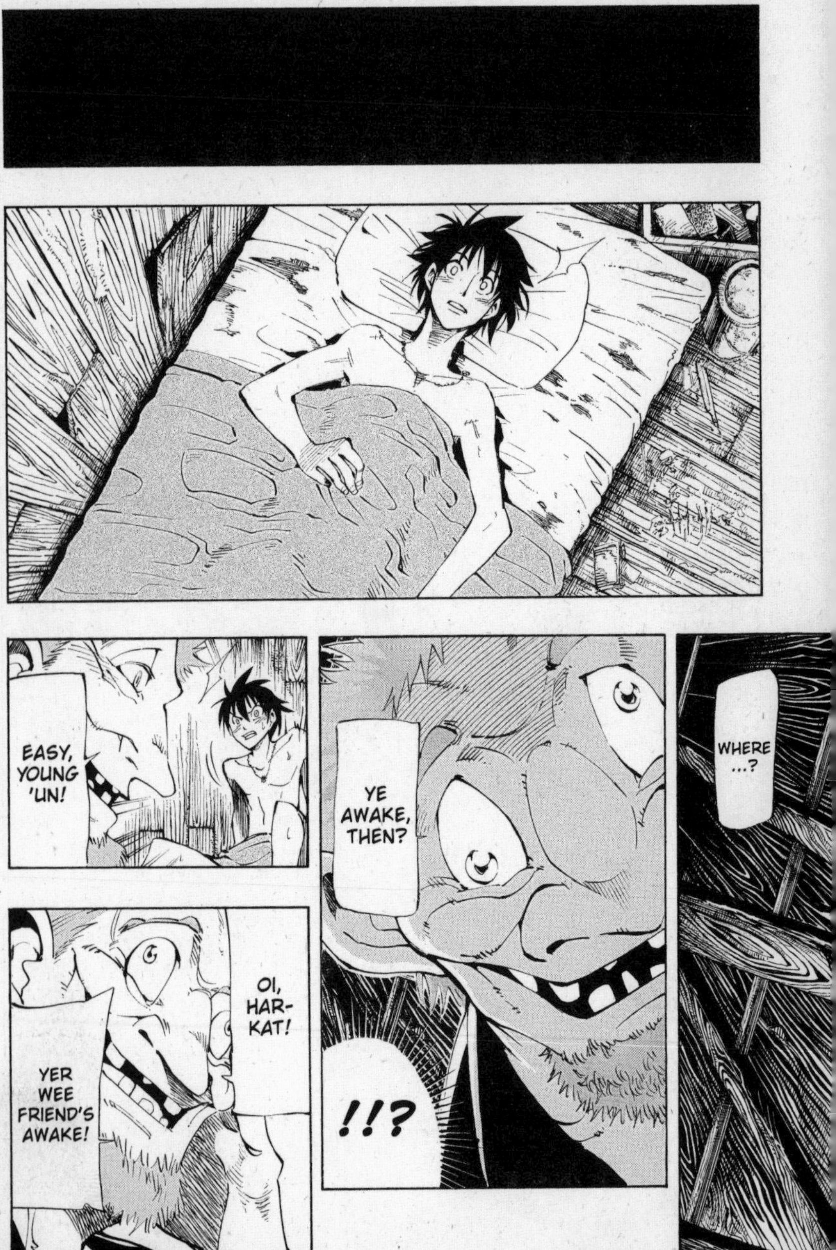
WHERE ...?
YE AWAKE, THEN?
!!?
EASY, YOUNG 'UN!
OI, HAR-KAT!
YER WEE FRIEND'S AWAKE!

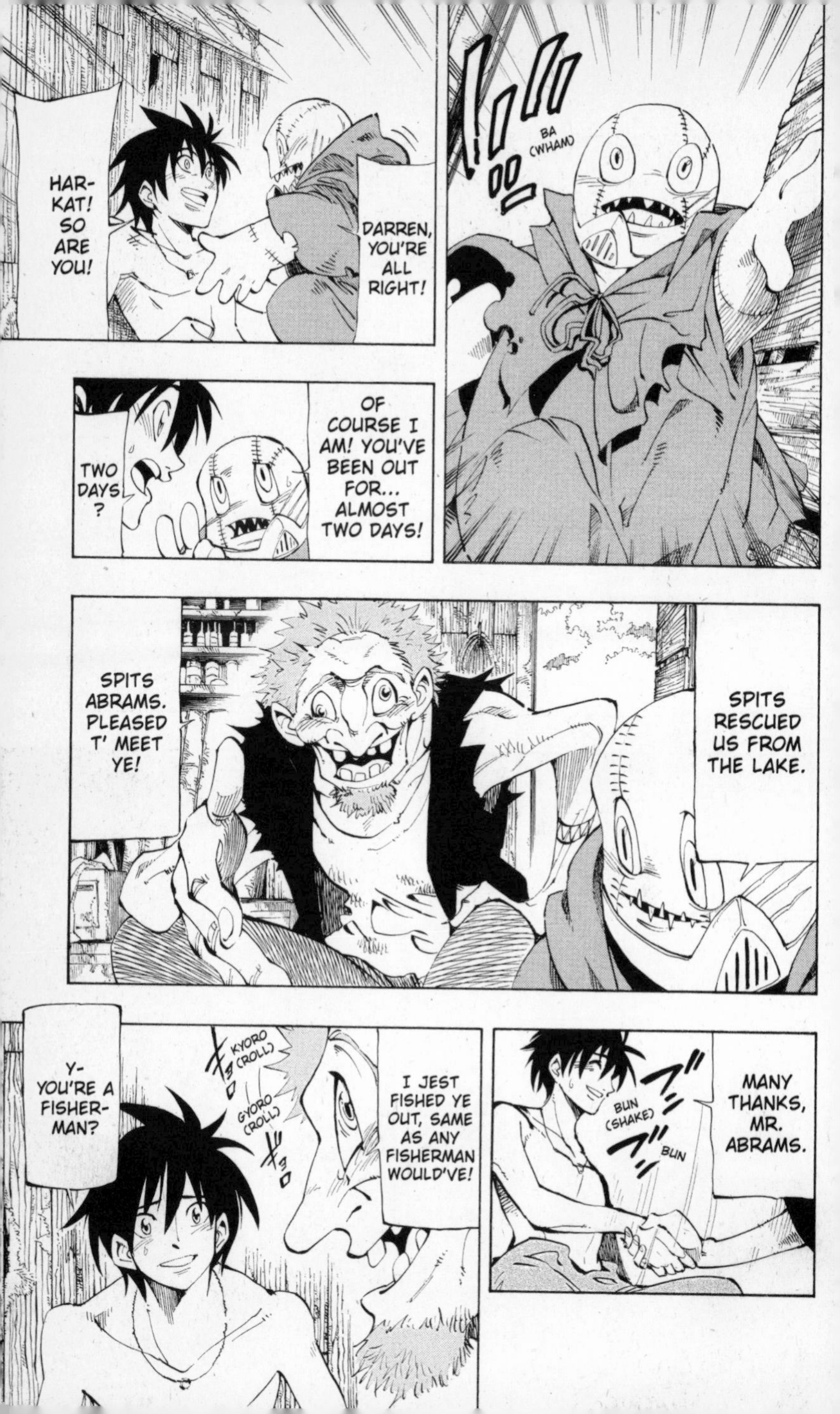
BA (WHAM)
DARREN, YOU'RE ALL RIGHT!
HAR-KAT! SO ARE YOU!
OF COURSE I AM! YOU'VE BEEN OUT FOR... ALMOST TWO DAYS!
TWO DAYS?
SPITS RESCUED US FROM THE LAKE.
SPITS ABRAMS. PLEASED T' MEET YE!
MANY THANKS, MR. ABRAMS.
BUN (SHAKE)
BUN
I JEST FISHED YE OUT, SAME AS ANY FISHERMAN WOULD'VE!
KYORO (ROLL)
GYORO (ROLL)
Y-YOU'RE A FISHER-MAN?

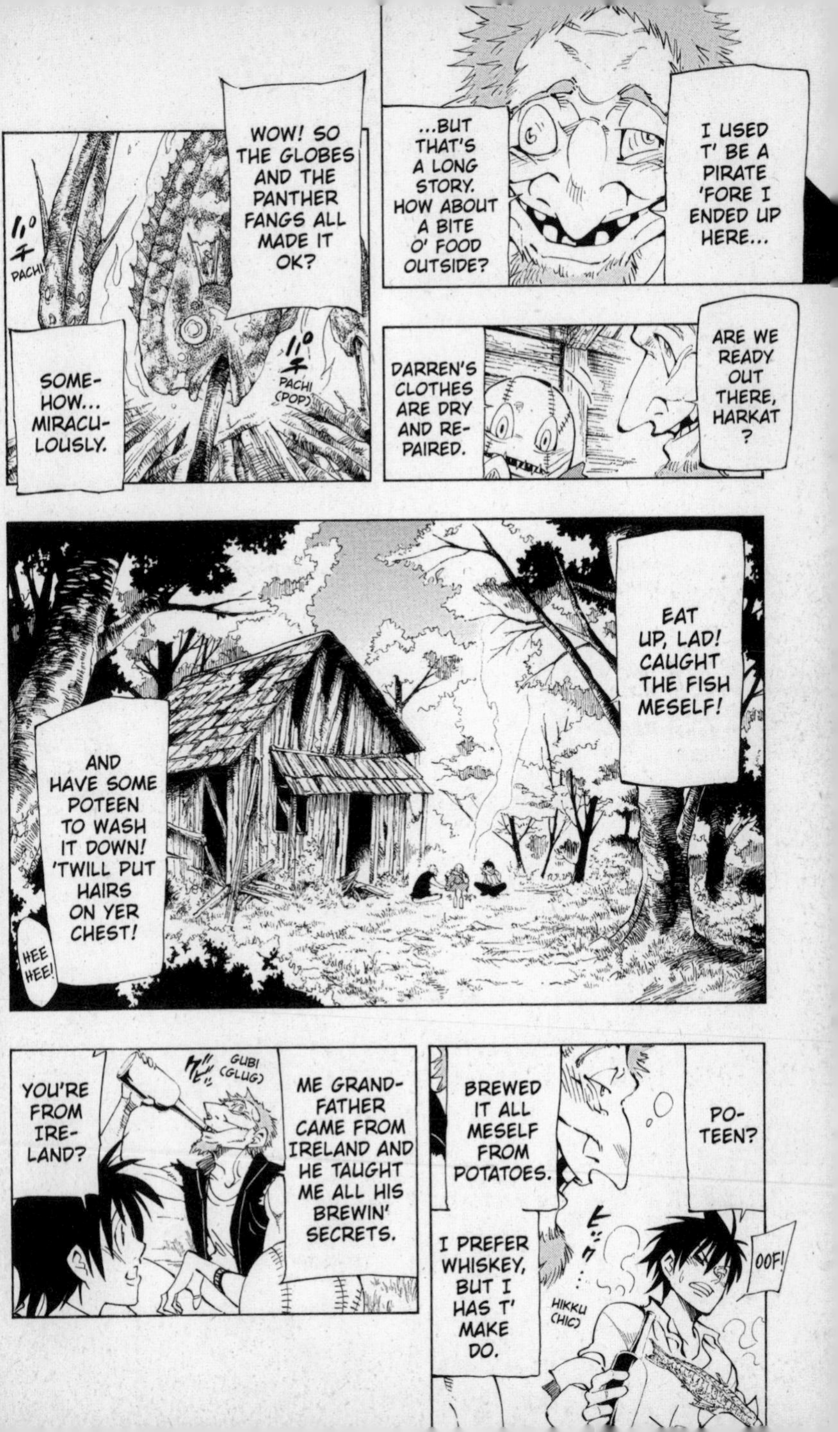
I USED T' BE A PIRATE 'FORE I ENDED UP HERE...
...BUT THAT'S A LONG STORY. HOW ABOUT A BITE O' FOOD OUTSIDE?
ARE WE READY OUT THERE, HARKAT?
DARREN'S CLOTHES ARE DRY AND REPAIRED.
WOW! SO THE GLOBES AND THE PANTHER FANGS ALL MADE IT OK?
PACHI (POP)
PACHI
SOME-HOW... MIRACULOUSLY.
EAT UP, LAD! CAUGHT THE FISH MESELF!
AND HAVE SOME POTEEN TO WASH IT DOWN! 'TWILL PUT HAIRS ON YER CHEST!
HEE HEE!
PO-TEEN?
BREWED IT ALL MESELF FROM POTATOES.
OOF!
HIKKU (HIC)
I PREFER WHISKEY, BUT I HAS T' MAKE DO.
GUBI (GLUG)
YOU'RE FROM IRE-LAND?
ME GRAND-FATHER CAME FROM IRELAND AND HE TAUGHT ME ALL HIS BREWIN' SECRETS.

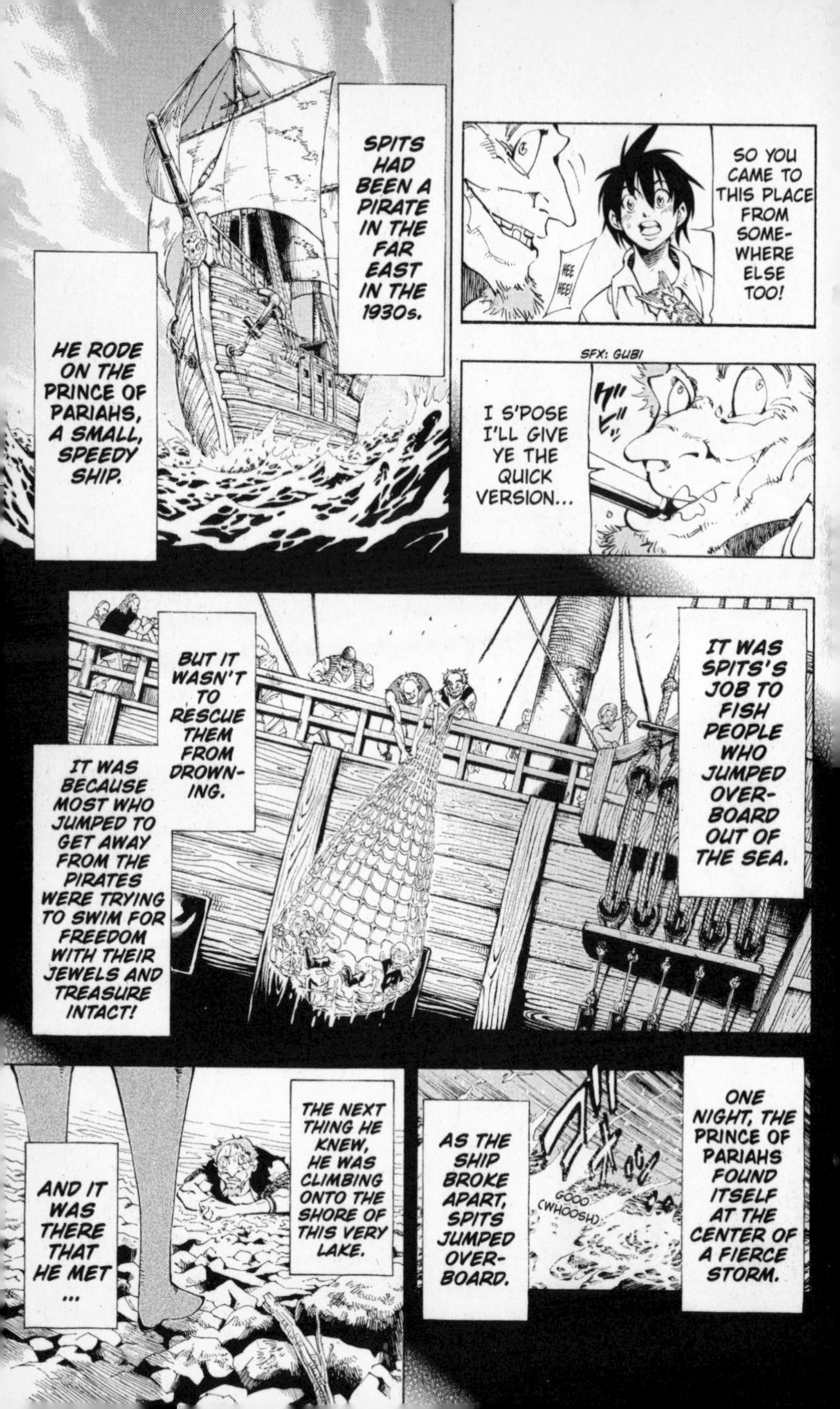
SO YOU CAME TO THIS PLACE FROM SOME-WHERE ELSE TOO!
HEE HEE!
SFX: GUBI
I S'POSE I'LL GIVE YE THE QUICK VERSION...
SPITS HAD BEEN A PIRATE IN THE FAR EAST IN THE 1930s.
HE RODE ON THE PRINCE OF PARIAHS, A SMALL, SPEEDY SHIP.
IT WAS SPITS'S JOB TO FISH PEOPLE WHO JUMPED OVER-BOARD OUT OF THE SEA.
BUT IT WASN'T TO RESCUE THEM FROM DROWN-ING.
IT WAS BECAUSE MOST WHO JUMPED TO GET AWAY FROM THE PIRATES WERE TRYING TO SWIM FOR FREEDOM WITH THEIR JEWELS AND TREASURE INTACT!
ONE NIGHT, THE PRINCE OF PARIAHS FOUND ITSELF AT THE CENTER OF A FIERCE STORM.
GOOO (WHOOSH)
AS THE SHIP BROKE APART, SPITS JUMPED OVER-BOARD.
THE NEXT THING HE KNEW, HE WAS CLIMBING ONTO THE SHORE OF THIS VERY LAKE.
AND IT WAS THERE THAT HE MET ...

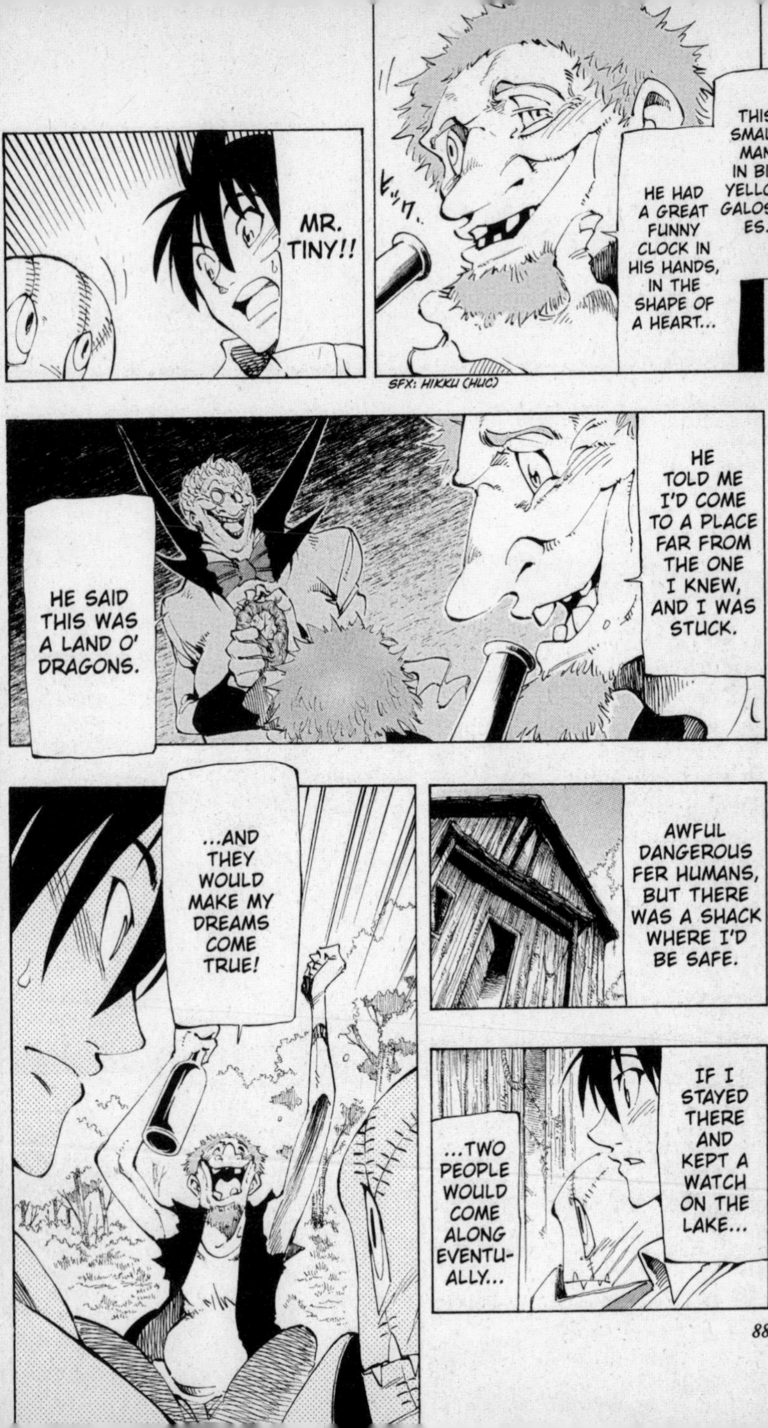
THIS SMALL MAN IN BIG YELLOW GALOSH-ES.
HE HAD A GREAT FUNNY CLOCK IN HIS HANDS, IN THE SHAPE OF A HEART...
SFX: HIKKU (HUC)
MR. TINY!!
HE TOLD ME I'D COME TO A PLACE FAR FROM THE ONE I KNEW, AND I WAS STUCK.
HE SAID THIS WAS A LAND O' DRAGONS.
AWFUL DANGEROUS FER HUMANS, BUT THERE WAS A SHACK WHERE I'D BE SAFE.
IF I STAYED THERE AND KEPT A WATCH ON THE LAKE...
...TWO PEOPLE WOULD COME ALONG EVENTU-ALLY...
...AND THEY WOULD MAKE MY DREAMS COME TRUE!

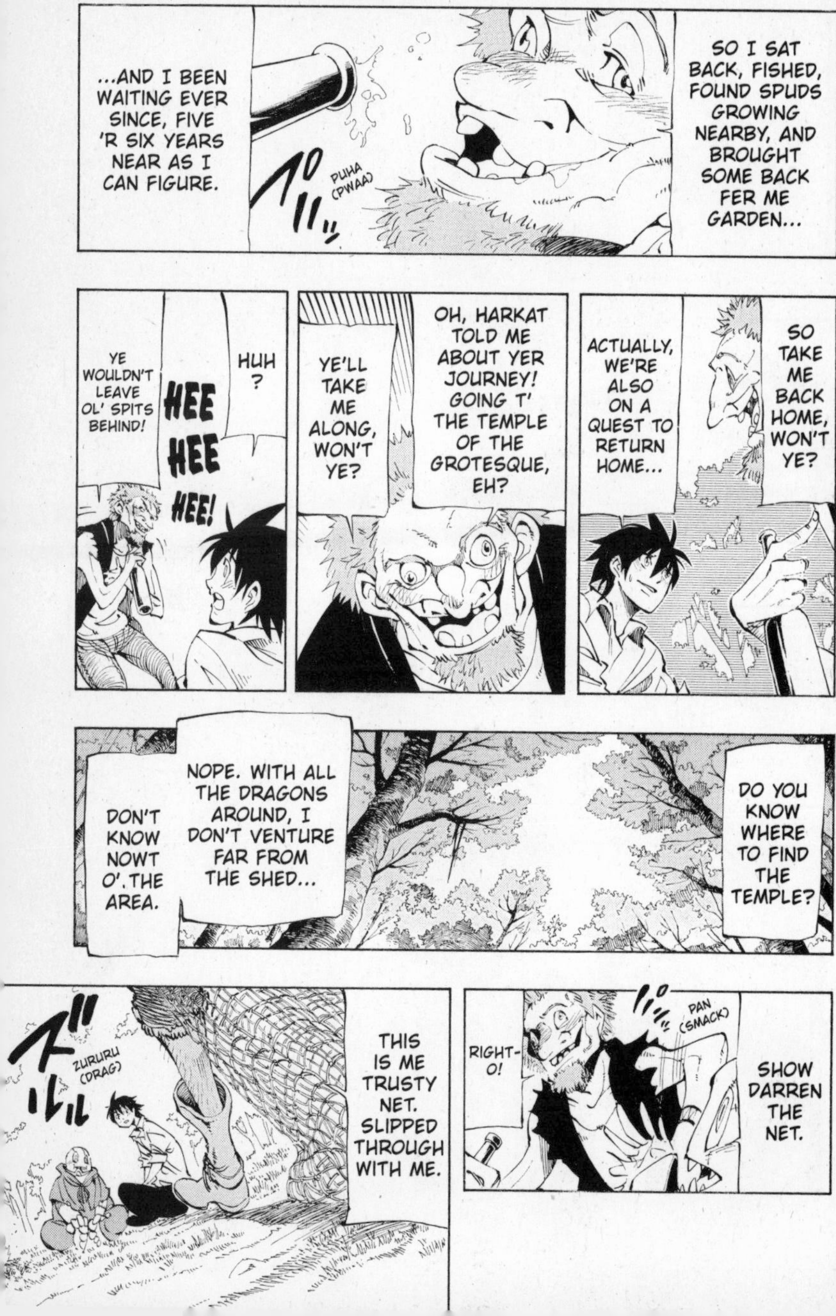
SO I SAT BACK, FISHED, FOUND SPUDS GROWING NEARBY, AND BROUGHT SOME BACK FER ME GARDEN...
PUHA (PWAA)
...AND I BEEN WAITING EVER SINCE, FIVE 'R SIX YEARS NEAR AS I CAN FIGURE.
SO TAKE ME BACK HOME, WON'T YE?
ACTUALLY, WE'RE ALSO ON A QUEST TO RETURN HOME...
OH, HARKAT TOLD ME ABOUT YER JOURNEY! GOING T' THE TEMPLE OF THE GROTESQUE, EH?
YE'LL TAKE ME ALONG, WON'T YE?
HUH?
HEE HEE HEE!
YE WOULDN'T LEAVE OL' SPITS BEHIND!
DO YOU KNOW WHERE TO FIND THE TEMPLE?
NOPE. WITH ALL THE DRAGONS AROUND, I DON'T VENTURE FAR FROM THE SHED...
DON'T KNOW NOWT O' THE AREA.
SHOW DARREN THE NET.
PAN (SMACK)
RIGHT-O!
THIS IS ME TRUSTY NET. SLIPPED THROUGH WITH ME.
ZURURU (DRAG)

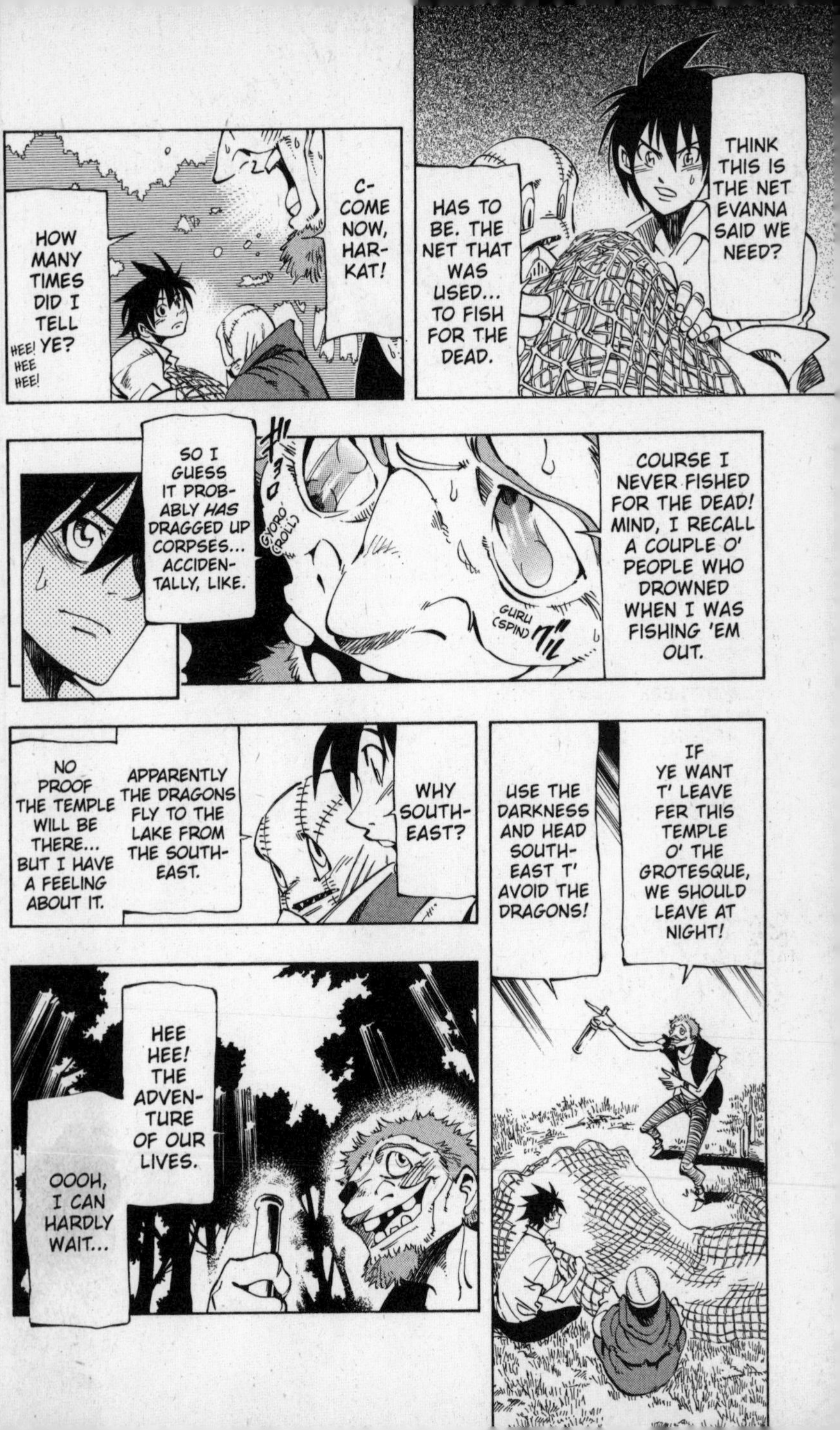
THINK THIS IS THE NET EVANNA SAID WE NEED?
HAS TO BE. THE NET THAT WAS USED... TO FISH FOR THE DEAD.
C-COME NOW, HAR-KAT!
HOW MANY TIMES DID I TELL YE?
HEE! HEE HEE!
COURSE I NEVER FISHED FOR THE DEAD! MIND, I RECALL A COUPLE O' PEOPLE WHO DROWNED WHEN I WAS FISHING 'EM OUT.
GURU (SPIN)
GYORO (ROLL)
SO I GUESS IT PROBABLY *HAS* DRAGGED UP CORPSES... ACCIDENTALLY, LIKE.
IF YE WANT T' LEAVE FER THIS TEMPLE O' THE GROTESQUE, WE SHOULD LEAVE AT NIGHT!
USE THE DARKNESS AND HEAD SOUTH-EAST T' AVOID THE DRAGONS!
WHY SOUTH-EAST?
APPARENTLY THE DRAGONS FLY TO THE LAKE FROM THE SOUTH-EAST.
NO PROOF THE TEMPLE WILL BE THERE... BUT I HAVE A FEELING ABOUT IT.
HEE HEE! THE ADVENTURE OF OUR LIVES.
OOOH, I CAN HARDLY WAIT...

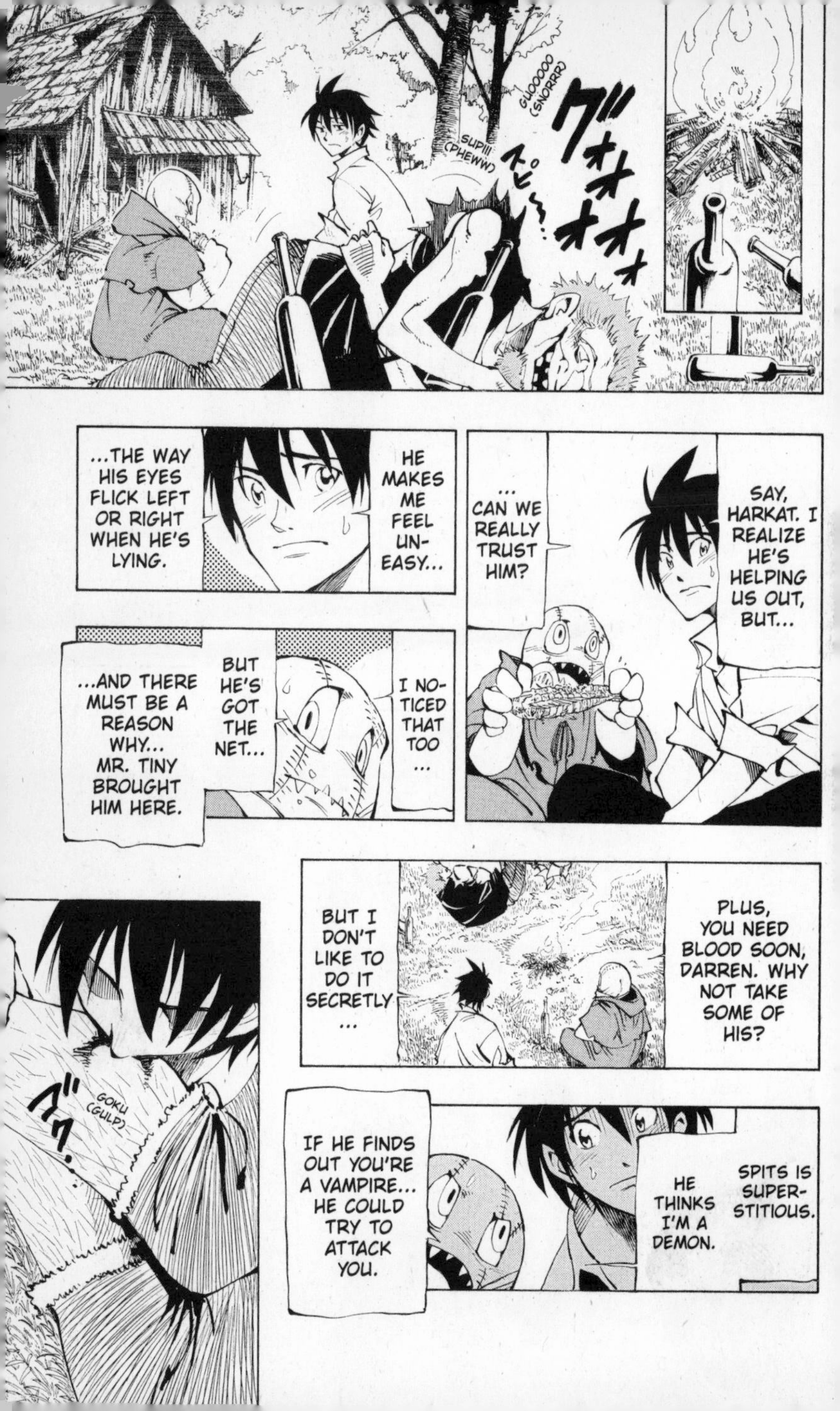
グォォォォォ
GUOOOOO (SNORRR)
スピ～…
SUPIII (PHEWW)
SAY, HARKAT. I REALIZE HE'S HELPING US OUT, BUT...
... CAN WE REALLY TRUST HIM?
HE MAKES ME FEEL UN-EASY...
...THE WAY HIS EYES FLICK LEFT OR RIGHT WHEN HE'S LYING.
I NO-TICED THAT TOO ...
BUT HE'S GOT THE NET...
...AND THERE MUST BE A REASON WHY... MR. TINY BROUGHT HIM HERE.
PLUS, YOU NEED BLOOD SOON, DARREN. WHY NOT TAKE SOME OF HIS?
BUT I DON'T LIKE TO DO IT SECRETLY ...
SPITS IS SUPER-STITIOUS.
HE THINKS I'M A DEMON.
IF HE FINDS OUT YOU'RE A VAMPIRE... HE COULD TRY TO ATTACK YOU.
ゴク
GOKU (GULP)

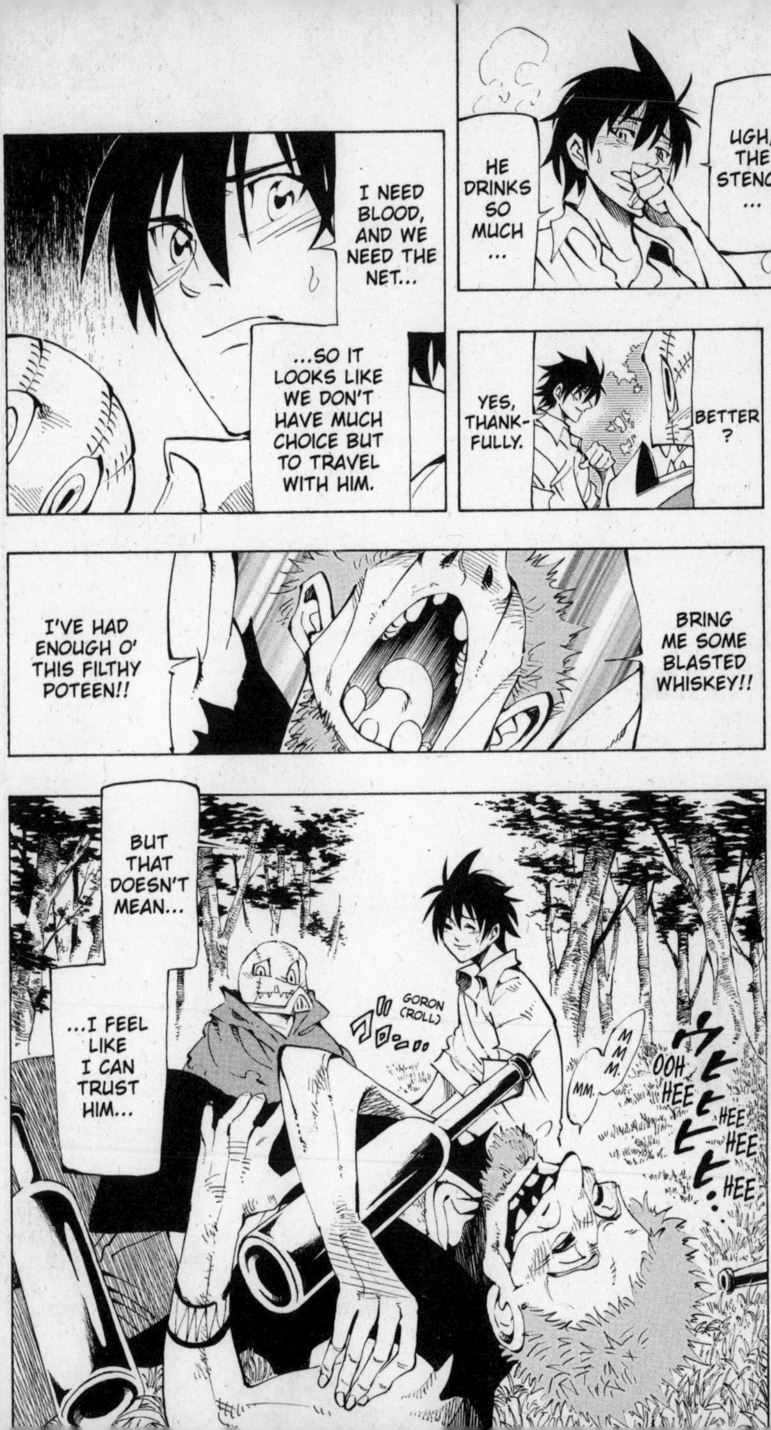
UGH, THE STENCH ...
HE DRINKS SO MUCH ...
BETTER?
YES, THANKFULLY.
I NEED BLOOD, AND WE NEED THE NET...
...SO IT LOOKS LIKE WE DON'T HAVE MUCH CHOICE BUT TO TRAVEL WITH HIM.
BRING ME SOME BLASTED WHISKEY!!
I'VE HAD ENOUGH O' THIS FILTHY POTEEN!!
BUT THAT DOESN'T MEAN...
OOH HEE HEE HEE HEE
MMM. MM.
GORON (ROLL)
...I FEEL LIKE I CAN TRUST HIM...

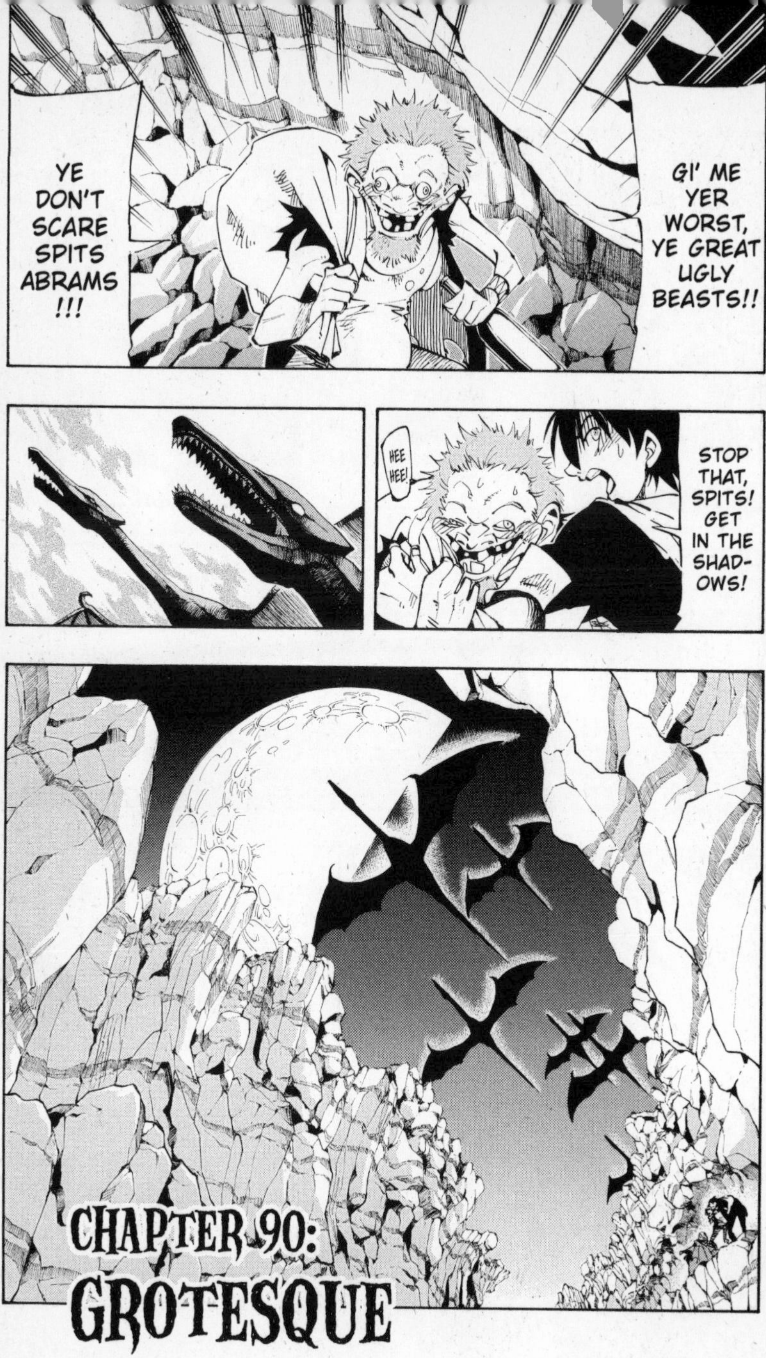
GI' ME YER WORST, YE GREAT UGLY BEASTS!!
YE DON'T SCARE SPITS ABRAMS!!!
STOP THAT, SPITS! GET IN THE SHAD-OWS!
HEE HEE!
CHAPTER 90:
GROTESQUE

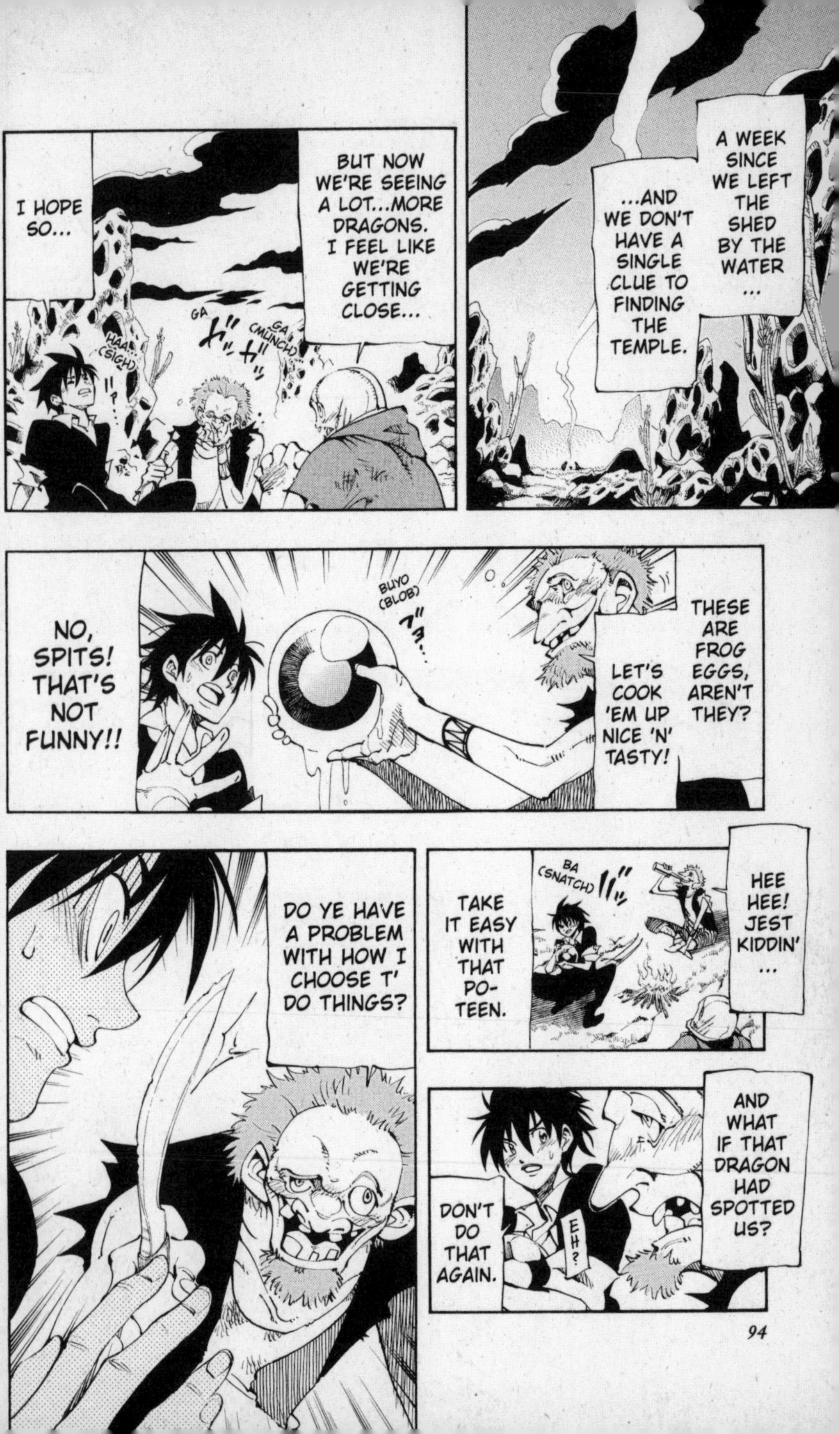
A WEEK SINCE WE LEFT THE SHED BY THE WATER ...
...AND WE DON'T HAVE A SINGLE CLUE TO FINDING THE TEMPLE.
BUT NOW WE'RE SEEING A LOT...MORE DRAGONS. I FEEL LIKE WE'RE GETTING CLOSE...
GA GA (MUNCH)
HAA... (SIGH)
I HOPE SO...
BUYO (BLOB)
THESE ARE FROG EGGS, AREN'T THEY?
LET'S COOK 'EM UP NICE 'N' TASTY!
NO, SPITS! THAT'S NOT FUNNY!!
HEE HEE! JEST KIDDIN' ...
BA (SNATCH)
TAKE IT EASY WITH THAT PO-TEEN.
AND WHAT IF THAT DRAGON HAD SPOTTED US?
EH?
DON'T DO THAT AGAIN.
DO YE HAVE A PROBLEM WITH HOW I CHOOSE T' DO THINGS?

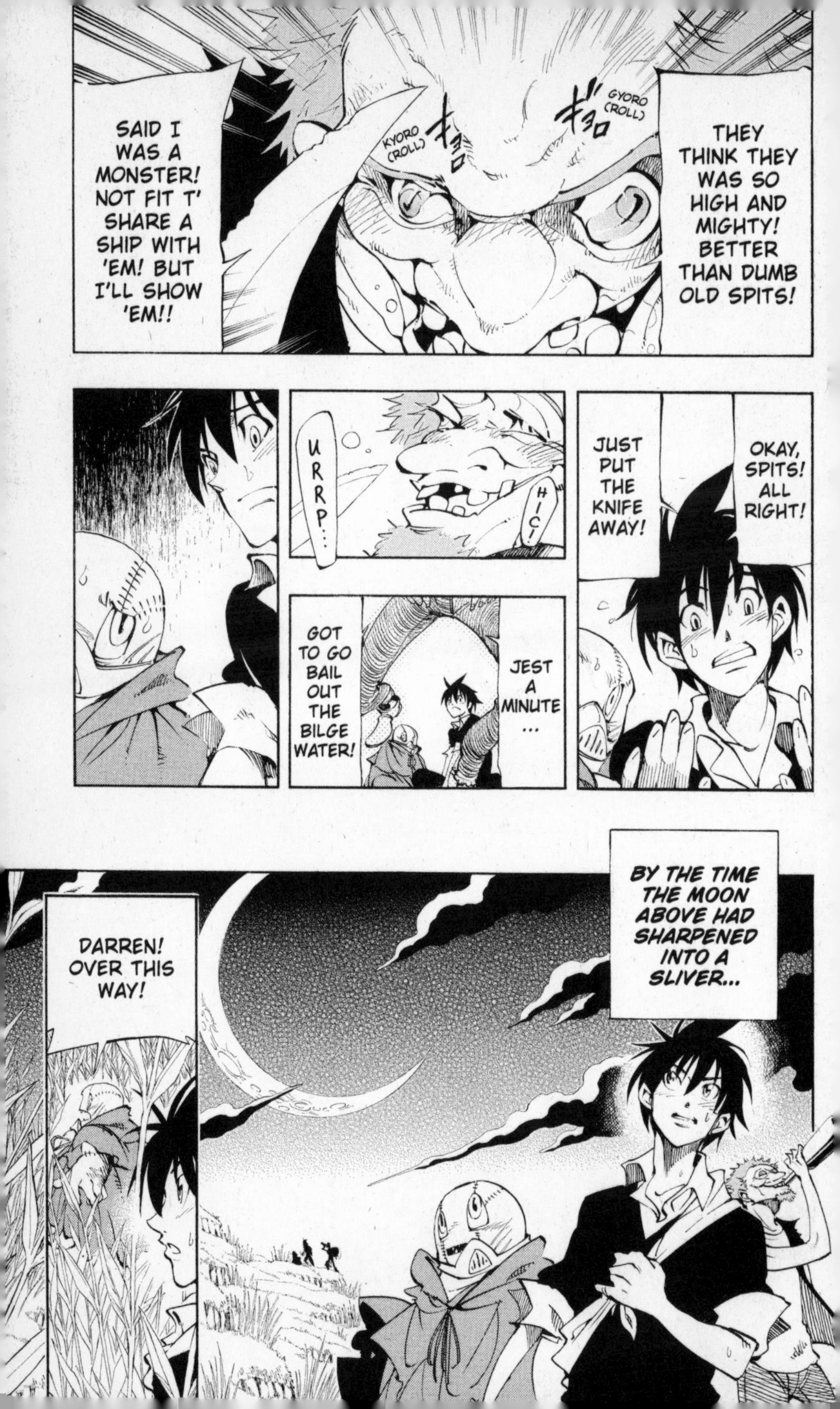
THEY THINK THEY WAS SO HIGH AND MIGHTY! BETTER THAN DUMB OLD SPITS!
GYORO (ROLL)
KYORO (ROLL)
SAID I WAS A MONSTER! NOT FIT T' SHARE A SHIP WITH 'EM! BUT I'LL SHOW 'EM!!
OKAY, SPITS! ALL RIGHT!
JUST PUT THE KNIFE AWAY!
HIC!
URRP...
JEST A MINUTE...
GOT TO GO BAIL OUT THE BILGE WATER!
BY THE TIME THE MOON ABOVE HAD SHARPENED INTO A SLIVER...
DARREN! OVER THIS WAY!

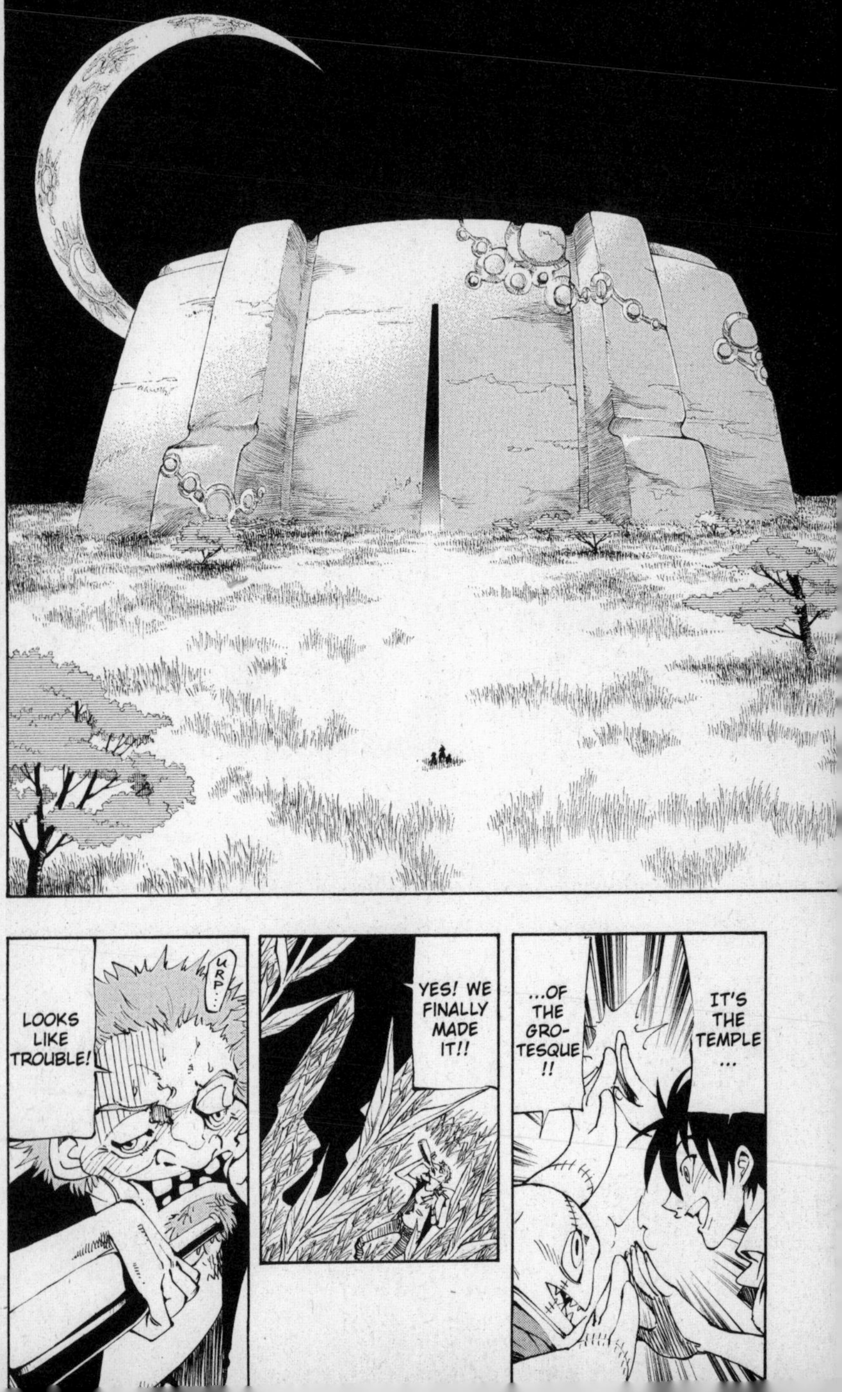
IT'S THE TEMPLE ...
...OF THE GRO-TESQUE !!
YES! WE FINALLY MADE IT!!
URP...
LOOKS LIKE TROUBLE!

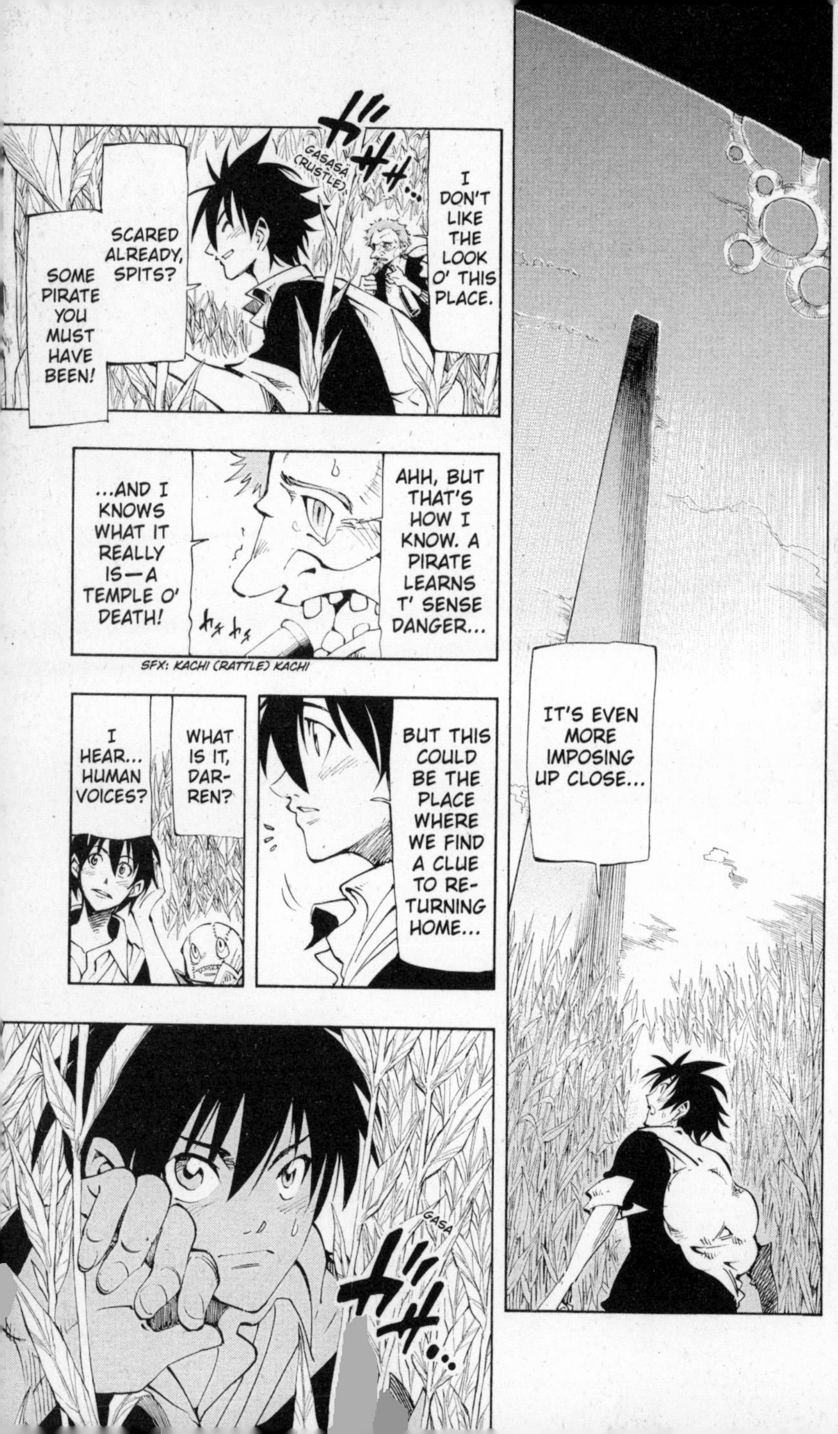
IT'S EVEN MORE IMPOSING UP CLOSE...
GASASA (RUSTLE)
I DON'T LIKE THE LOOK O' THIS PLACE.
SCARED ALREADY, SPITS?
SOME PIRATE YOU MUST HAVE BEEN!
AHH, BUT THAT'S HOW I KNOW. A PIRATE LEARNS T' SENSE DANGER...
...AND I KNOWS WHAT IT REALLY IS—A TEMPLE O' DEATH!
SFX: KACHI (RATTLE) KACHI
BUT THIS COULD BE THE PLACE WHERE WE FIND A CLUE TO RE-TURNING HOME...
WHAT IS IT, DAR-REN?
I HEAR... HUMAN VOICES?
GASA

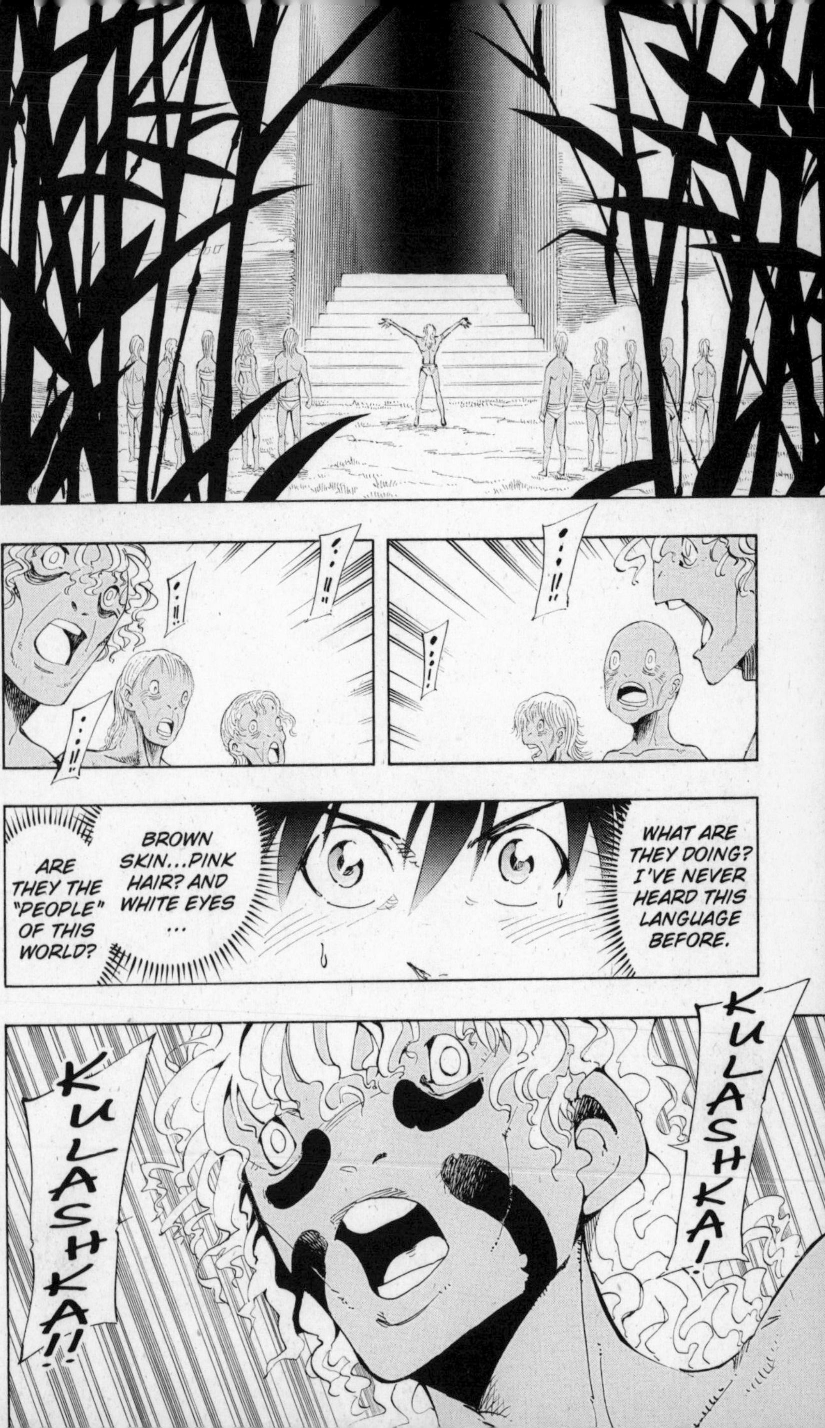
!...!!
!...!
!...!!
!...!!
!...!!
WHAT ARE THEY DOING? I'VE NEVER HEARD THIS LANGUAGE BEFORE.
BROWN SKIN...PINK HAIR? AND WHITE EYES ...
ARE THEY THE "PEOPLE" OF THIS WORLD?
KULASHKAI!
KULASHKA!!

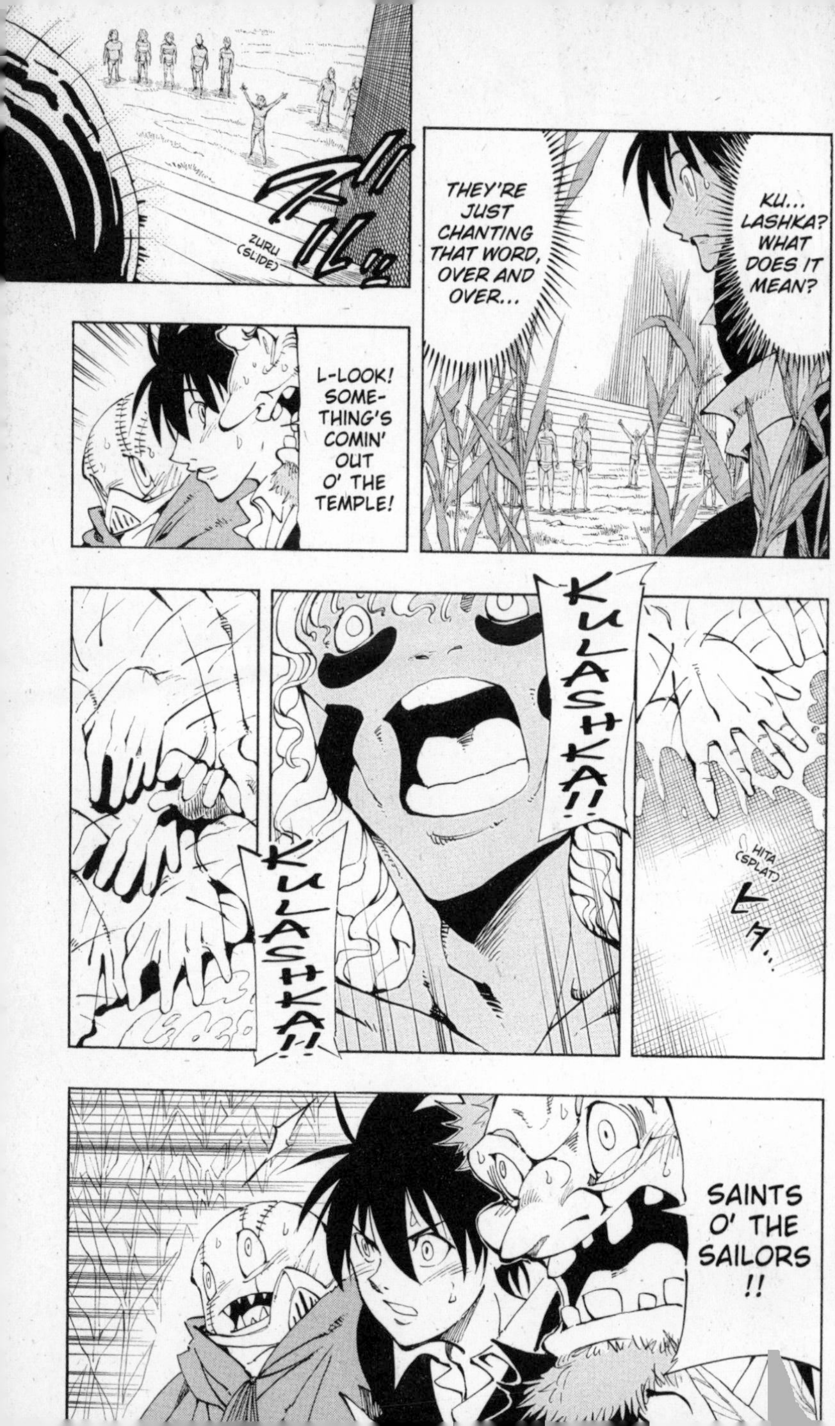
ZURU (SLIDE)
KU... LASHKA? WHAT DOES IT MEAN?
THEY'RE JUST CHANTING THAT WORD, OVER AND OVER...
L-LOOK! SOME-THING'S COMIN' OUT O' THE TEMPLE!
HITA (SPLAT)
KULASHKA!!
KULASHKA!!
SAINTS O' THE SAILORS !!

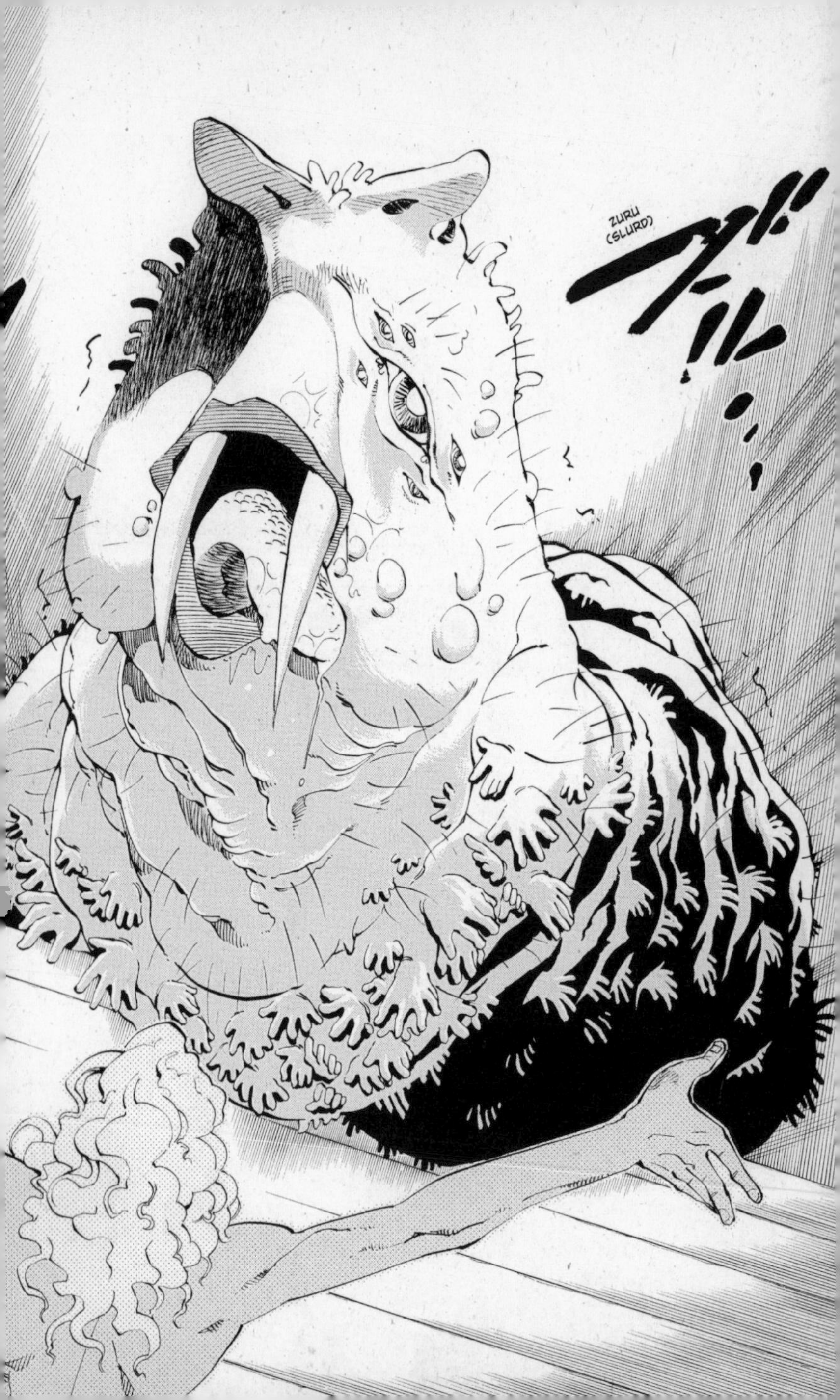
ZURU
(SLURP)

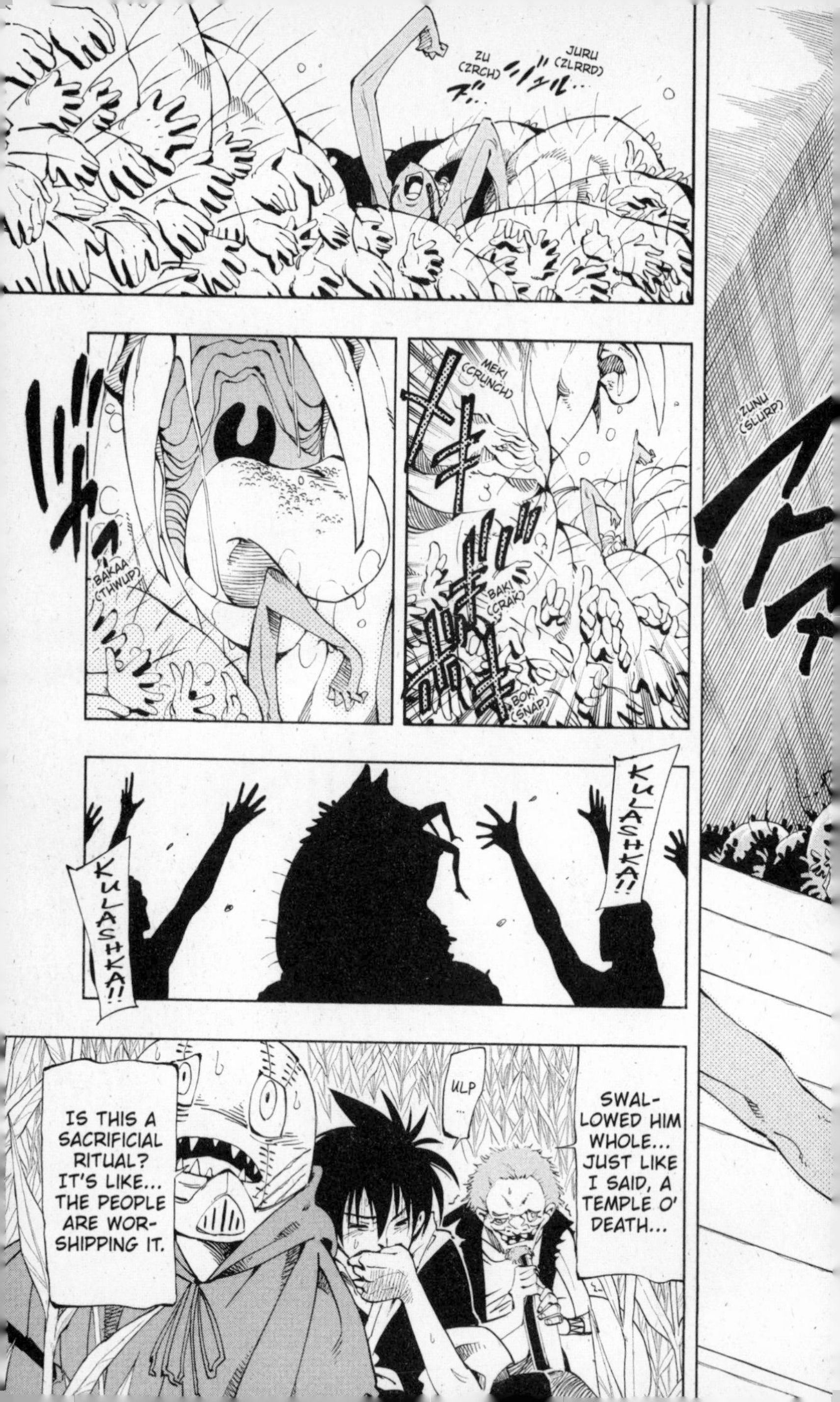
ZUNU (SLURP)
ZU (ZRCH)
JURU (ZLRRD)
MEKI (CRUNCH)
BAKI (CRAK)
BOKI (SNAP)
BAKAA (THWUP)
KULASHKA!!
KULASHKA!!
SWAL-LOWED HIM WHOLE... JUST LIKE I SAID, A TEMPLE O' DEATH...
ULP ...
IS THIS A SACRIFICIAL RITUAL? IT'S LIKE... THE PEOPLE ARE WOR-SHIPPING IT.

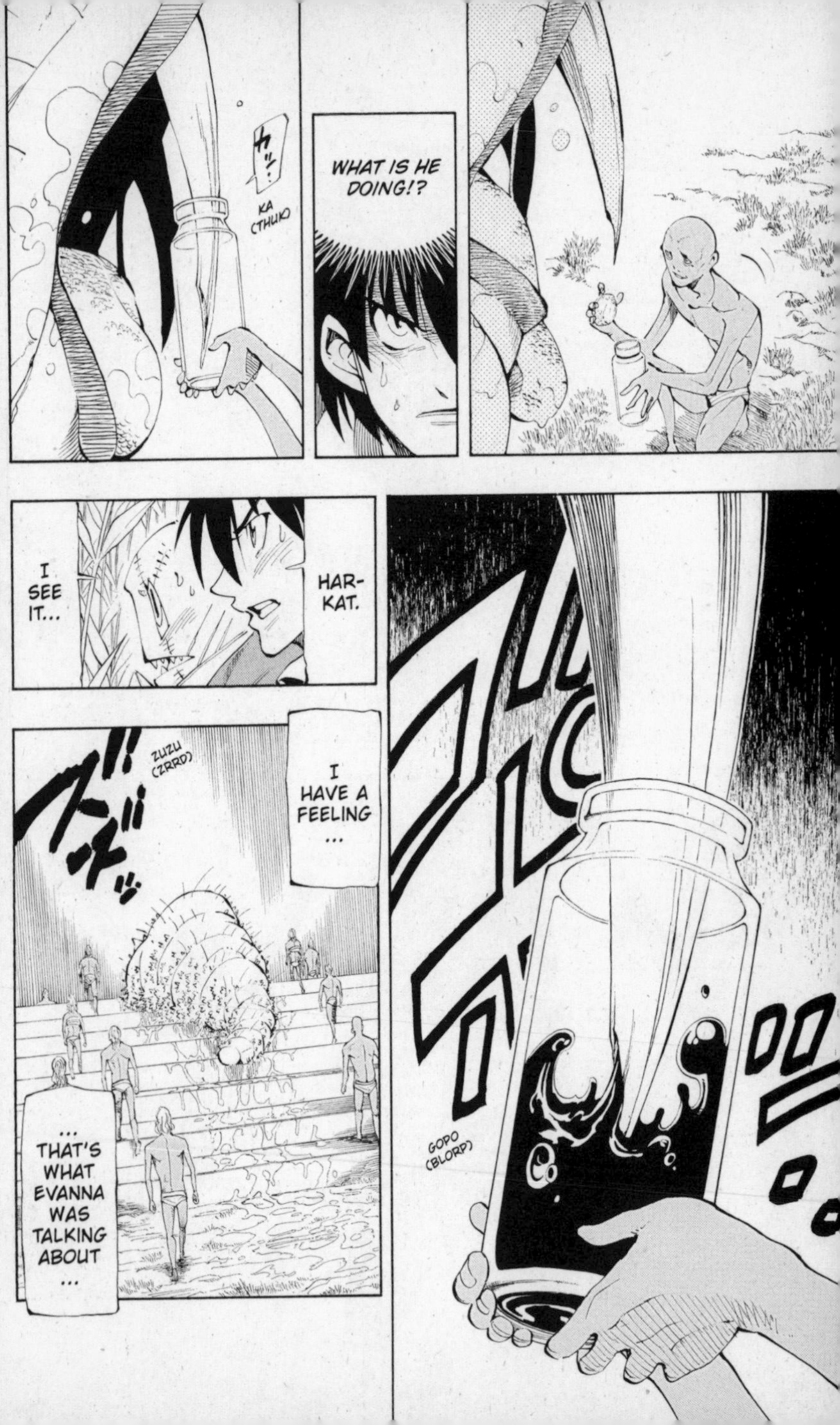
WHAT IS HE DOING!?
KA (THUK)
GOPO (BLORP)
HAR-KAT.
I SEE IT...
I HAVE A FEELING ...
ZUZU (ZRRD)
... THAT'S WHAT EVANNA WAS TALKING ABOUT ...

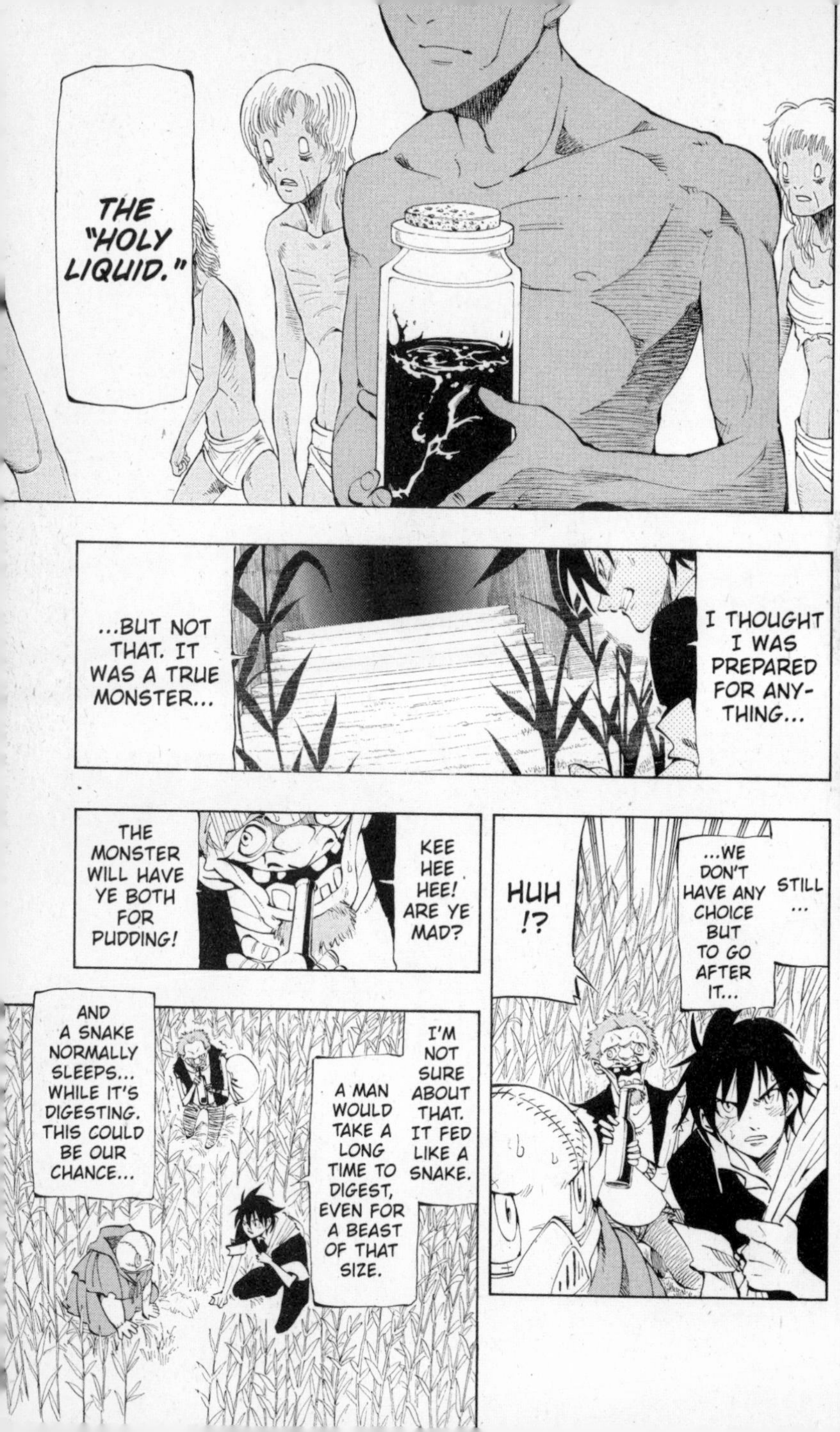
THE "HOLY LIQUID."
I THOUGHT I WAS PREPARED FOR ANYTHING...
...BUT NOT THAT. IT WAS A TRUE MONSTER...
STILL...
...WE DON'T HAVE ANY CHOICE BUT TO GO AFTER IT...
HUH!?
KEE HEE HEE! ARE YE MAD?
THE MONSTER WILL HAVE YE BOTH FOR PUDDING!
I'M NOT SURE ABOUT THAT. IT FED LIKE A SNAKE.
A MAN WOULD TAKE A LONG TIME TO DIGEST, EVEN FOR A BEAST OF THAT SIZE.
AND A SNAKE NORMALLY SLEEPS... WHILE IT'S DIGESTING. THIS COULD BE OUR CHANCE...

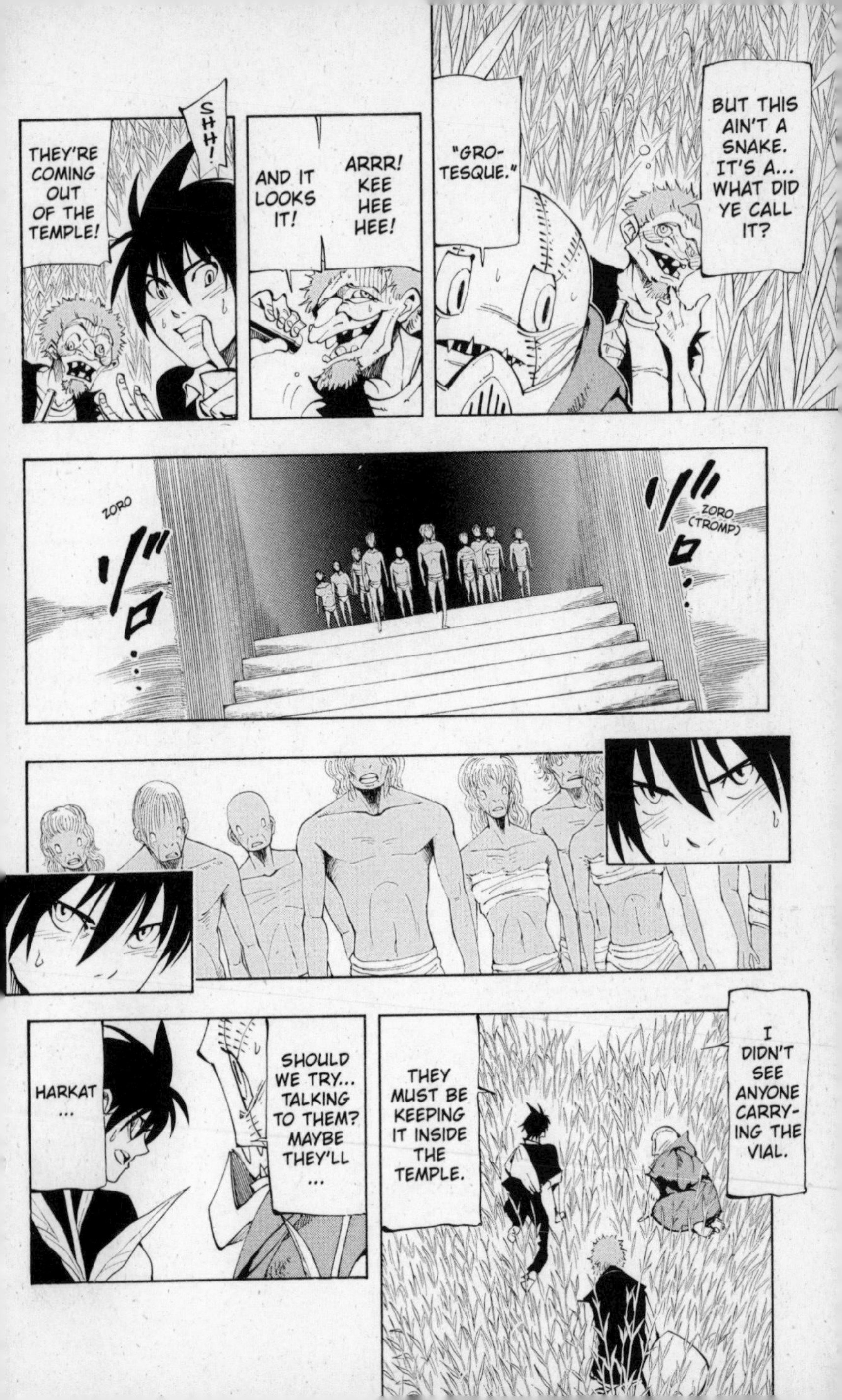
BUT THIS AIN'T A SNAKE. IT'S A... WHAT DID YE CALL IT?
"GRO-TESQUE."
ARRR! KEE HEE HEE!
AND IT LOOKS IT!
SHH!
THEY'RE COMING OUT OF THE TEMPLE!
ZORO (TROMP)
ZORO
I DIDN'T SEE ANYONE CARRY-ING THE VIAL.
THEY MUST BE KEEPING IT INSIDE THE TEMPLE.
SHOULD WE TRY... TALKING TO THEM? MAYBE THEY'LL ...
HARKAT ...

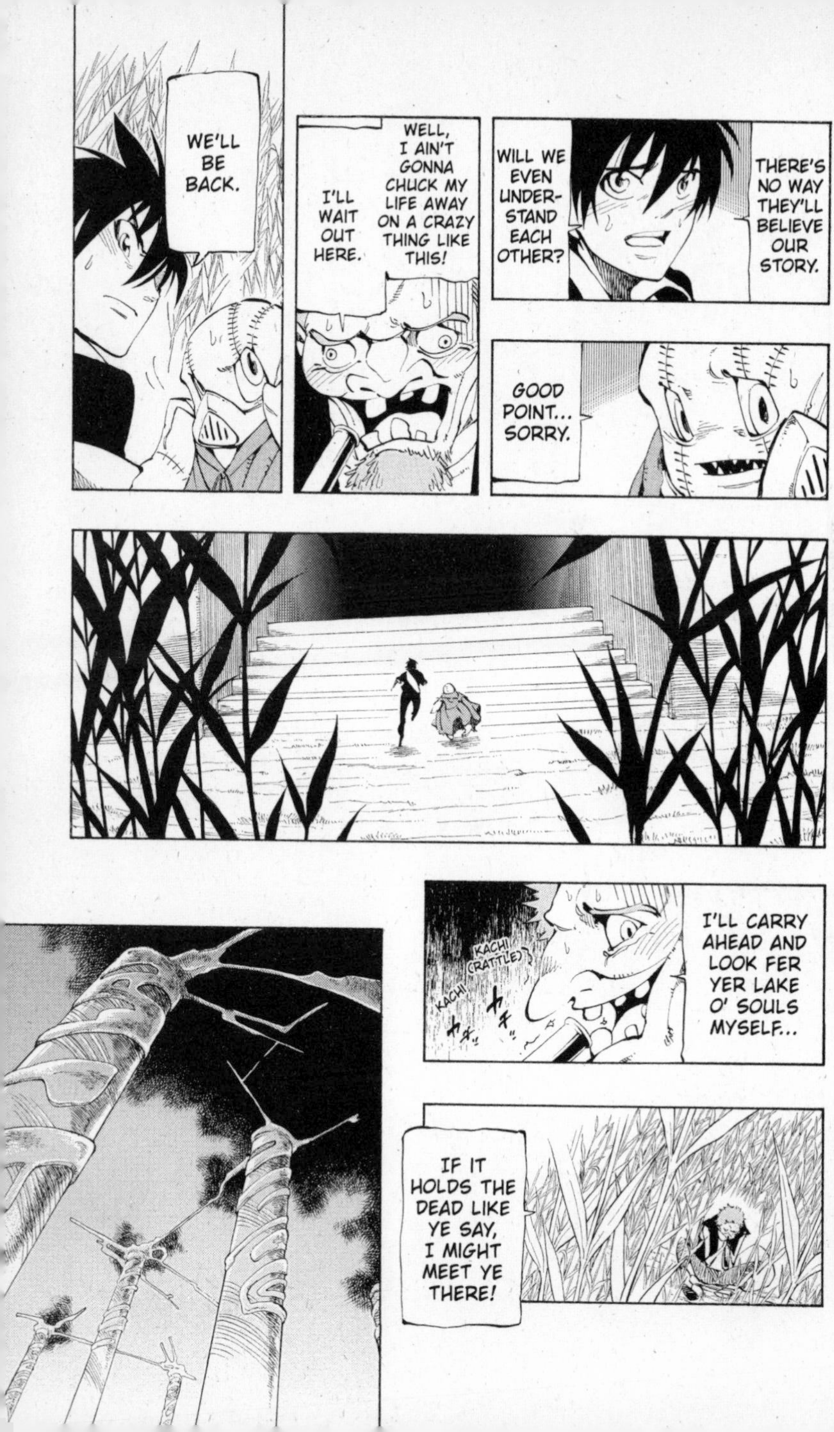
THERE'S NO WAY THEY'LL BELIEVE OUR STORY.
WILL WE EVEN UNDERSTAND EACH OTHER?
GOOD POINT... SORRY.
WELL, I AIN'T GONNA CHUCK MY LIFE AWAY ON A CRAZY THING LIKE THIS!
I'LL WAIT OUT HERE.
WE'LL BE BACK.
I'LL CARRY AHEAD AND LOOK FER YER LAKE O' SOULS MYSELF...
KACHI (RATTLE)
KACHI
IF IT HOLDS THE DEAD LIKE YE SAY, I MIGHT MEET YE THERE!

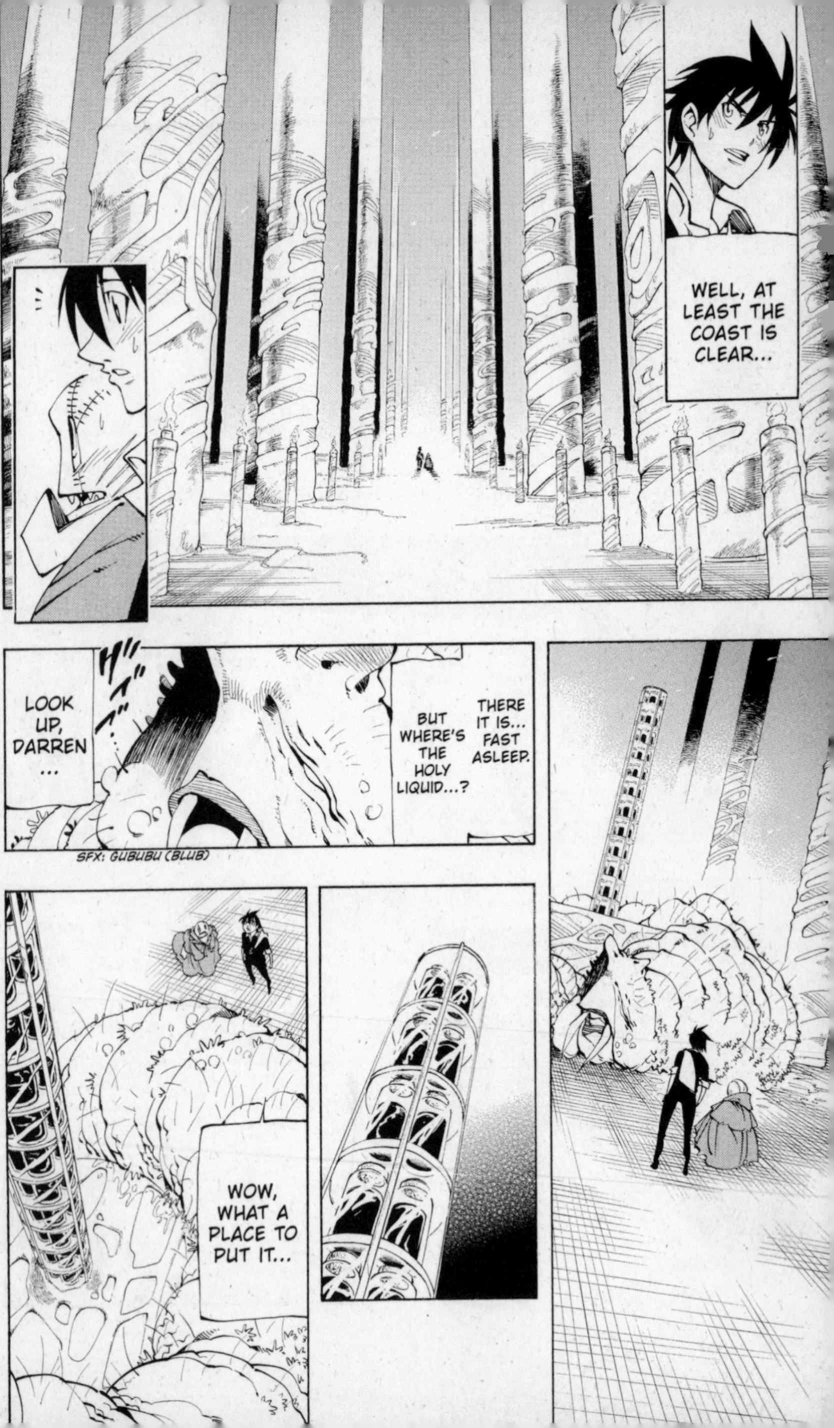
WELL, AT LEAST THE COAST IS CLEAR...
THERE IT IS... FAST ASLEEP.
BUT WHERE'S THE HOLY LIQUID...?
LOOK UP, DARREN ...
SFX: GUBUBU (BLUB)
WOW, WHAT A PLACE TO PUT IT...

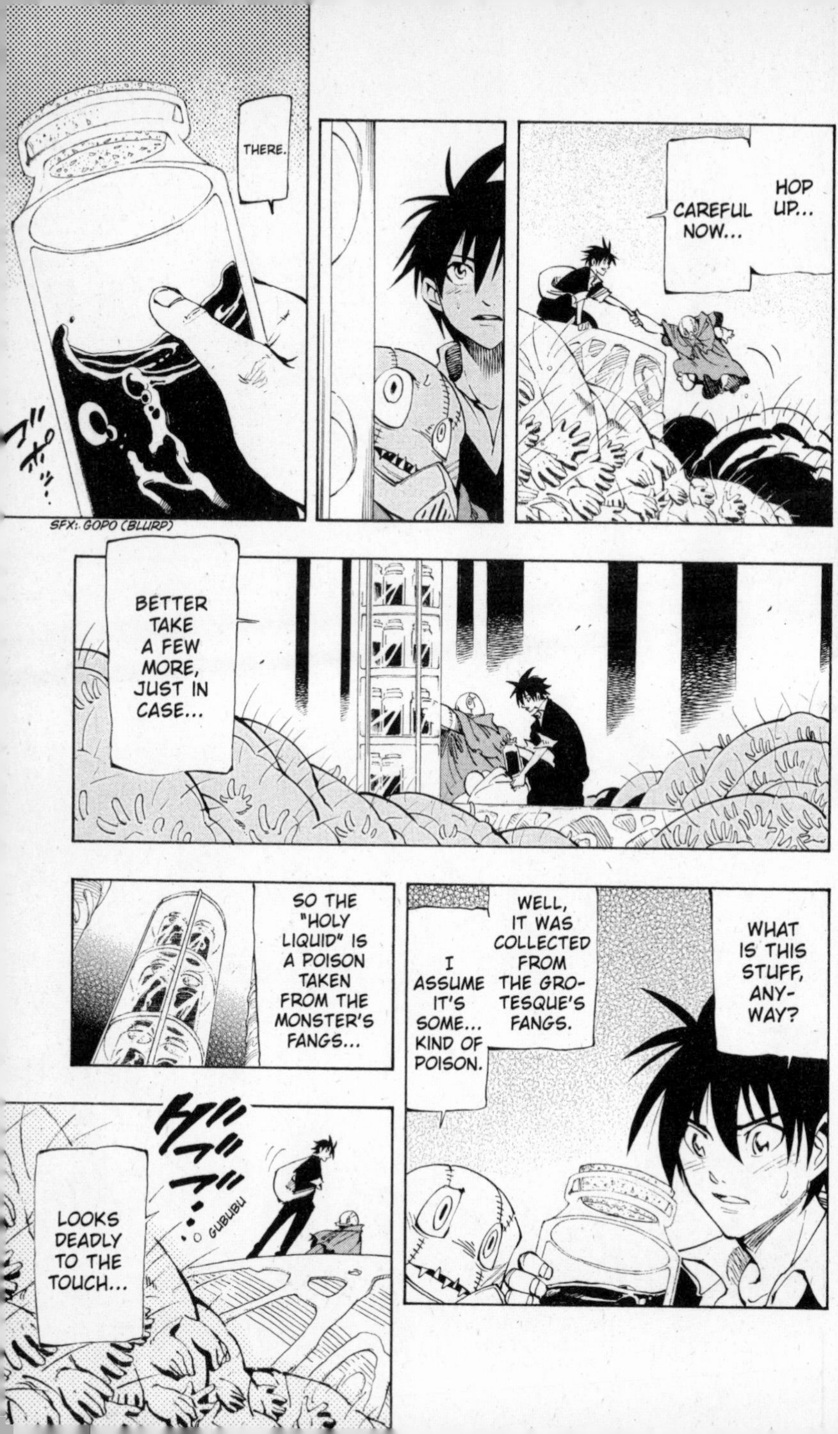
HOP UP...
CAREFUL NOW...
THERE.
SFX: GOPO (BLURP)
BETTER TAKE A FEW MORE, JUST IN CASE...
WHAT IS THIS STUFF, ANYWAY?
WELL, IT WAS COLLECTED FROM THE GROTESQUE'S FANGS.
I ASSUME IT'S SOME... KIND OF POISON.
SO THE "HOLY LIQUID" IS A POISON TAKEN FROM THE MONSTER'S FANGS...
GUBUBU
LOOKS DEADLY TO THE TOUCH...

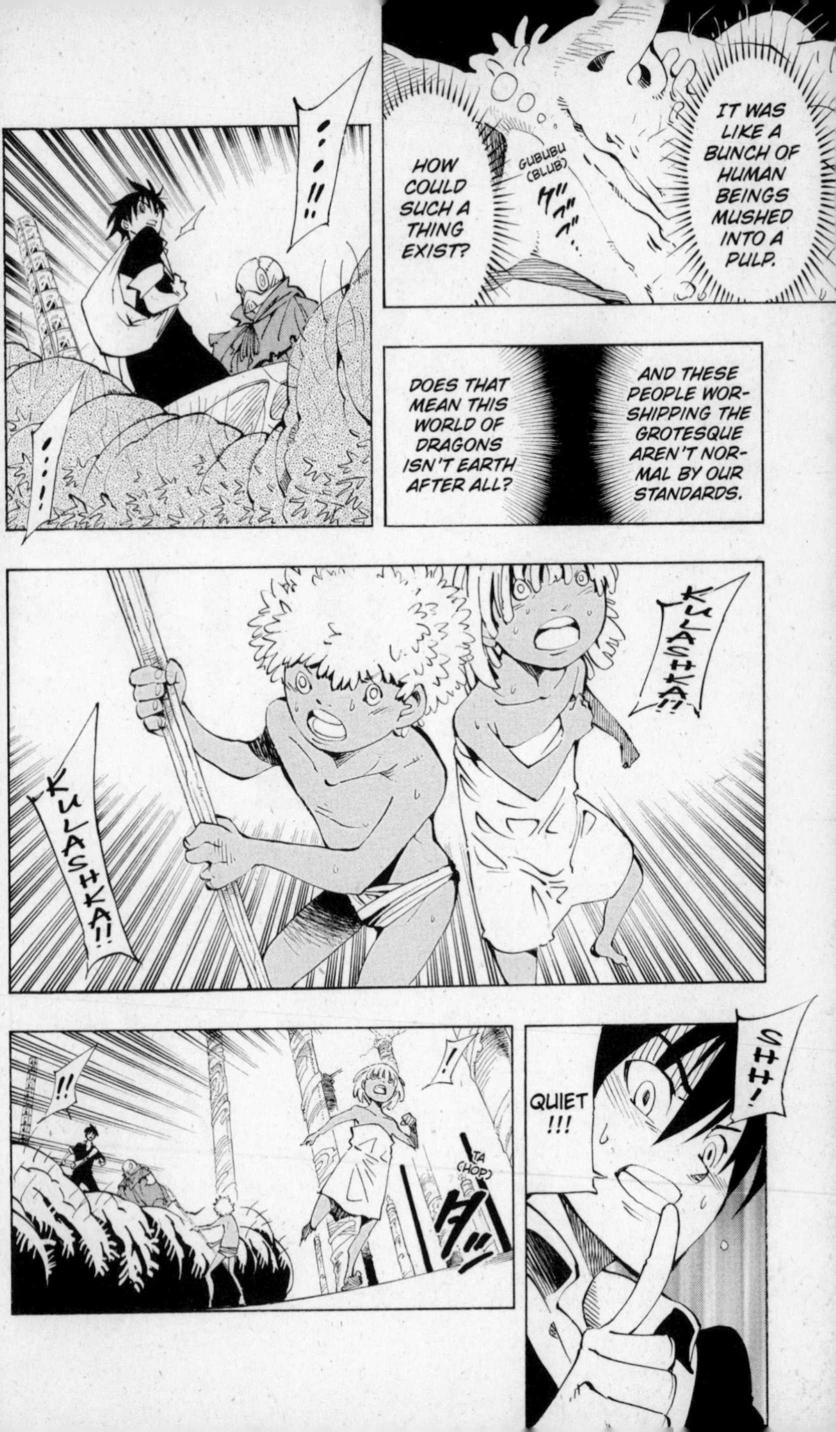
IT WAS LIKE A BUNCH OF HUMAN BEINGS MUSHED INTO A PULP.
GUBUBU (BLUB)
HOW COULD SUCH A THING EXIST?
AND THESE PEOPLE WOR-SHIPPING THE GROTESQUE AREN'T NOR-MAL BY OUR STANDARDS.
DOES THAT MEAN THIS WORLD OF DRAGONS ISN'T EARTH AFTER ALL?
...!!
...!
KULASHKA!!
KULASHKA!!
SHH!
QUIET!!!
!
TA (HOP)
!!

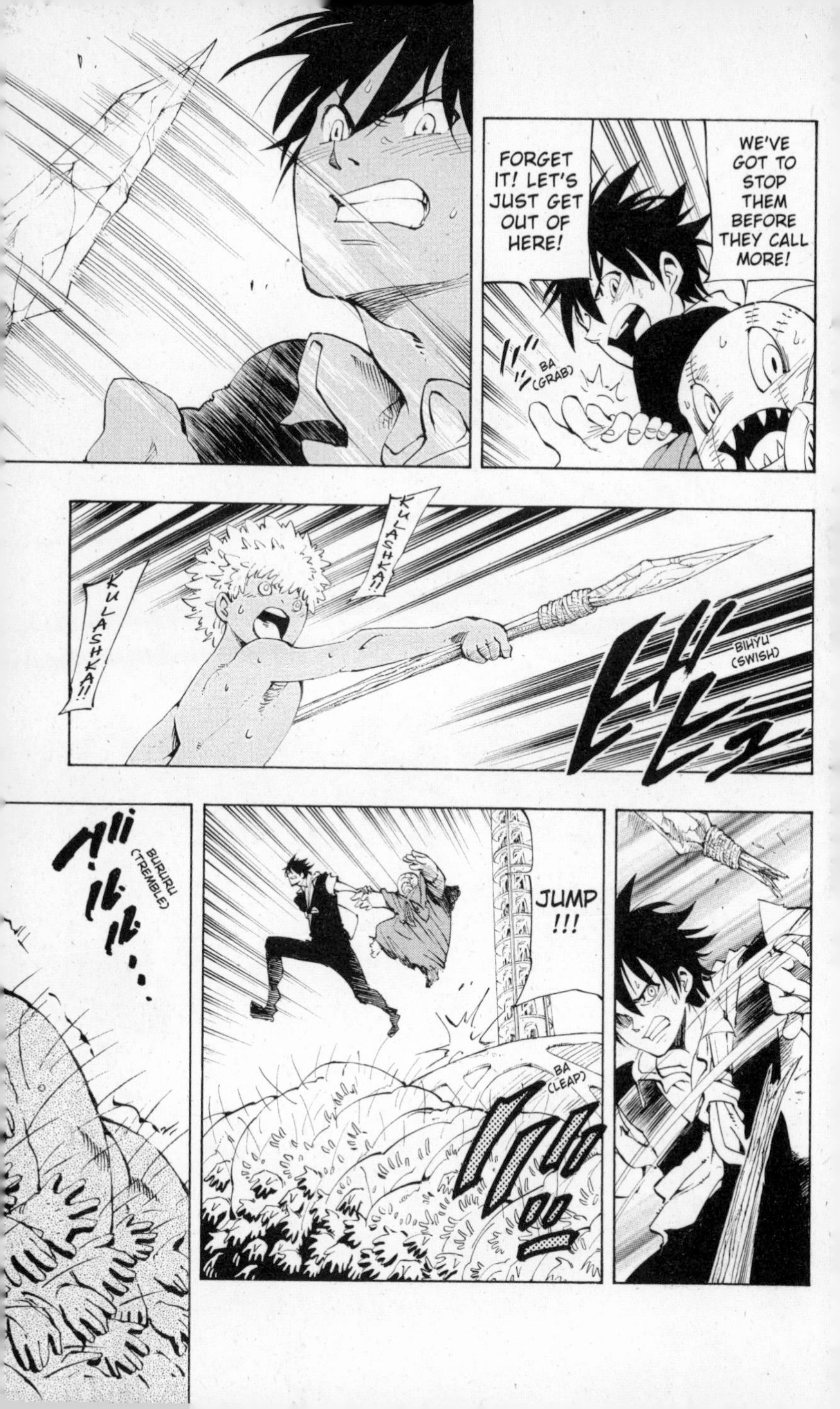

WE'VE GOT TO STOP THEM BEFORE THEY CALL MORE!
FORGET IT! LET'S JUST GET OUT OF HERE!
BA (GRAB)
KULASHKA!!
KULASHKA!!
BIHYU (SWISH)
JUMP !!!
BA (LEAP)
BURURU (TREMBLE)

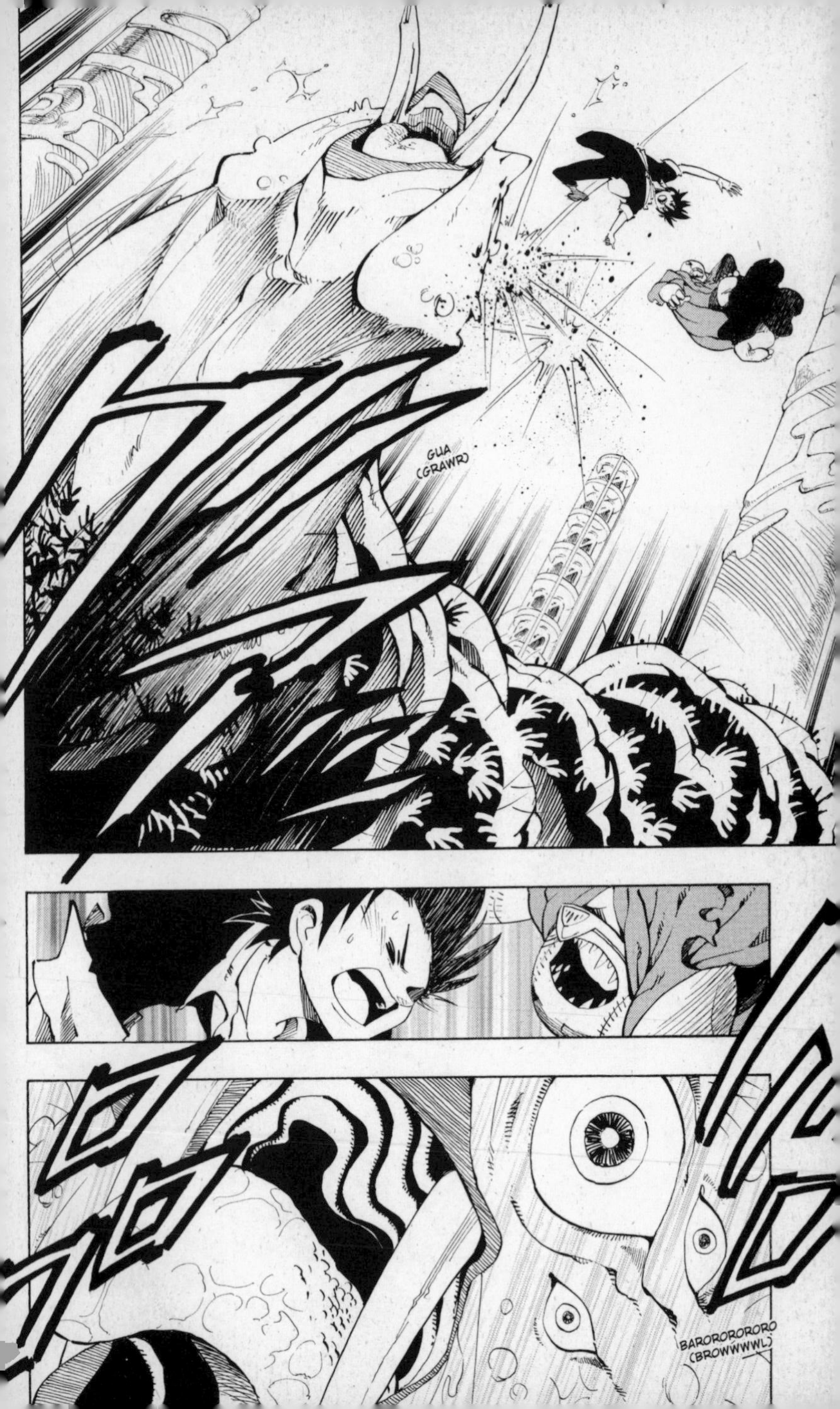
GUA
(GRAWR)
BARORORORORO
(BROWWWWL)

CHAPTER 91:
GETAWAY

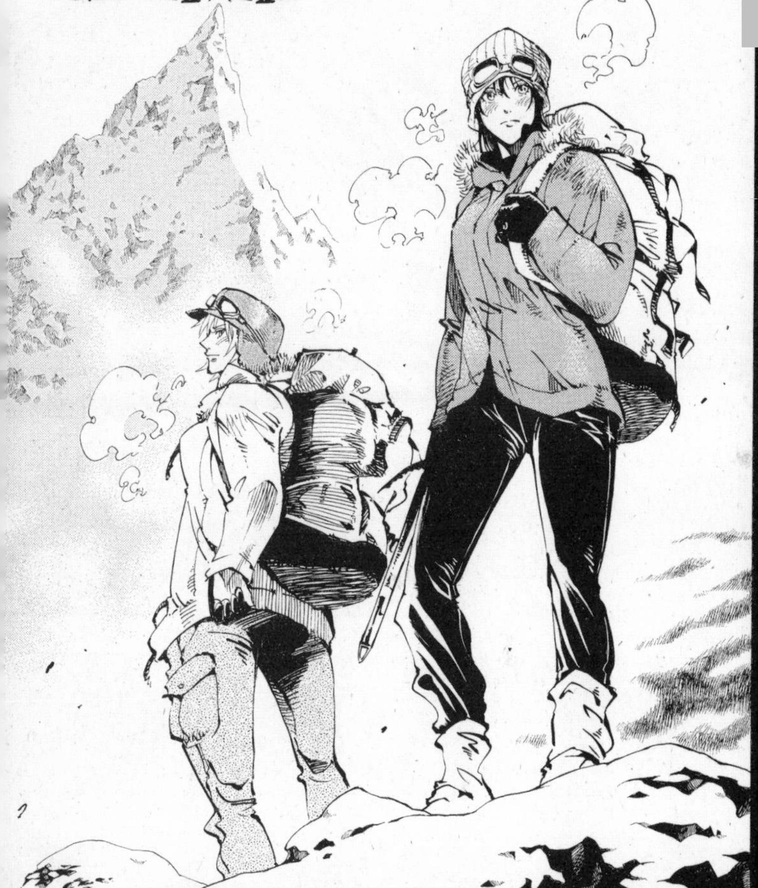

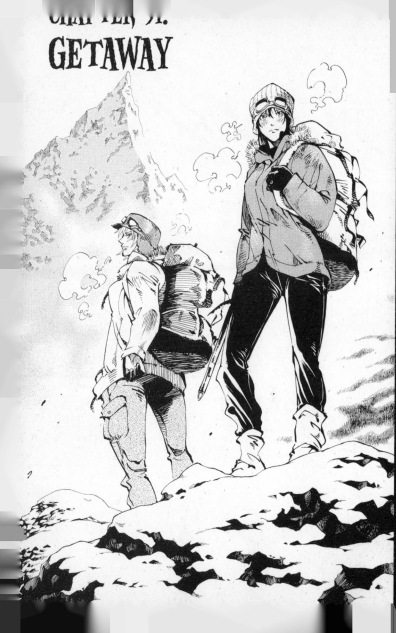

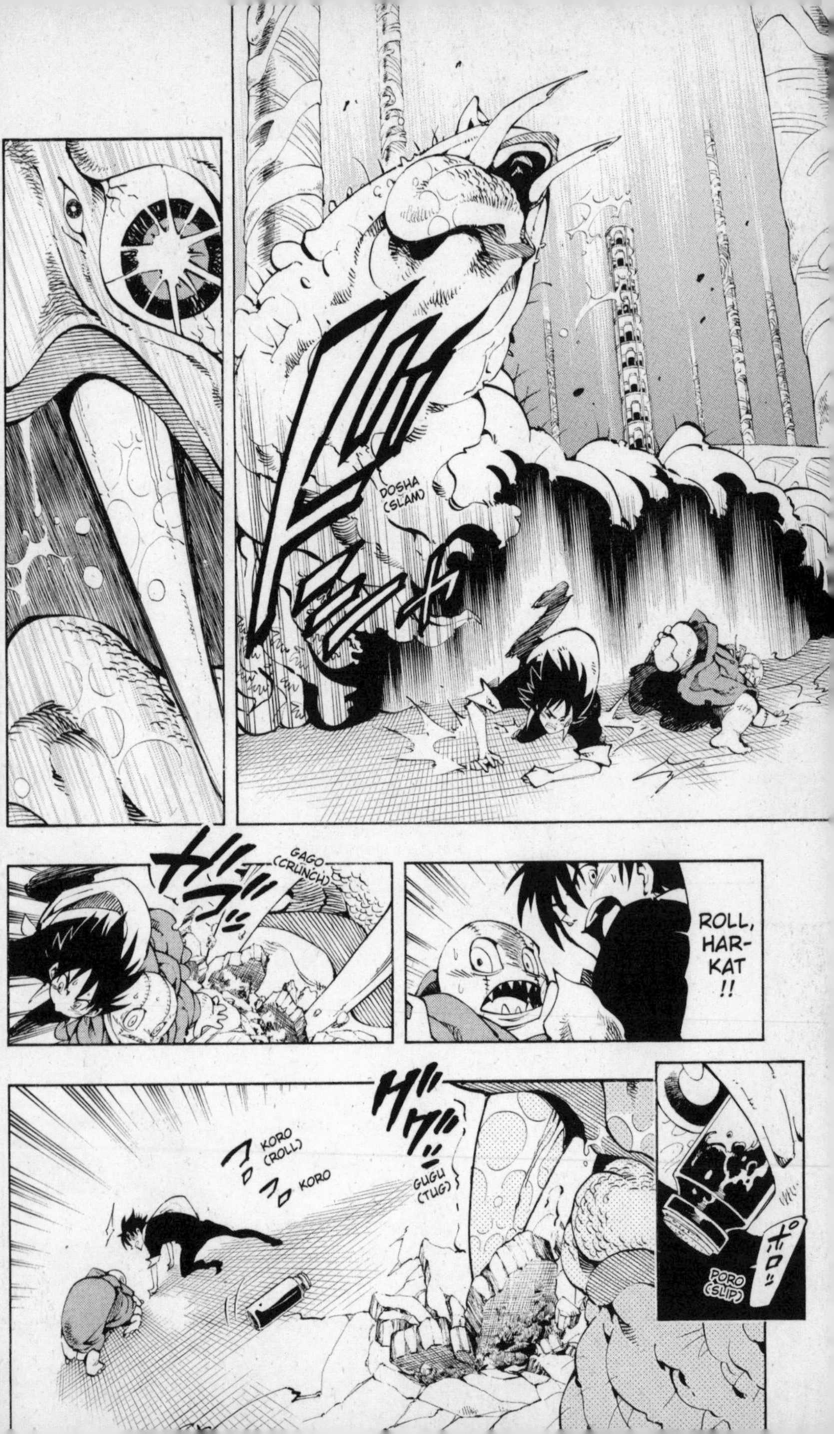
DOSHA (SLAM)
ROLL, HARKAT !!
GAGO (CRUNCH)
PORO (SLIP)
GUGU (TUG)
KORO (ROLL)
KORO

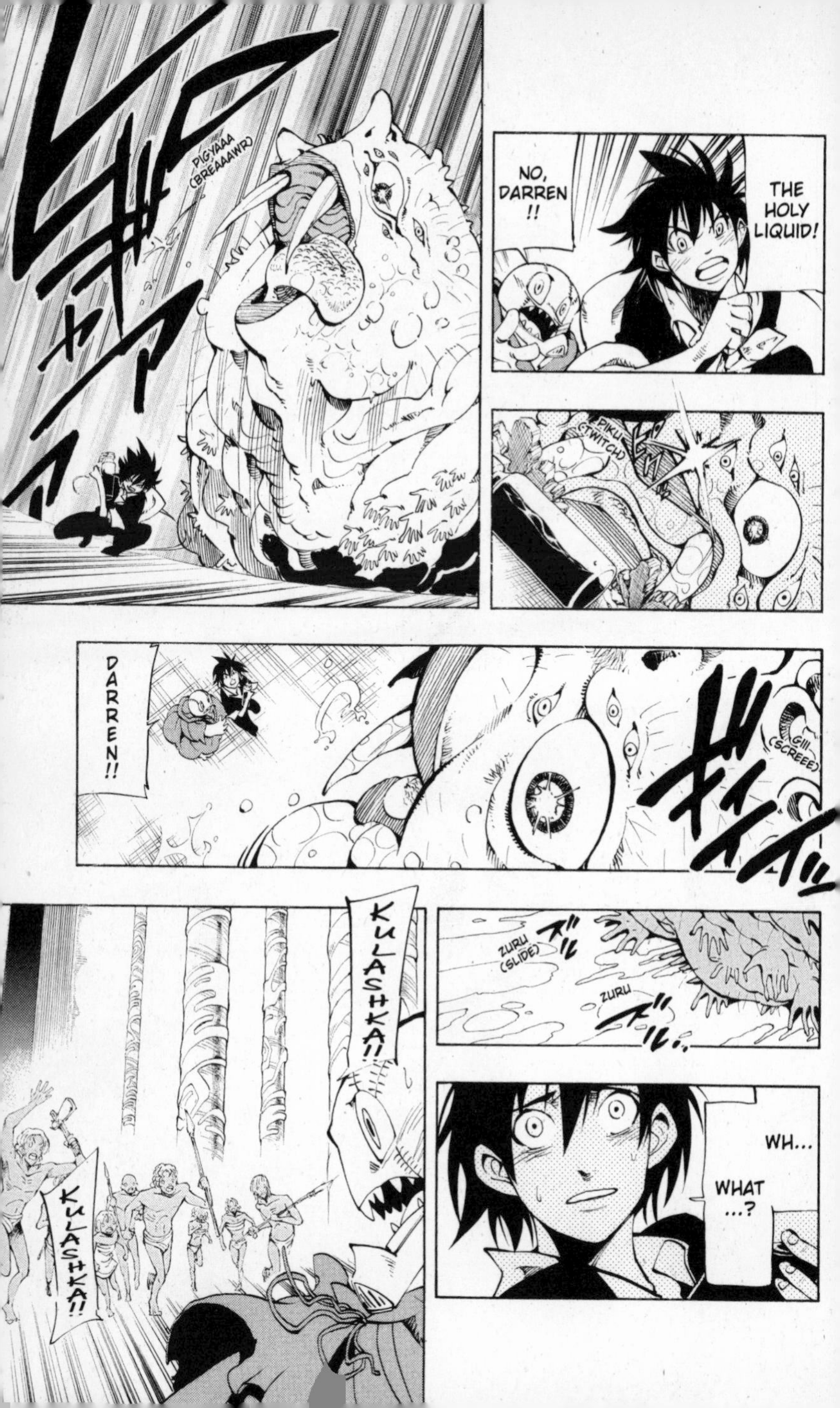

THE HOLY LIQUID!
NO, DARREN!!
PIKU (TWITCH)
PIGYAAA (BREAAAWR)
GIII (SCREEE)
DARREN!!
ZURU (SLIDE)
ZURU
WH... WHAT...?
KULASHKA!!
KULASHKA!!

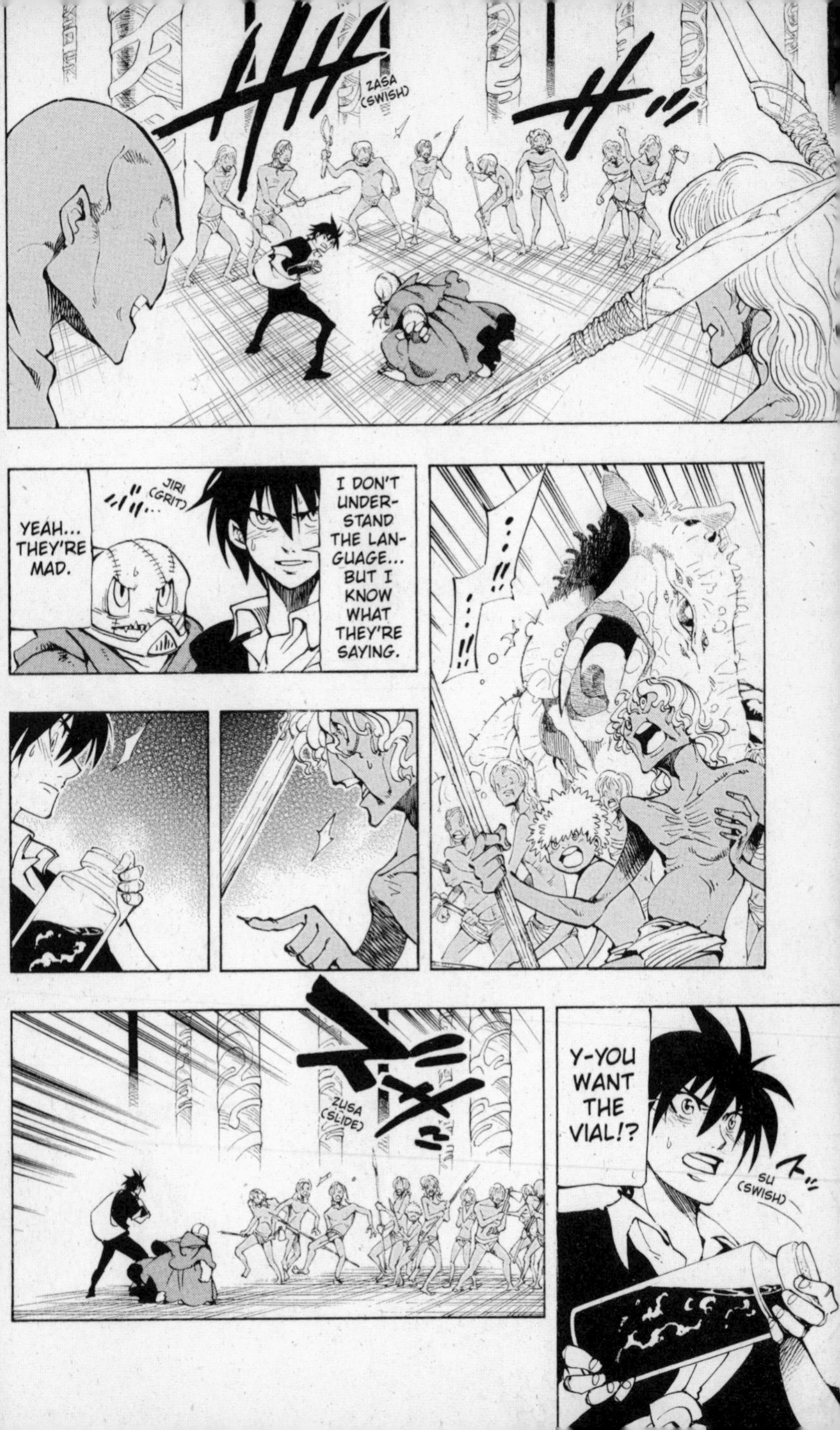

ZASA (SWISH)
...!! ...!!
I DON'T UNDER-STAND THE LAN-GUAGE... BUT I KNOW WHAT THEY'RE SAYING.
JIRI (GRIT)
YEAH... THEY'RE MAD.
Y-YOU WANT THE VIAL!?
SU (SWISH)
ZUSA (SLIDE)

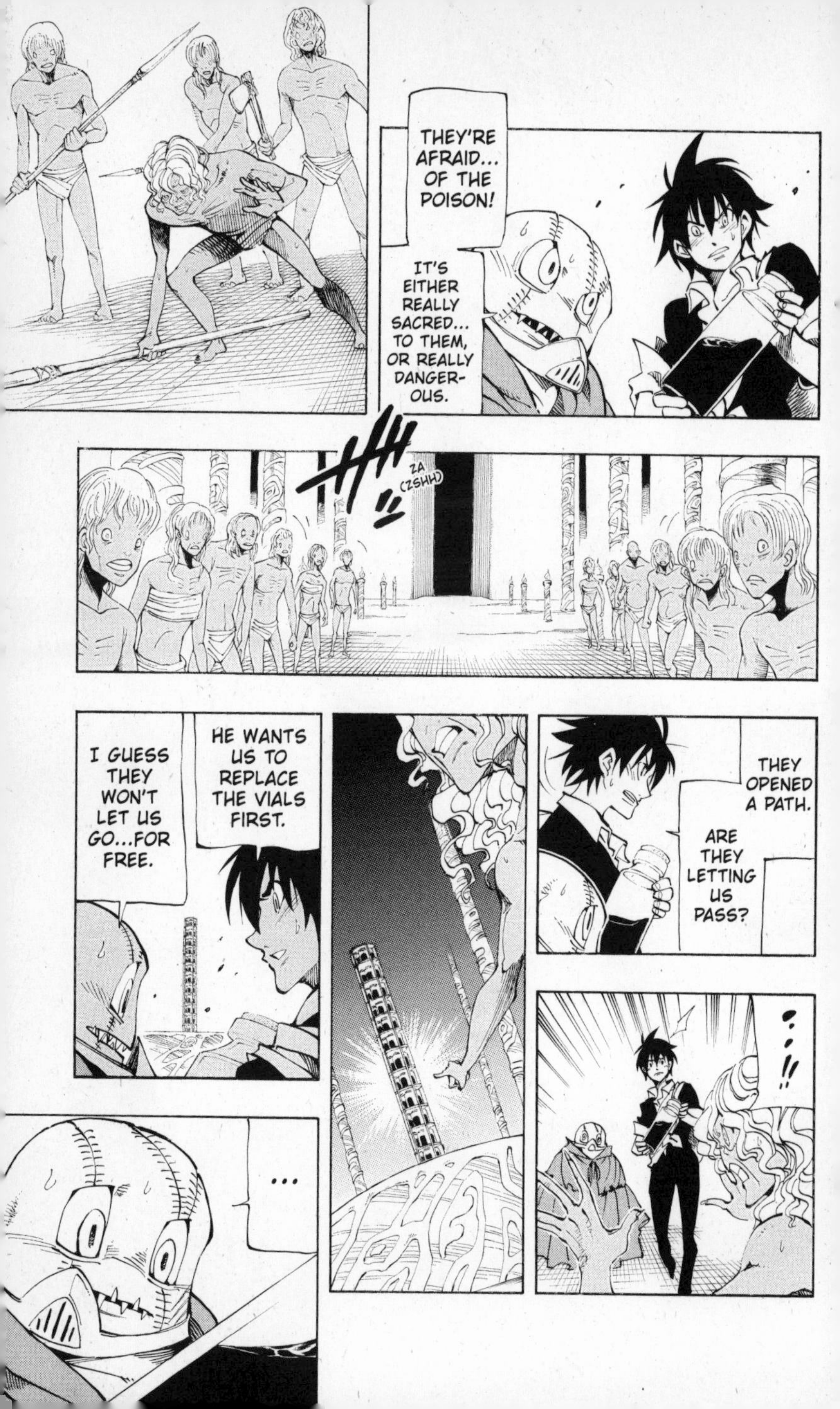
THEY'RE AFRAID... OF THE POISON!
IT'S EITHER REALLY SACRED... TO THEM, OR REALLY DANGER-OUS.
ZA (ZSHH)
THEY OPENED A PATH.
ARE THEY LETTING US PASS?
...!!
HE WANTS US TO REPLACE THE VIALS FIRST.
I GUESS THEY WON'T LET US GO...FOR FREE.
...

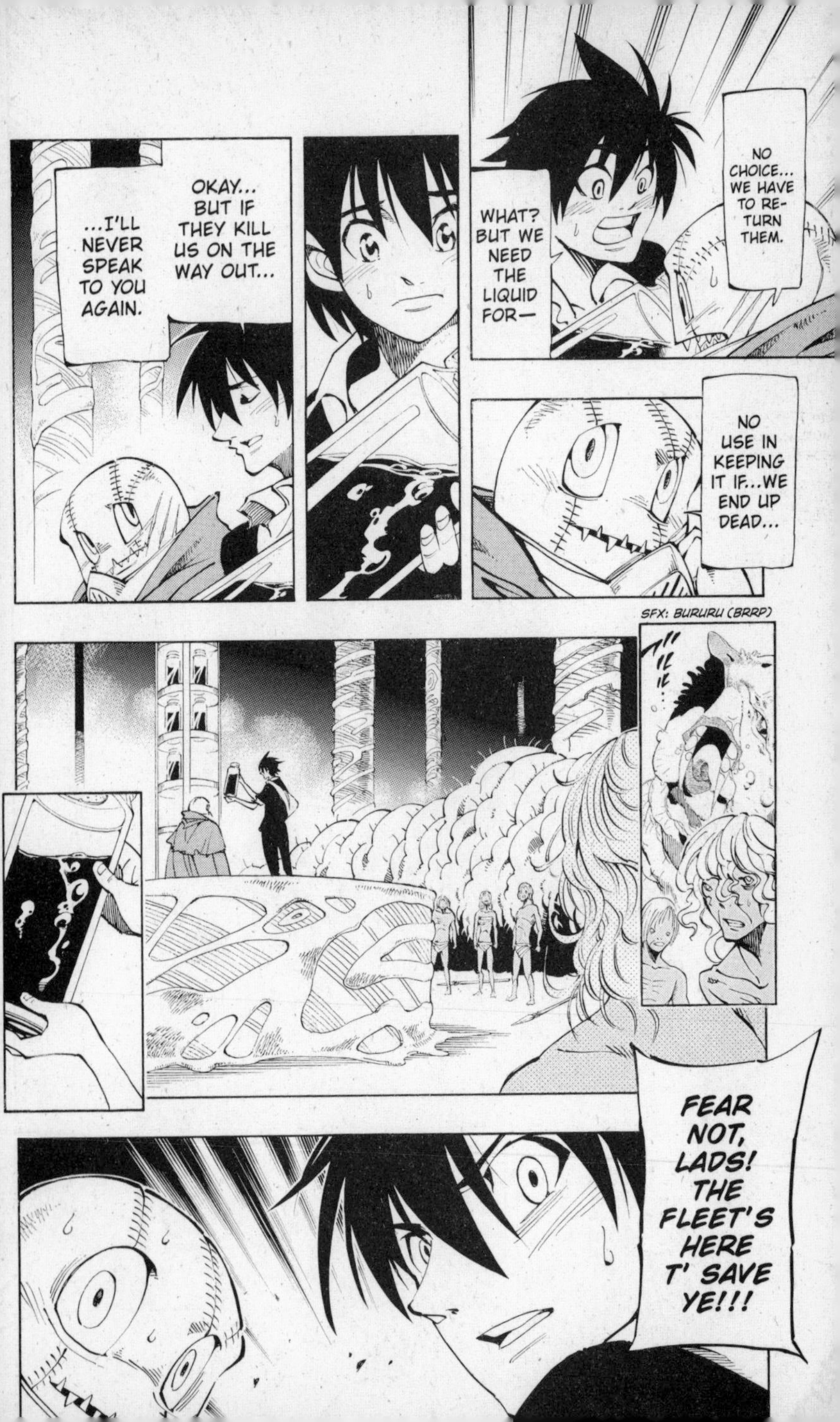
NO CHOICE... WE HAVE TO RE-TURN THEM.
WHAT? BUT WE NEED THE LIQUID FOR—
NO USE IN KEEPING IT IF...WE END UP DEAD...
OKAY... BUT IF THEY KILL US ON THE WAY OUT...
...I'LL NEVER SPEAK TO YOU AGAIN.
SFX: BURURU (BRRP)
FEAR NOT, LADS! THE FLEET'S HERE T' SAVE YE!!!

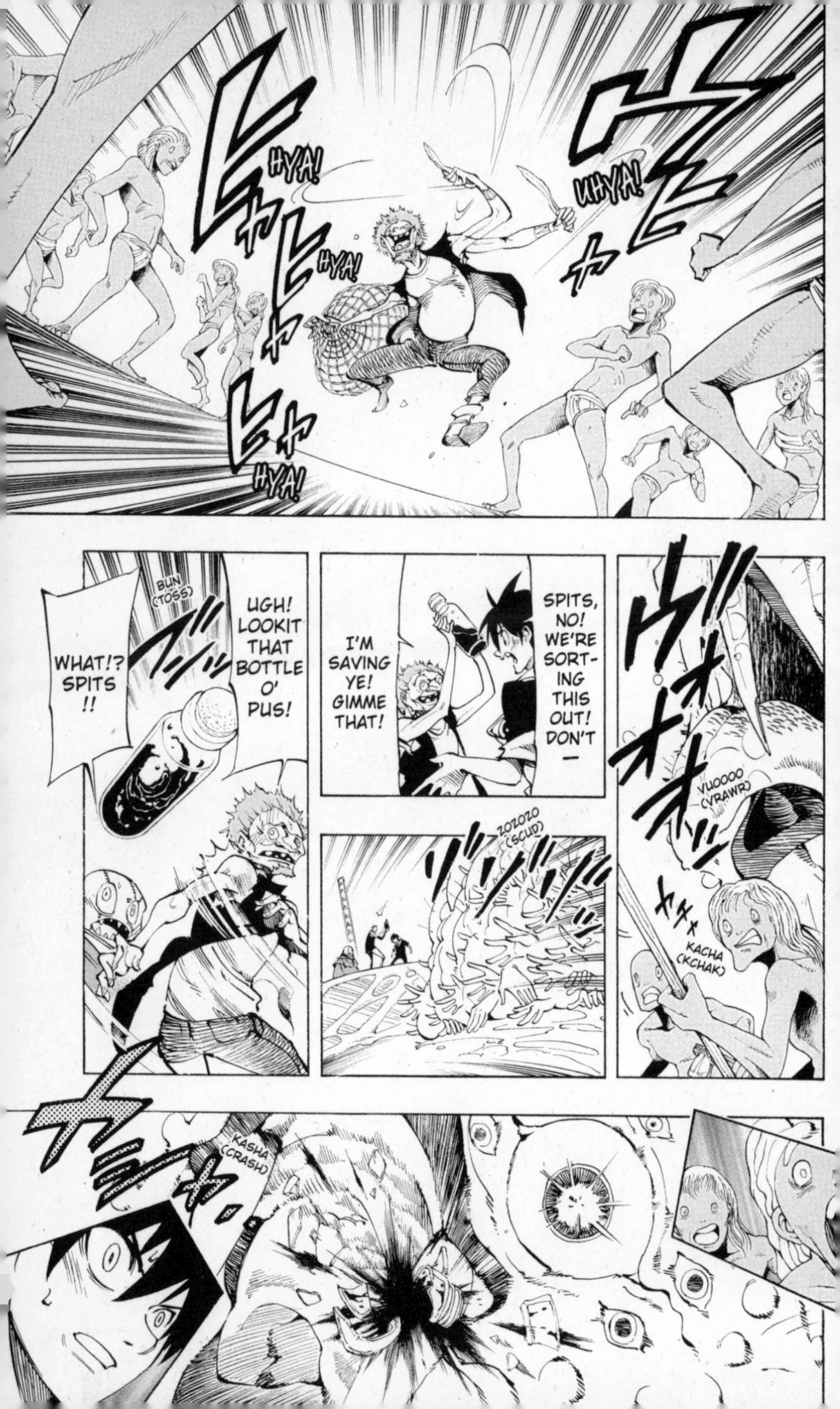
UHYA!
HYA!
HYA!
HYA!
VUOOOO (VRAWR)
KACHA (KCHAK)
SPITS, NO! WE'RE SORTING THIS OUT! DON'T —
I'M SAVING YE! GIMME THAT!
ZOZOZO (SCUD)
UGH! LOOKIT THAT BOTTLE O' PUS!
BUN (TOSS)
WHAT!? SPITS !!
KASHA (CRASH)

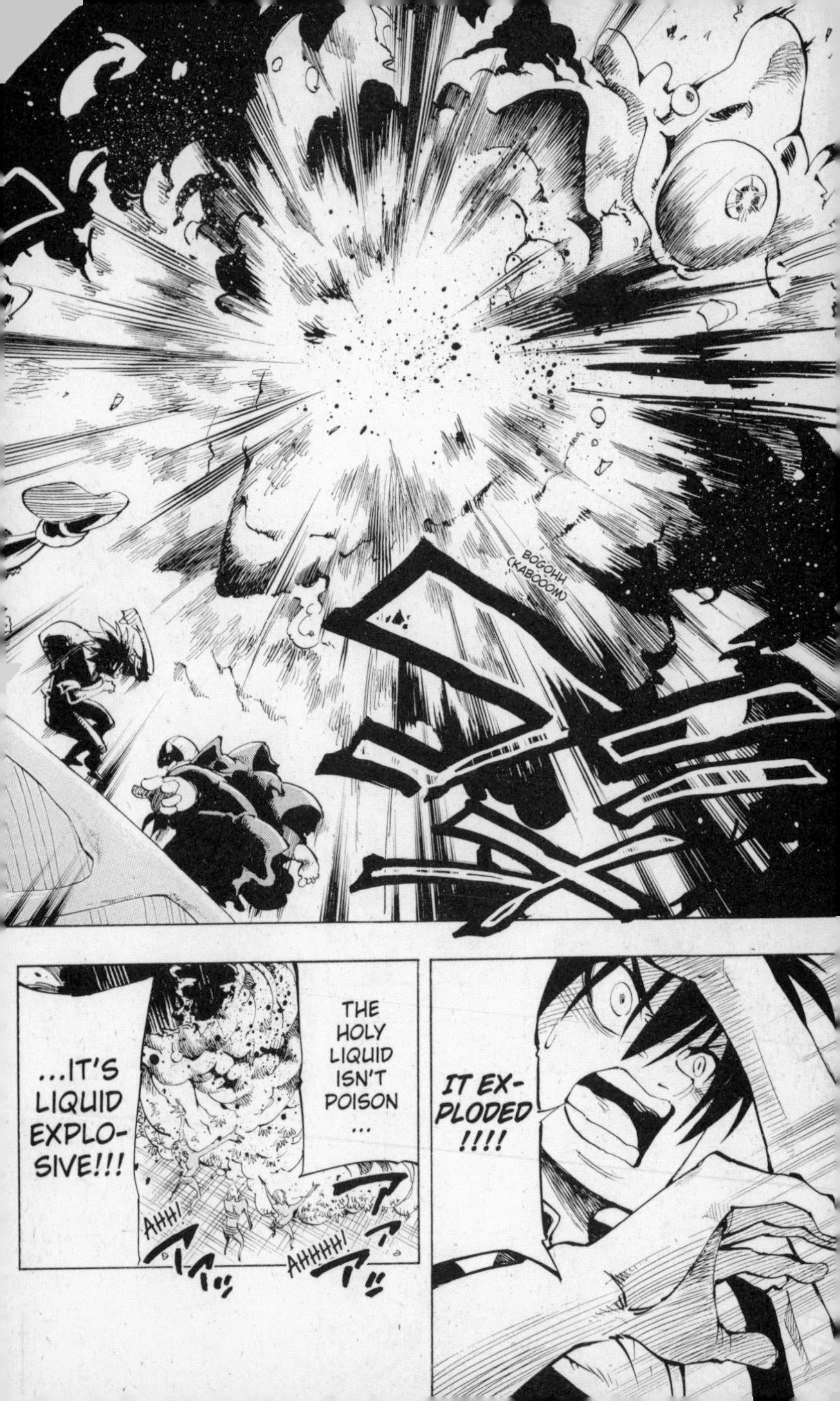
BOGOHH
(KABOOOM)
IT EX-
PLODED
!!!!
THE HOLY LIQUID ISN'T POISON ...
...IT'S LIQUID EXPLO-SIVE!!!
AHH!
AHHHH!

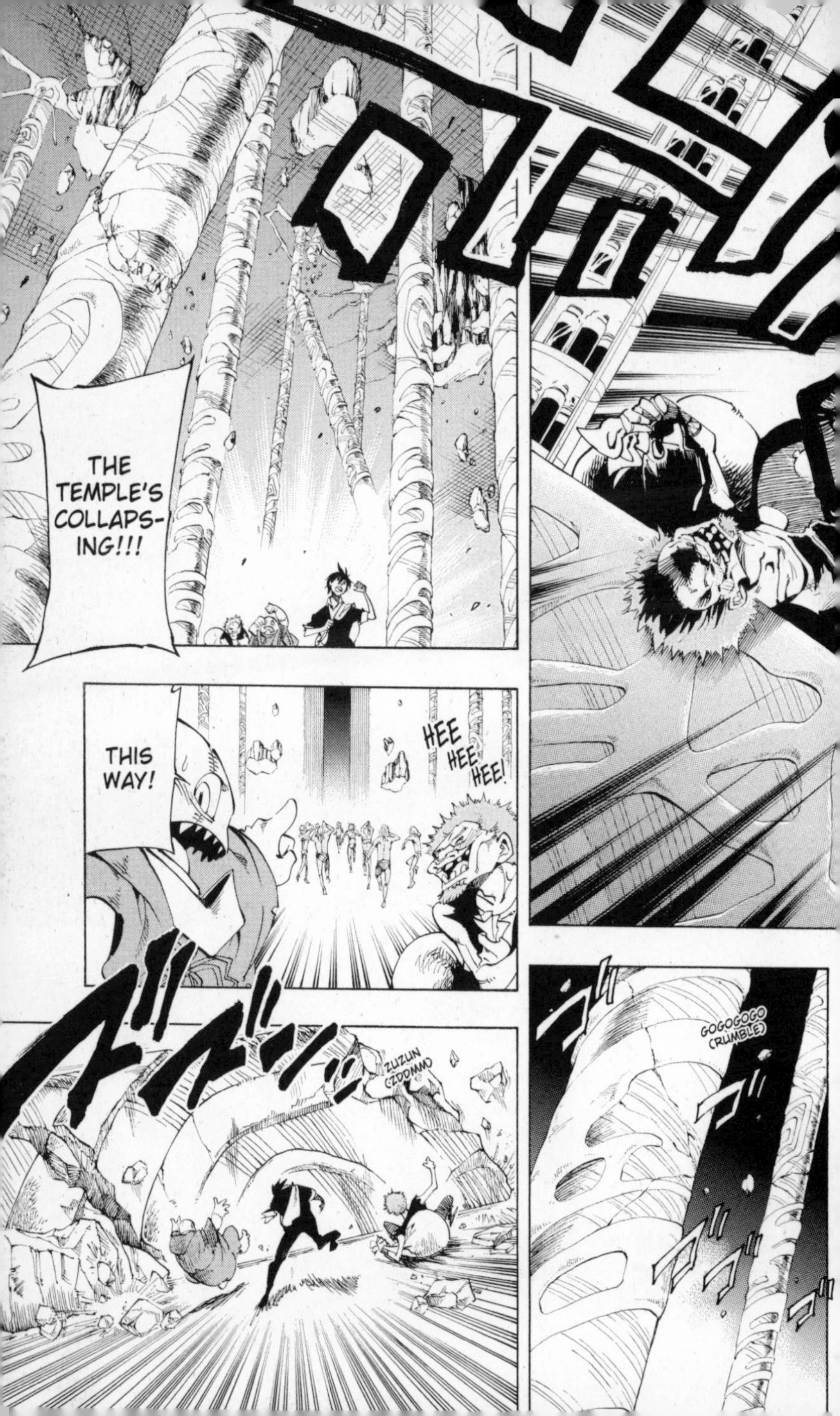
THE TEMPLE'S COLLAPSING!!!
HEE HEE HEE!
THIS WAY!
GOGOGOGO (RUMBLE)
ZUZUN (ZDOOM)

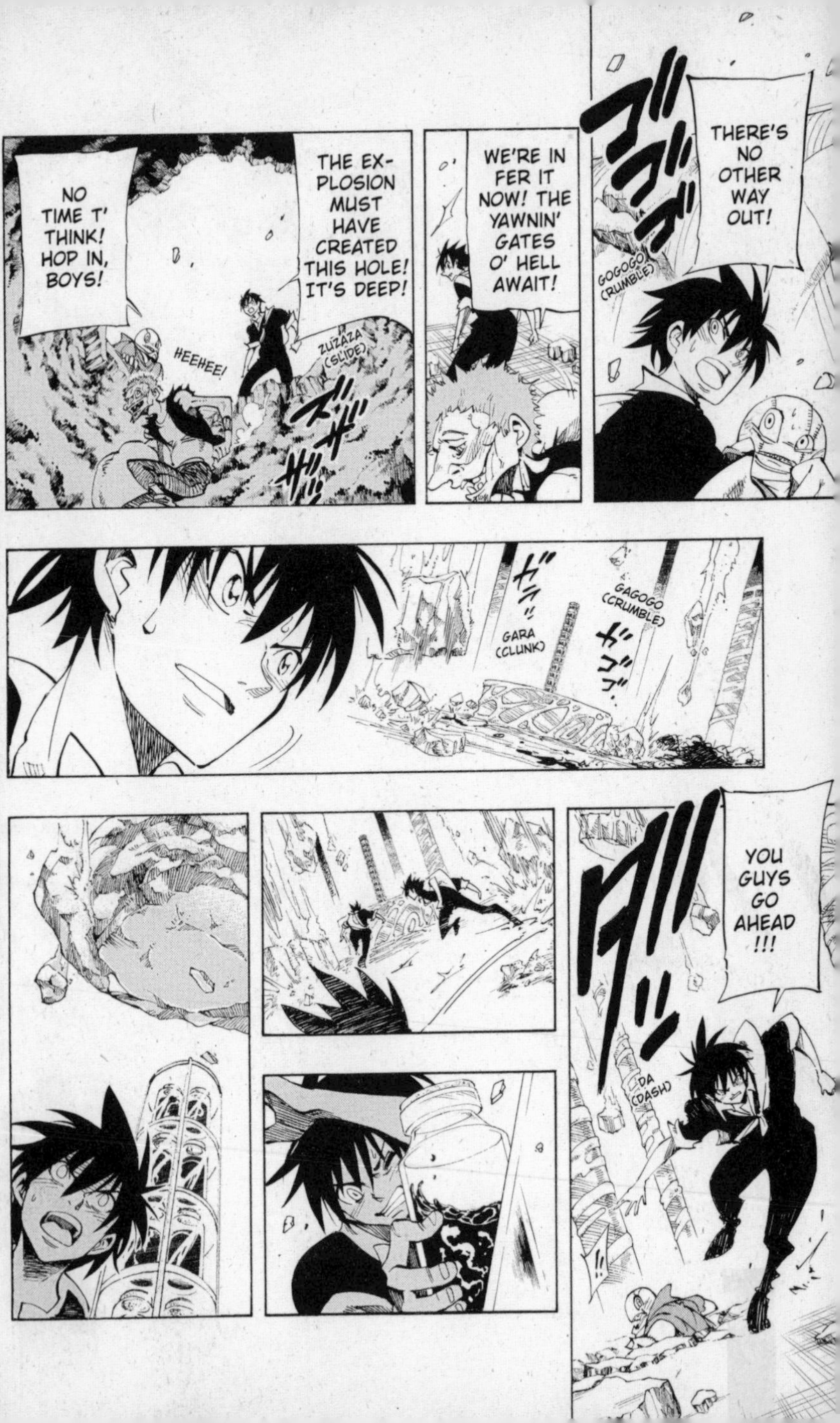
THERE'S NO OTHER WAY OUT!
GOGOGO (RUMBLE)
WE'RE IN FER IT NOW! THE YAWNIN' GATES O' HELL AWAIT!
THE EX-PLOSION MUST HAVE CREATED THIS HOLE! IT'S DEEP!
ZUZAZA (SLIDE)
NO TIME T' THINK! HOP IN, BOYS!
HEEHEE!
GAGOGO (CRUMBLE)
GARA (CLUNK)
YOU GUYS GO AHEAD!!!
DA (DASH)
!!

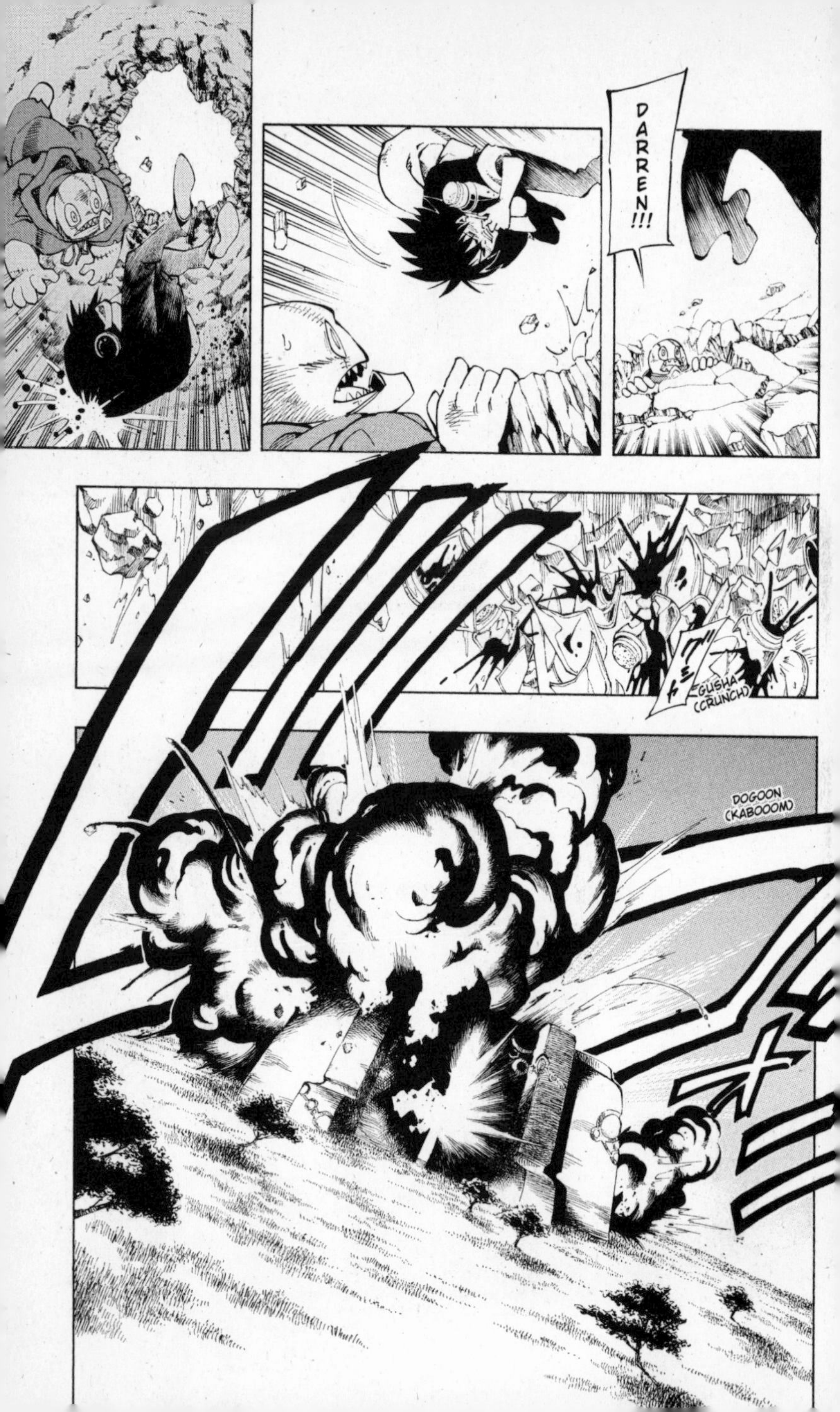
DARREN!!!
GUSHA (CRUNCH)
DOGOON (KABOOOM)

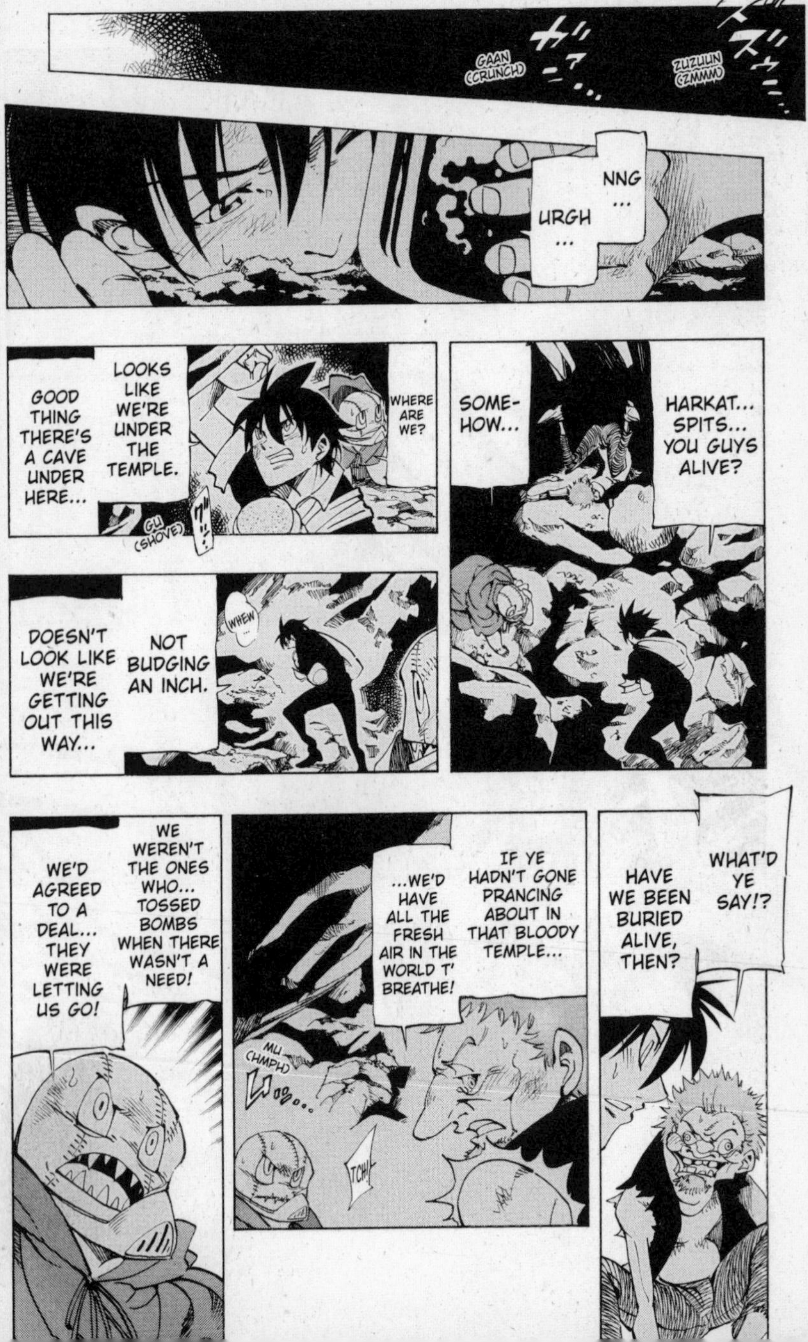
ZUZUUN (ZMMMM)
GAAN (CRUNCH)
NNG...
URGH...
HARKAT... SPITS... YOU GUYS ALIVE?
SOME-HOW...
WHERE ARE WE?
LOOKS LIKE WE'RE UNDER THE TEMPLE.
GOOD THING THERE'S A CAVE UNDER HERE...
GU (SHOVE)
WHEW...
NOT BUDGING AN INCH.
DOESN'T LOOK LIKE WE'RE GETTING OUT THIS WAY...
WHAT'D YE SAY!?
HAVE WE BEEN BURIED ALIVE, THEN?
IF YE HADN'T GONE PRANCING ABOUT IN THAT BLOODY TEMPLE...
...WE'D HAVE ALL THE FRESH AIR IN THE WORLD T' BREATHE!
MU CHMPH
TCH!
WE WEREN'T THE ONES WHO... TOSSED BOMBS WHEN THERE WASN'T A NEED!
WE'D AGREED TO A DEAL... THEY WERE LETTING US GO!

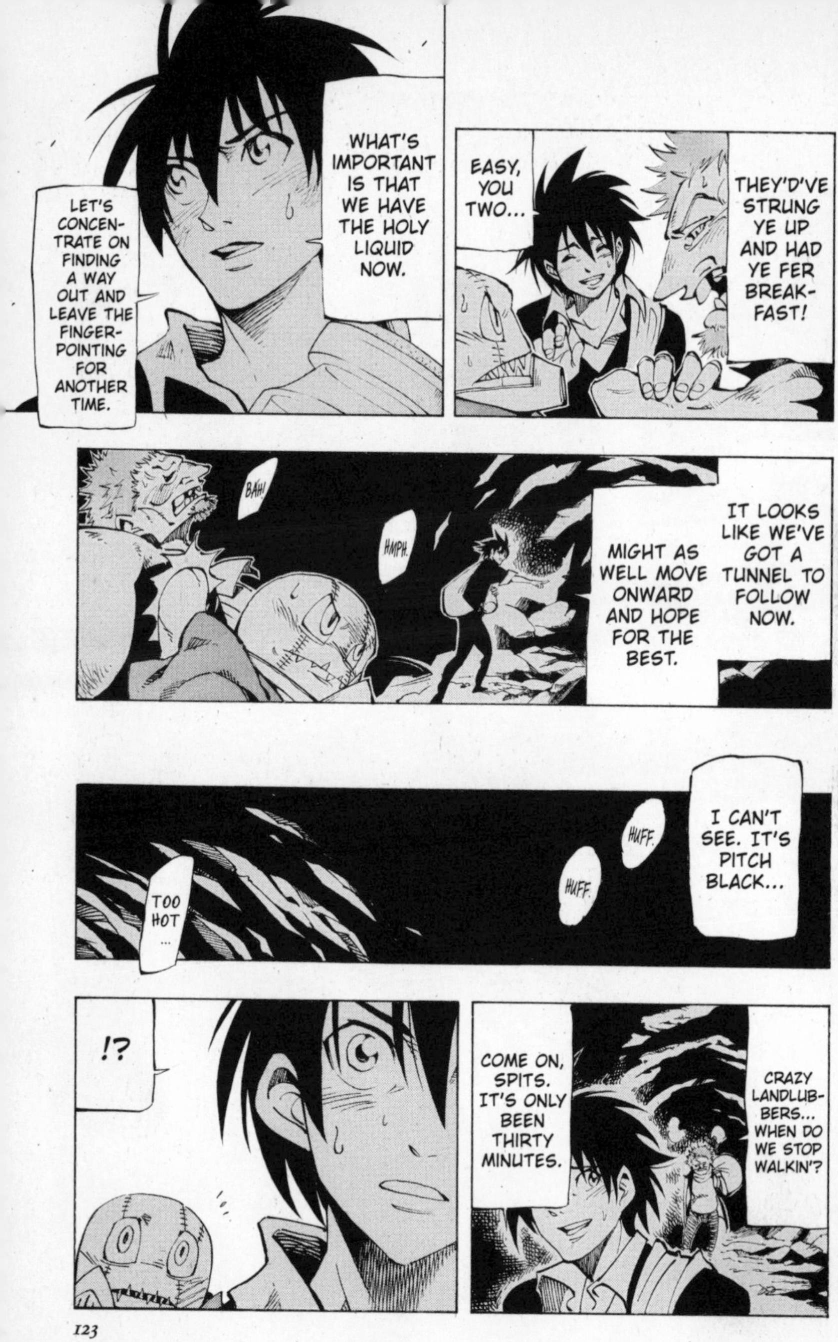
THEY'D'VE STRUNG YE UP AND HAD YE FER BREAK-FAST!
EASY, YOU TWO...
WHAT'S IMPORTANT IS THAT WE HAVE THE HOLY LIQUID NOW.
LET'S CONCEN-TRATE ON FINDING A WAY OUT AND LEAVE THE FINGER-POINTING FOR ANOTHER TIME.
IT LOOKS LIKE WE'VE GOT A TUNNEL TO FOLLOW NOW.
MIGHT AS WELL MOVE ONWARD AND HOPE FOR THE BEST.
HMPH.
BAH!
I CAN'T SEE. IT'S PITCH BLACK...
HUFF.
HUFF.
TOO HOT ...
CRAZY LANDLUB-BERS... WHEN DO WE STOP WALKIN'?
COME ON, SPITS. IT'S ONLY BEEN THIRTY MINUTES.
!?

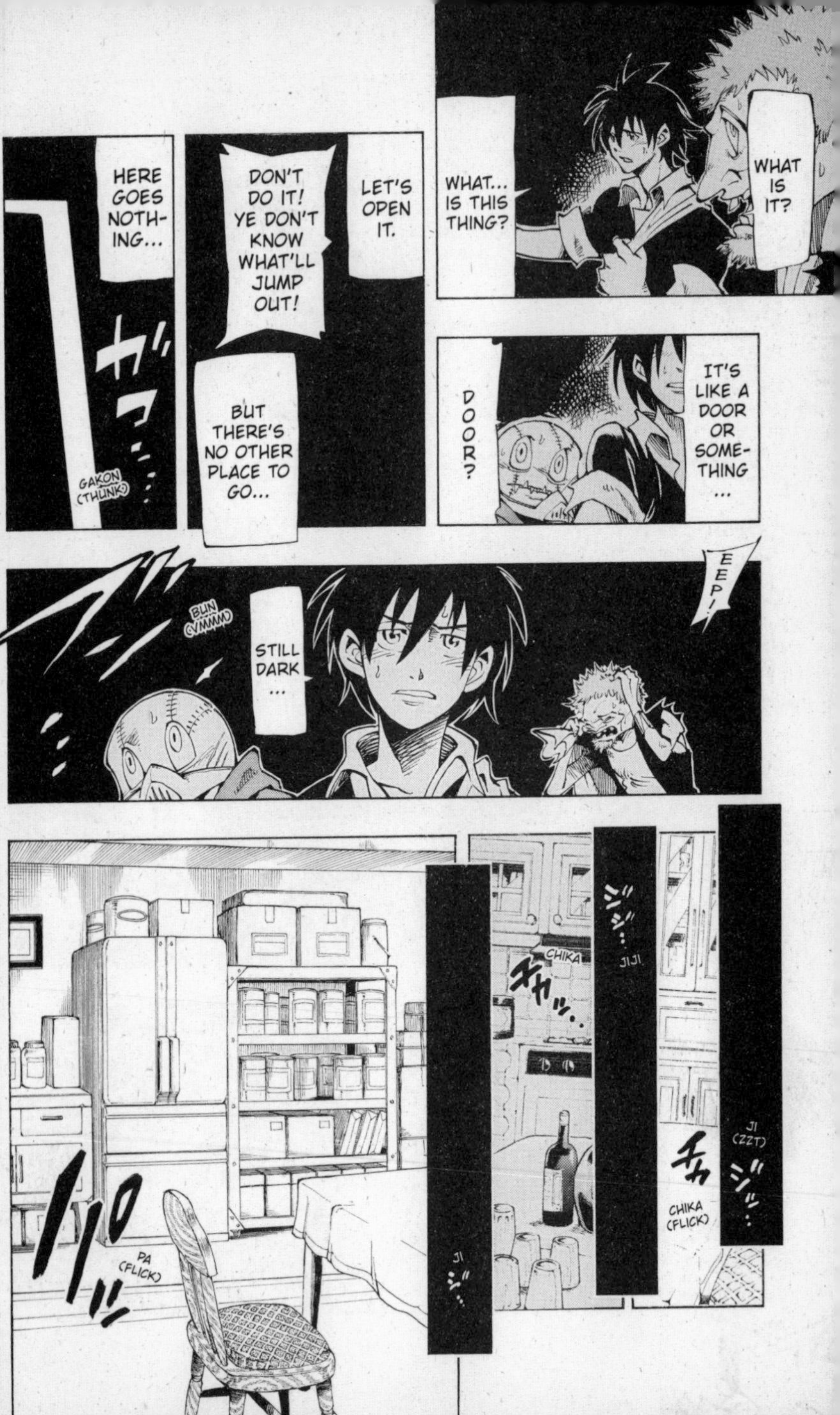
WHAT IS IT?
WHAT... IS THIS THING?
IT'S LIKE A DOOR OR SOME-THING...
DOOR?
LET'S OPEN IT.
DON'T DO IT! YE DON'T KNOW WHAT'LL JUMP OUT!
BUT THERE'S NO OTHER PLACE TO GO...
HERE GOES NOTH-ING...
GAKON (THUNK)
EEP!
STILL DARK...
BUN (VMMM)
JI (ZZT)
CHIKA (FLICK)
JIJI
CHIKA
JI
PA (FLICK)

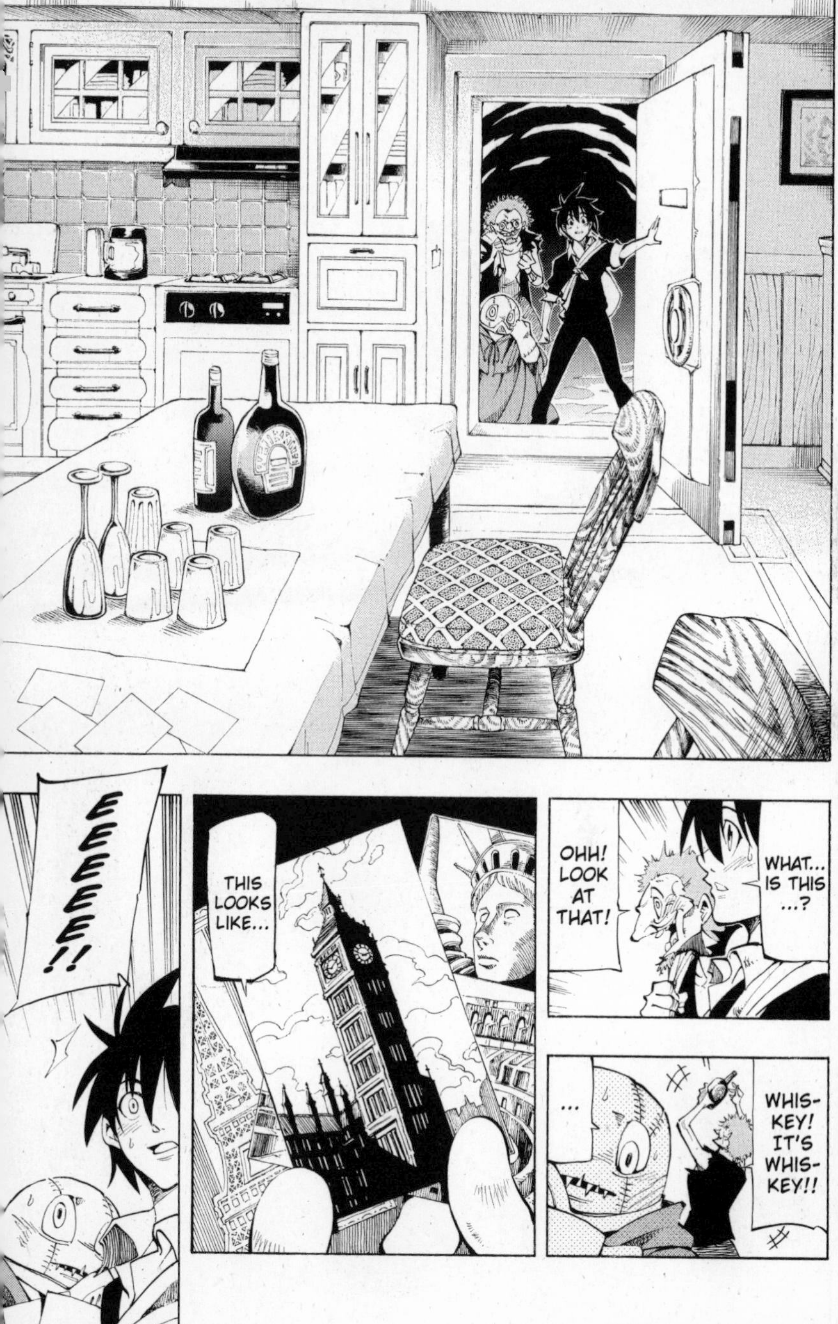
WHAT... IS THIS ...?
OHH! LOOK AT THAT!
...
WHIS-KEY! IT'S WHIS-KEY!!
THIS LOOKS LIKE...
EEEEEE!!

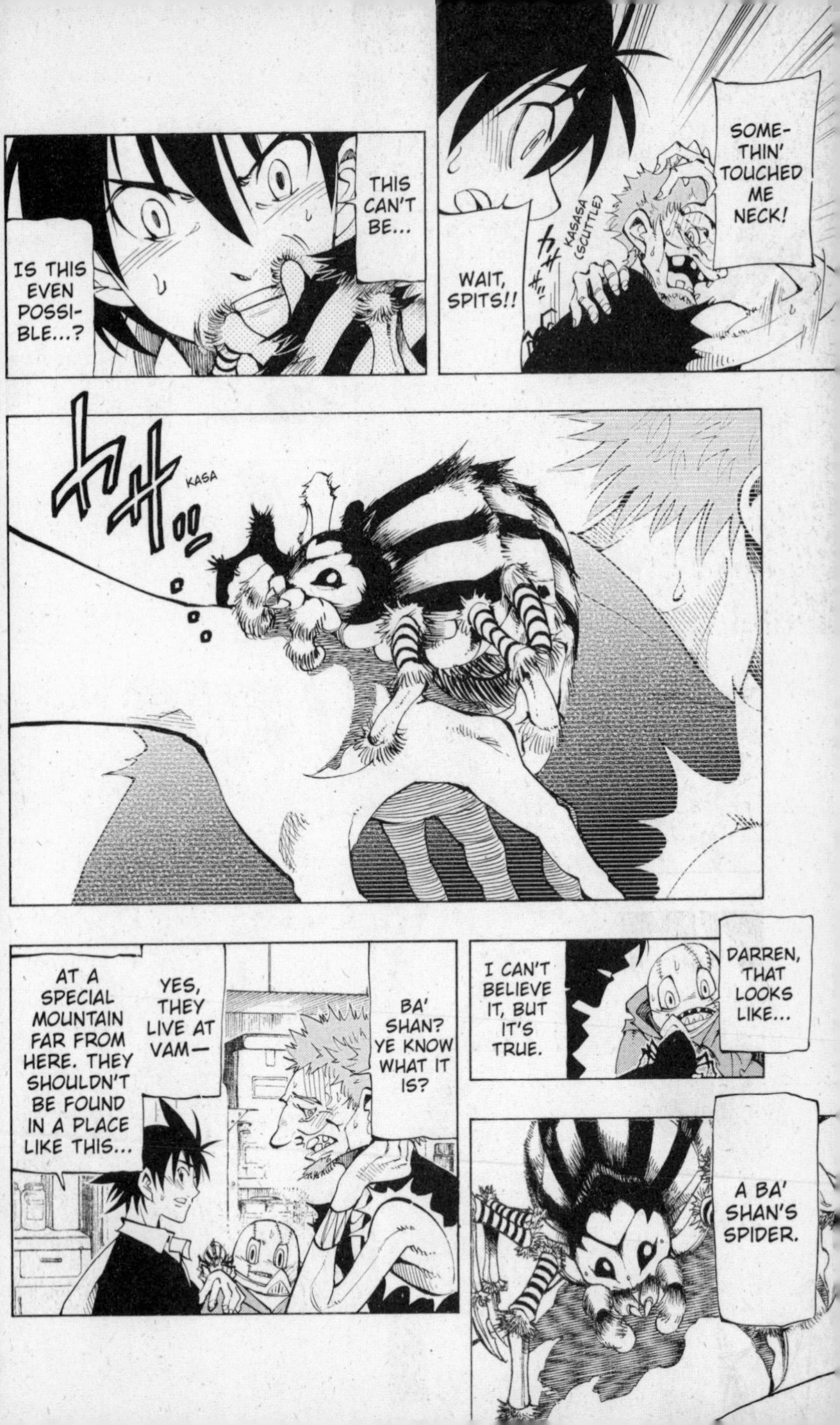
SOME-THIN' TOUCHED ME NECK!
KASASA (SCUTTLE)
WAIT, SPITS!!
THIS CAN'T BE...
IS THIS EVEN POSSI-BLE...?
KASA
DARREN, THAT LOOKS LIKE...
I CAN'T BELIEVE IT, BUT IT'S TRUE.
A BA' SHAN'S SPIDER.
BA' SHAN? YE KNOW WHAT IT IS?
YES, THEY LIVE AT VAM—
AT A SPECIAL MOUNTAIN FAR FROM HERE. THEY SHOULDN'T BE FOUND IN A PLACE LIKE THIS...

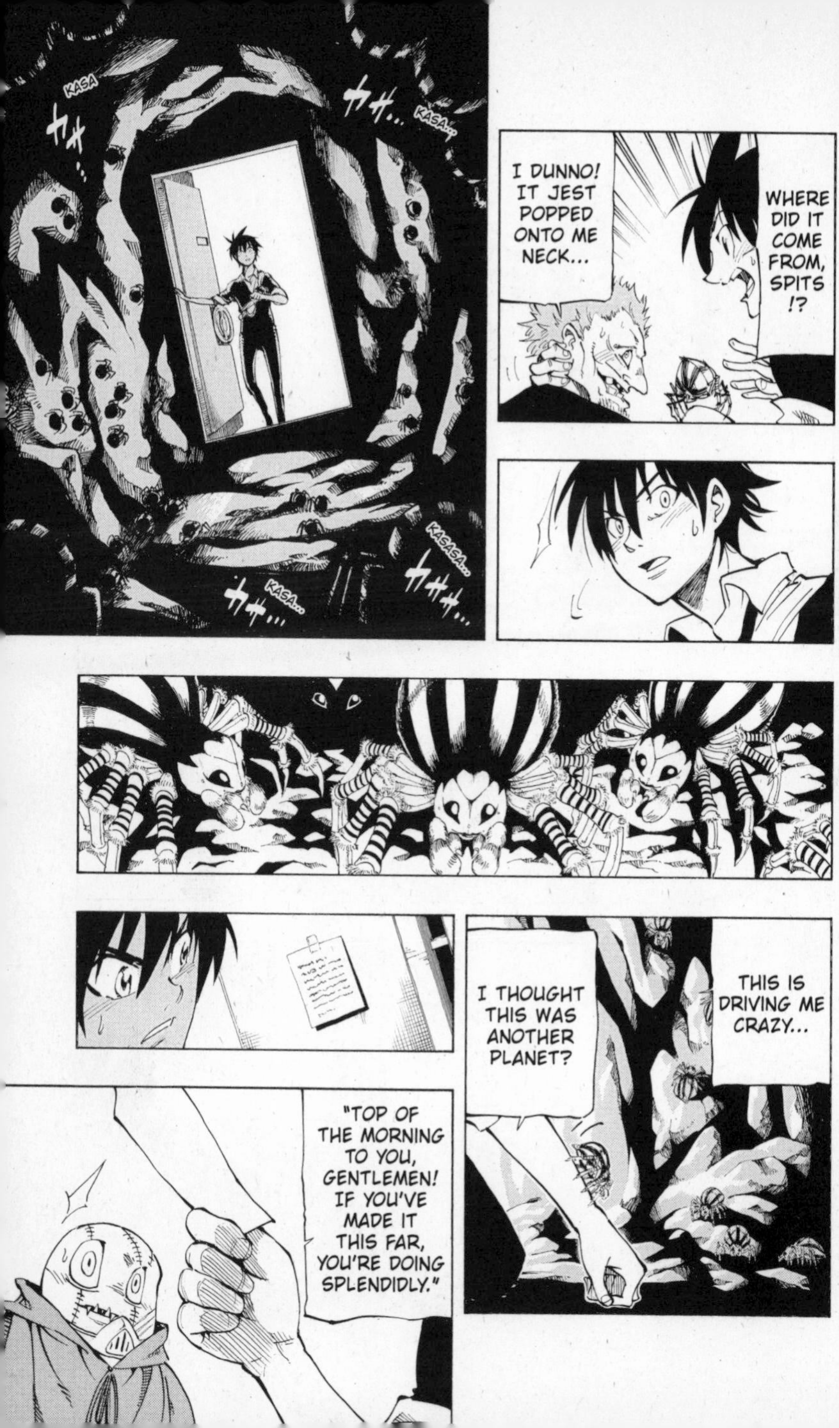
WHERE DID IT COME FROM, SPITS !?
I DUNNO! IT JEST POPPED ONTO ME NECK...
KASA...
KASA
KASASA...
KASA...
THIS IS DRIVING ME CRAZY...
I THOUGHT THIS WAS ANOTHER PLANET?
"TOP OF THE MORNING TO YOU, GENTLEMEN! IF YOU'VE MADE IT THIS FAR, YOU'RE DOING SPLENDIDLY."

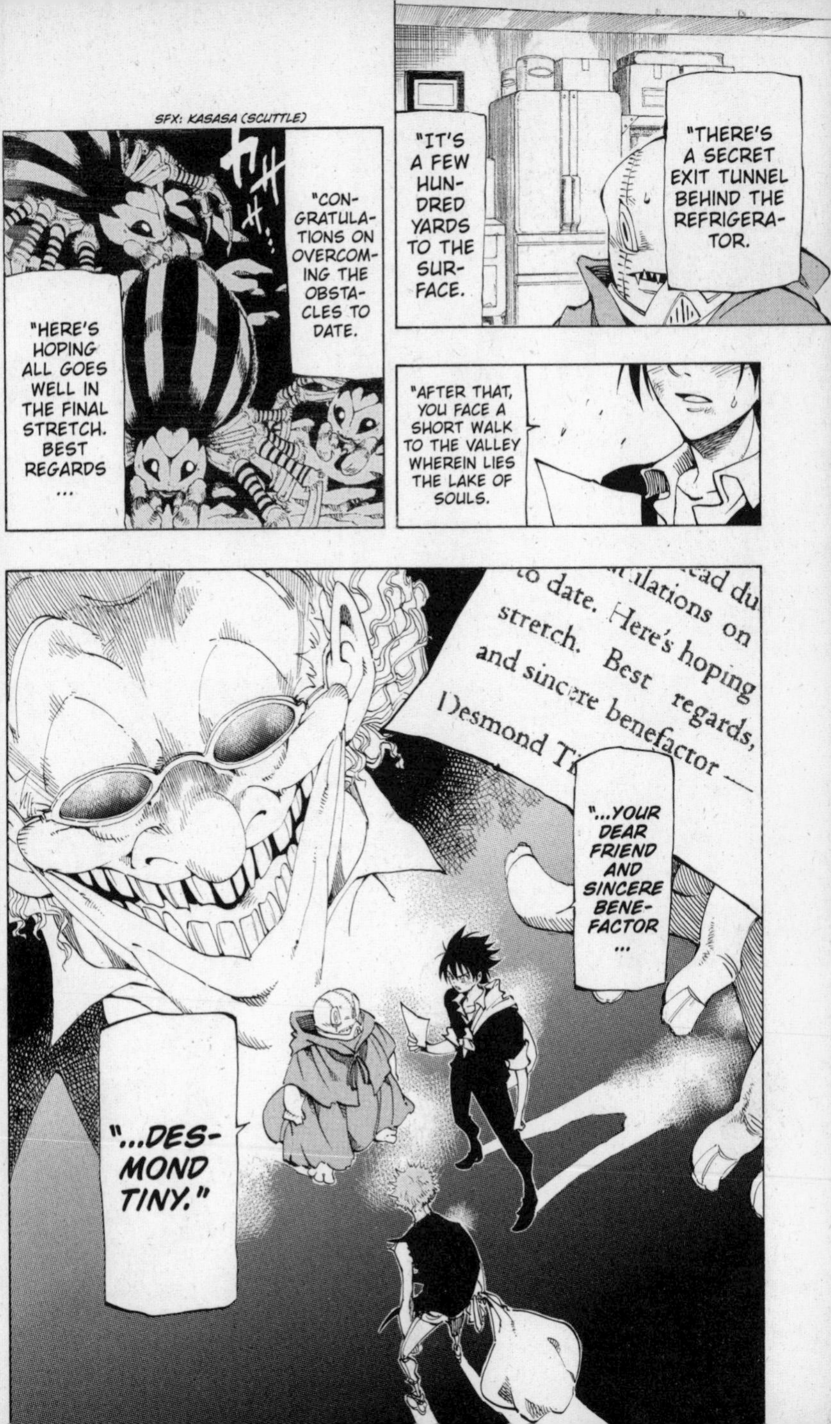
"THERE'S A SECRET EXIT TUNNEL BEHIND THE REFRIGERATOR.
"IT'S A FEW HUNDRED YARDS TO THE SURFACE.
"AFTER THAT, YOU FACE A SHORT WALK TO THE VALLEY WHEREIN LIES THE LAKE OF SOULS.
SFX: KASASA (SCUTTLE)
"CONGRATULATIONS ON OVERCOMING THE OBSTACLES TO DATE.
"HERE'S HOPING ALL GOES WELL IN THE FINAL STRETCH. BEST REGARDS ...
ulations on
to date. Here's hoping
strerch. Best regards,
and sincere benefactor —
"...YOUR DEAR FRIEND AND SINCERE BENEFACTOR ...
"...DESMOND TINY."

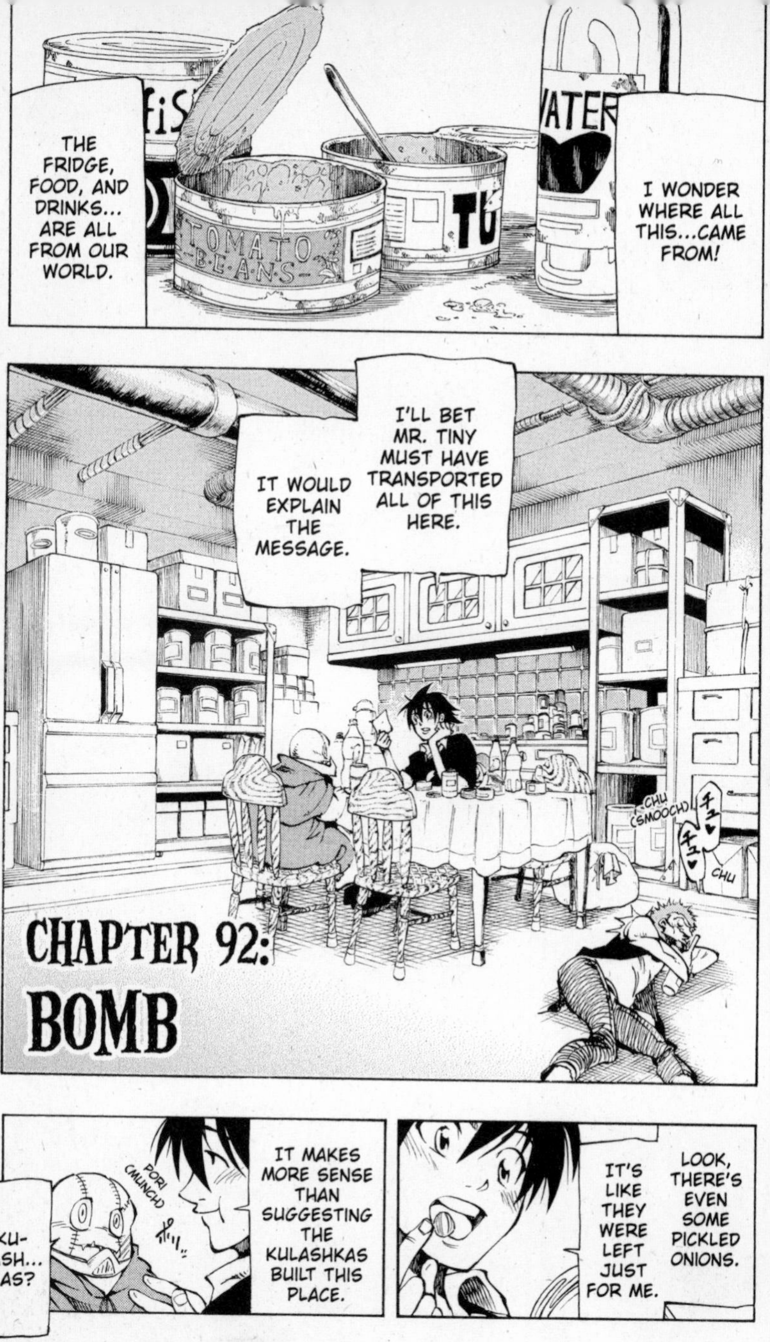
WATER
TU
TOMATO BEANS
FiS
I WONDER WHERE ALL THIS...CAME FROM!
THE FRIDGE, FOOD, AND DRINKS... ARE ALL FROM OUR WORLD.
I'LL BET MR. TINY MUST HAVE TRANSPORTED ALL OF THIS HERE.
IT WOULD EXPLAIN THE MESSAGE.
チュ♥ チュ♥
CHU (SMOOCH)
CHU
CHAPTER 92: BOMB
LOOK, THERE'S EVEN SOME PICKLED ONIONS.
IT'S LIKE THEY WERE LEFT JUST FOR ME.
IT MAKES MORE SENSE THAN SUGGESTING THE KULASHKAS BUILT THIS PLACE.
ポリ
PORI (MUNCH)
KU-LASH... KAS?

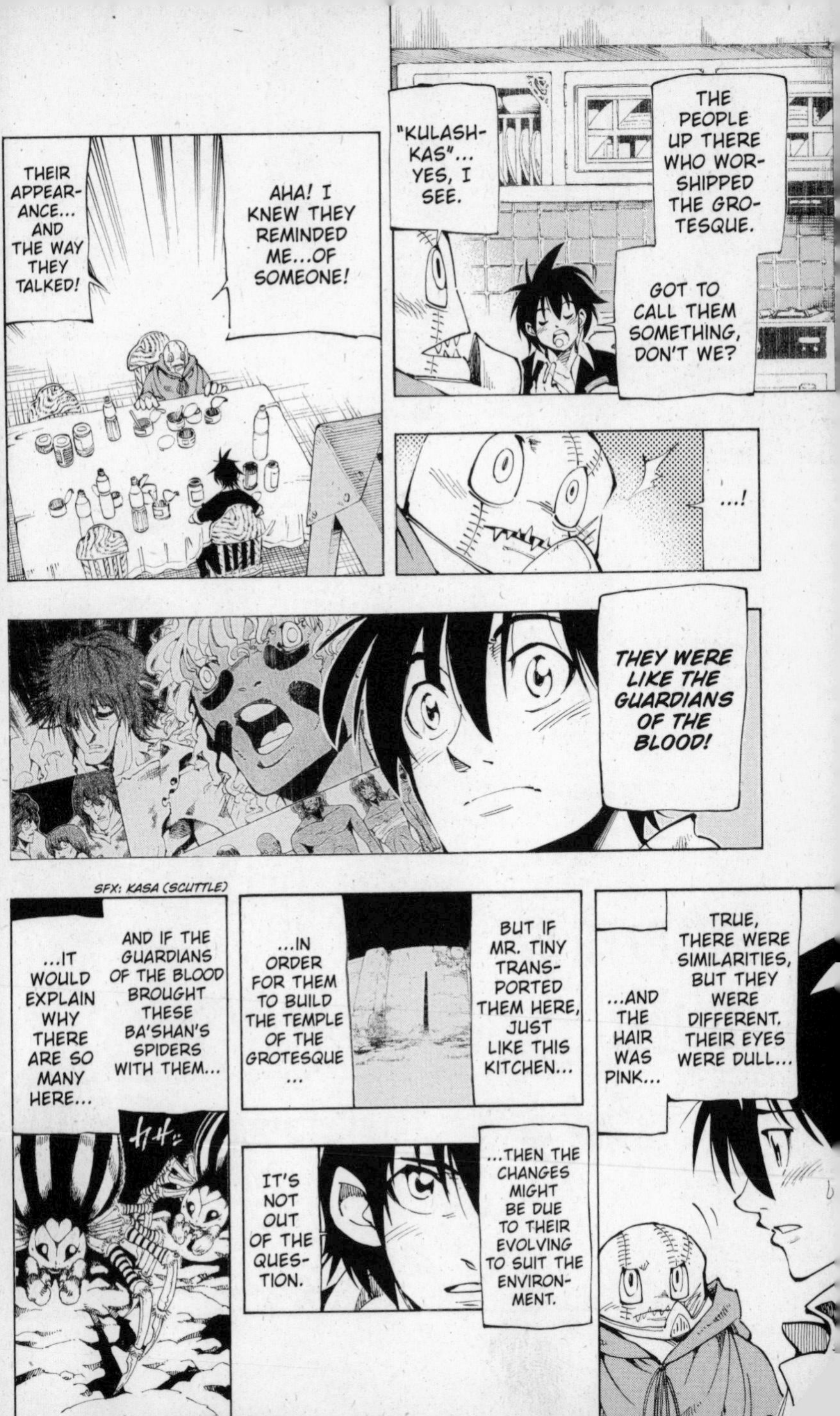
THE PEOPLE UP THERE WHO WOR-SHIPPED THE GRO-TESQUE.
GOT TO CALL THEM SOMETHING, DON'T WE?
"KULASH-KAS"... YES, I SEE.
...!
AHA! I KNEW THEY REMINDED ME...OF SOMEONE!
THEIR APPEAR-ANCE... AND THE WAY THEY TALKED!
THEY WERE LIKE THE GUARDIANS OF THE BLOOD!
TRUE, THERE WERE SIMILARITIES, BUT THEY WERE DIFFERENT. THEIR EYES WERE DULL...
...AND THE HAIR WAS PINK...
BUT IF MR. TINY TRANS-PORTED THEM HERE, JUST LIKE THIS KITCHEN...
...IN ORDER FOR THEM TO BUILD THE TEMPLE OF THE GROTESQUE ...
...THEN THE CHANGES MIGHT BE DUE TO THEIR EVOLVING TO SUIT THE ENVIRON-MENT.
IT'S NOT OUT OF THE QUES-TION.
AND IF THE GUARDIANS OF THE BLOOD BROUGHT THESE BA'SHAN'S SPIDERS WITH THEM...
...IT WOULD EXPLAIN WHY THERE ARE SO MANY HERE...
SFX: KASA (SCUTTLE)

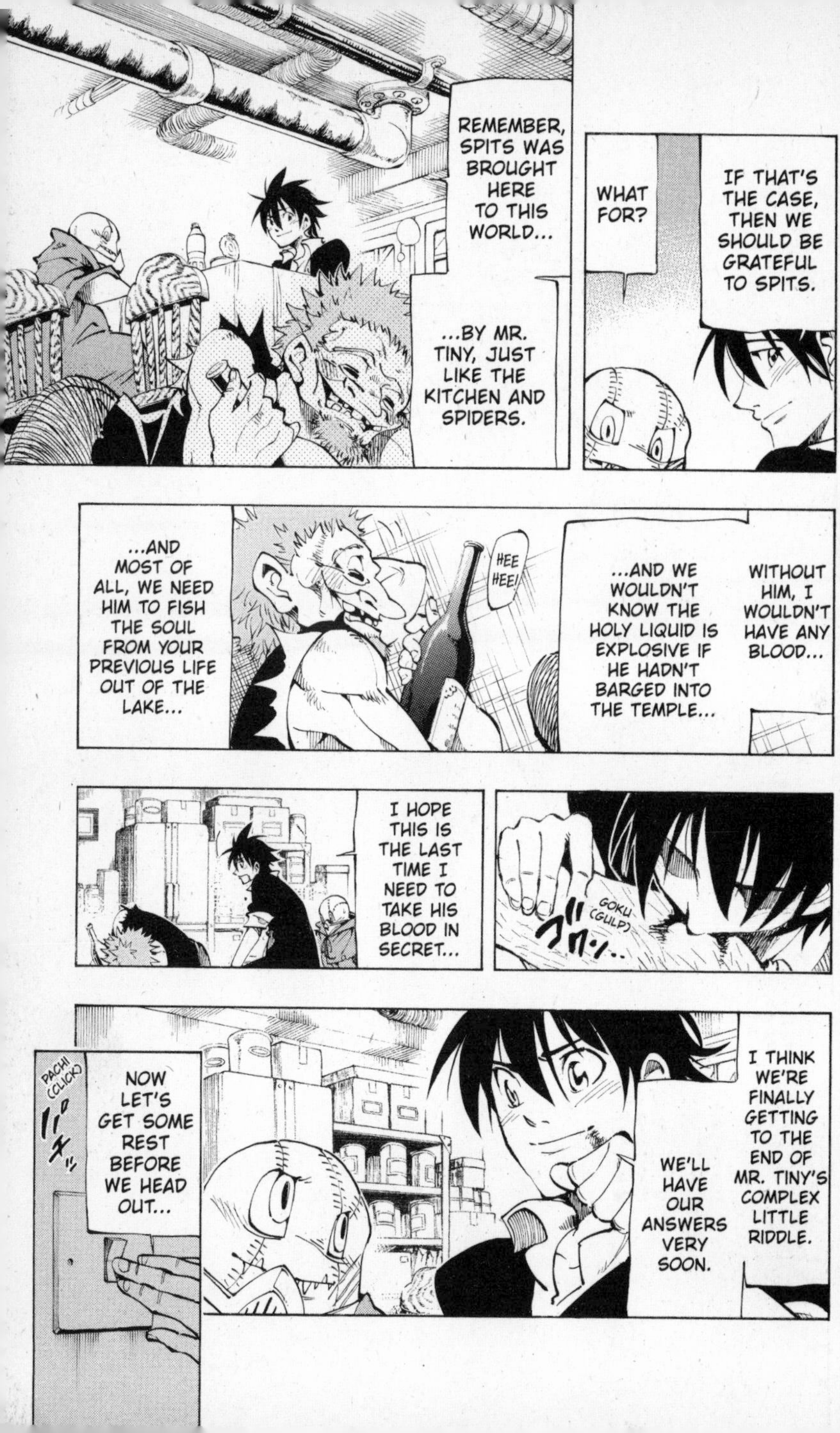
IF THAT'S THE CASE, THEN WE SHOULD BE GRATEFUL TO SPITS.
WHAT FOR?
REMEMBER, SPITS WAS BROUGHT HERE TO THIS WORLD...
...BY MR. TINY, JUST LIKE THE KITCHEN AND SPIDERS.
WITHOUT HIM, I WOULDN'T HAVE ANY BLOOD...
...AND WE WOULDN'T KNOW THE HOLY LIQUID IS EXPLOSIVE IF HE HADN'T BARGED INTO THE TEMPLE...
HEE HEE!
...AND MOST OF ALL, WE NEED HIM TO FISH THE SOUL FROM YOUR PREVIOUS LIFE OUT OF THE LAKE...
GOKU (GULP)
I HOPE THIS IS THE LAST TIME I NEED TO TAKE HIS BLOOD IN SECRET...
I THINK WE'RE FINALLY GETTING TO THE END OF MR. TINY'S COMPLEX LITTLE RIDDLE.
WE'LL HAVE OUR ANSWERS VERY SOON.
NOW LET'S GET SOME REST BEFORE WE HEAD OUT...
PACHI (CLICK)

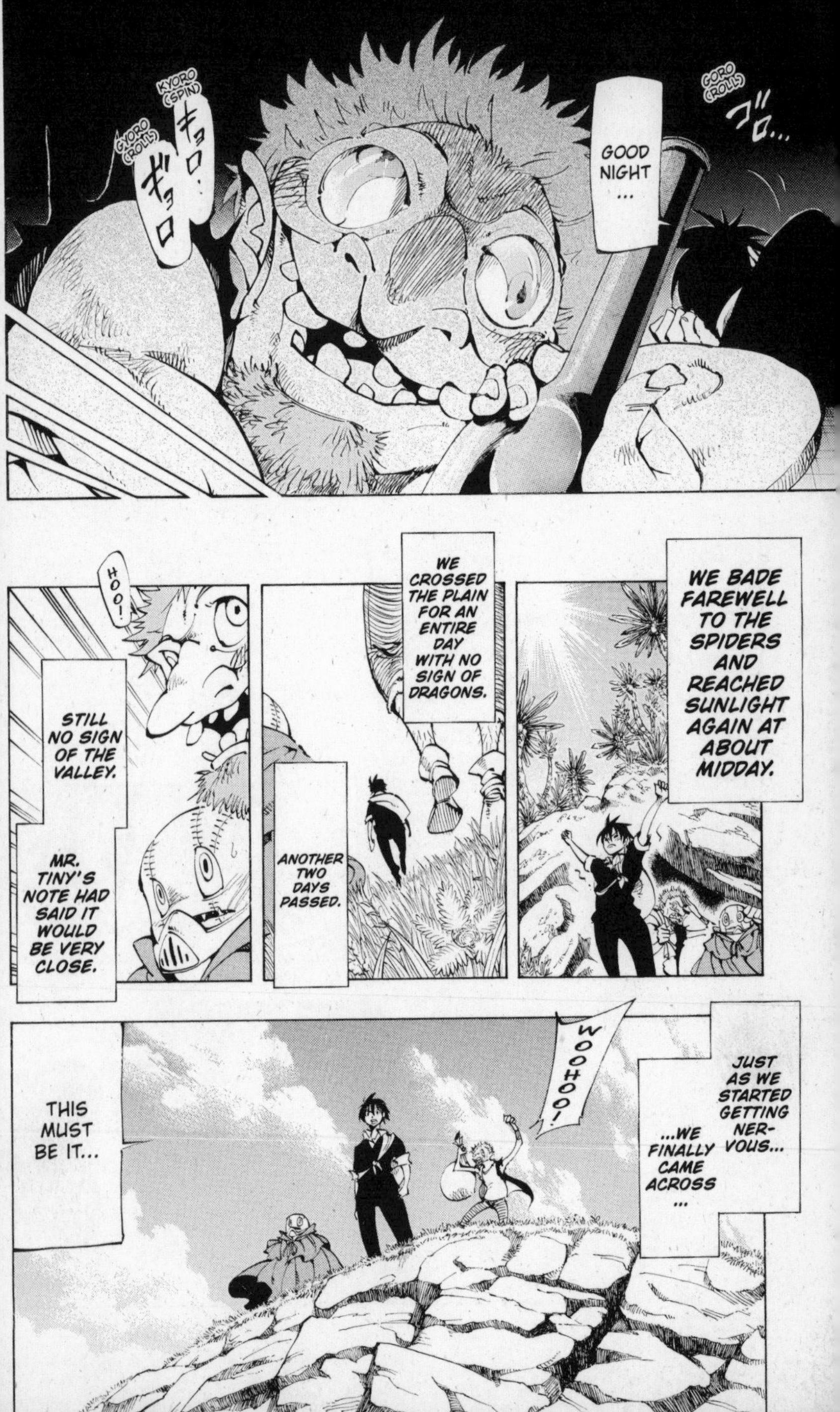

ゴロ...
GORO (ROLL)
GOOD NIGHT ...
キョロ
KYORO (SPIN)
ギョロ
GYORO (ROLL)
WE BADE FAREWELL TO THE SPIDERS AND REACHED SUNLIGHT AGAIN AT ABOUT MIDDAY.
WE CROSSED THE PLAIN FOR AN ENTIRE DAY WITH NO SIGN OF DRAGONS.
ANOTHER TWO DAYS PASSED.
HOO!
STILL NO SIGN OF THE VALLEY.
MR. TINY'S NOTE HAD SAID IT WOULD BE VERY CLOSE.
JUST AS WE STARTED GETTING NER-VOUS...
...WE FINALLY CAME ACROSS ...
WOOHOO!
THIS MUST BE IT...

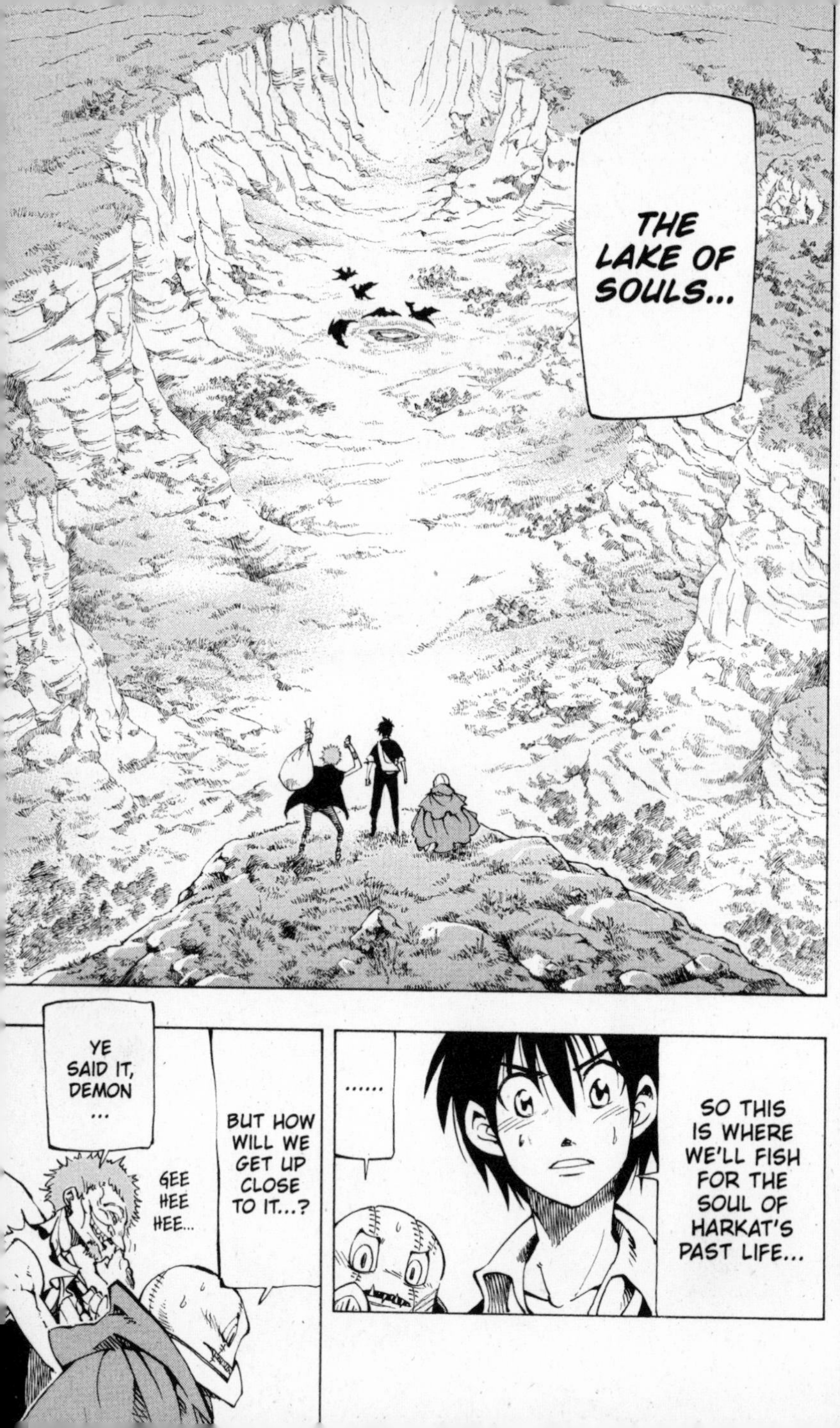
THE LAKE OF SOULS...
SO THIS IS WHERE WE'LL FISH FOR THE SOUL OF HARKAT'S PAST LIFE...
......
YE SAID IT, DEMON ...
GEE HEE HEE...
BUT HOW WILL WE GET UP CLOSE TO IT...?

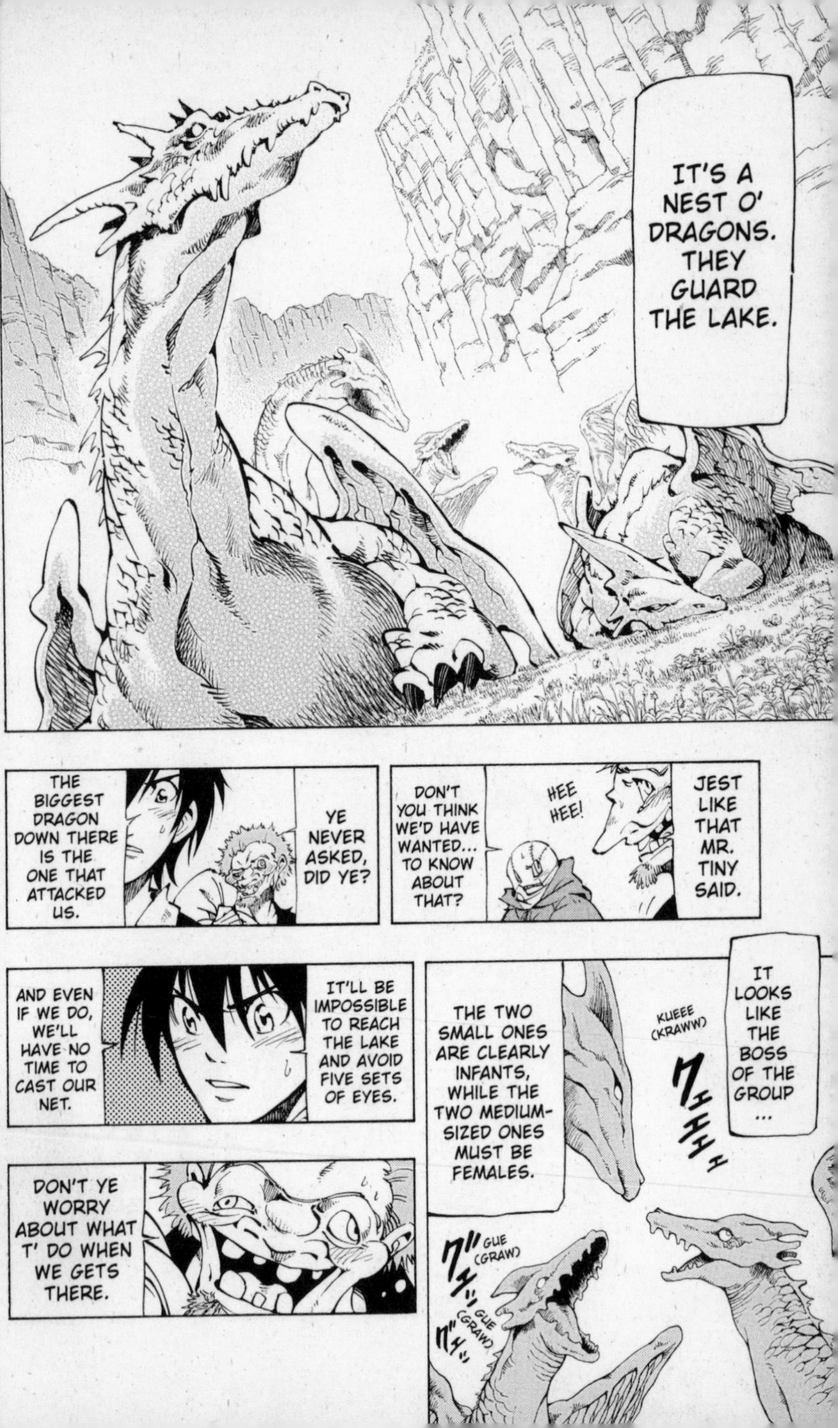
IT'S A NEST O' DRAGONS. THEY GUARD THE LAKE.
JEST LIKE THAT MR. TINY SAID.
HEE HEE!
DON'T YOU THINK WE'D HAVE WANTED... TO KNOW ABOUT THAT?
YE NEVER ASKED, DID YE?
THE BIGGEST DRAGON DOWN THERE IS THE ONE THAT ATTACKED US.
IT LOOKS LIKE THE BOSS OF THE GROUP...
KUEEE (KRAWW)
THE TWO SMALL ONES ARE CLEARLY INFANTS, WHILE THE TWO MEDIUM-SIZED ONES MUST BE FEMALES.
GUE (GRAW)
GUE (GRAW)
IT'LL BE IMPOSSIBLE TO REACH THE LAKE AND AVOID FIVE SETS OF EYES.
AND EVEN IF WE DO, WE'LL HAVE NO TIME TO CAST OUR NET.
DON'T YE WORRY ABOUT WHAT T' DO WHEN WE GETS THERE.

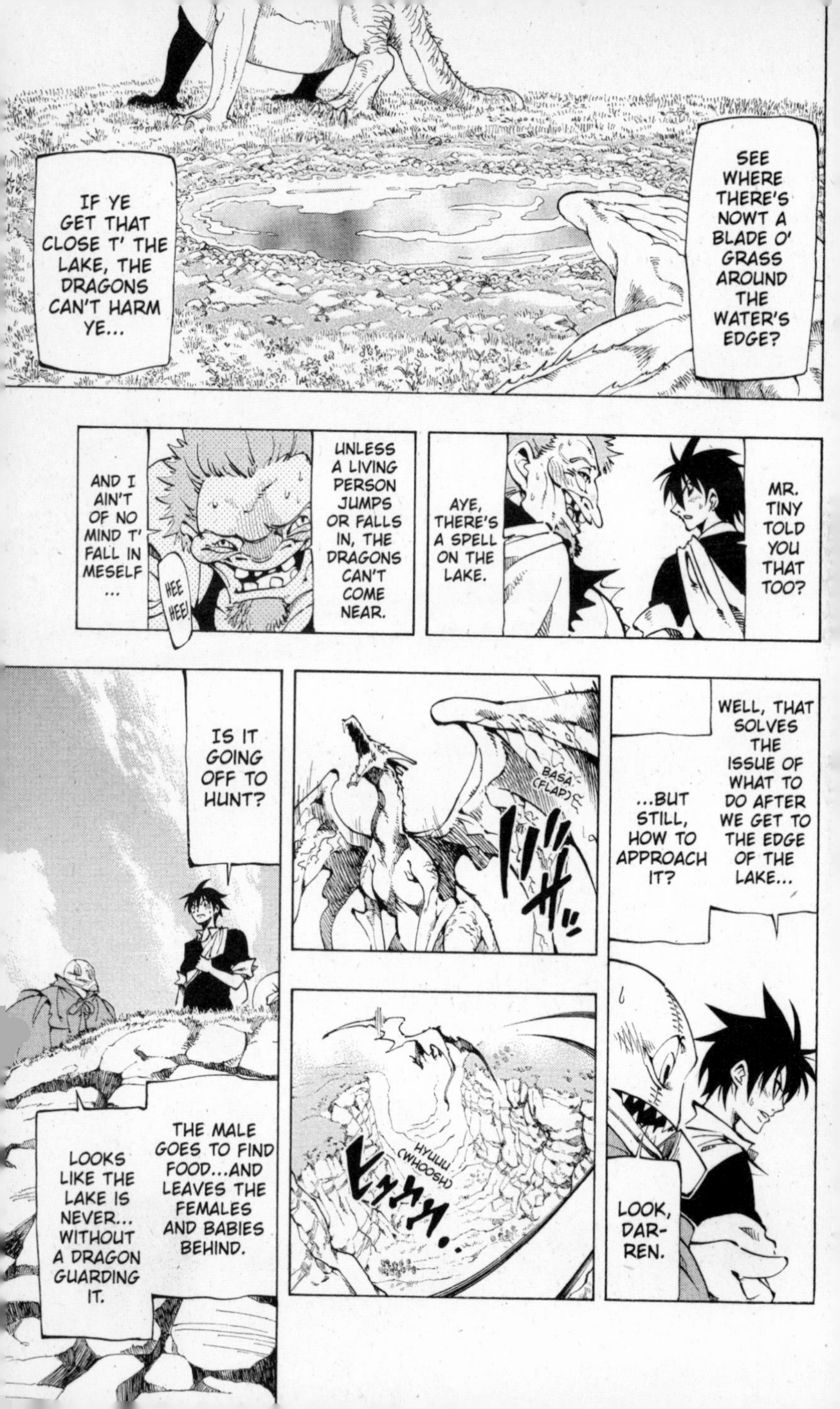
SEE WHERE THERE'S NOWT A BLADE O' GRASS AROUND THE WATER'S EDGE?
IF YE GET THAT CLOSE T' THE LAKE, THE DRAGONS CAN'T HARM YE...
MR. TINY TOLD YOU THAT TOO?
AYE, THERE'S A SPELL ON THE LAKE.
UNLESS A LIVING PERSON JUMPS OR FALLS IN, THE DRAGONS CAN'T COME NEAR.
AND I AIN'T OF NO MIND T' FALL IN MESELF...
HEE HEE!
WELL, THAT SOLVES THE ISSUE OF WHAT TO DO AFTER WE GET TO THE EDGE OF THE LAKE...
...BUT STILL, HOW TO APPROACH IT?
LOOK, DARREN.
BASA (FLAP)
HYUUU (WHOOSH)
IS IT GOING OFF TO HUNT?
THE MALE GOES TO FIND FOOD...AND LEAVES THE FEMALES AND BABIES BEHIND.
LOOKS LIKE THE LAKE IS NEVER... WITHOUT A DRAGON GUARDING IT.

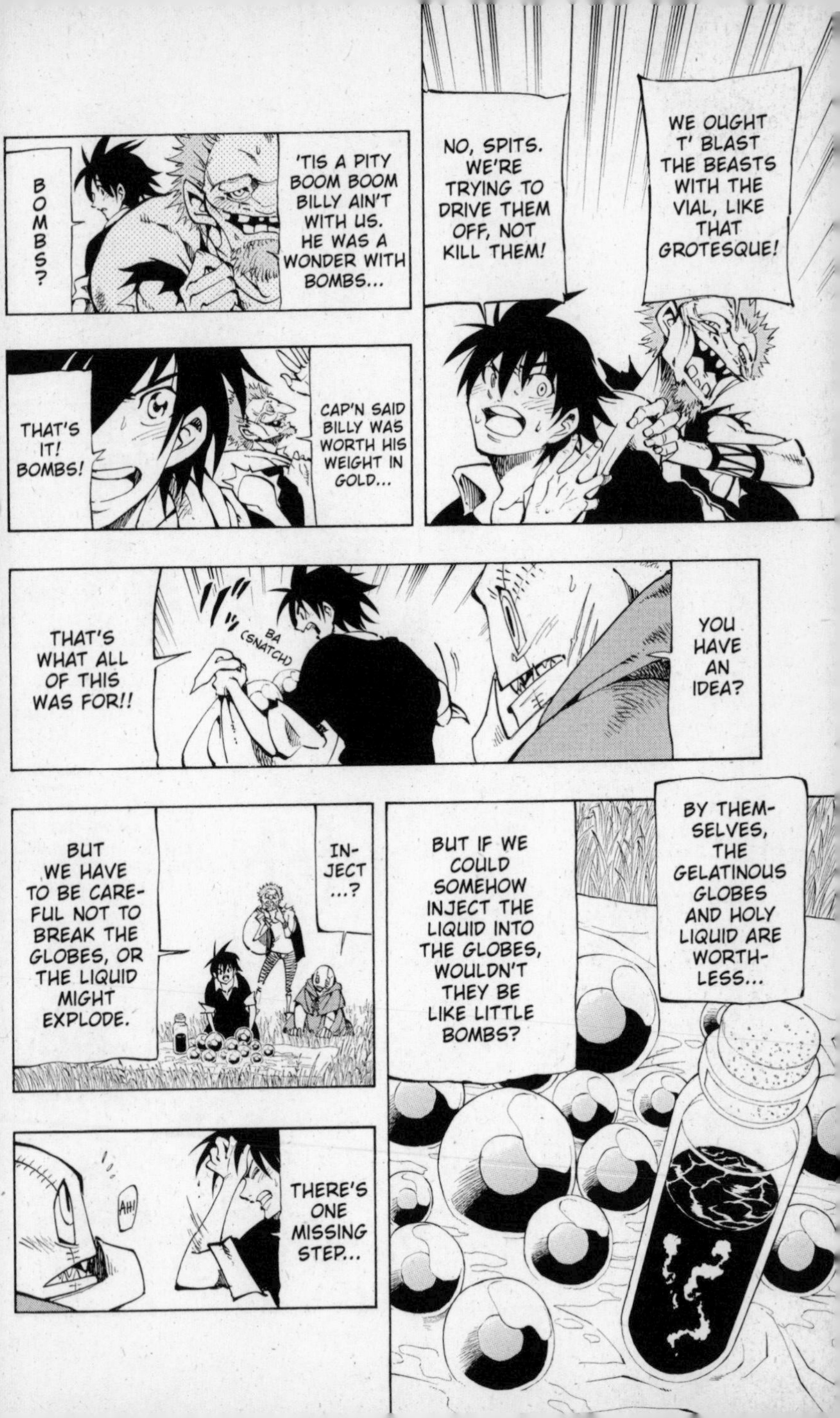
WE OUGHT T' BLAST THE BEASTS WITH THE VIAL, LIKE THAT GROTESQUE!
NO, SPITS. WE'RE TRYING TO DRIVE THEM OFF, NOT KILL THEM!
'TIS A PITY BOOM BOOM BILLY AIN'T WITH US. HE WAS A WONDER WITH BOMBS...
BOMBS?
CAP'N SAID BILLY WAS WORTH HIS WEIGHT IN GOLD...
THAT'S IT! BOMBS!
YOU HAVE AN IDEA?
BA (SNATCH)
THAT'S WHAT ALL OF THIS WAS FOR!!
BY THEM-SELVES, THE GELATINOUS GLOBES AND HOLY LIQUID ARE WORTH-LESS...
BUT IF WE COULD SOMEHOW INJECT THE LIQUID INTO THE GLOBES, WOULDN'T THEY BE LIKE LITTLE BOMBS?
IN-JECT ...?
BUT WE HAVE TO BE CARE-FUL NOT TO BREAK THE GLOBES, OR THE LIQUID MIGHT EXPLODE.
THERE'S ONE MISSING STEP...
AH!

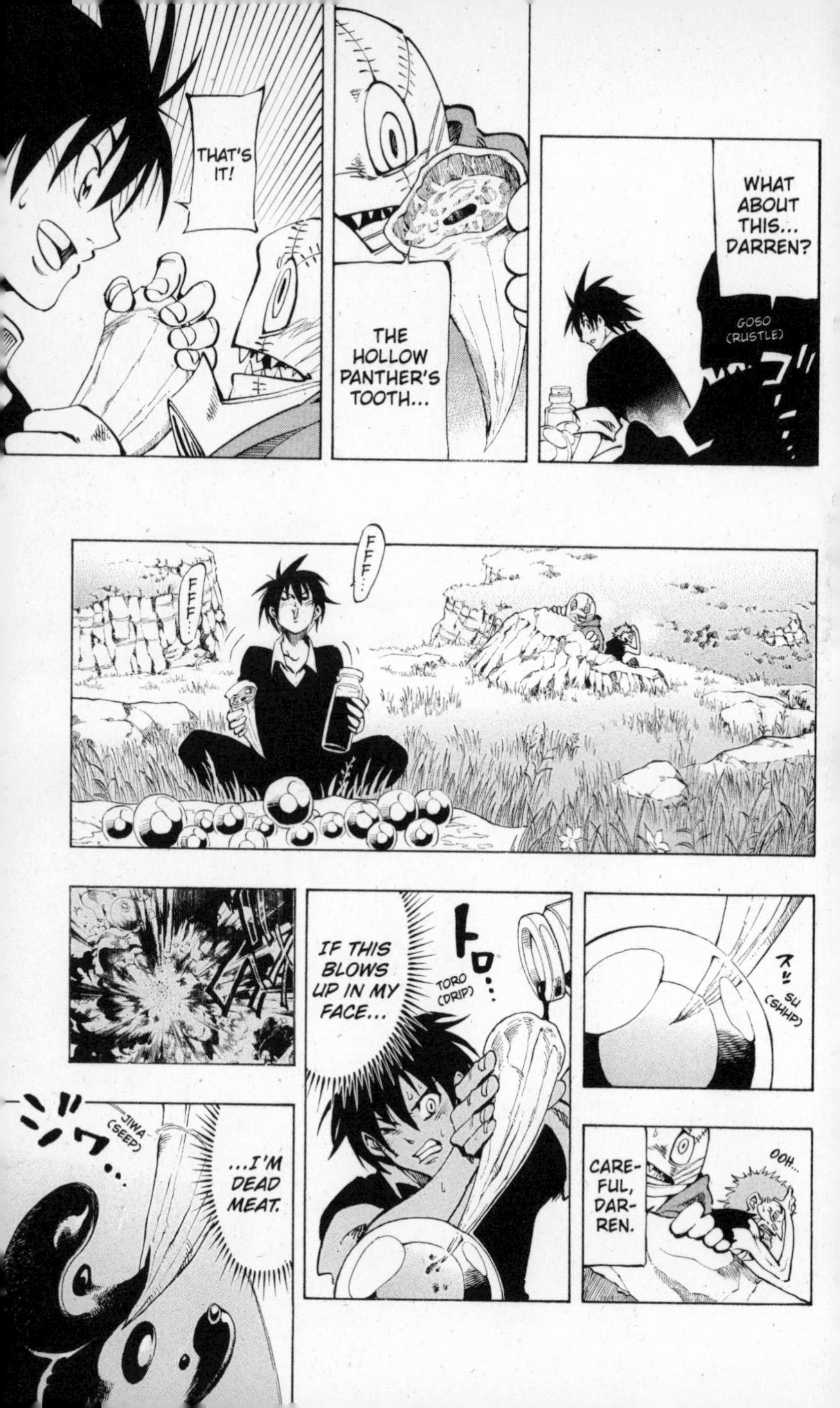
WHAT ABOUT THIS... DARREN?
GOSO (RUSTLE)
THE HOLLOW PANTHER'S TOOTH...
THAT'S IT!
FFF...
FFF...
SU (SHHP)
OOH...
CARE-FUL, DAR-REN.
TORO (DRIP)
IF THIS BLOWS UP IN MY FACE...
JIWA (SEEP)
...I'M DEAD MEAT.

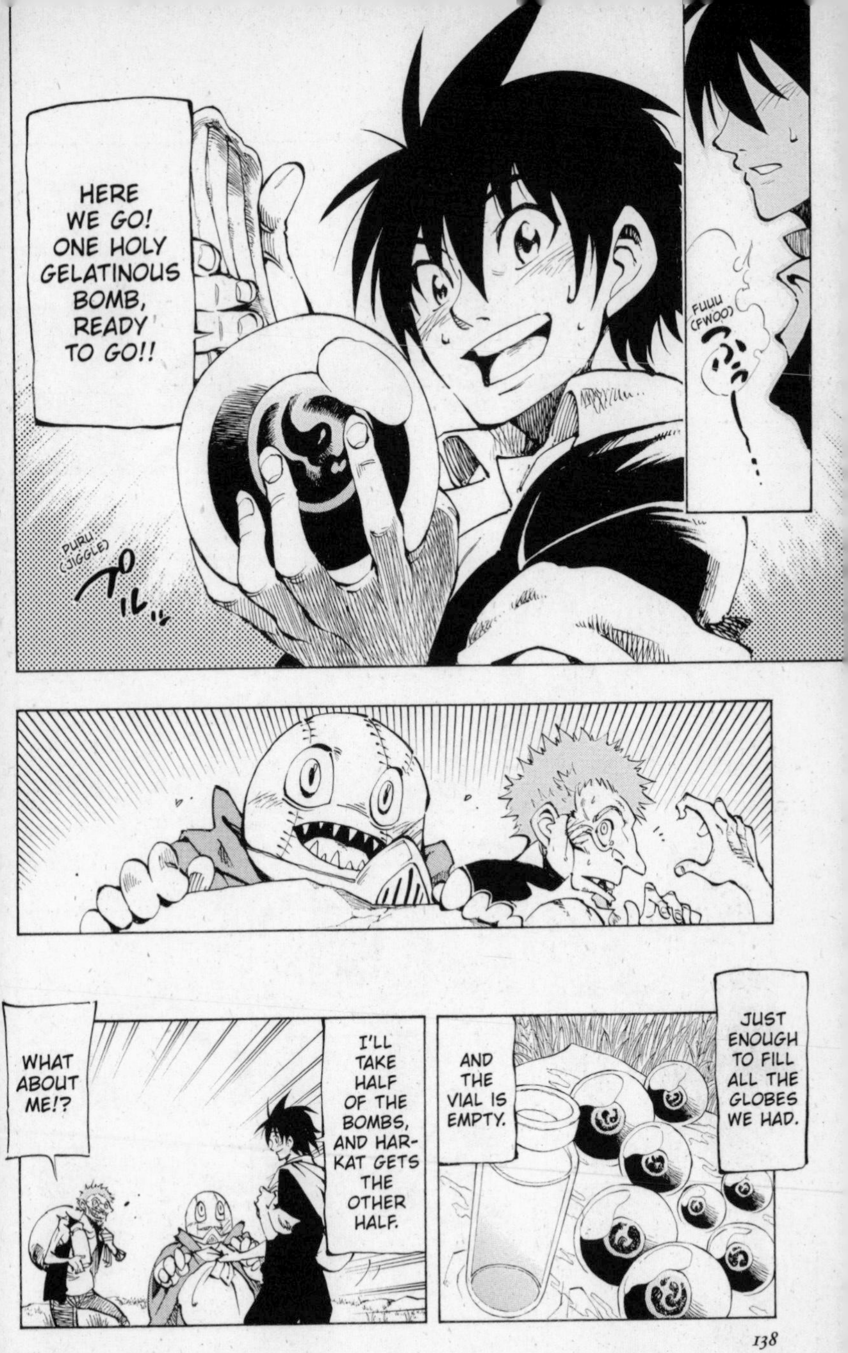
FUUU (FWOO)
HERE WE GO! ONE HOLY GELATINOUS BOMB, READY TO GO!!
PURU (JIGGLE)
JUST ENOUGH TO FILL ALL THE GLOBES WE HAD.
AND THE VIAL IS EMPTY.
I'LL TAKE HALF OF THE BOMBS, AND HAR-KAT GETS THE OTHER HALF.
WHAT ABOUT ME!?

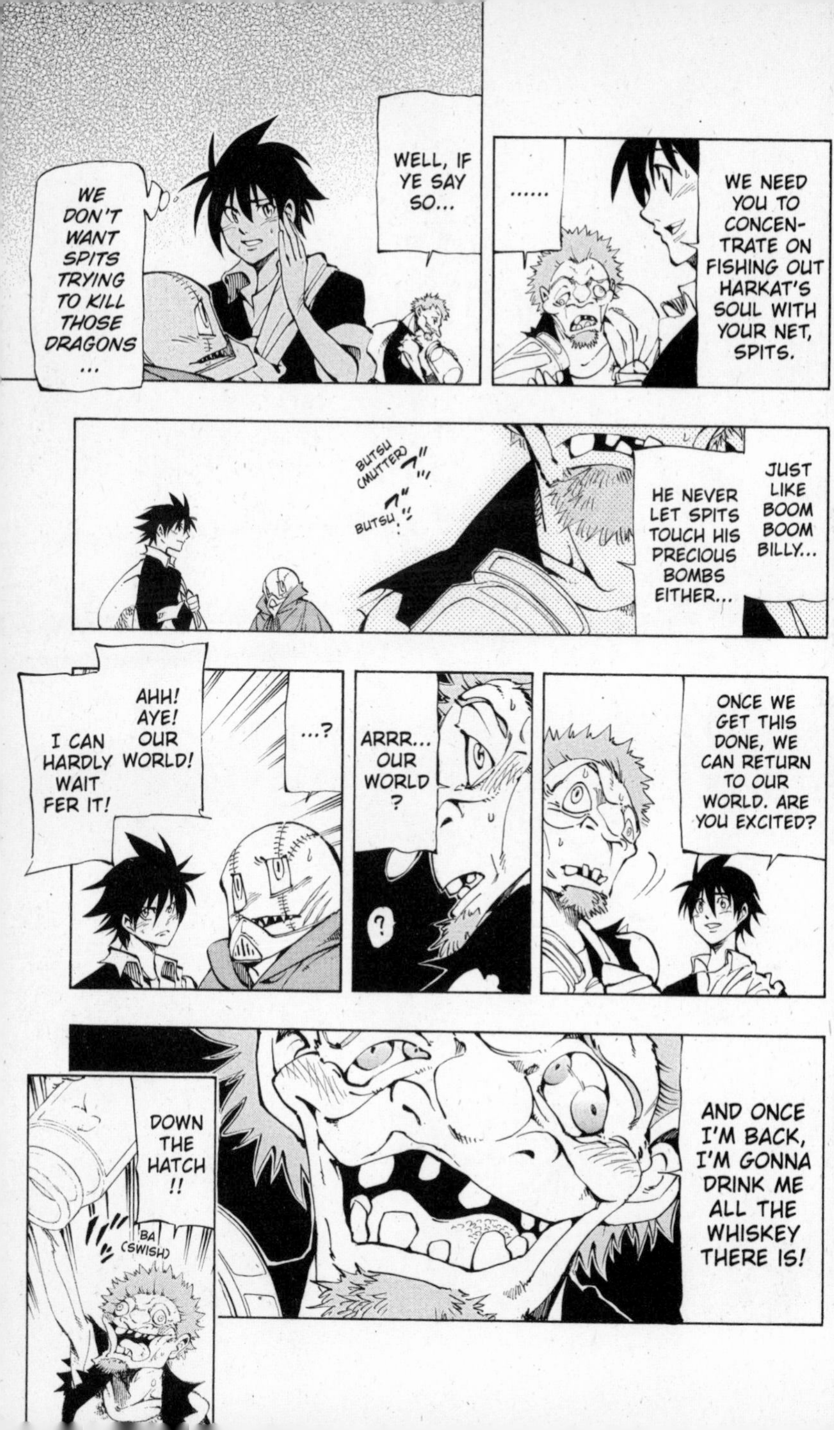
WE NEED YOU TO CONCENTRATE ON FISHING OUT HARKAT'S SOUL WITH YOUR NET, SPITS.
......
WELL, IF YE SAY SO...
WE DON'T WANT SPITS TRYING TO KILL THOSE DRAGONS...
JUST LIKE BOOM BOOM BILLY...
HE NEVER LET SPITS TOUCH HIS PRECIOUS BOMBS EITHER...
BUTSU (MUTTER)
BUTSU
ONCE WE GET THIS DONE, WE CAN RETURN TO OUR WORLD. ARE YOU EXCITED?
ARRR... OUR WORLD?
...?
AHH! AYE! OUR WORLD!
I CAN HARDLY WAIT FER IT!
AND ONCE I'M BACK, I'M GONNA DRINK ME ALL THE WHISKEY THERE IS!
DOWN THE HATCH!!
BA (SWISH)

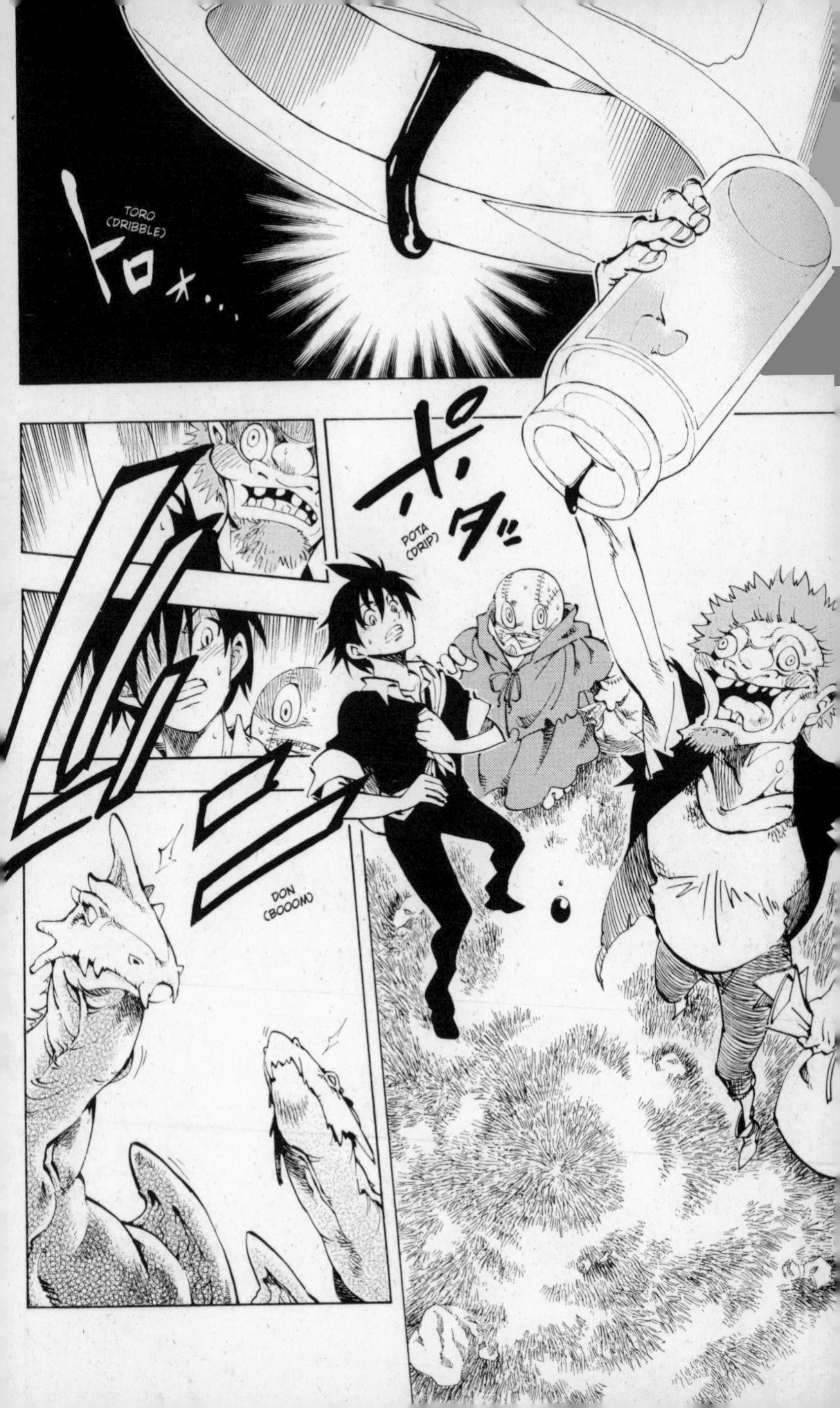
TORO
(DRIBBLE)
POTA
(DRIP)
DON
(BOOOM)

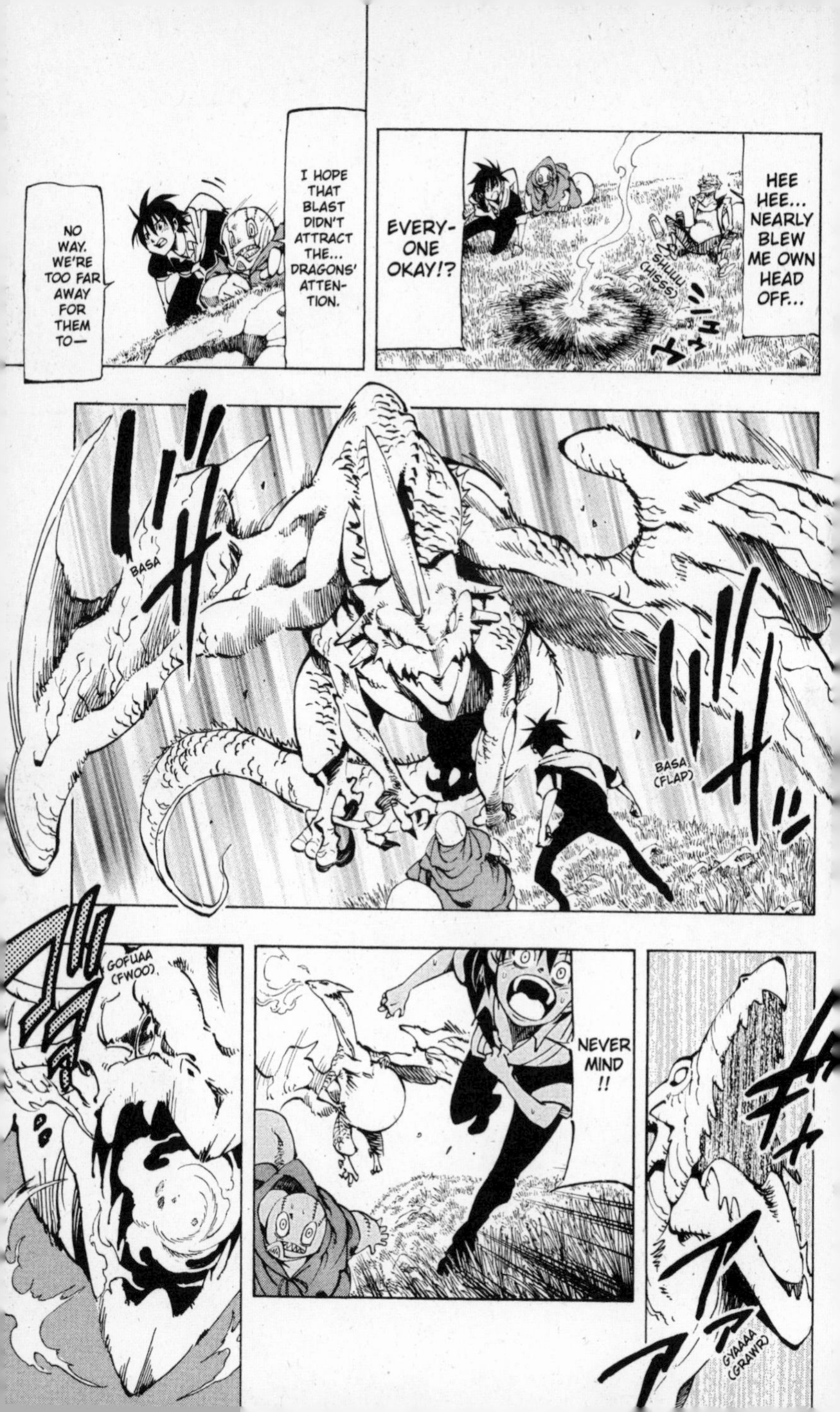
HEE HEE... NEARLY BLEW ME OWN HEAD OFF...
SHUUU (HISSS)
EVERY-ONE OKAY!?
I HOPE THAT BLAST DIDN'T ATTRACT THE... DRAGONS' ATTENTION.
NO WAY. WE'RE TOO FAR AWAY FOR THEM TO—
BASA (FLAP)
BASA
GYAAAA (GRAWR)
NEVER MIND !!
GOFUAA (FWOO)

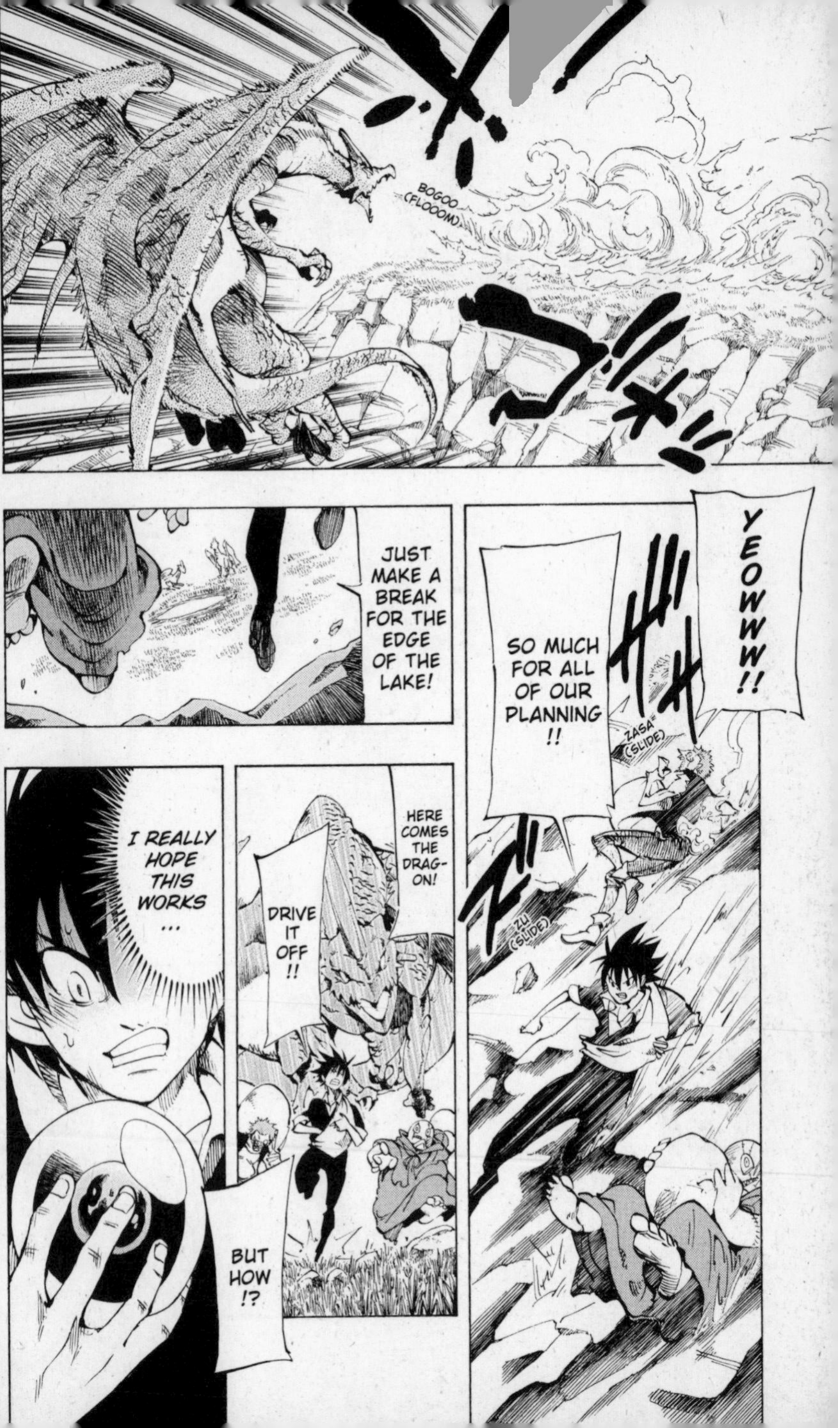
BOGOO (FLOOOM)
YEOWWW!!
SO MUCH FOR ALL OF OUR PLANNING !!
ZASA (SLIDE)
ZU (SLIDE)
JUST MAKE A BREAK FOR THE EDGE OF THE LAKE!
HERE COMES THE DRAG-ON!
DRIVE IT OFF !!
I REALLY HOPE THIS WORKS ...
BUT HOW !?

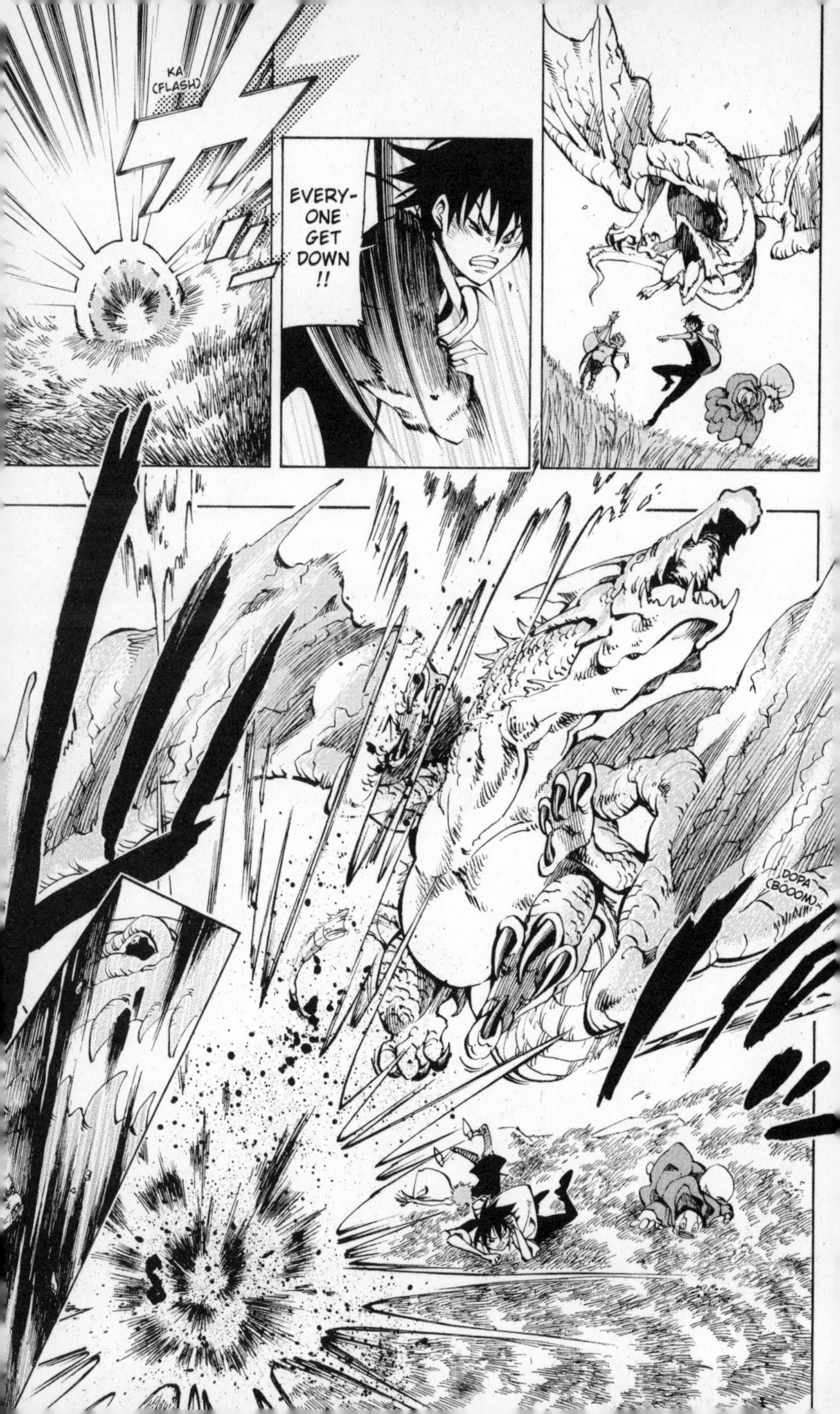
EVERY-ONE GET DOWN !!
KA (FLASH)
DOPA (BOOOM)

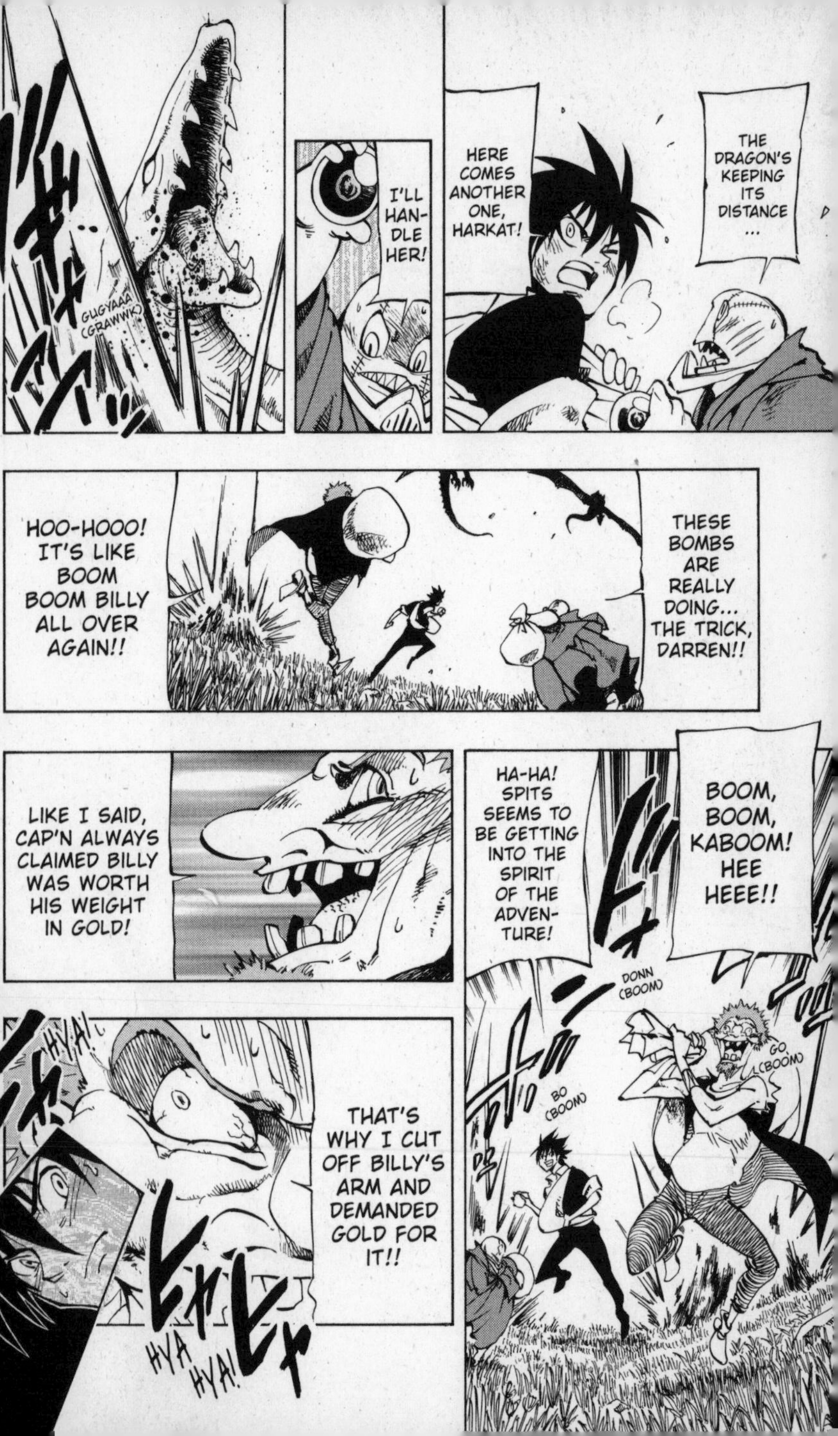
THE DRAGON'S KEEPING ITS DISTANCE ...
HERE COMES ANOTHER ONE, HARKAT!
I'LL HAN-DLE HER!
GUGYAAA (GRAWWIK)
THESE BOMBS ARE REALLY DOING... THE TRICK, DARREN!!
HOO-HOOO! IT'S LIKE BOOM BOOM BILLY ALL OVER AGAIN!!
BOOM, BOOM, KABOOM! HEE HEEE!!
HA-HA! SPITS SEEMS TO BE GETTING INTO THE SPIRIT OF THE ADVEN-TURE!
DONN (BOOM)
GO (BOOM)
BO (BOOM)
LIKE I SAID, CAP'N ALWAYS CLAIMED BILLY WAS WORTH HIS WEIGHT IN GOLD!
HYA!
THAT'S WHY I CUT OFF BILLY'S ARM AND DEMANDED GOLD FOR IT!!
HYA HYA!

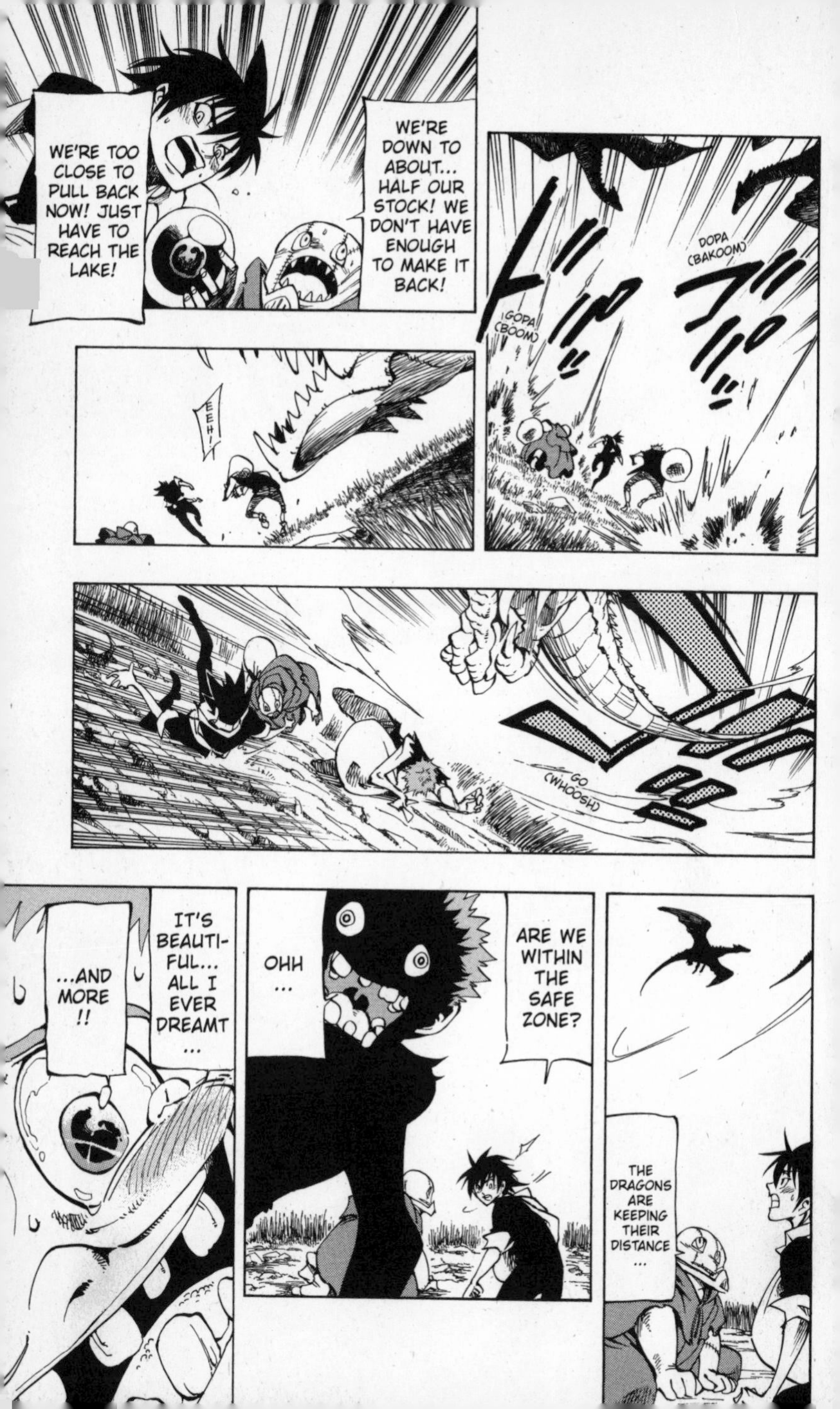
WE'RE DOWN TO ABOUT... HALF OUR STOCK! WE DON'T HAVE ENOUGH TO MAKE IT BACK!
WE'RE TOO CLOSE TO PULL BACK NOW! JUST HAVE TO REACH THE LAKE!
DOPA (BAKOOM)
GOPA (BOOM)
EEH!
GO (WHOOSH)
THE DRAGONS ARE KEEPING THEIR DISTANCE ...
ARE WE WITHIN THE SAFE ZONE?
OHH ...
IT'S BEAUTI-FUL... ALL I EVER DREAMT ...
...AND MORE !!

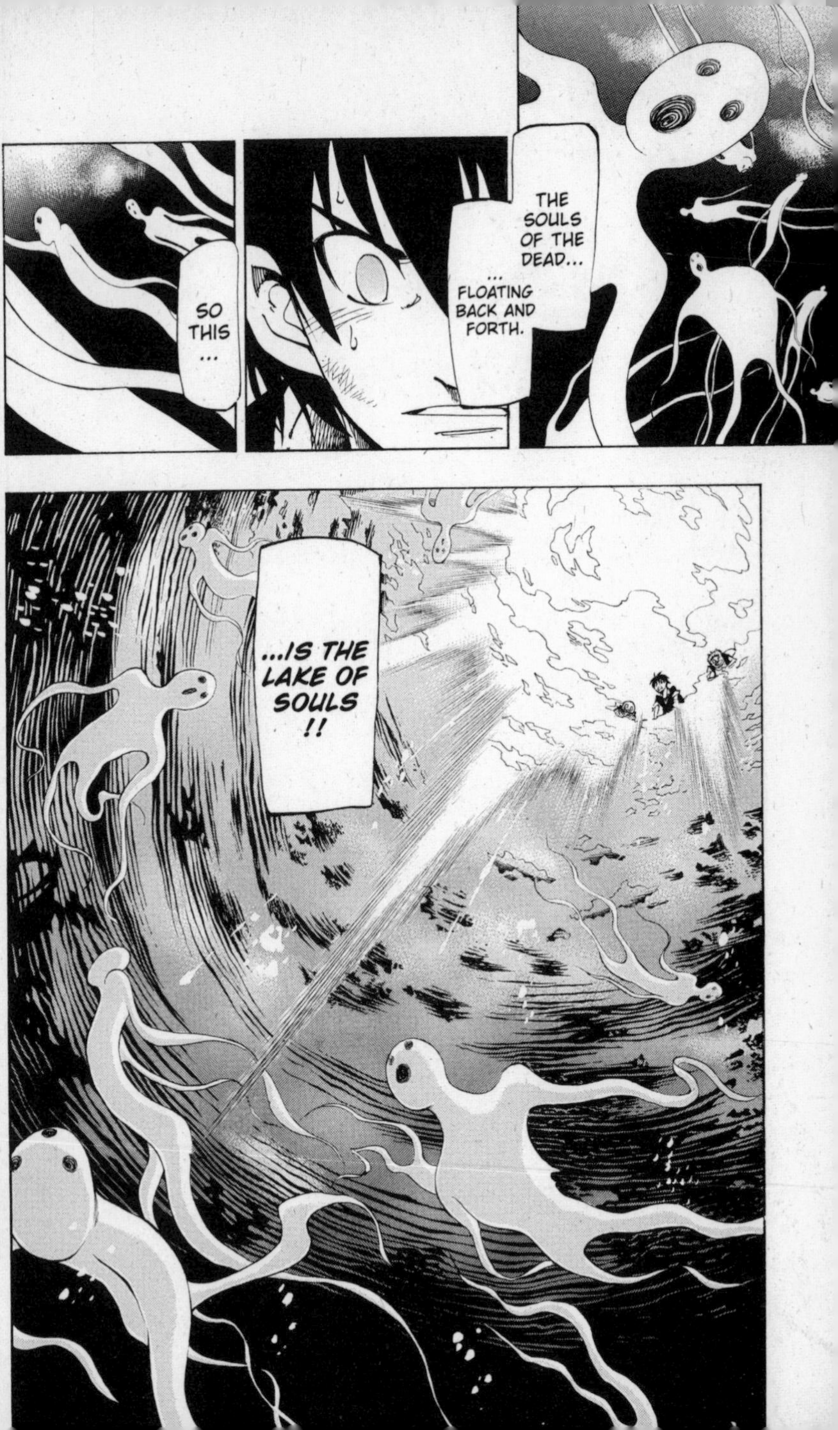
THE SOULS OF THE DEAD...
...FLOATING BACK AND FORTH.
SO THIS ...
...IS THE LAKE OF SOULS !!

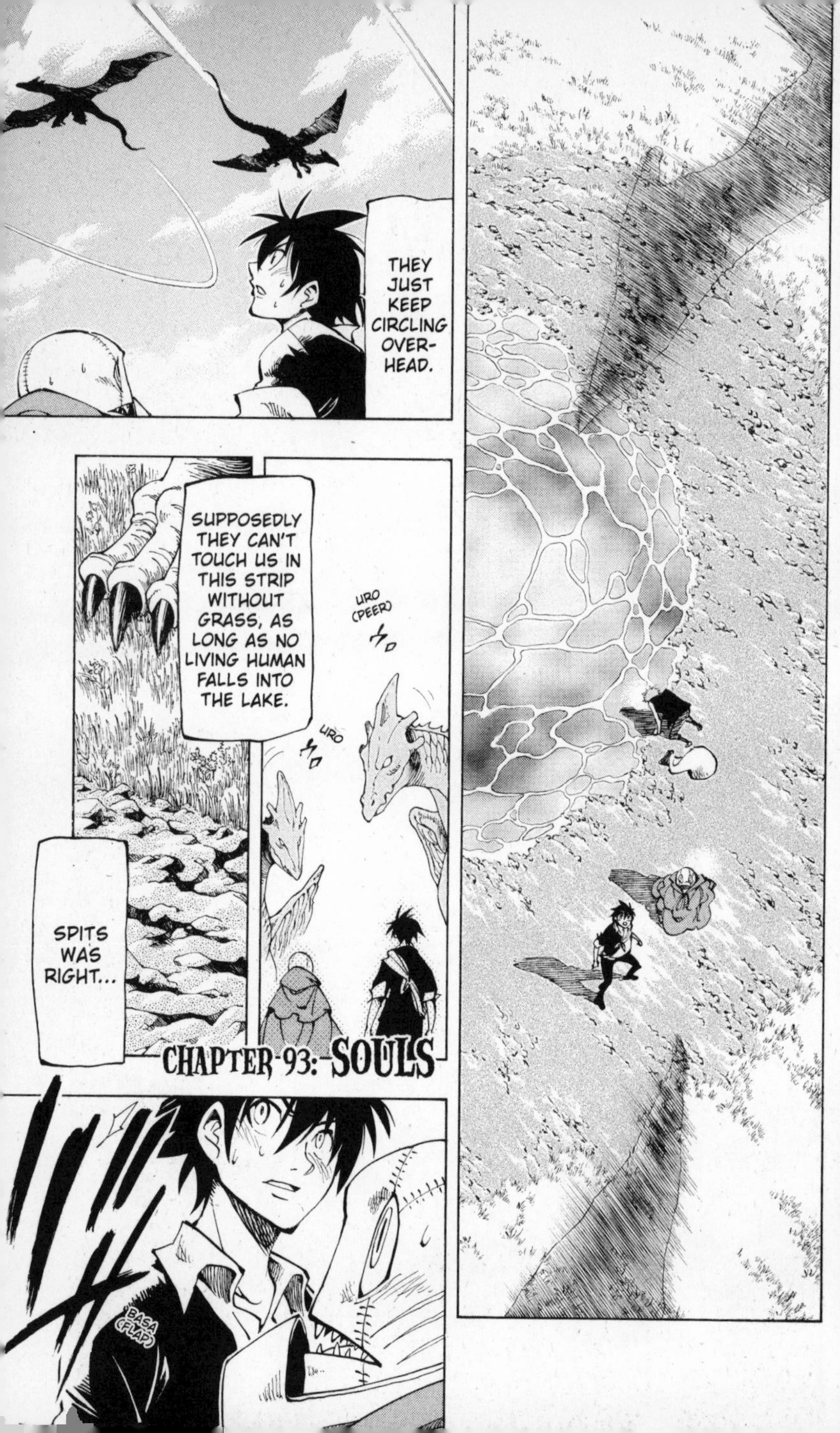
THEY JUST KEEP CIRCLING OVER-HEAD.
URO (PEER)
URO
SUPPOSEDLY THEY CAN'T TOUCH US IN THIS STRIP WITHOUT GRASS, AS LONG AS NO LIVING HUMAN FALLS INTO THE LAKE.
SPITS WAS RIGHT...
CHAPTER 93: SOULS
BASA (FLAP)

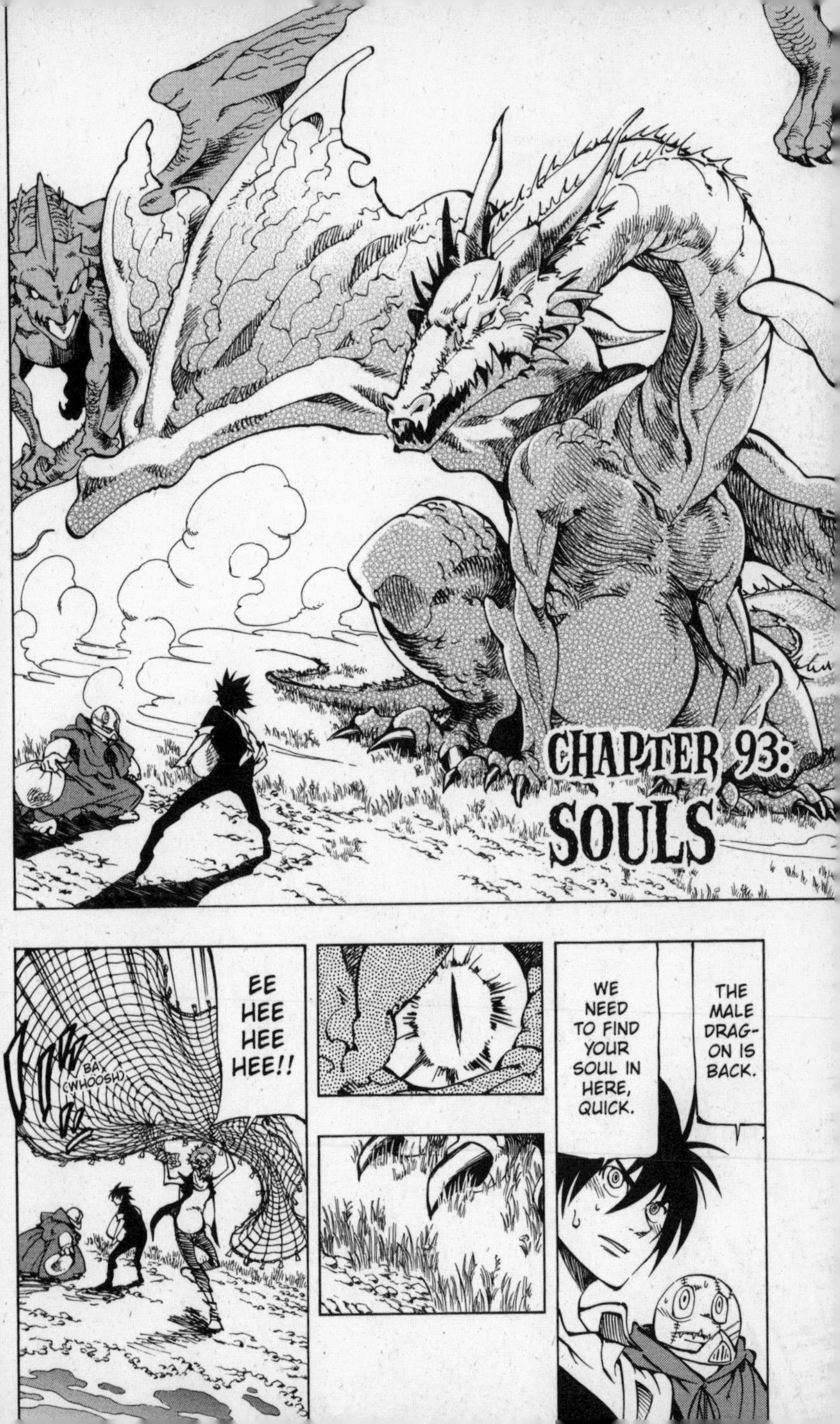
CHAPTER 93:
SOULS
THE MALE DRAG-ON IS BACK.
WE NEED TO FIND YOUR SOUL IN HERE, QUICK.
EE HEE HEE HEE!!
BA (WHOOSH)

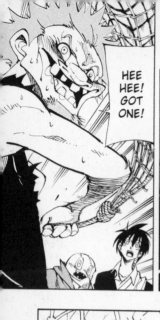

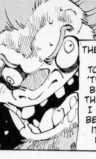

THE LITTLE MAN TOLD ME 'TWOULD BE LIKE THIS, BUT I NEVER BELIEVED IT TILL NOW.
ALL ME DREAMS ARE COMING TRUE! HE WASN'T LYING!
DREAMS?
GEEHEEHEE!
THESE SOULS MAY BE NOWT BUT GHOSTIES IN THE WATER...
BUT ONCE YE HAUL 'EM UP ON LAND...
ZU (SLIP)
HEE HEE! GOT ONE!
WAIT, NO! STOP IT, SPITS!
LET GO OF THE NET!!
!!
GU (GRAB)

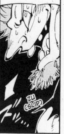

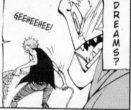

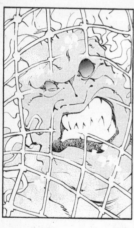

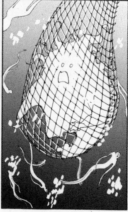

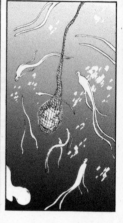

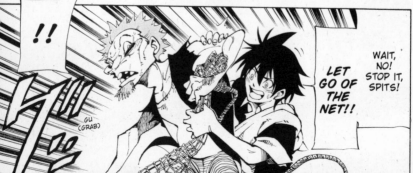

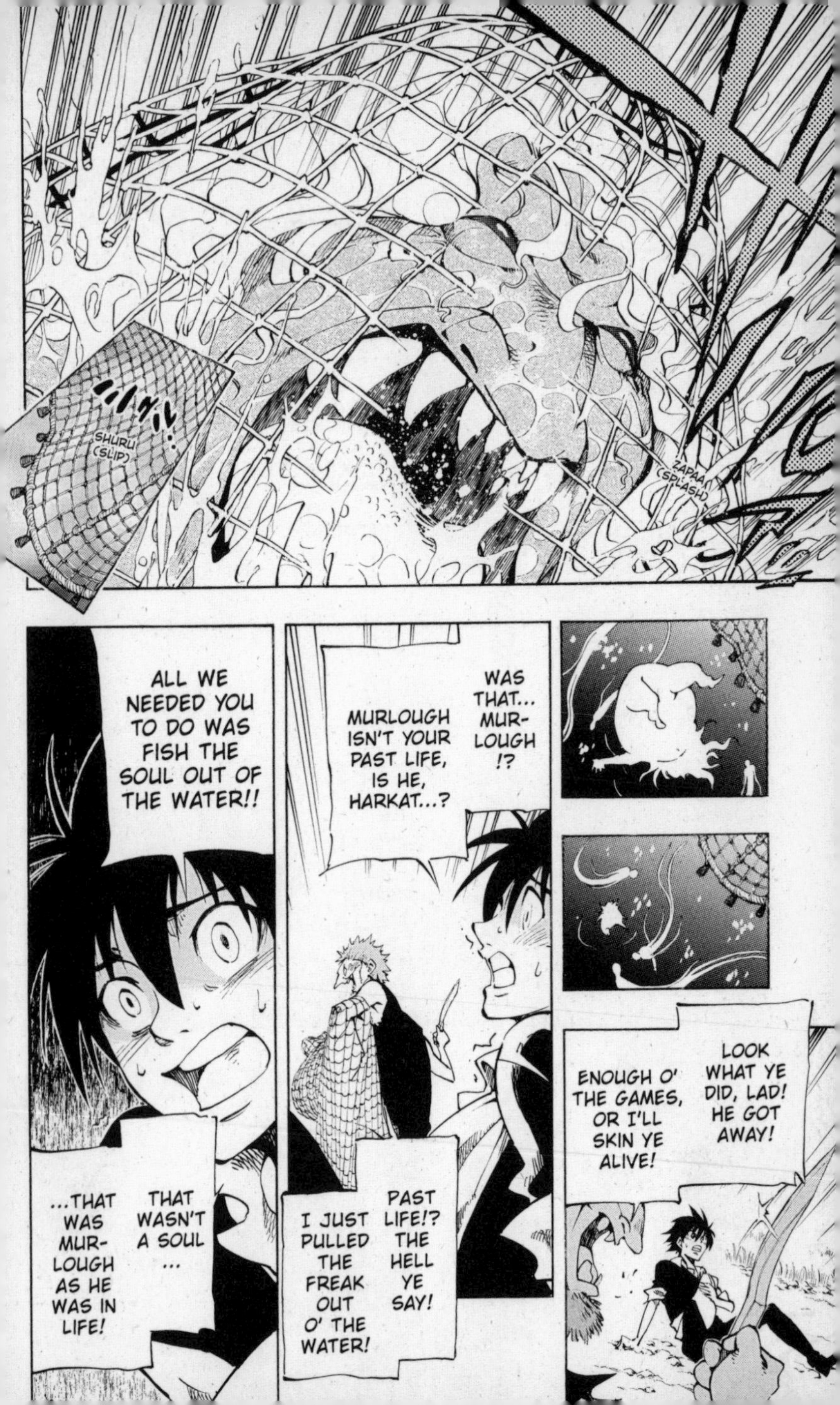
ZAPAAA (SPLASH)
SHURU (SLIP)
LOOK WHAT YE DID, LAD! HE GOT AWAY!
ENOUGH O' THE GAMES, OR I'LL SKIN YE ALIVE!
WAS THAT... MUR-LOUGH!?
MURLOUGH ISN'T YOUR PAST LIFE, IS HE, HARKAT...?
PAST LIFE!? THE HELL YE SAY!
I JUST PULLED THE FREAK OUT O' THE WATER!
ALL WE NEEDED YOU TO DO WAS FISH THE SOUL OUT OF THE WATER!!
THAT WASN'T A SOUL...
...THAT WAS MUR-LOUGH AS HE WAS IN LIFE!

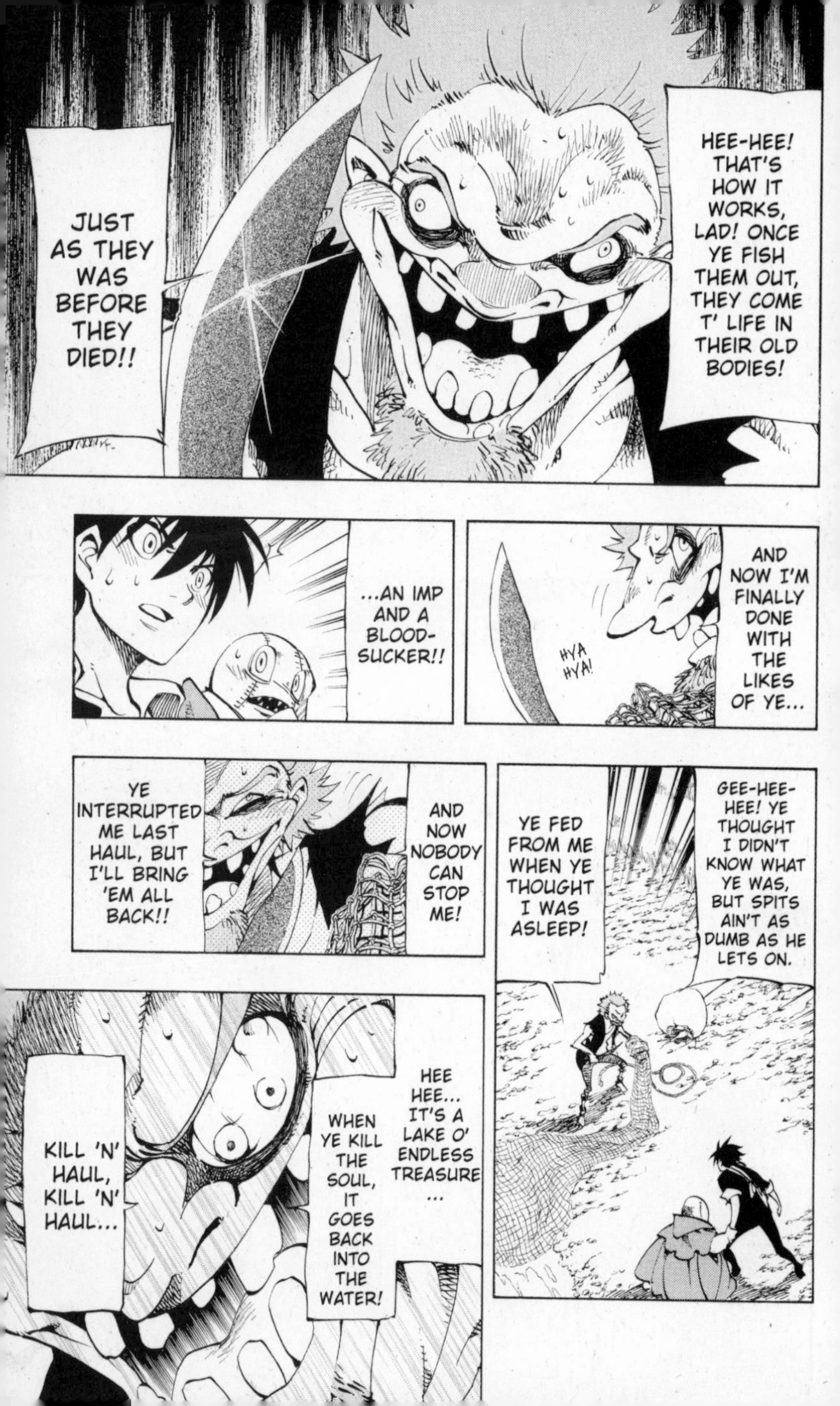
HEE-HEE! THAT'S HOW IT WORKS, LAD! ONCE YE FISH THEM OUT, THEY COME T' LIFE IN THEIR OLD BODIES!
JUST AS THEY WAS BEFORE THEY DIED!!
AND NOW I'M FINALLY DONE WITH THE LIKES OF YE...
HYA HYA!
...AN IMP AND A BLOOD-SUCKER!!
GEE-HEE-HEE! YE THOUGHT I DIDN'T KNOW WHAT YE WAS, BUT SPITS AIN'T AS DUMB AS HE LETS ON.
YE FED FROM ME WHEN YE THOUGHT I WAS ASLEEP!
AND NOW NOBODY CAN STOP ME!
YE INTERRUPTED ME LAST HAUL, BUT I'LL BRING 'EM ALL BACK!!
HEE HEE... IT'S A LAKE O' ENDLESS TREASURE...
WHEN YE KILL THE SOUL, IT GOES BACK INTO THE WATER!
KILL 'N' HAUL, KILL 'N' HAUL...

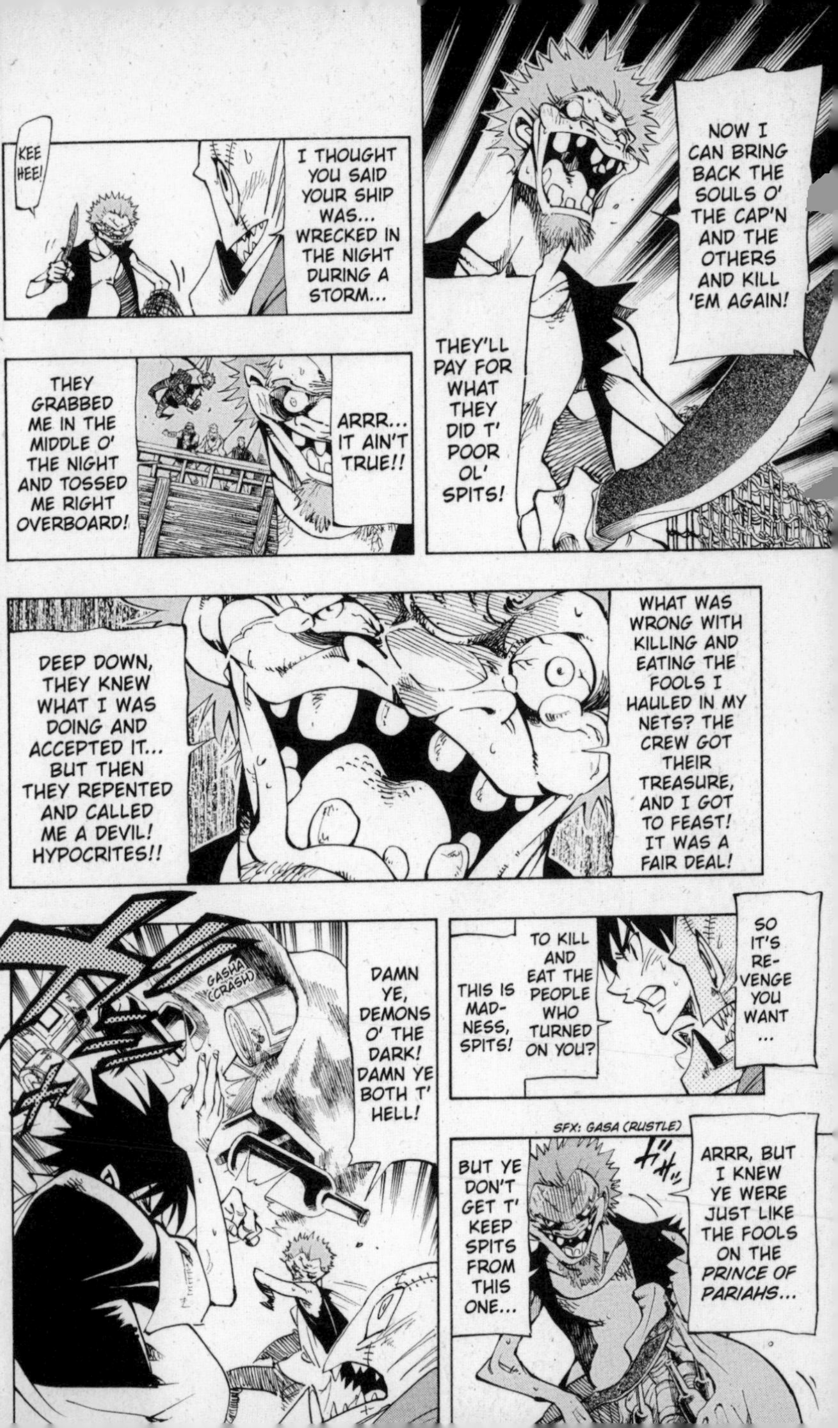
NOW I CAN BRING BACK THE SOULS O' THE CAP'N AND THE OTHERS AND KILL 'EM AGAIN!
THEY'LL PAY FOR WHAT THEY DID T' POOR OL' SPITS!
I THOUGHT YOU SAID YOUR SHIP WAS... WRECKED IN THE NIGHT DURING A STORM...
KEE HEE!
ARRR... IT AIN'T TRUE!!
THEY GRABBED ME IN THE MIDDLE O' THE NIGHT AND TOSSED ME RIGHT OVERBOARD!
WHAT WAS WRONG WITH KILLING AND EATING THE FOOLS I HAULED IN MY NETS? THE CREW GOT THEIR TREASURE, AND I GOT TO FEAST! IT WAS A FAIR DEAL!
DEEP DOWN, THEY KNEW WHAT I WAS DOING AND ACCEPTED IT... BUT THEN THEY REPENTED AND CALLED ME A DEVIL! HYPOCRITES!!
SO IT'S RE-VENGE YOU WANT...
TO KILL AND EAT THE PEOPLE WHO TURNED ON YOU?
THIS IS MAD-NESS, SPITS!
ARRR, BUT I KNEW YE WERE JUST LIKE THE FOOLS ON THE *PRINCE OF PARIAHS*...
BUT YE DON'T GET T' KEEP SPITS FROM THIS ONE...
SFX: GASA (RUSTLE)
DAMN YE, DEMONS O' THE DARK! DAMN YE BOTH T' HELL!
GASHA (CRASH)

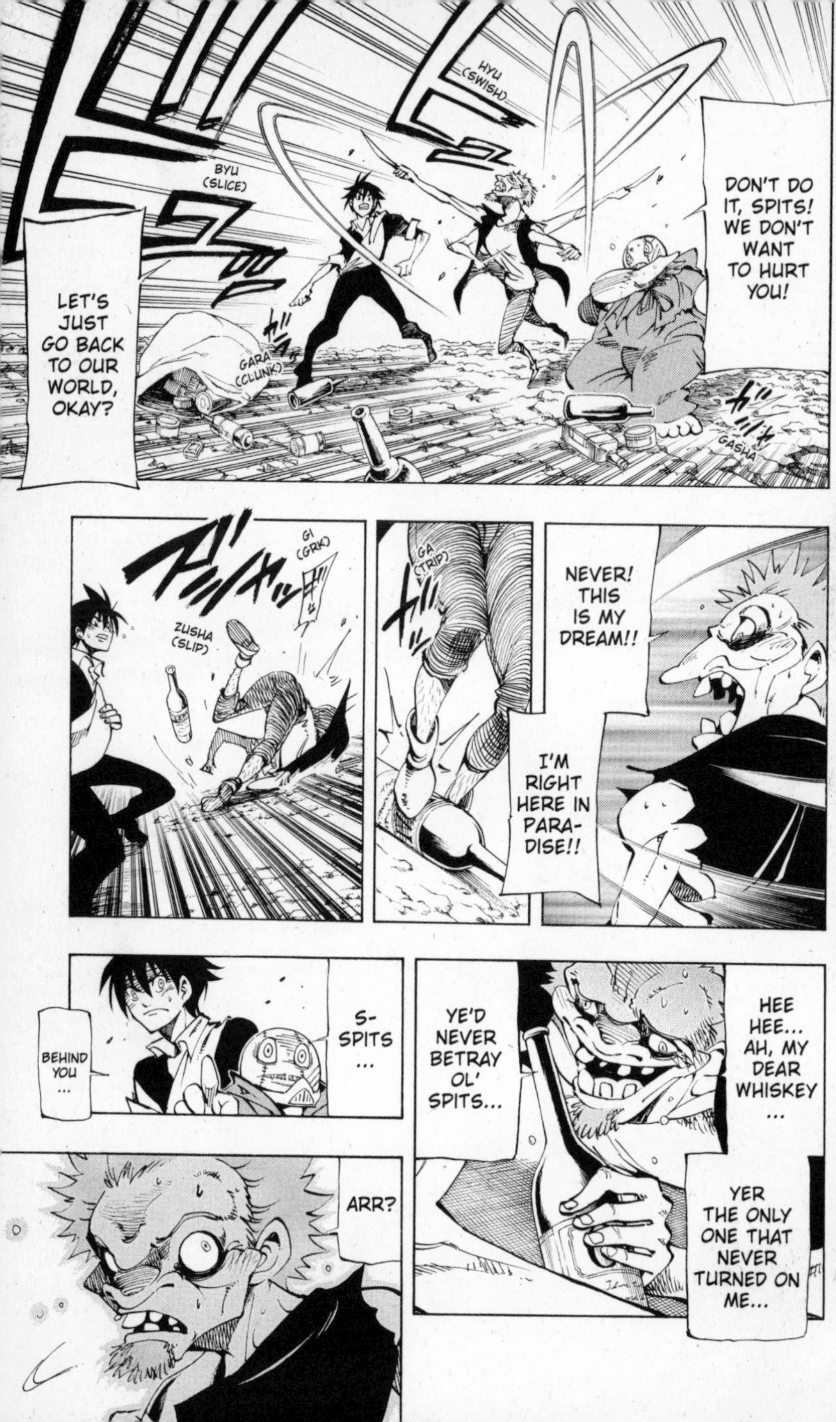
HYU (SWISH)
DON'T DO IT, SPITS! WE DON'T WANT TO HURT YOU!
BYU (SLICE)
LET'S JUST GO BACK TO OUR WORLD, OKAY?
GARA (CLUNK)
GASHA
NEVER! THIS IS MY DREAM!!
I'M RIGHT HERE IN PARA-DISE!!
GA (TRIP)
GI (GRK)
ZUSHA (SLIP)
HEE HEE... AH, MY DEAR WHISKEY ...
YE'D NEVER BETRAY OL' SPITS...
S-SPITS ...
BEHIND YOU ...
YER THE ONLY ONE THAT NEVER TURNED ON ME...
ARR?

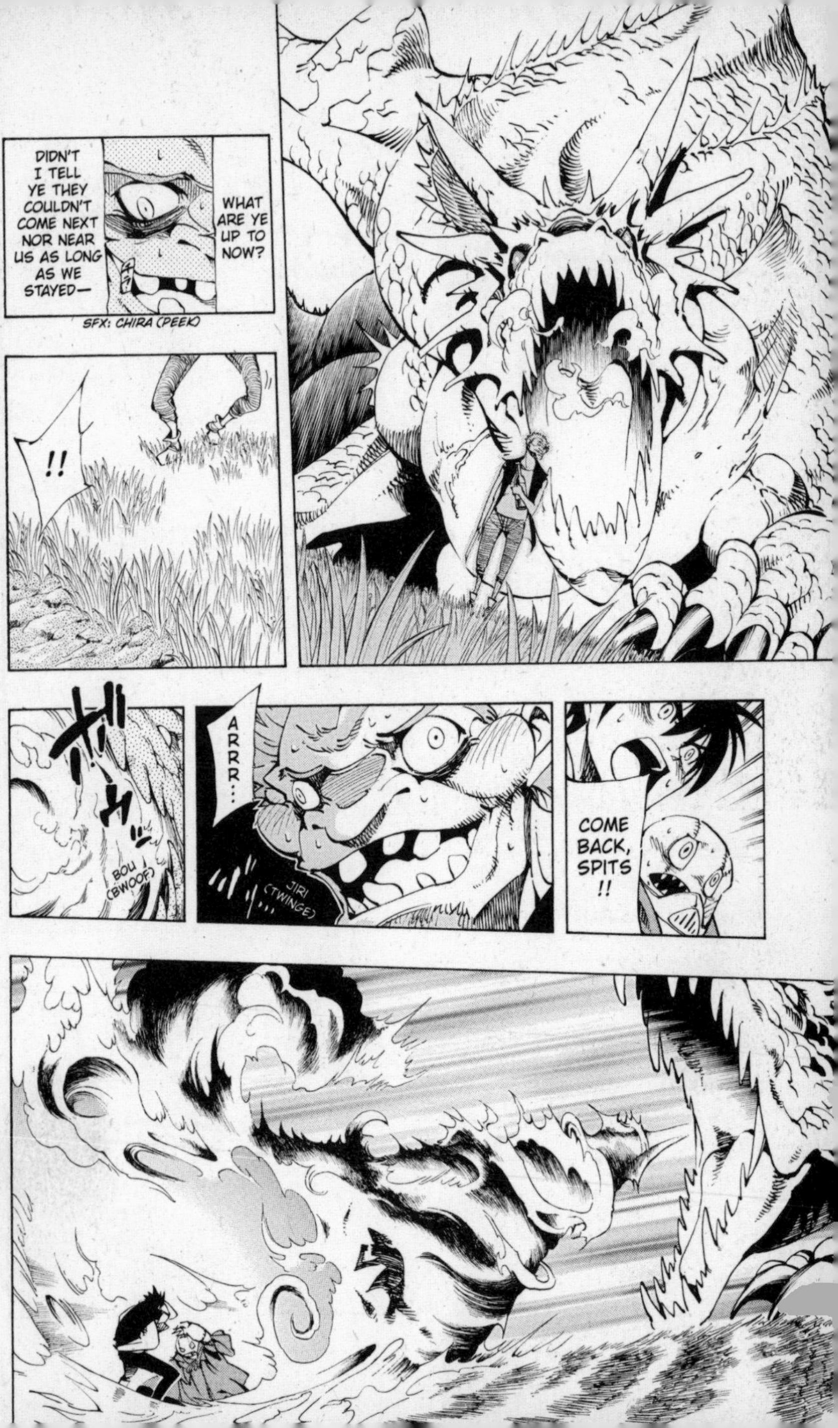
WHAT ARE YE UP TO NOW?
DIDN'T I TELL YE THEY COULDN'T COME NEXT NOR NEAR US AS LONG AS WE STAYED—
SFX: CHIRA (PEEK)
!!
COME BACK, SPITS !!
ARRR...
JIRI (TWINGE)
BOU (BWOOF)

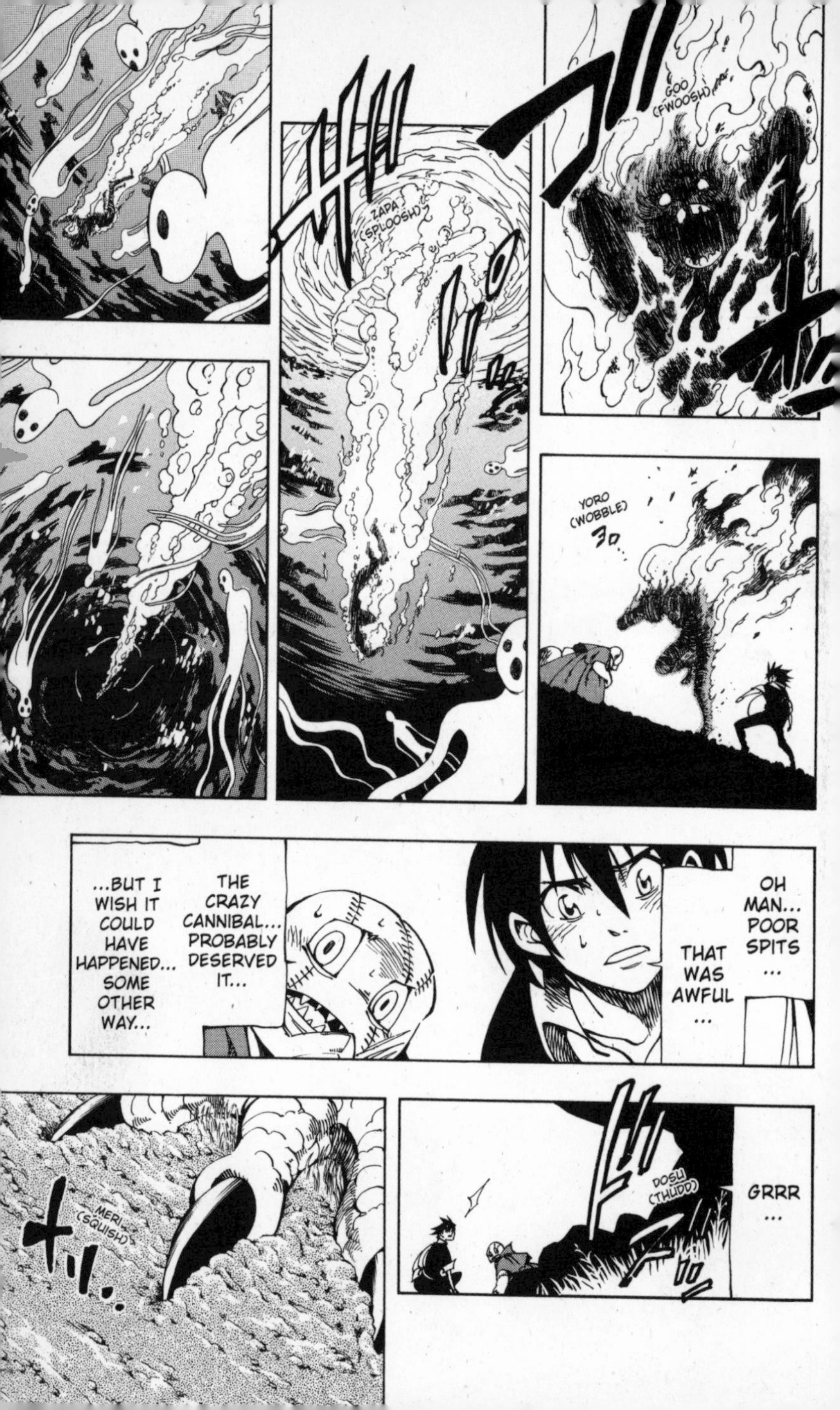
GOO (FWOOSH)
YORO (WOBBLE)
ZAPA (SPLOOSH)
OH MAN... POOR SPITS...
THAT WAS AWFUL...
THE CRAZY CANNIBAL... PROBABLY DESERVED IT...
...BUT I WISH IT COULD HAVE HAPPENED... SOME OTHER WAY...
DOSU (THUDD)
GRRR...
MERI (SQUISH)

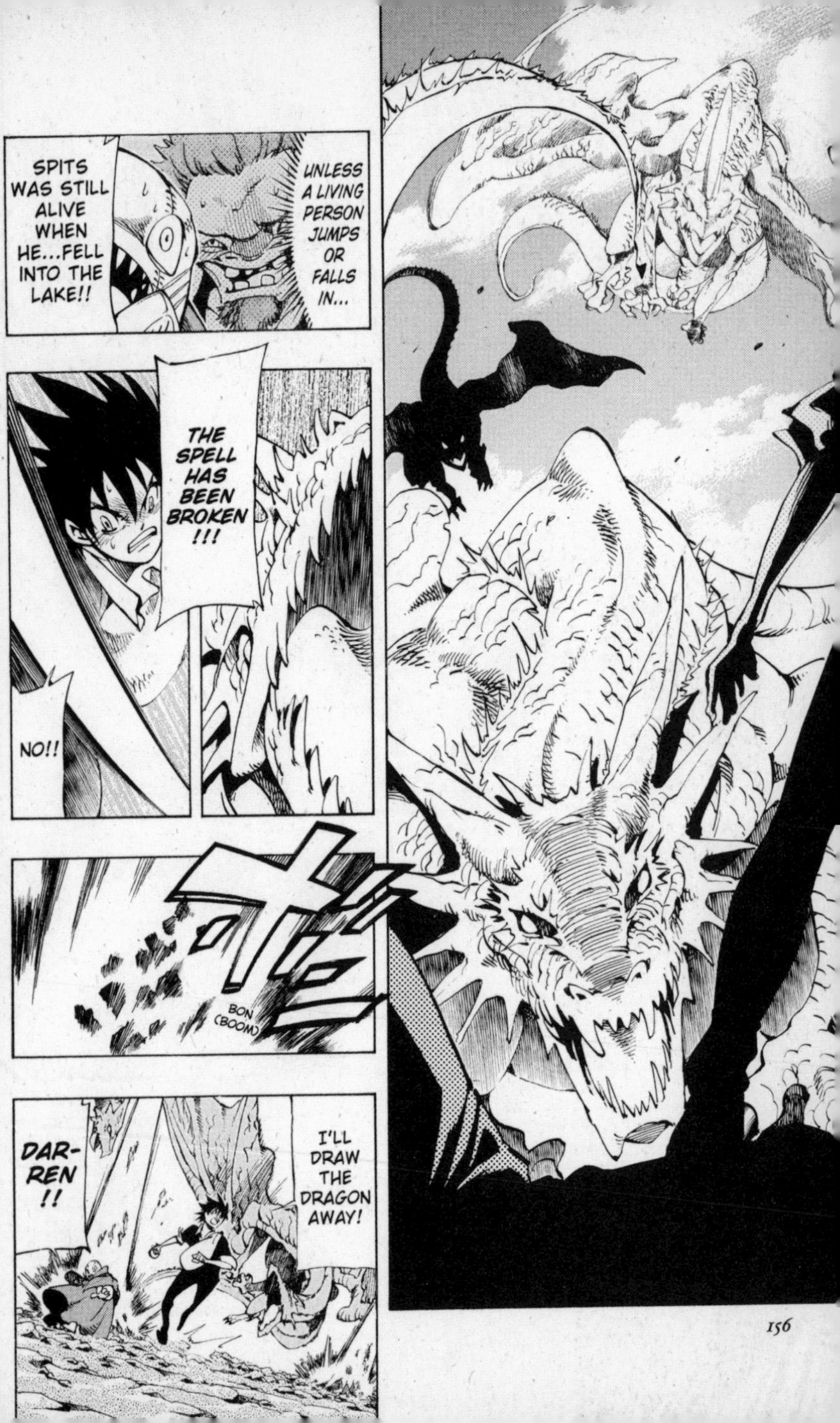
UNLESS A LIVING PERSON JUMPS OR FALLS IN...
SPITS WAS STILL ALIVE WHEN HE...FELL INTO THE LAKE!!
THE SPELL HAS BEEN BROKEN!!!
NO!!
BON (BOOM)
I'LL DRAW THE DRAGON AWAY!
DAR-REN!!

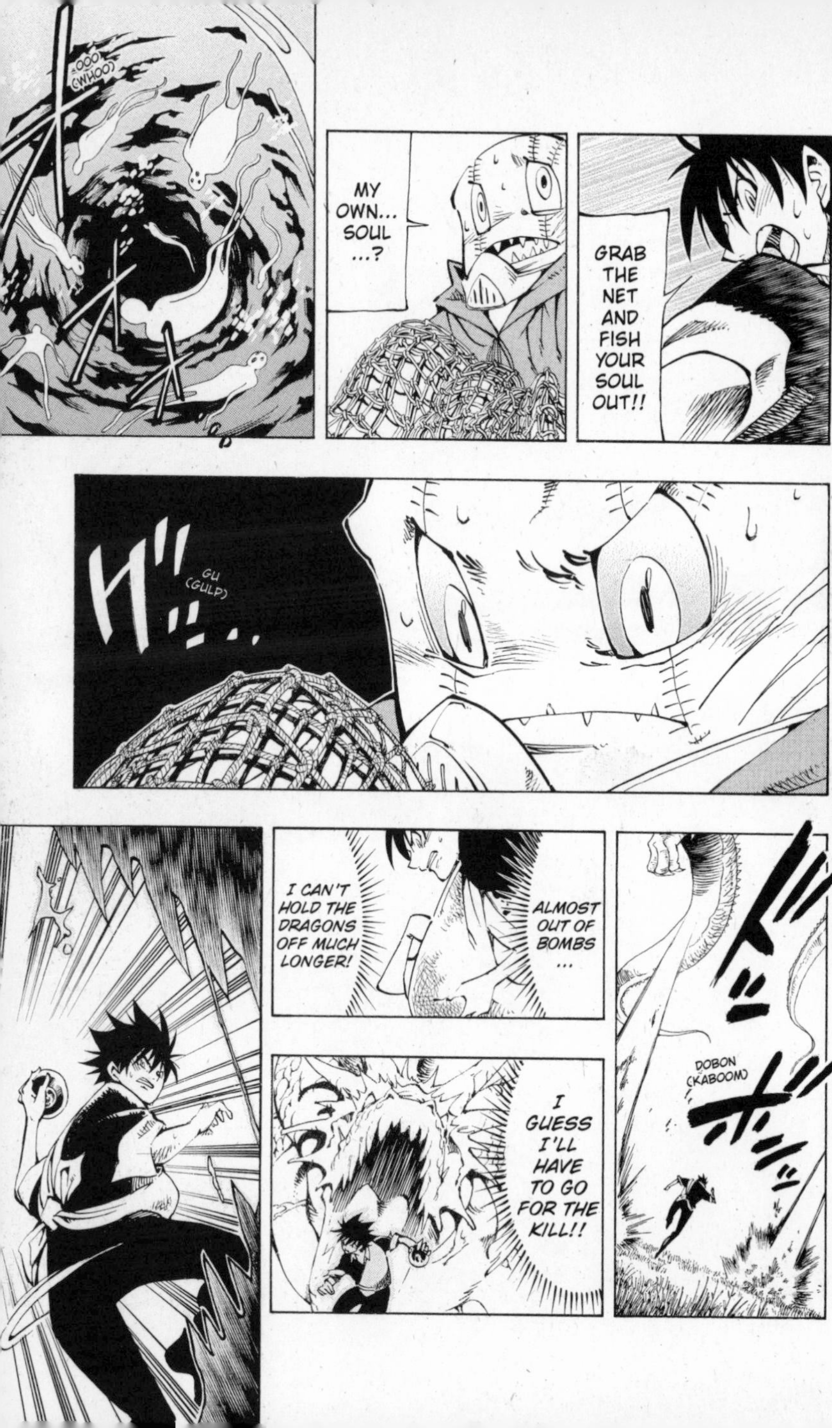
GRAB THE NET AND FISH YOUR SOUL OUT!!
MY OWN... SOUL ...?
OOO (WHOO)
GU (GULP)
DOBON (KABOOM)
ALMOST OUT OF BOMBS ...
I CAN'T HOLD THE DRAGONS OFF MUCH LONGER!
I GUESS I'LL HAVE TO GO FOR THE KILL!!

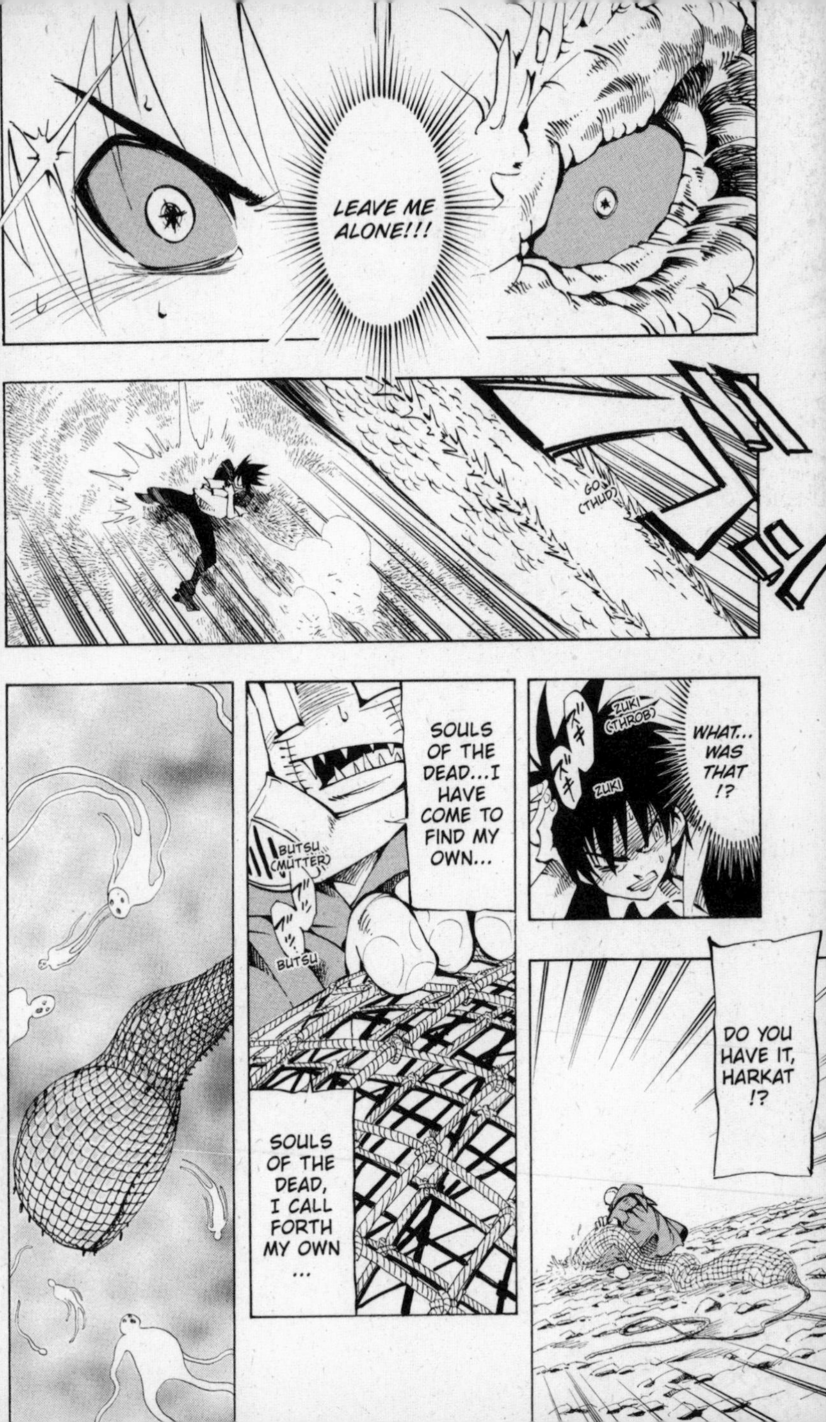
LEAVE ME ALONE!!!
GO (THUD)
ZUKI (THROB)
ZUKI
WHAT... WAS THAT !?
DO YOU HAVE IT, HARKAT !?
SOULS OF THE DEAD...I HAVE COME TO FIND MY OWN...
BUTSU (MUTTER)
BUTSU
SOULS OF THE DEAD, I CALL FORTH MY OWN ...

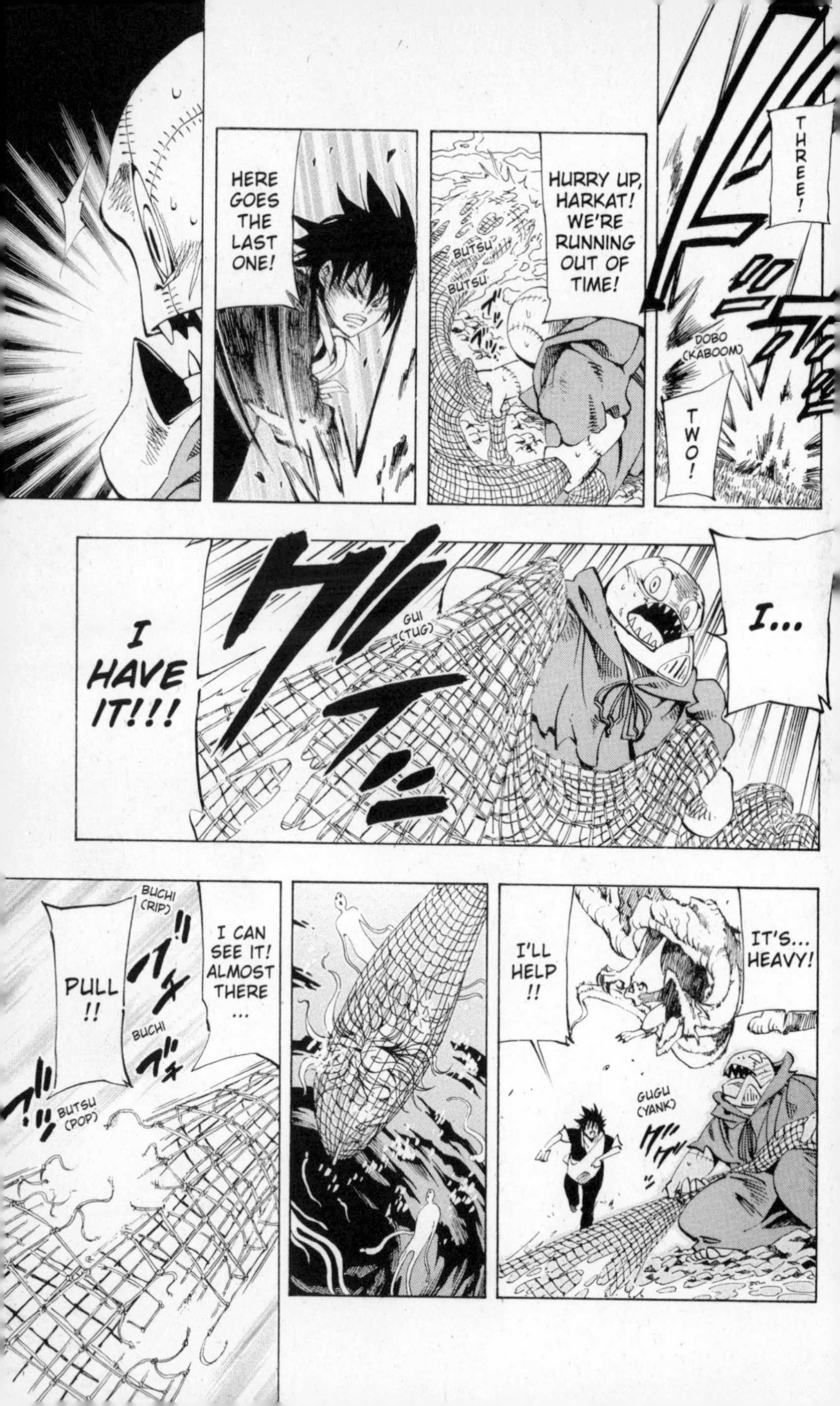
THREE!
DOBO (KABOOM)
TWO!
HURRY UP, HARKAT! WE'RE RUNNING OUT OF TIME!
BUTSU
BUTSU
HERE GOES THE LAST ONE!
I...
GUI (TUG)
I HAVE IT!!!
IT'S... HEAVY!
I'LL HELP !!
GUGU (YANK)
I CAN SEE IT! ALMOST THERE ...
BUCHI (RIP)
BUCHI
PULL !!
BUTSU (POP)

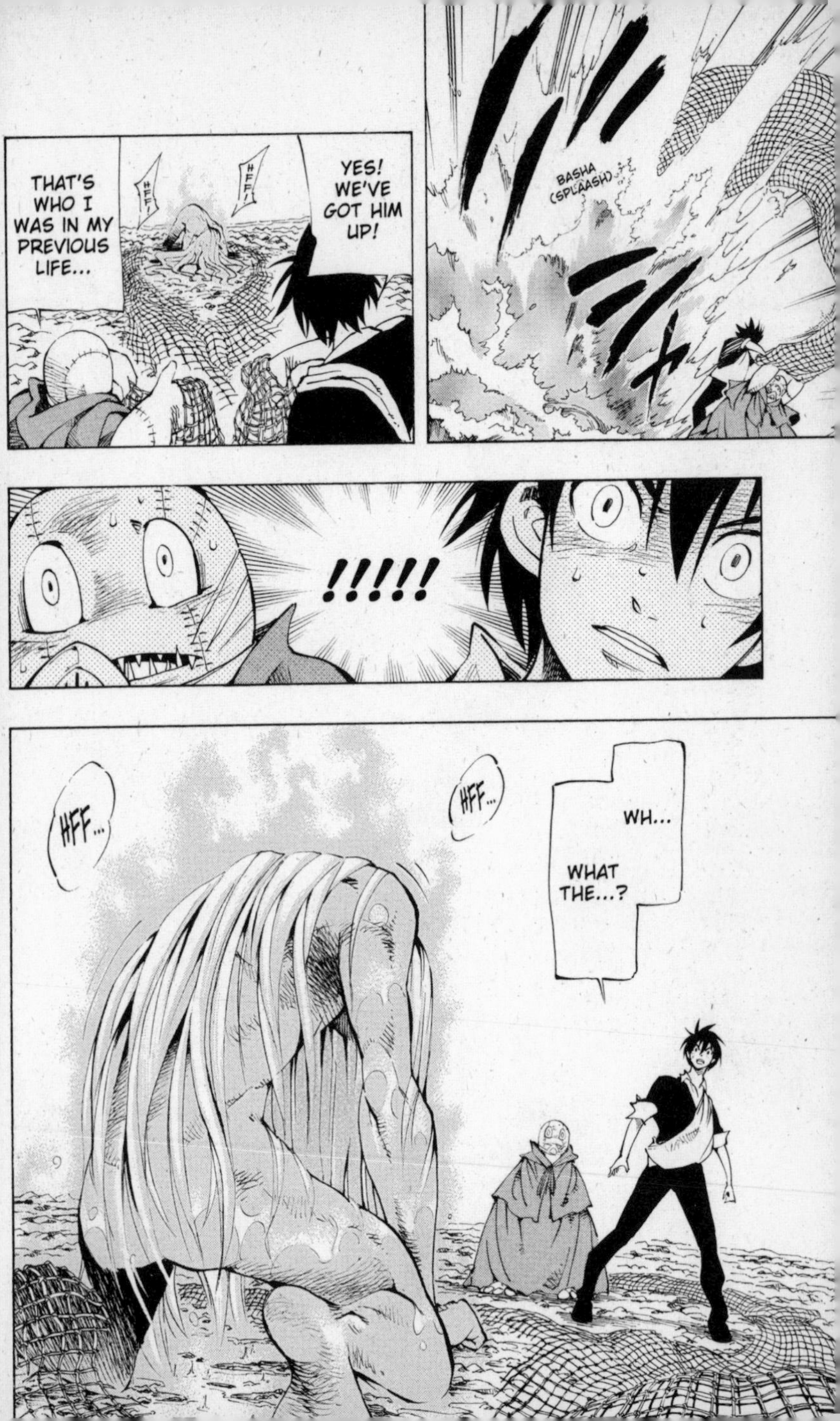
BASHA (SPLAASH)
YES! WE'VE GOT HIM UP!
HFF!
HFF!
THAT'S WHO I WAS IN MY PREVIOUS LIFE...
!!!!!
WH... WHAT THE...?
HFF...
HFF...

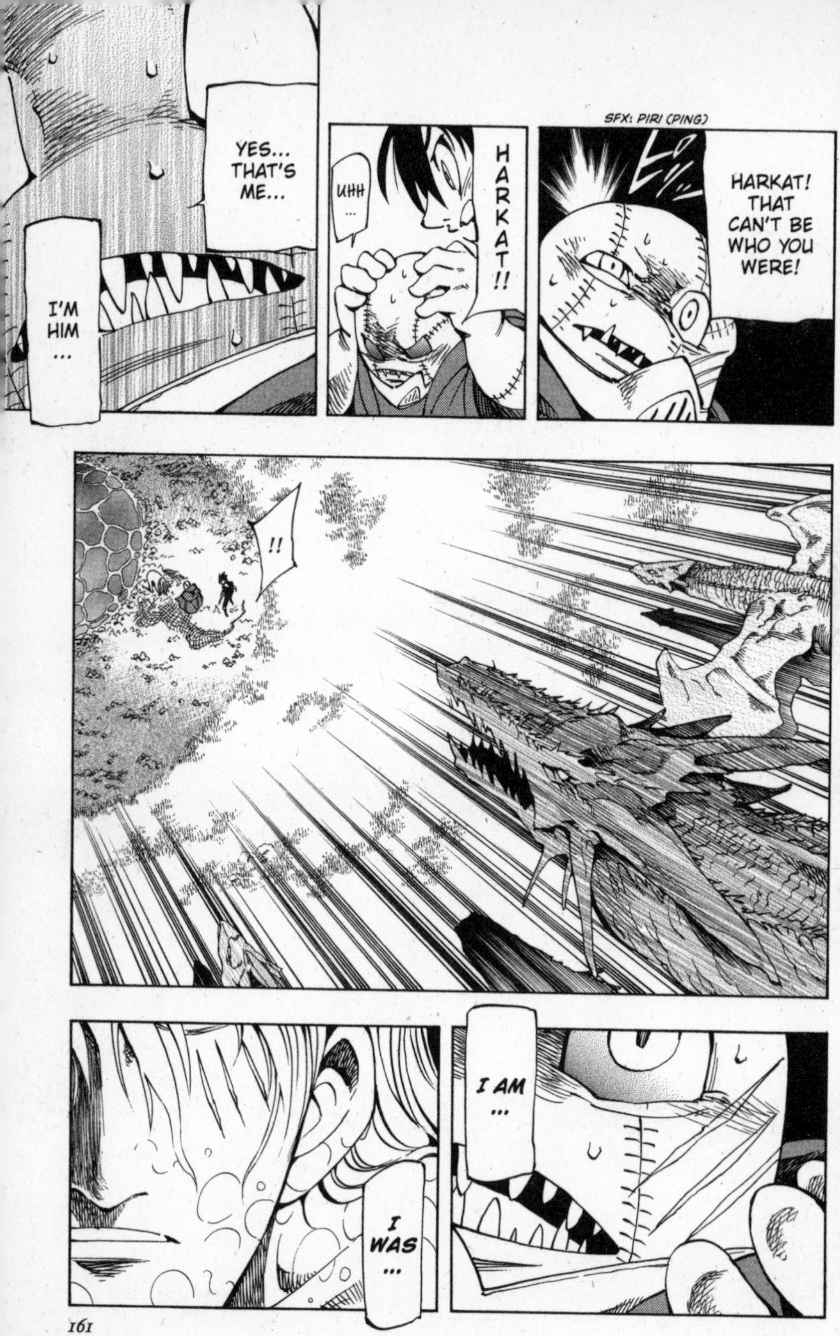
SFX: PIRI (PING)
HARKAT! THAT CAN'T BE WHO YOU WERE!
HARKAT!!
UHH ...
YES... THAT'S ME...
I'M HIM ...
!!
I AM ...
I WAS ...

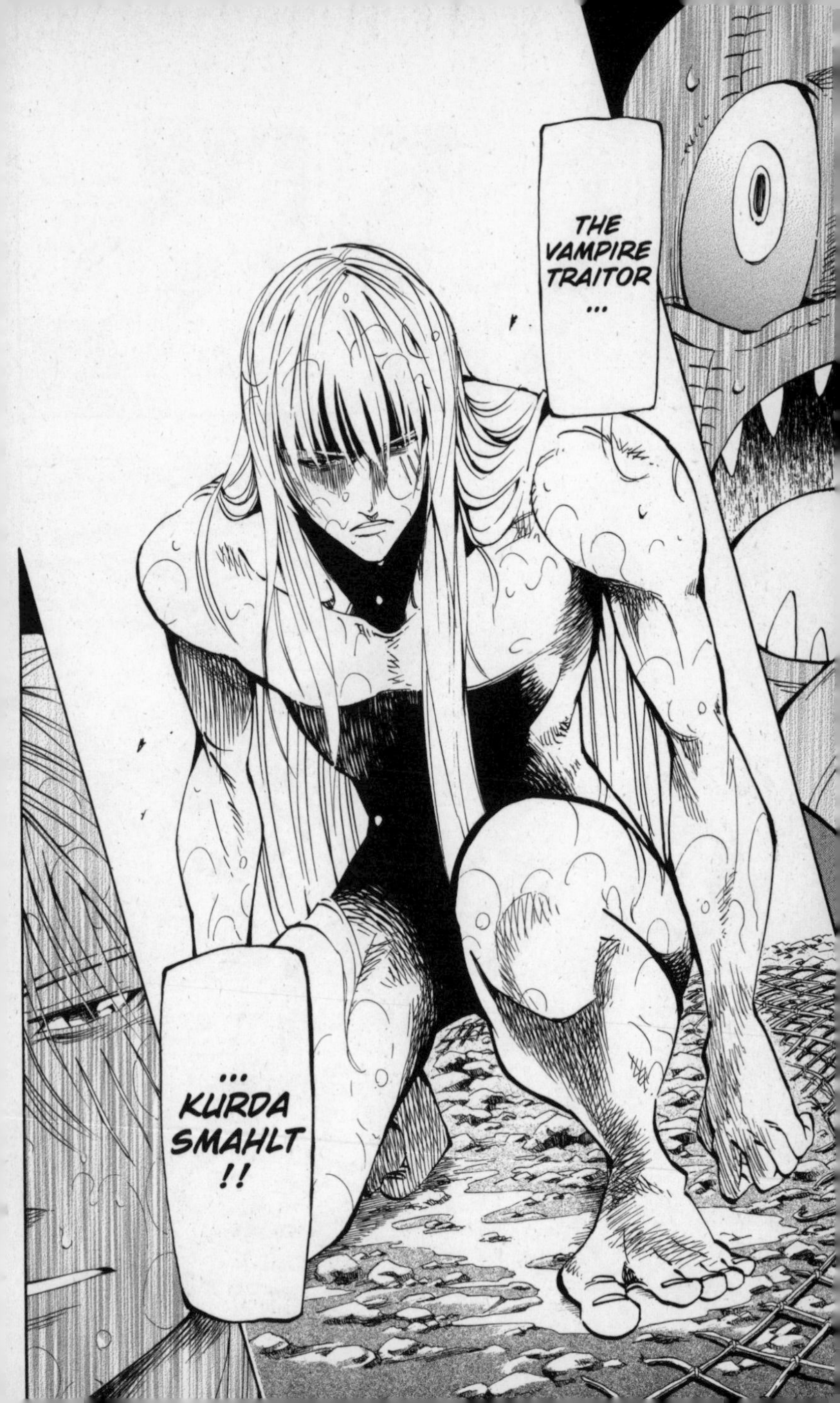
THE VAMPIRE TRAITOR ...
... KURDA SMAHLT !!

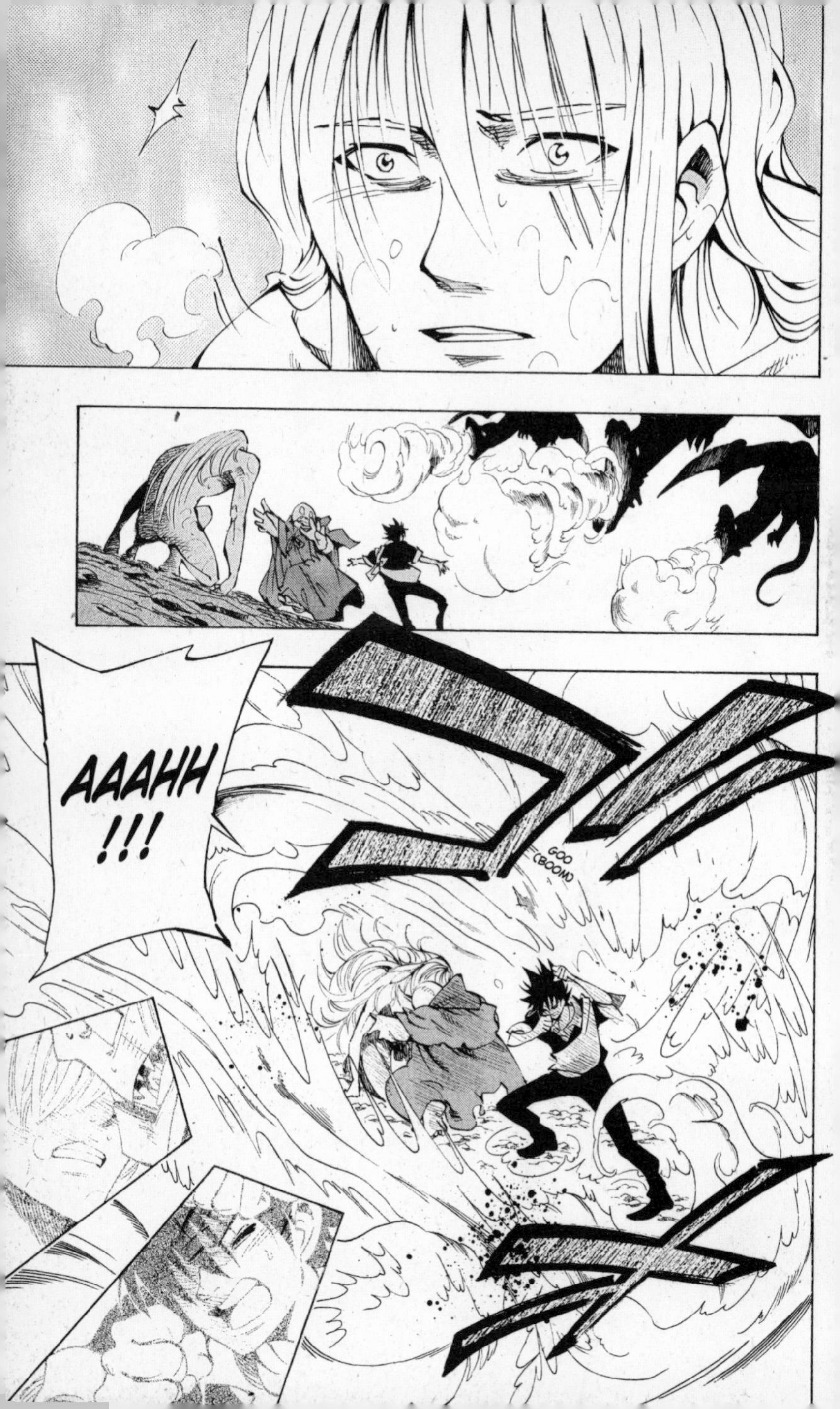
AAAHH
!!!
GOO
(BOOM)

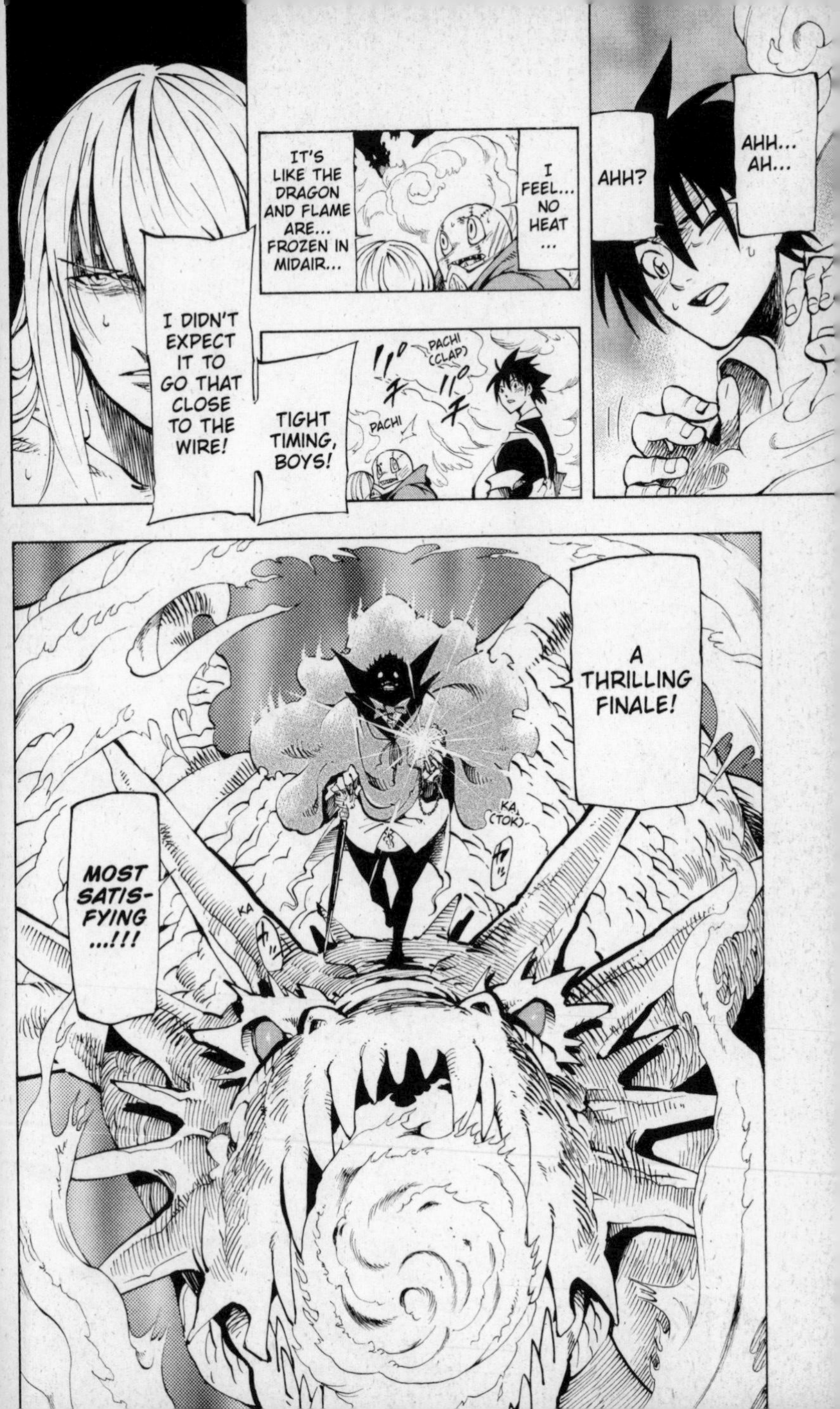
AHH... AH...
AHH?
I FEEL... NO HEAT...
IT'S LIKE THE DRAGON AND FLAME ARE... FROZEN IN MIDAIR...
PACHI (CLAP)
PACHI
TIGHT TIMING, BOYS!
I DIDN'T EXPECT IT TO GO THAT CLOSE TO THE WIRE!
A THRILLING FINALE!
KA (TOK)
KA
MOST SATIS-FYING ...!!!

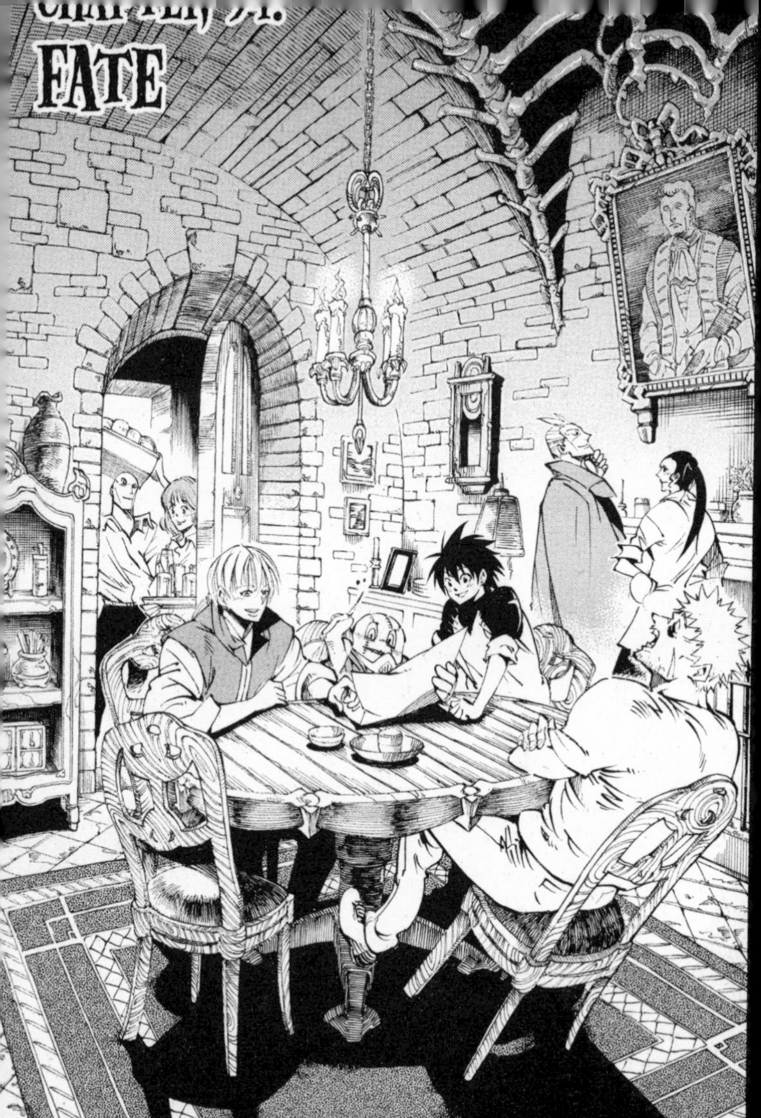
FATE

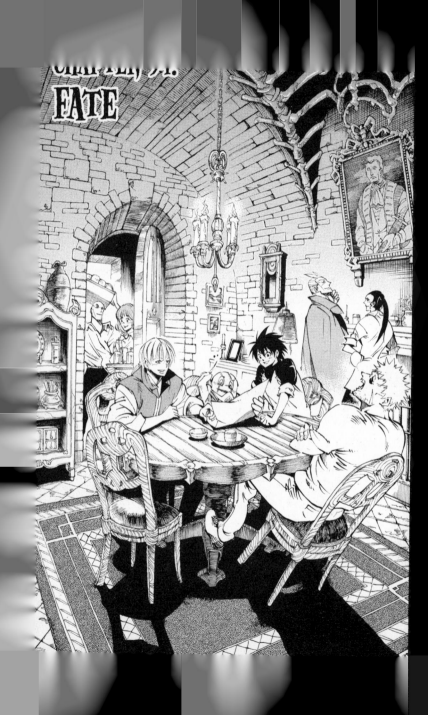

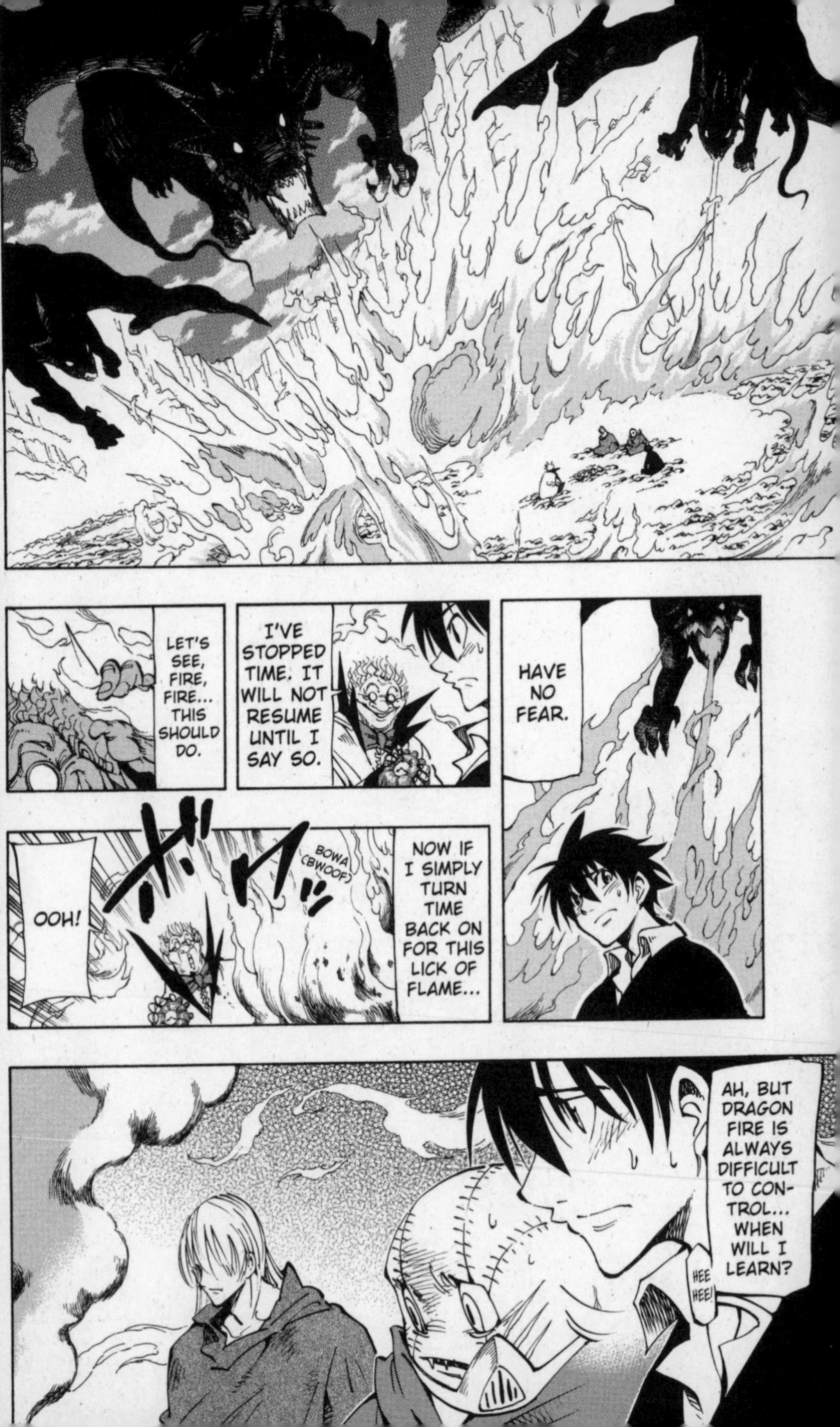
HAVE NO FEAR.
I'VE STOPPED TIME. IT WILL NOT RESUME UNTIL I SAY SO.
LET'S SEE, FIRE, FIRE... THIS SHOULD DO.
NOW IF I SIMPLY TURN TIME BACK ON FOR THIS LICK OF FLAME...
BOWA (BWOOF)
OOH!
AH, BUT DRAGON FIRE IS ALWAYS DIFFICULT TO CON-TROL... WHEN WILL I LEARN?
HEE HEE!

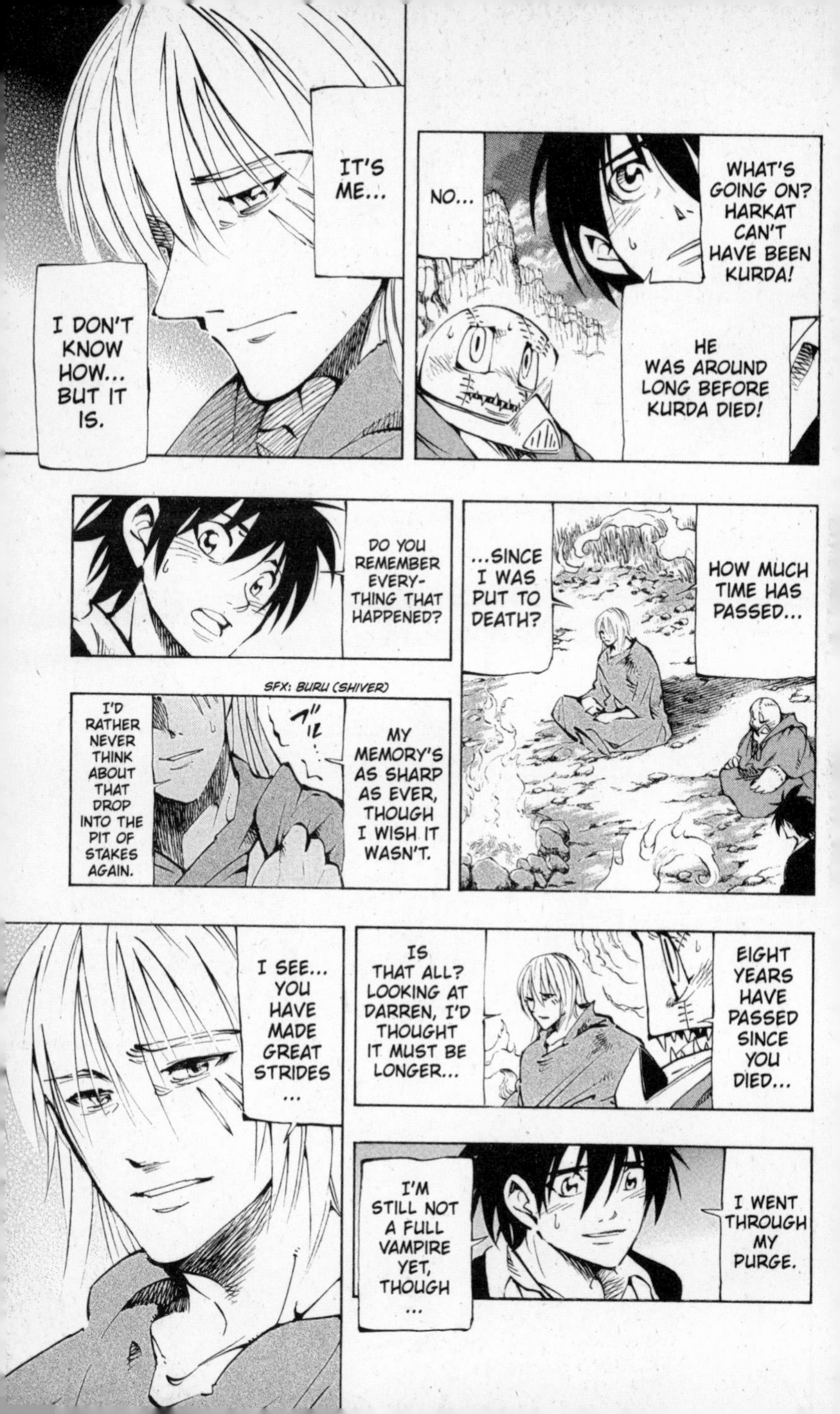
WHAT'S GOING ON? HARKAT CAN'T HAVE BEEN KURDA!
NO...
HE WAS AROUND LONG BEFORE KURDA DIED!
IT'S ME...
I DON'T KNOW HOW... BUT IT IS.
HOW MUCH TIME HAS PASSED...
...SINCE I WAS PUT TO DEATH?
DO YOU REMEMBER EVERY-THING THAT HAPPENED?
SFX: BURU (SHIVER)
MY MEMORY'S AS SHARP AS EVER, THOUGH I WISH IT WASN'T.
I'D RATHER NEVER THINK ABOUT THAT DROP INTO THE PIT OF STAKES AGAIN.
EIGHT YEARS HAVE PASSED SINCE YOU DIED...
IS THAT ALL? LOOKING AT DARREN, I'D THOUGHT IT MUST BE LONGER...
I WENT THROUGH MY PURGE.
I'M STILL NOT A FULL VAMPIRE YET, THOUGH ...
I SEE... YOU HAVE MADE GREAT STRIDES ...

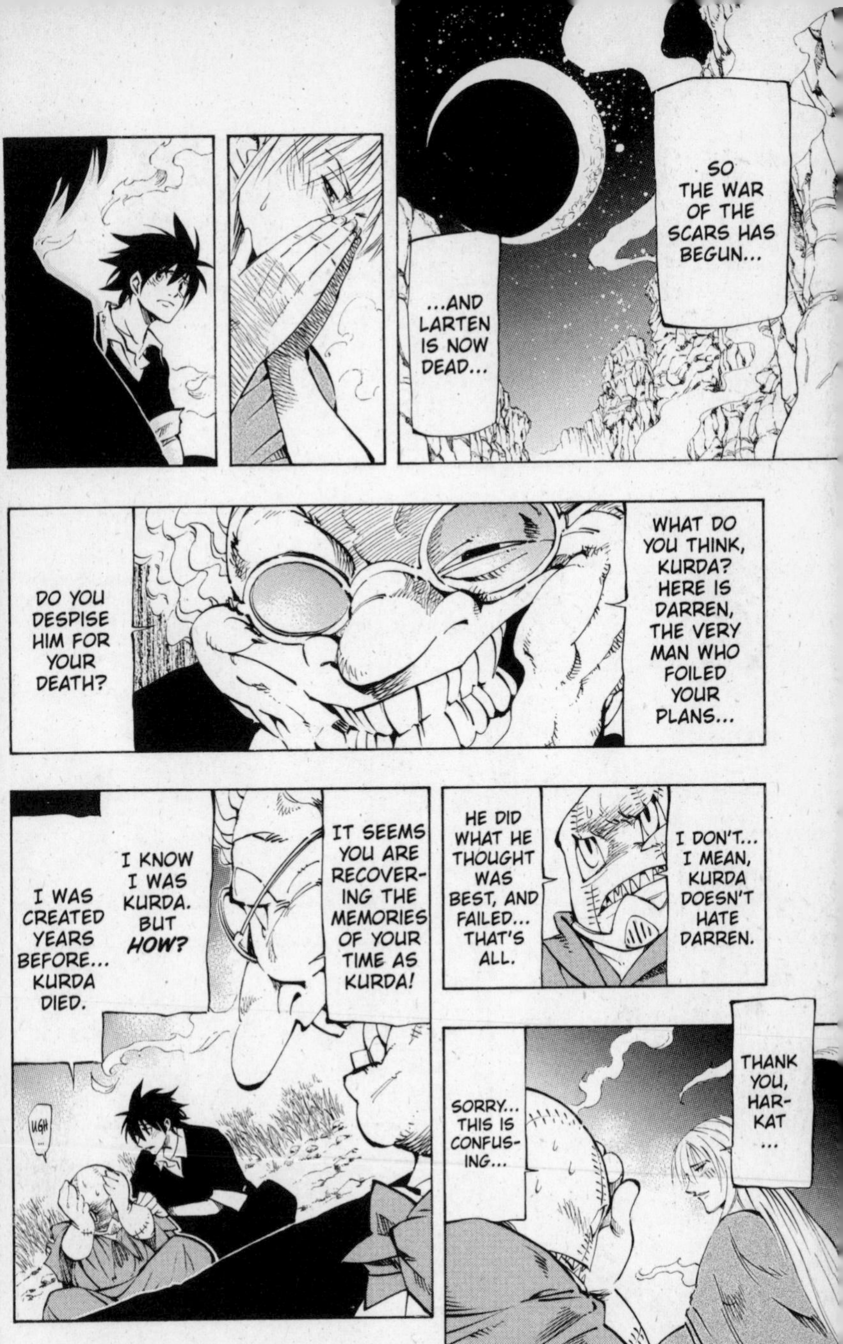
SO THE WAR OF THE SCARS HAS BEGUN...
...AND LARTEN IS NOW DEAD...
WHAT DO YOU THINK, KURDA? HERE IS DARREN, THE VERY MAN WHO FOILED YOUR PLANS...
DO YOU DESPISE HIM FOR YOUR DEATH?
I DON'T... I MEAN, KURDA DOESN'T HATE DARREN.
HE DID WHAT HE THOUGHT WAS BEST, AND FAILED... THAT'S ALL.
THANK YOU, HAR-KAT...
SORRY... THIS IS CONFUS-ING...
IT SEEMS YOU ARE RECOVER-ING THE MEMORIES OF YOUR TIME AS KURDA!
I KNOW I WAS KURDA. BUT *HOW?*
I WAS CREATED YEARS BEFORE... KURDA DIED.
UGH...

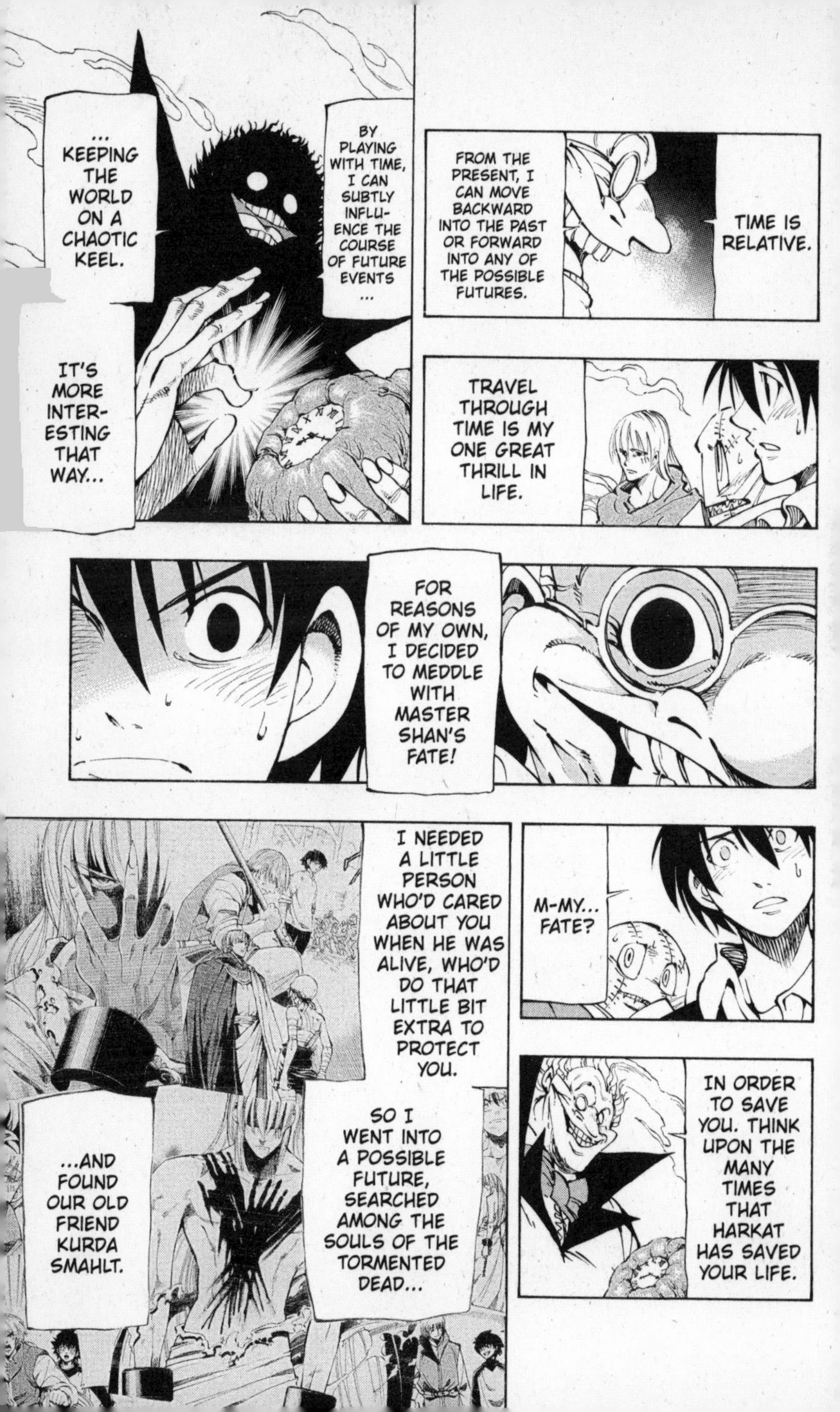
TIME IS RELATIVE.
FROM THE PRESENT, I CAN MOVE BACKWARD INTO THE PAST OR FORWARD INTO ANY OF THE POSSIBLE FUTURES.
TRAVEL THROUGH TIME IS MY ONE GREAT THRILL IN LIFE.
BY PLAYING WITH TIME, I CAN SUBTLY INFLU-ENCE THE COURSE OF FUTURE EVENTS ...
... KEEPING THE WORLD ON A CHAOTIC KEEL.
IT'S MORE INTER-ESTING THAT WAY...
FOR REASONS OF MY OWN, I DECIDED TO MEDDLE WITH MASTER SHAN'S FATE!
M-MY... FATE?
IN ORDER TO SAVE YOU. THINK UPON THE MANY TIMES THAT HARKAT HAS SAVED YOUR LIFE.
I NEEDED A LITTLE PERSON WHO'D CARED ABOUT YOU WHEN HE WAS ALIVE, WHO'D DO THAT LITTLE BIT EXTRA TO PROTECT YOU.
SO I WENT INTO A POSSIBLE FUTURE, SEARCHED AMONG THE SOULS OF THE TORMENTED DEAD...
...AND FOUND OUR OLD FRIEND KURDA SMAHLT.

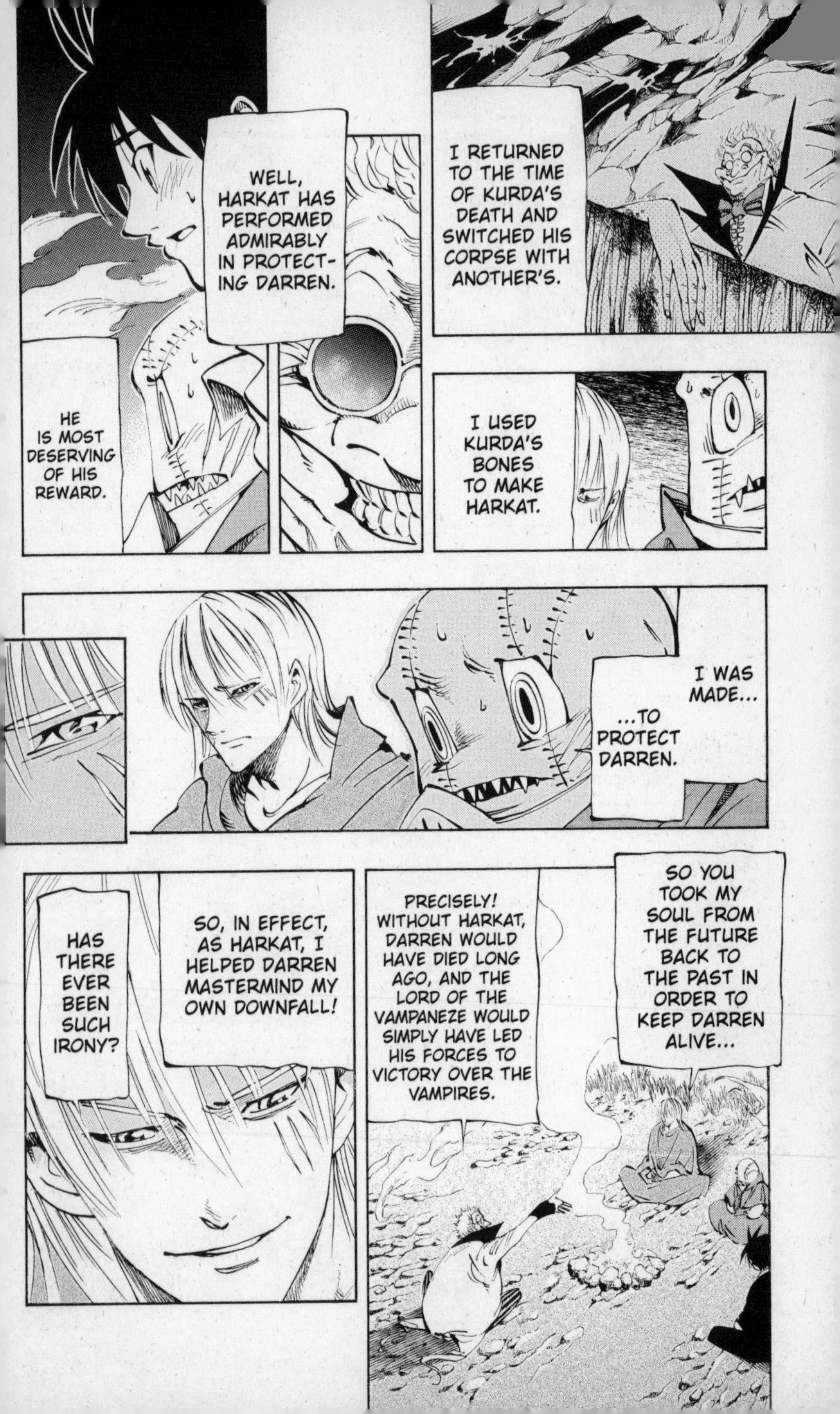

I RETURNED TO THE TIME OF KURDA'S DEATH AND SWITCHED HIS CORPSE WITH ANOTHER'S.
WELL, HARKAT HAS PERFORMED ADMIRABLY IN PROTECTING DARREN.
I USED KURDA'S BONES TO MAKE HARKAT.
HE IS MOST DESERVING OF HIS REWARD.
I WAS MADE...
...TO PROTECT DARREN.
SO YOU TOOK MY SOUL FROM THE FUTURE BACK TO THE PAST IN ORDER TO KEEP DARREN ALIVE...
PRECISELY! WITHOUT HARKAT, DARREN WOULD HAVE DIED LONG AGO, AND THE LORD OF THE VAMPANEZE WOULD SIMPLY HAVE LED HIS FORCES TO VICTORY OVER THE VAMPIRES.
SO, IN EFFECT, AS HARKAT, I HELPED DARREN MASTERMIND MY OWN DOWNFALL!
HAS THERE EVER BEEN SUCH IRONY?

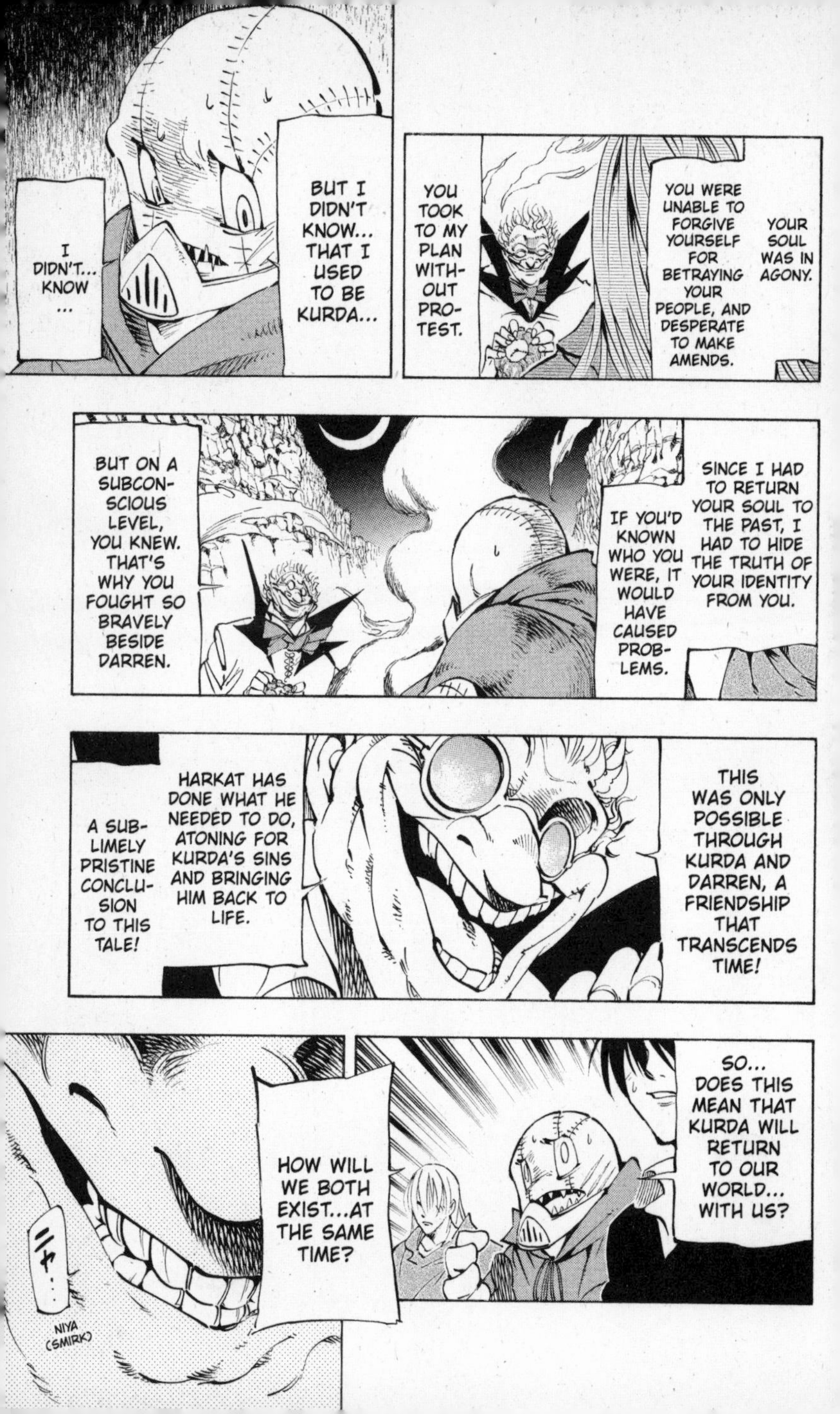
YOUR SOUL WAS IN AGONY.
YOU WERE UNABLE TO FORGIVE YOURSELF FOR BETRAYING YOUR PEOPLE, AND DESPERATE TO MAKE AMENDS.
YOU TOOK TO MY PLAN WITHOUT PROTEST.
BUT I DIDN'T KNOW... THAT I USED TO BE KURDA...
I DIDN'T... KNOW ...
SINCE I HAD TO RETURN YOUR SOUL TO THE PAST, I HAD TO HIDE THE TRUTH OF YOUR IDENTITY FROM YOU.
IF YOU'D KNOWN WHO YOU WERE, IT WOULD HAVE CAUSED PROBLEMS.
BUT ON A SUBCONSCIOUS LEVEL, YOU KNEW. THAT'S WHY YOU FOUGHT SO BRAVELY BESIDE DARREN.
THIS WAS ONLY POSSIBLE THROUGH KURDA AND DARREN, A FRIENDSHIP THAT TRANSCENDS TIME!
HARKAT HAS DONE WHAT HE NEEDED TO DO, ATONING FOR KURDA'S SINS AND BRINGING HIM BACK TO LIFE.
A SUBLIMELY PRISTINE CONCLUSION TO THIS TALE!
SO... DOES THIS MEAN THAT KURDA WILL RETURN TO OUR WORLD... WITH US?
HOW WILL WE BOTH EXIST...AT THE SAME TIME?
ニヤ・・・
NIYA (SMIRK)

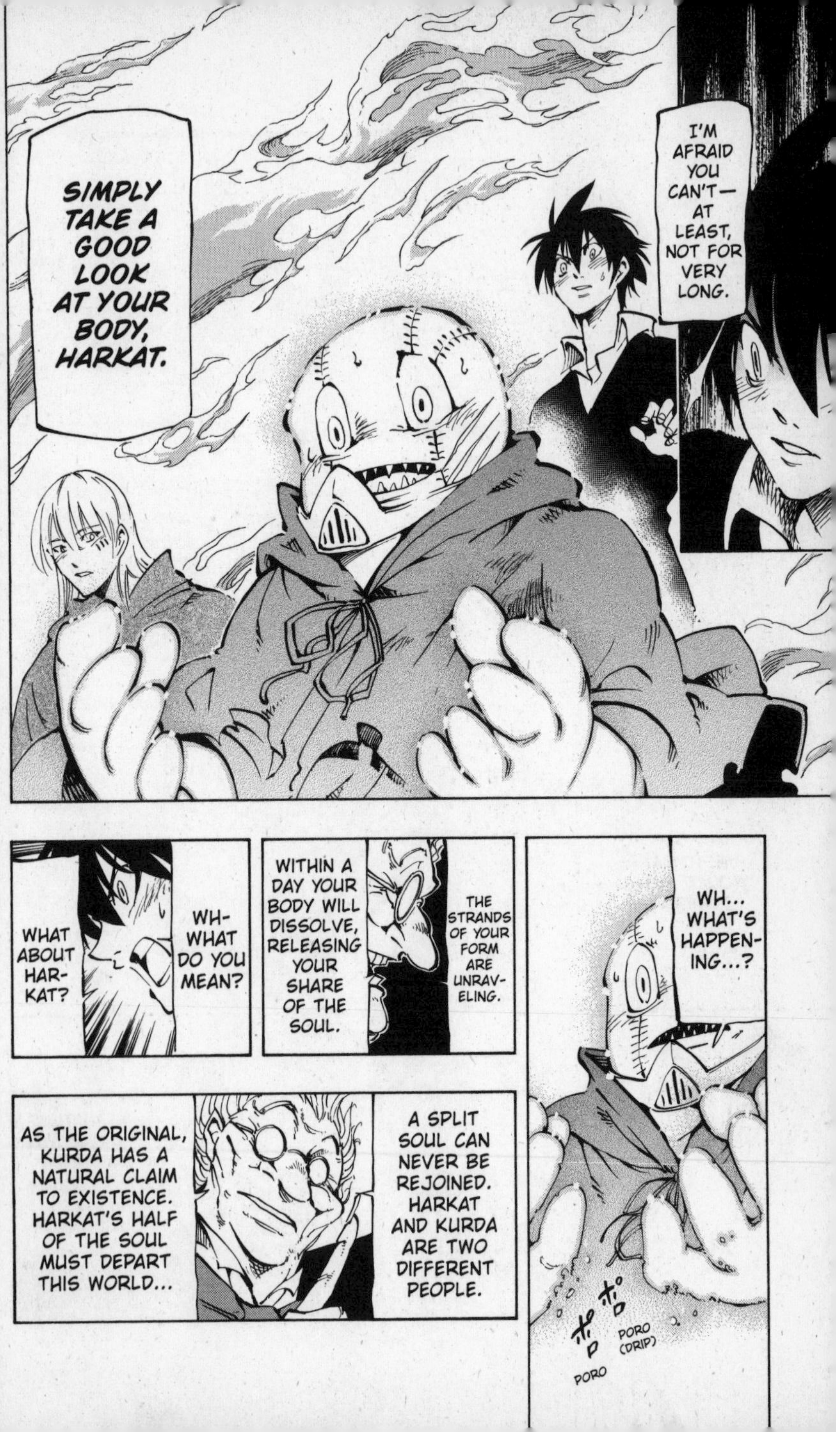
I'M AFRAID YOU CAN'T— AT LEAST, NOT FOR VERY LONG.
SIMPLY TAKE A GOOD LOOK AT YOUR BODY, HARKAT.
WH... WHAT'S HAPPEN-ING...?
PORO
PORO (DRIP)
WH-WHAT DO YOU MEAN?
WHAT ABOUT HAR-KAT?
THE STRANDS OF YOUR FORM ARE UNRAV-ELING.
WITHIN A DAY YOUR BODY WILL DISSOLVE, RELEASING YOUR SHARE OF THE SOUL.
A SPLIT SOUL CAN NEVER BE REJOINED. HARKAT AND KURDA ARE TWO DIFFERENT PEOPLE.
AS THE ORIGINAL, KURDA HAS A NATURAL CLAIM TO EXISTENCE. HARKAT'S HALF OF THE SOUL MUST DEPART THIS WORLD...

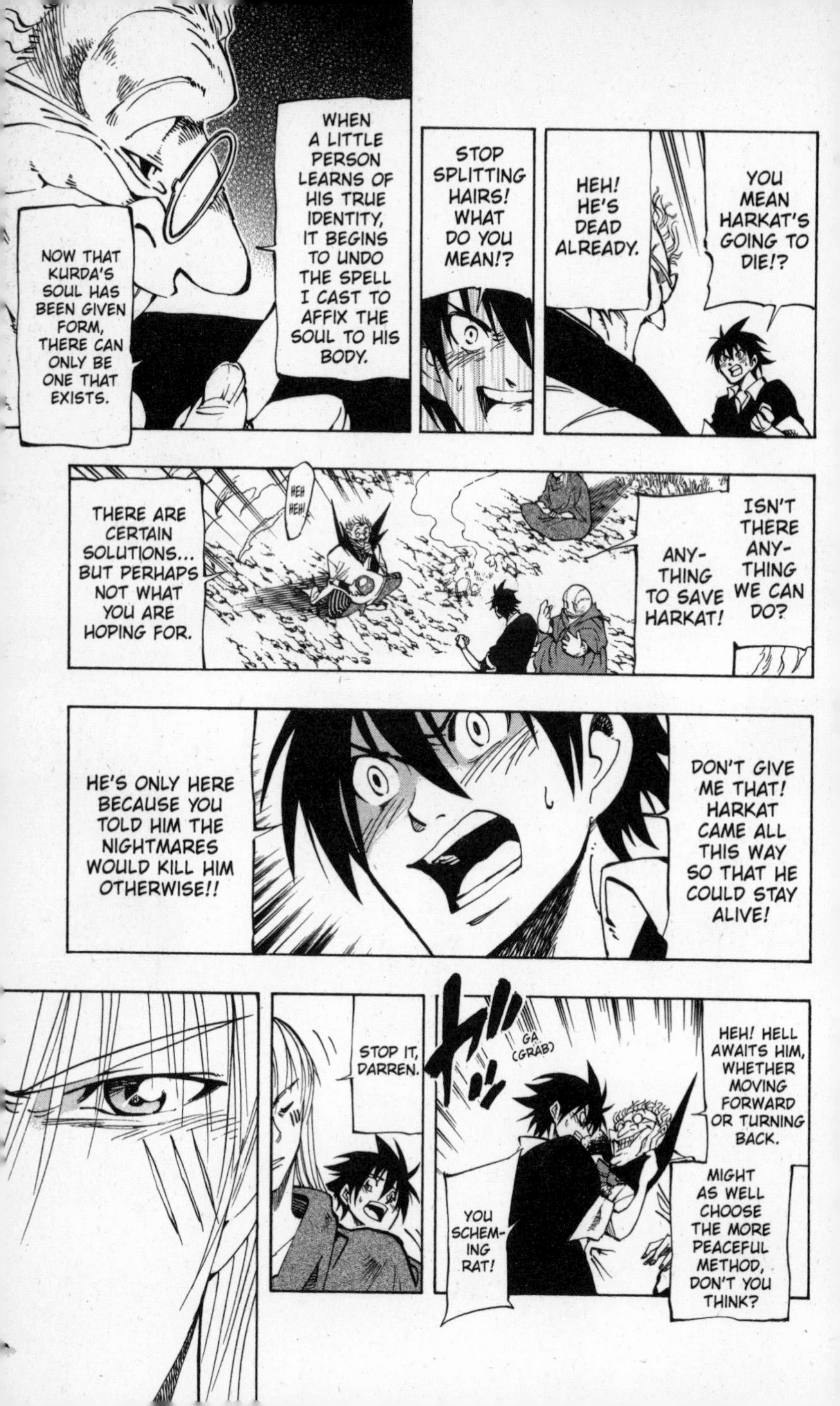
YOU MEAN HARKAT'S GOING TO DIE!?
HEH! HE'S DEAD ALREADY.
STOP SPLITTING HAIRS! WHAT DO YOU MEAN!?
WHEN A LITTLE PERSON LEARNS OF HIS TRUE IDENTITY, IT BEGINS TO UNDO THE SPELL I CAST TO AFFIX THE SOUL TO HIS BODY.
NOW THAT KURDA'S SOUL HAS BEEN GIVEN FORM, THERE CAN ONLY BE ONE THAT EXISTS.
ISN'T THERE ANYTHING WE CAN DO?
ANYTHING TO SAVE HARKAT!
HEH HEH!
THERE ARE CERTAIN SOLUTIONS... BUT PERHAPS NOT WHAT YOU ARE HOPING FOR.
DON'T GIVE ME THAT! HARKAT CAME ALL THIS WAY SO THAT HE COULD STAY ALIVE!
HE'S ONLY HERE BECAUSE YOU TOLD HIM THE NIGHTMARES WOULD KILL HIM OTHERWISE!!
HEH! HELL AWAITS HIM, WHETHER MOVING FORWARD OR TURNING BACK.
GA (GRAB)
MIGHT AS WELL CHOOSE THE MORE PEACEFUL METHOD, DON'T YOU THINK?
YOU SCHEM-ING RAT!
STOP IT, DARREN.

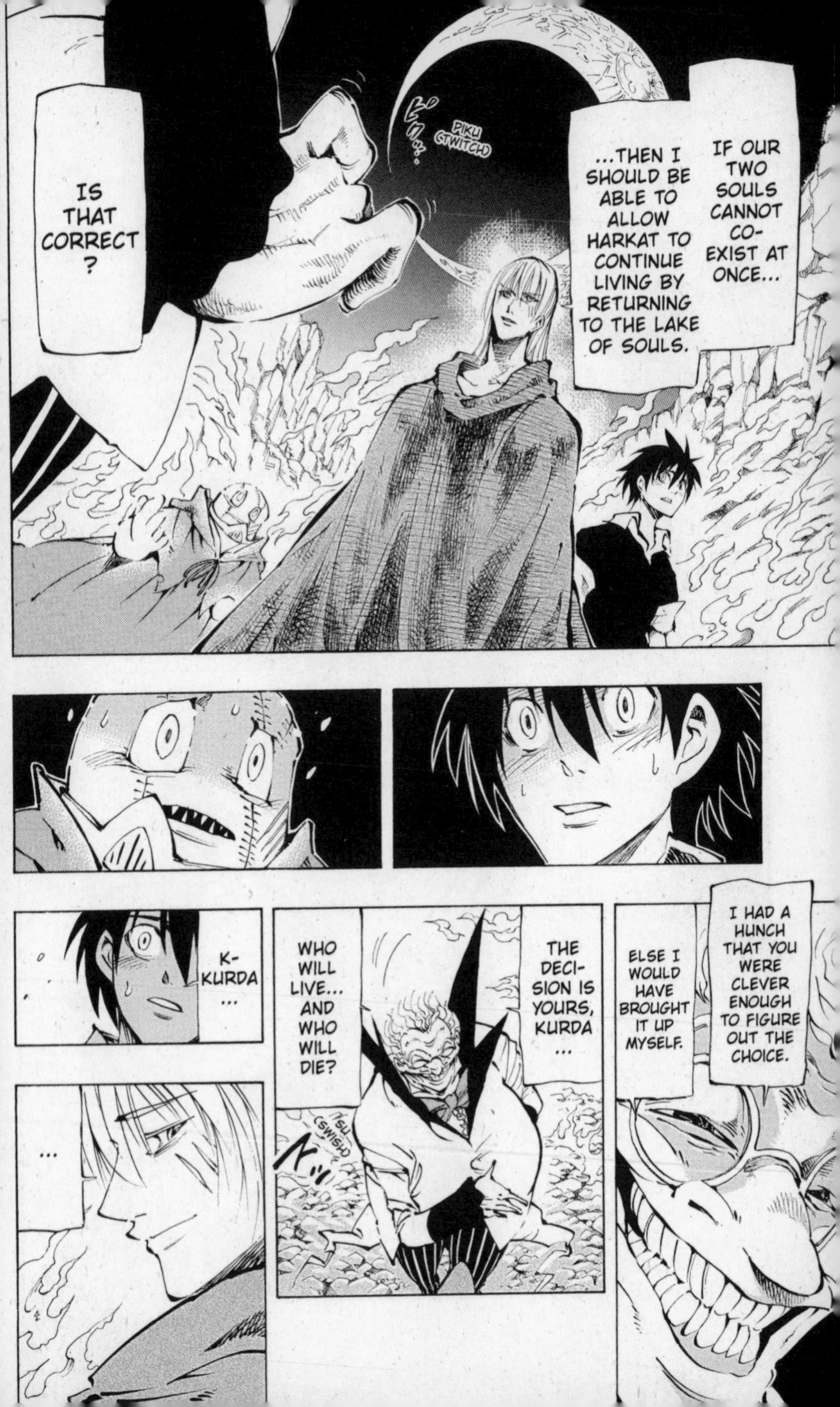
IF OUR TWO SOULS CANNOT CO-EXIST AT ONCE...
...THEN I SHOULD BE ABLE TO ALLOW HARKAT TO CONTINUE LIVING BY RETURNING TO THE LAKE OF SOULS.
PIKU (TWITCH)
IS THAT CORRECT?
I HAD A HUNCH THAT YOU WERE CLEVER ENOUGH TO FIGURE OUT THE CHOICE.
ELSE I WOULD HAVE BROUGHT IT UP MYSELF.
THE DECISION IS YOURS, KURDA...
WHO WILL LIVE... AND WHO WILL DIE?
TSU (SWISH)
K-KURDA...
...

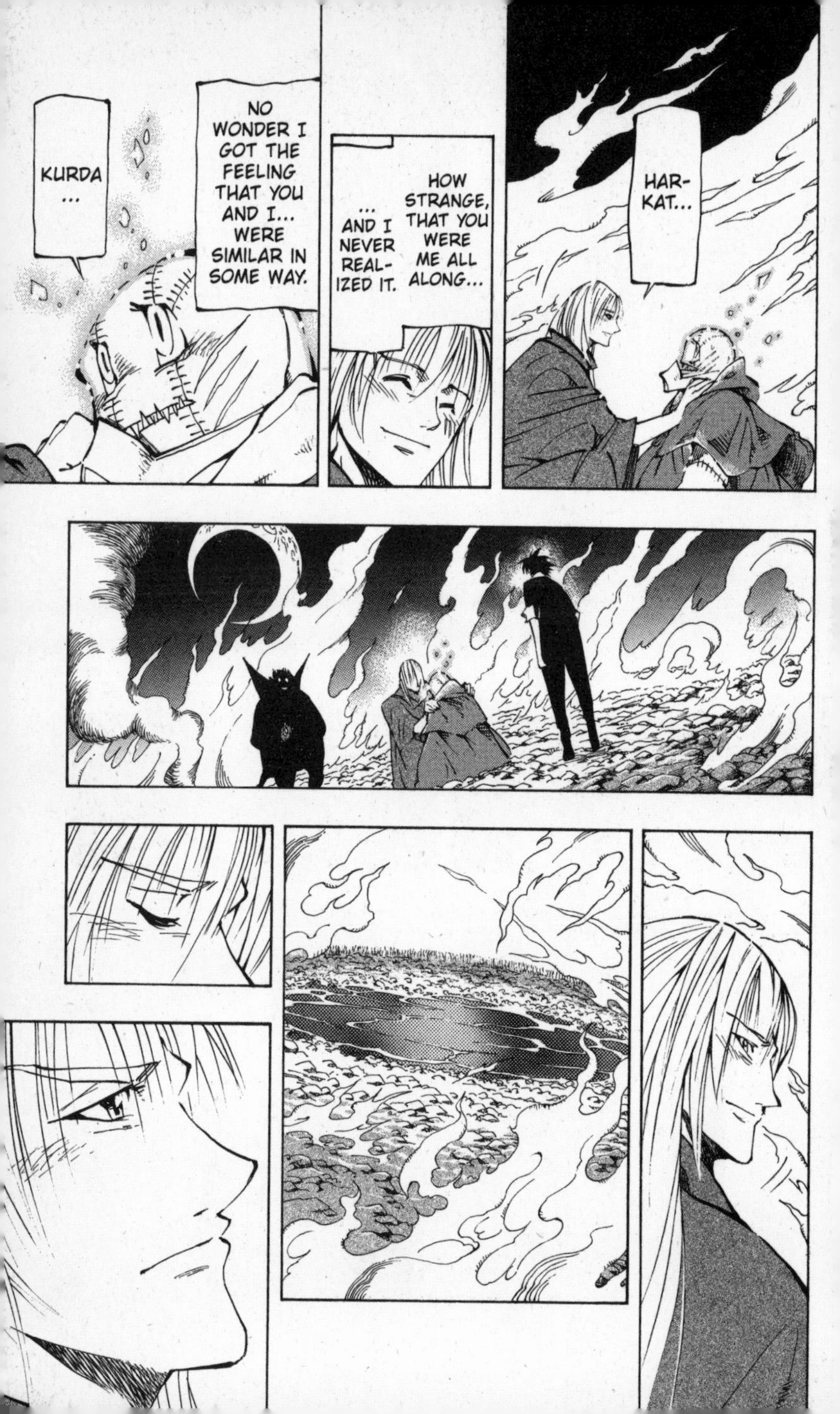
HAR-KAT...
HOW STRANGE, THAT YOU WERE ME ALL ALONG...
... AND I NEVER REAL-IZED IT.
NO WONDER I GOT THE FEELING THAT YOU AND I... WERE SIMILAR IN SOME WAY.
KURDA ...

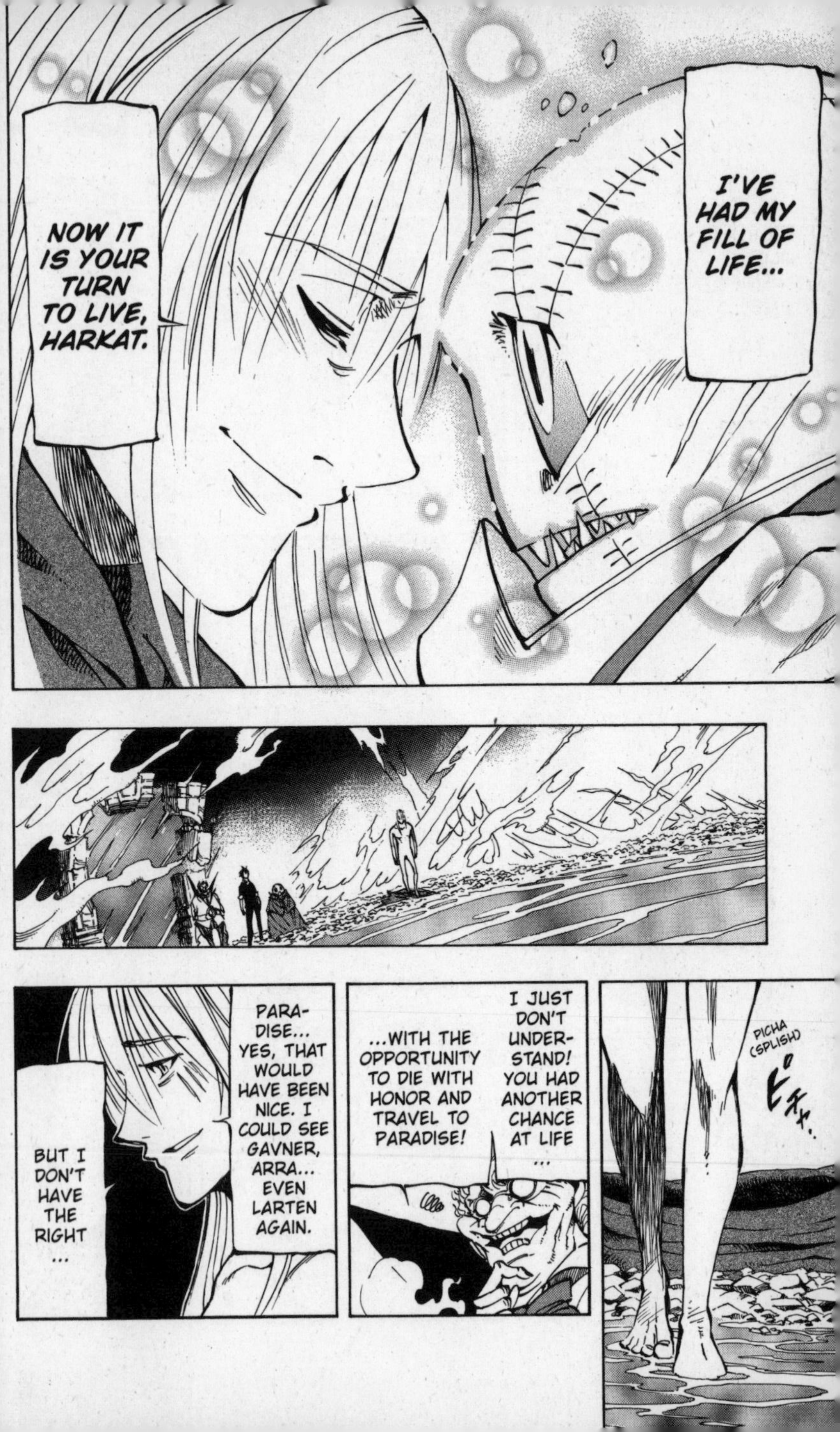
I'VE HAD MY FILL OF LIFE...
NOW IT IS YOUR TURN TO LIVE, HARKAT.
PICHA (SPLISH)
ピチャ..
I JUST DON'T UNDER-STAND! YOU HAD ANOTHER CHANCE AT LIFE...
...WITH THE OPPORTUNITY TO DIE WITH HONOR AND TRAVEL TO PARADISE!
PARA-DISE... YES, THAT WOULD HAVE BEEN NICE. I COULD SEE GAVNER, ARRA... EVEN LARTEN AGAIN.
BUT I DON'T HAVE THE RIGHT...

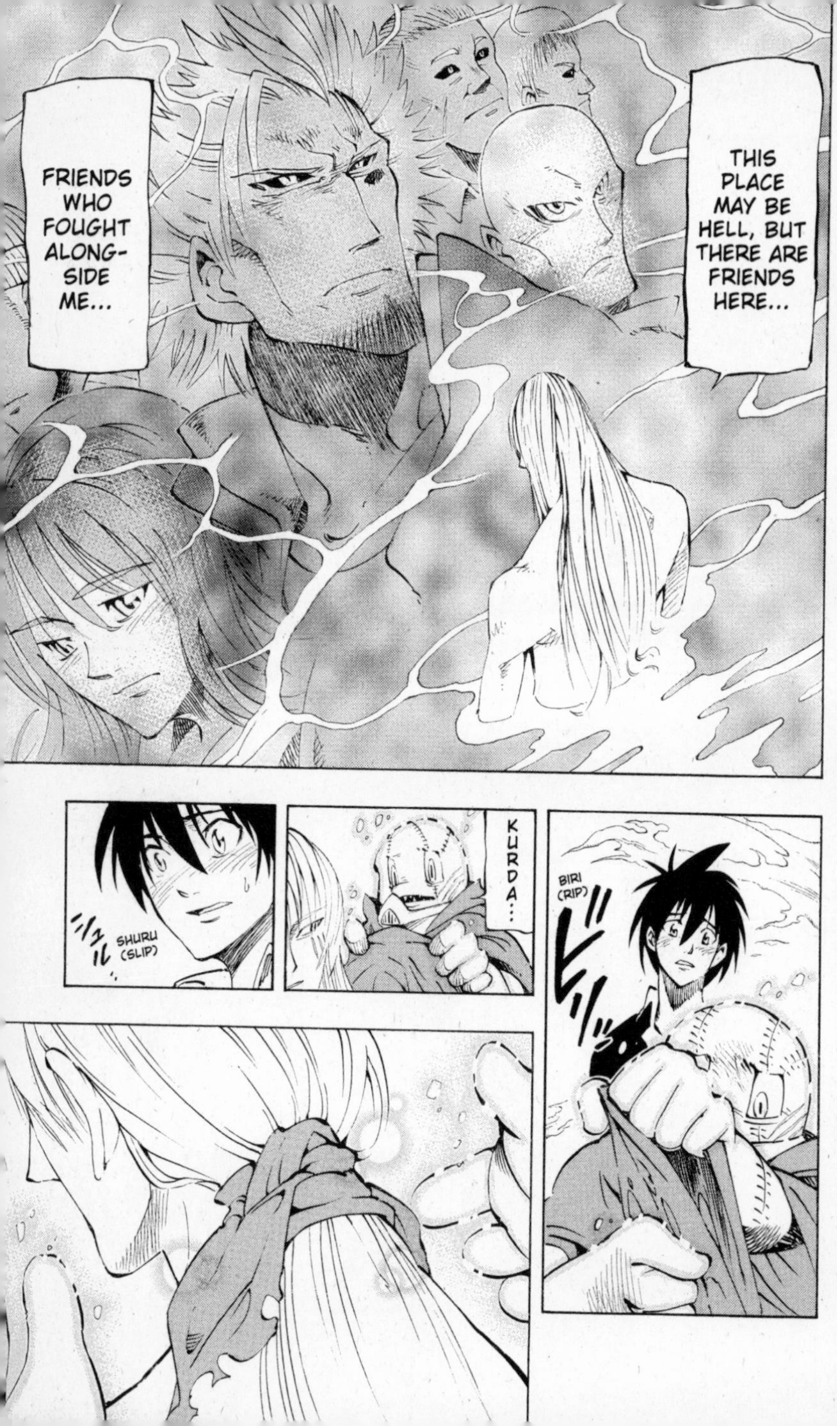
THIS PLACE MAY BE HELL, BUT THERE ARE FRIENDS HERE...
FRIENDS WHO FOUGHT ALONG-SIDE ME...
BIRI (RIP)
KURDA...
SHURU (SLIP)

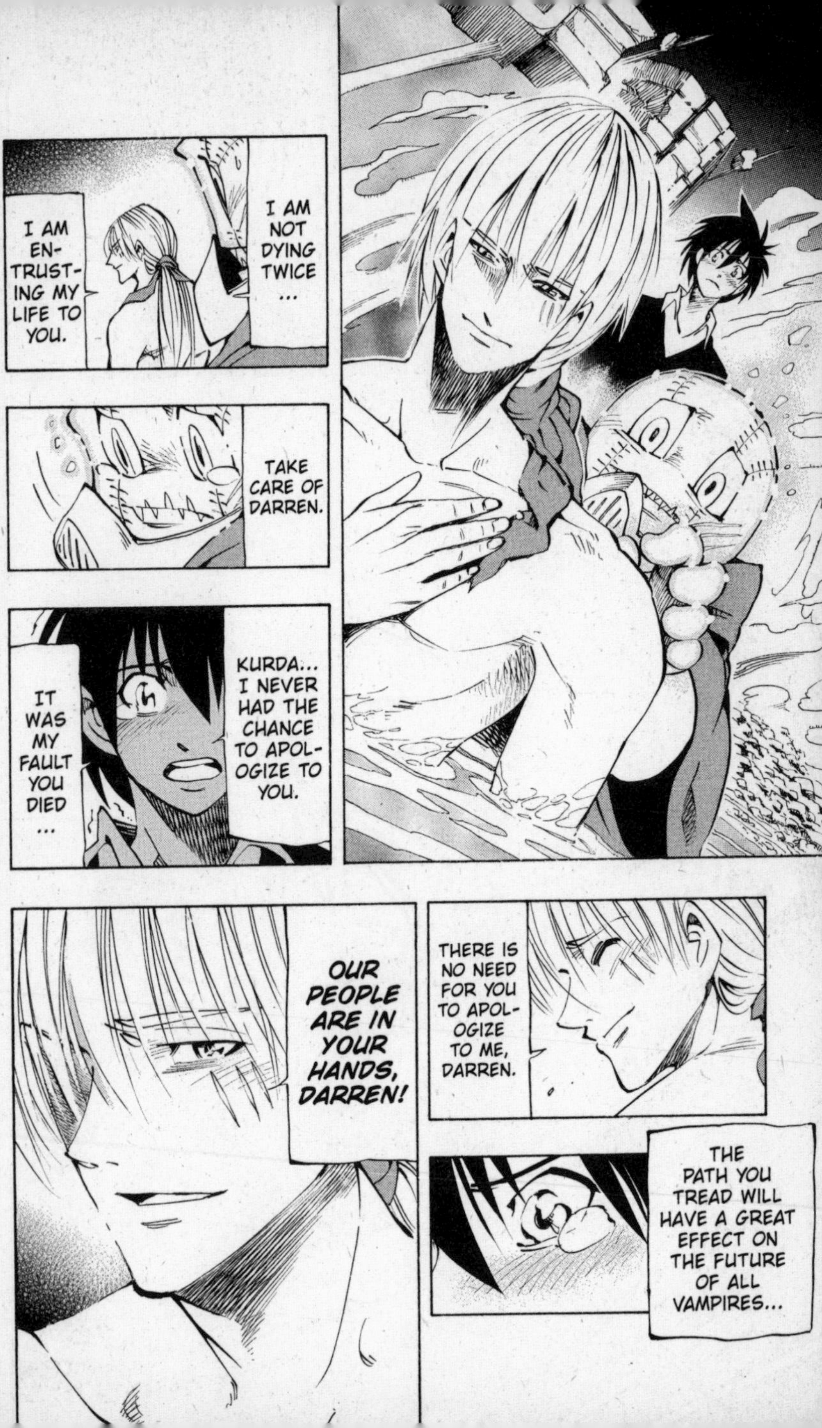
I AM NOT DYING TWICE ...
I AM EN-TRUST-ING MY LIFE TO YOU.
TAKE CARE OF DARREN.
KURDA... I NEVER HAD THE CHANCE TO APOL-OGIZE TO YOU.
IT WAS MY FAULT YOU DIED ...
THERE IS NO NEED FOR YOU TO APOL-OGIZE TO ME, DARREN.
THE PATH YOU TREAD WILL HAVE A GREAT EFFECT ON THE FUTURE OF ALL VAMPIRES...
OUR PEOPLE ARE IN YOUR HANDS, DARREN!

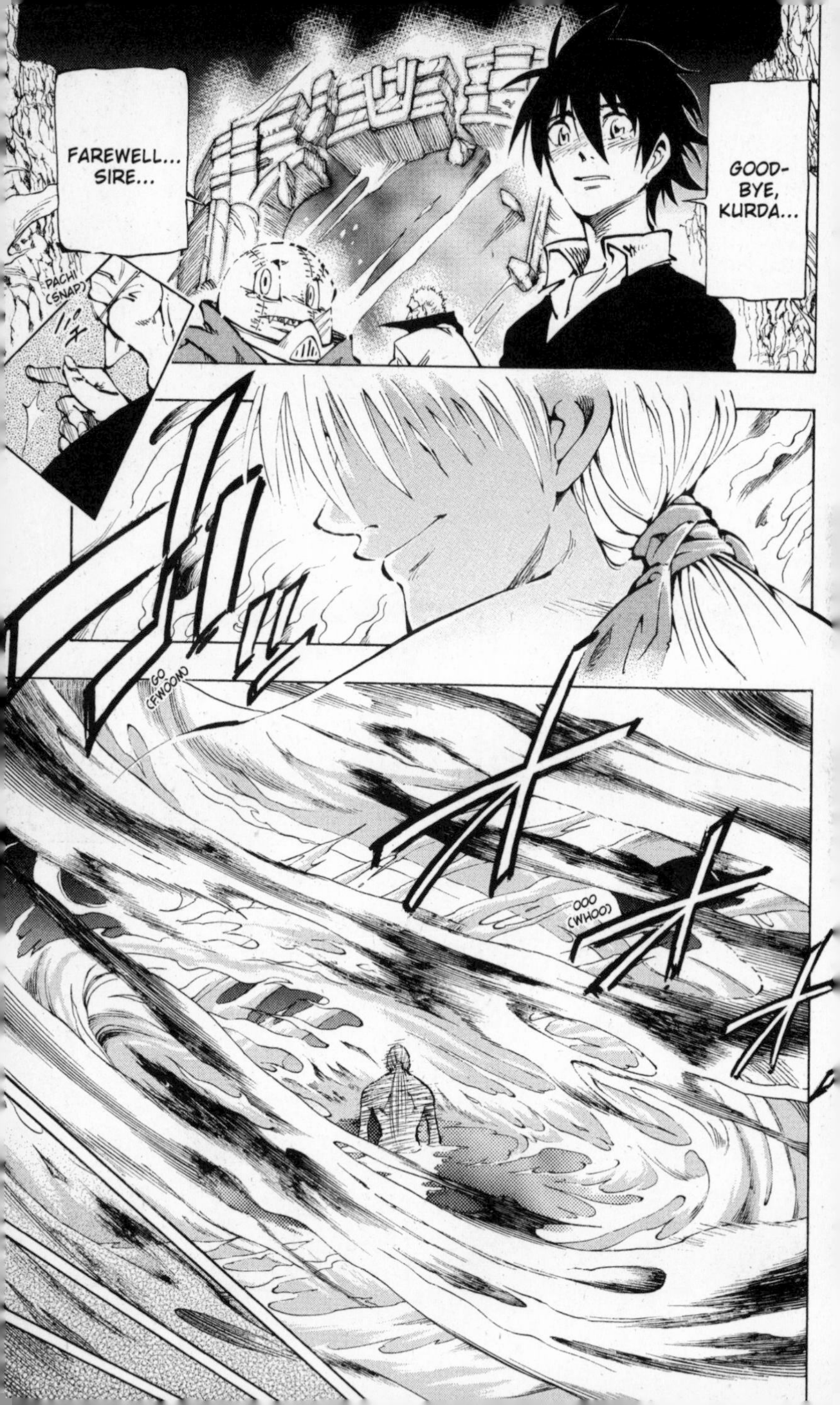
GOOD-BYE, KURDA...
FAREWELL... SIRE...
PACHI (SNAP)
GO (FWOOM)
OOO (WHOO)

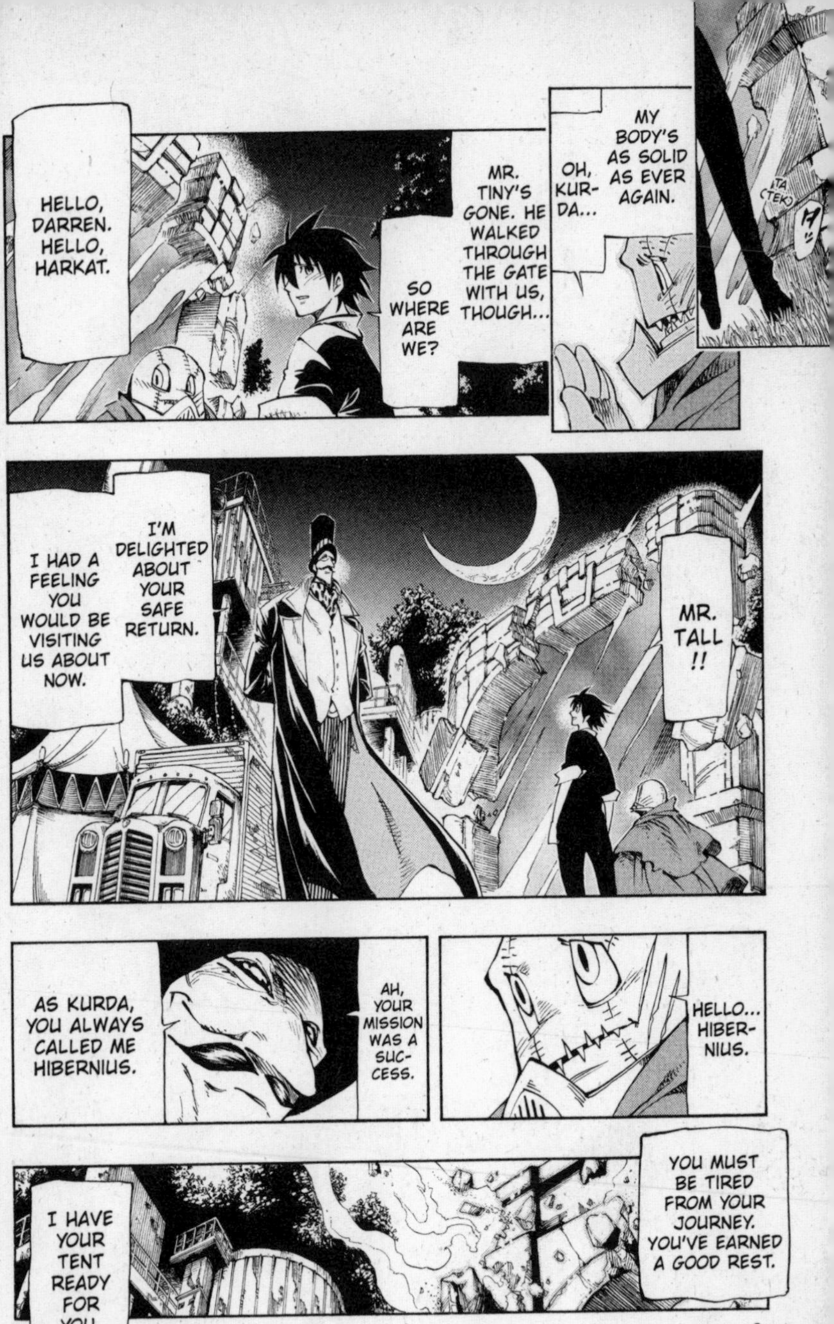
TA (TEK)
MY BODY'S AS SOLID AS EVER AGAIN.
OH, KUR-DA...
MR. TINY'S GONE. HE WALKED THROUGH THE GATE WITH US, THOUGH...
SO WHERE ARE WE?
HELLO, DARREN. HELLO, HARKAT.
MR. TALL!!
I'M DELIGHTED ABOUT YOUR SAFE RETURN.
I HAD A FEELING YOU WOULD BE VISITING US ABOUT NOW.
HELLO... HIBER-NIUS.
AH, YOUR MISSION WAS A SUC-CESS.
AS KURDA, YOU ALWAYS CALLED ME HIBERNIUS.
YOU MUST BE TIRED FROM YOUR JOURNEY. YOU'VE EARNED A GOOD REST.
I HAVE YOUR TENT READY FOR YOU.

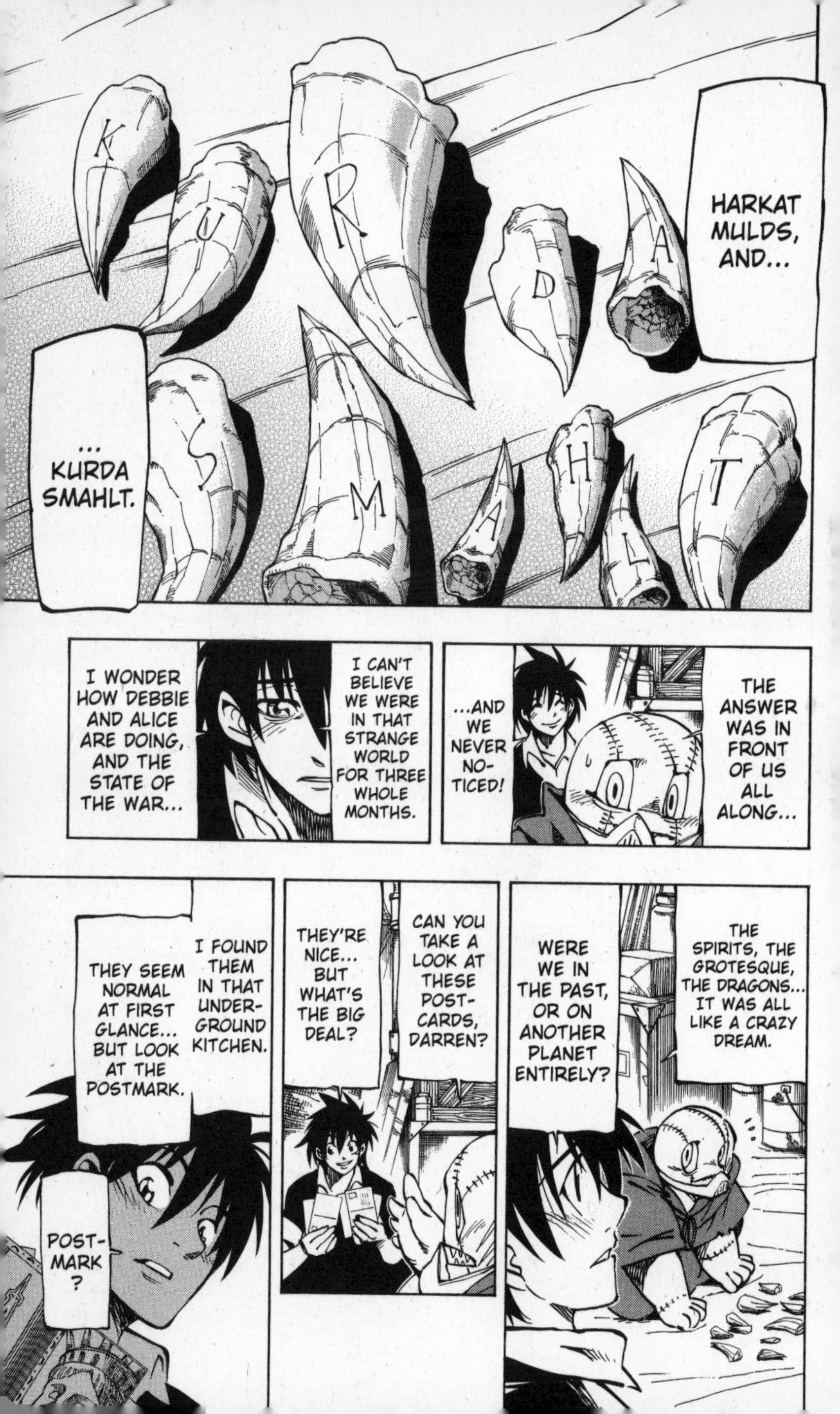
HARKAT MULDS, AND...
... KURDA SMAHLT.
THE ANSWER WAS IN FRONT OF US ALL ALONG...
...AND WE NEVER NOTICED!
I CAN'T BELIEVE WE WERE IN THAT STRANGE WORLD FOR THREE WHOLE MONTHS.
I WONDER HOW DEBBIE AND ALICE ARE DOING, AND THE STATE OF THE WAR...
THE SPIRITS, THE GROTESQUE, THE DRAGONS... IT WAS ALL LIKE A CRAZY DREAM.
WERE WE IN THE PAST, OR ON ANOTHER PLANET ENTIRELY?
CAN YOU TAKE A LOOK AT THESE POSTCARDS, DARREN?
THEY'RE NICE... BUT WHAT'S THE BIG DEAL?
I FOUND THEM IN THAT UNDERGROUND KITCHEN.
THEY SEEM NORMAL AT FIRST GLANCE... BUT LOOK AT THE POSTMARK.
POSTMARK?

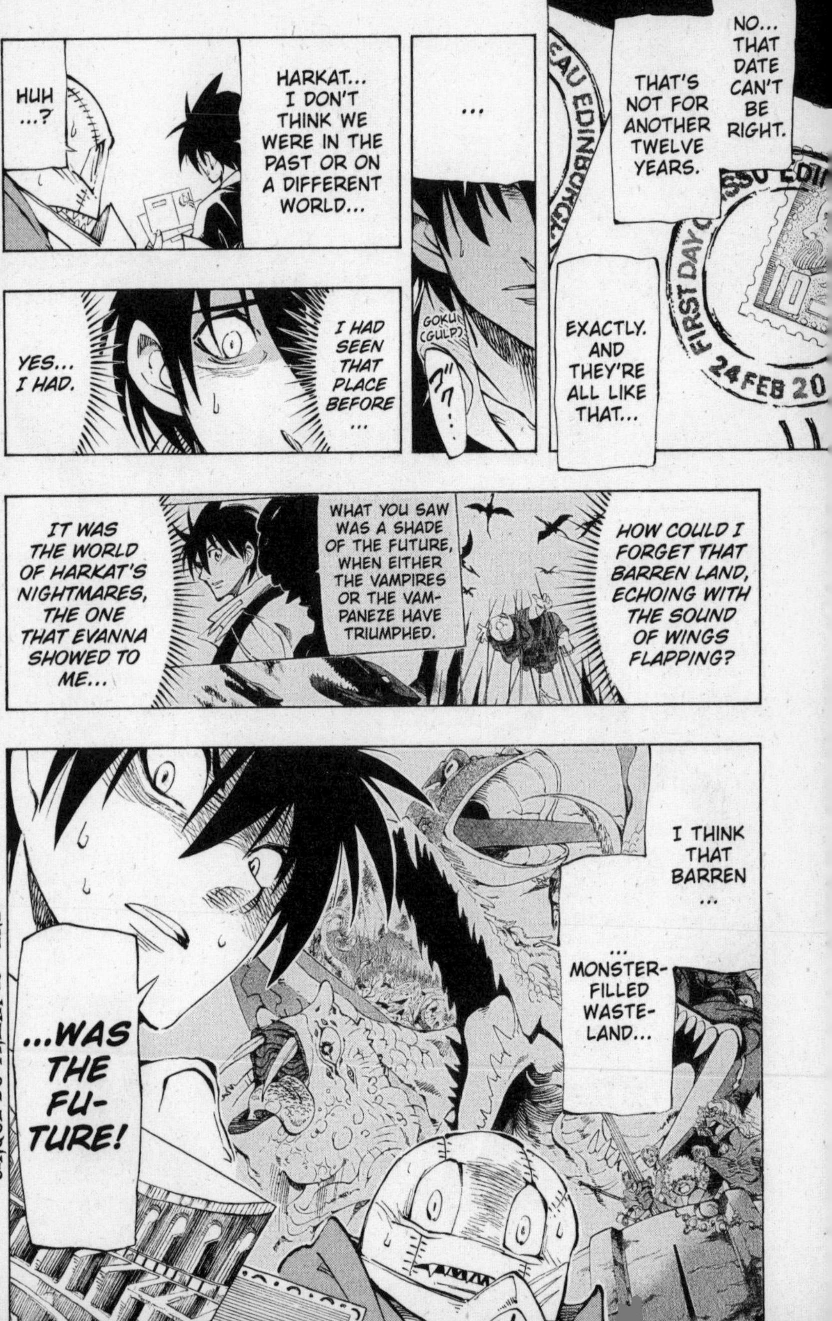
NO... THAT DATE CAN'T BE RIGHT.
THAT'S NOT FOR ANOTHER TWELVE YEARS.
24 FEB 20
EXACTLY. AND THEY'RE ALL LIKE THAT...
...
GOKU (GULP)
HARKAT... I DON'T THINK WE WERE IN THE PAST OR ON A DIFFERENT WORLD...
HUH ...?
I HAD SEEN THAT PLACE BEFORE ...
YES... I HAD.
HOW COULD I FORGET THAT BARREN LAND, ECHOING WITH THE SOUND OF WINGS FLAPPING?
WHAT YOU SAW WAS A SHADE OF THE FUTURE, WHEN EITHER THE VAMPIRES OR THE VAMPANEZE HAVE TRIUMPHED.
IT WAS THE WORLD OF HARKAT'S NIGHTMARES, THE ONE THAT EVANNA SHOWED TO ME...
I THINK THAT BARREN ...
... MONSTER-FILLED WASTE-LAND...
...WAS THE FUTURE!

CIRQUE DU FREAK 10 · END

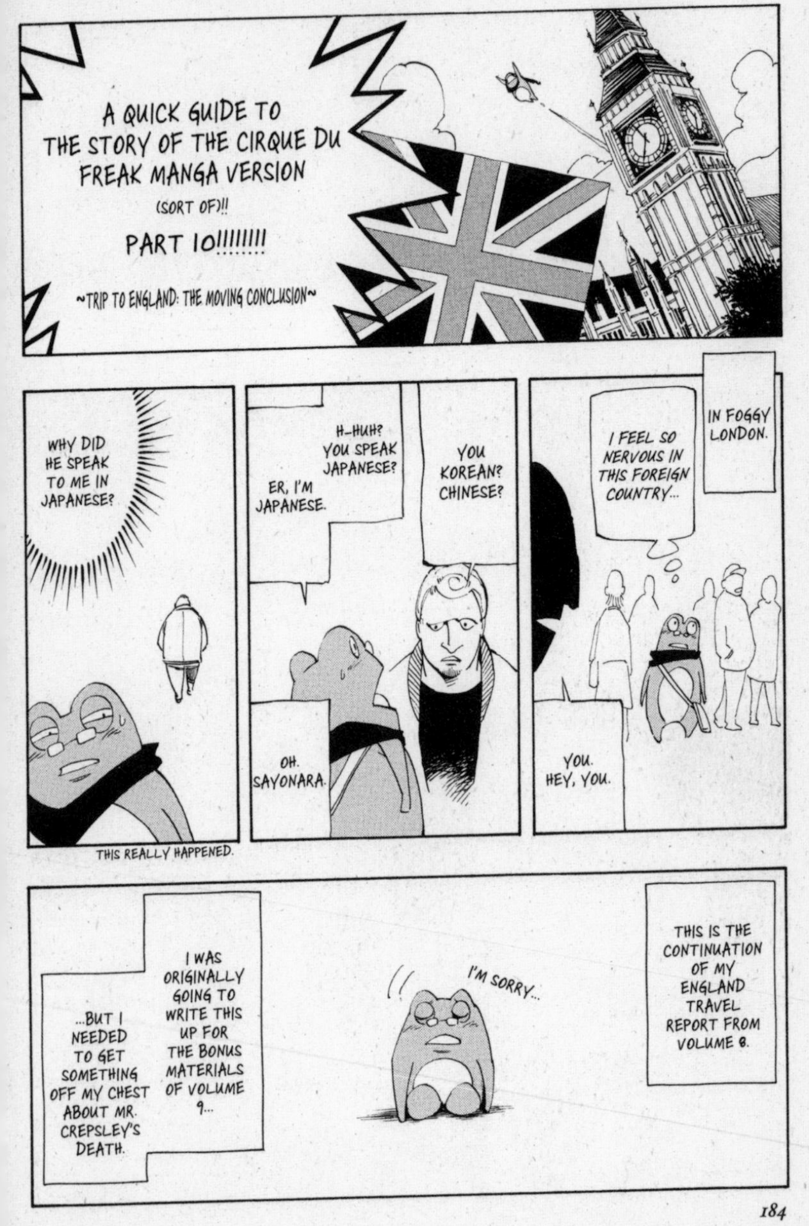
A QUICK GUIDE TO THE STORY OF THE CIRQUE DU FREAK MANGA VERSION
(SORT OF)!!
PART 10!!!!!!!!
~TRIP TO ENGLAND: THE MOVING CONCLUSION~
IN FOGGY LONDON.
I FEEL SO NERVOUS IN THIS FOREIGN COUNTRY...
YOU. HEY, YOU.
YOU KOREAN? CHINESE?
ER, I'M JAPANESE.
H-HUH? YOU SPEAK JAPANESE?
OH. SAYONARA.
WHY DID HE SPEAK TO ME IN JAPANESE?
THIS REALLY HAPPENED.
THIS IS THE CONTINUATION OF MY ENGLAND TRAVEL REPORT FROM VOLUME 8.
I'M SORRY...
I WAS ORIGINALLY GOING TO WRITE THIS UP FOR THE BONUS MATERIALS OF VOLUME 9...
...BUT I NEEDED TO GET SOMETHING OFF MY CHEST ABOUT MR. CREPSLEY'S DEATH.

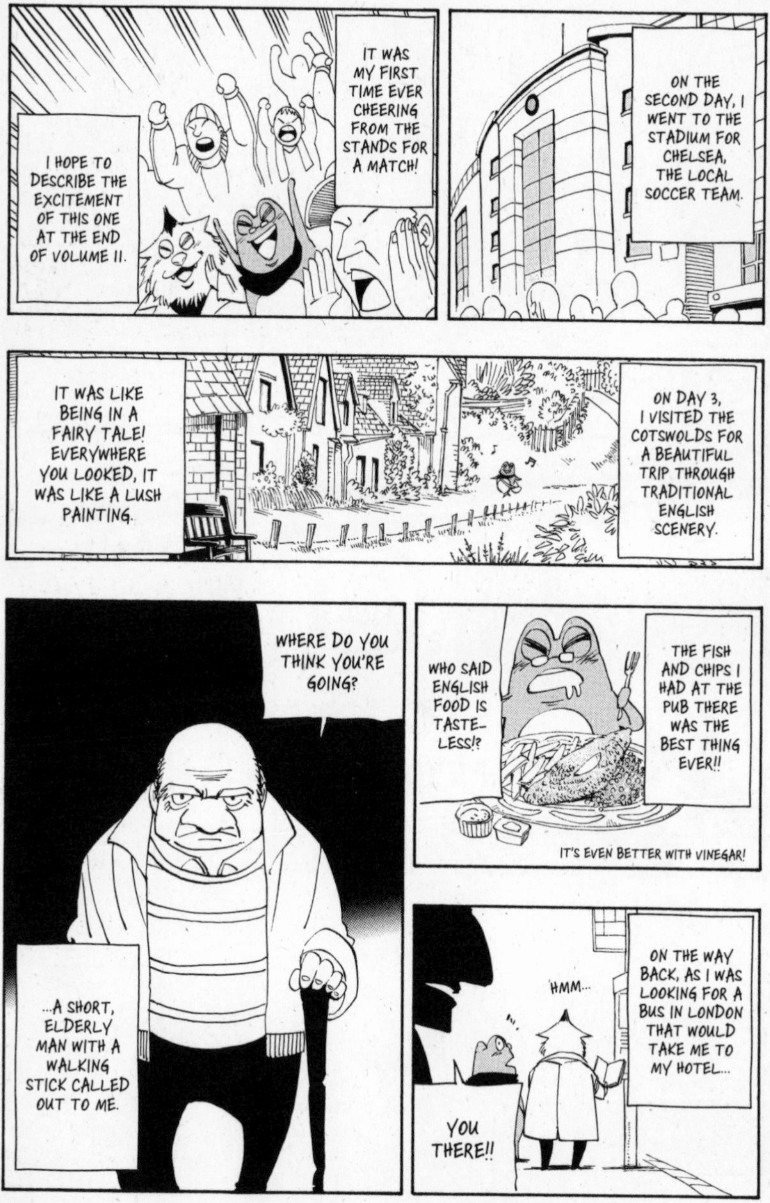
ON THE SECOND DAY, I WENT TO THE STADIUM FOR CHELSEA, THE LOCAL SOCCER TEAM.
IT WAS MY FIRST TIME EVER CHEERING FROM THE STANDS FOR A MATCH!
I HOPE TO DESCRIBE THE EXCITEMENT OF THIS ONE AT THE END OF VOLUME 11.
ON DAY 3, I VISITED THE COTSWOLDS FOR A BEAUTIFUL TRIP THROUGH TRADITIONAL ENGLISH SCENERY.
IT WAS LIKE BEING IN A FAIRY TALE! EVERYWHERE YOU LOOKED, IT WAS LIKE A LUSH PAINTING.
THE FISH AND CHIPS I HAD AT THE PUB THERE WAS THE BEST THING EVER!!
WHO SAID ENGLISH FOOD IS TASTE-LESS!?
IT'S EVEN BETTER WITH VINEGAR!
ON THE WAY BACK, AS I WAS LOOKING FOR A BUS IN LONDON THAT WOULD TAKE ME TO MY HOTEL...
HMM...
YOU THERE!!
WHERE DO YOU THINK YOU'RE GOING?
...A SHORT, ELDERLY MAN WITH A WALKING STICK CALLED OUT TO ME.

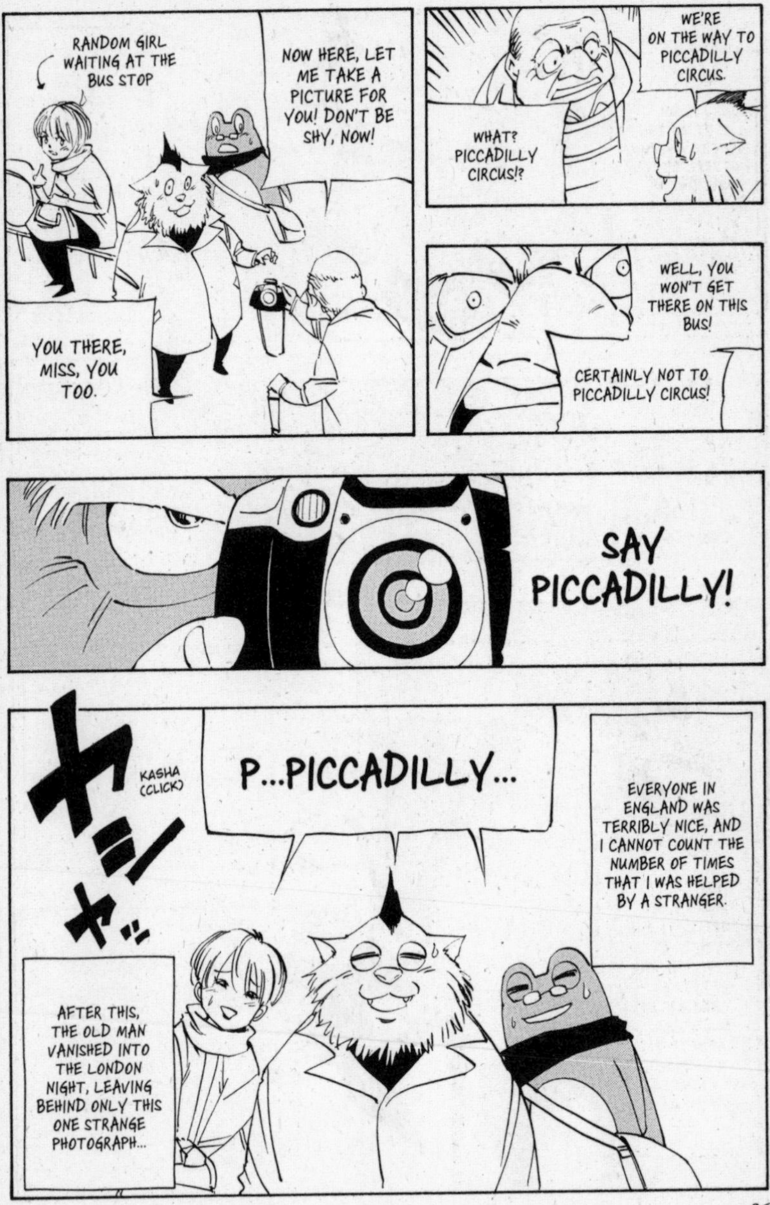
WE'RE ON THE WAY TO PICCADILLY CIRCUS.
WHAT? PICCADILLY CIRCUS!?
WELL, YOU WON'T GET THERE ON THIS BUS!
CERTAINLY NOT TO PICCADILLY CIRCUS!
NOW HERE, LET ME TAKE A PICTURE FOR YOU! DON'T BE SHY, NOW!
RANDOM GIRL WAITING AT THE BUS STOP
YOU THERE, MISS, YOU TOO.
SAY PICCADILLY!
EVERYONE IN ENGLAND WAS TERRIBLY NICE, AND I CANNOT COUNT THE NUMBER OF TIMES THAT I WAS HELPED BY A STRANGER.
P...PICCADILLY...
KASHA (CLICK)
AFTER THIS, THE OLD MAN VANISHED INTO THE LONDON NIGHT, LEAVING BEHIND ONLY THIS ONE STRANGE PHOTOGRAPH...

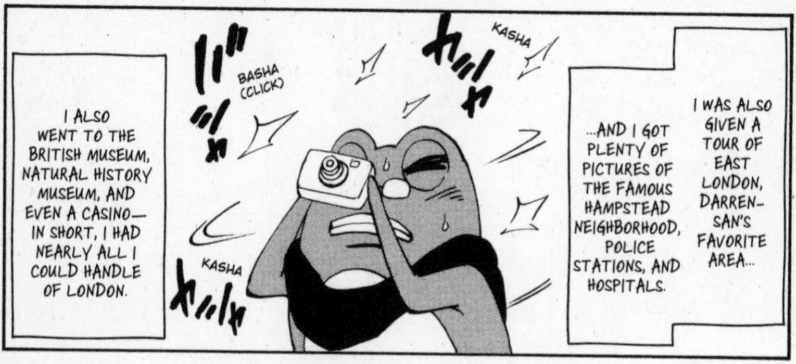
I WAS ALSO GIVEN A TOUR OF EAST LONDON, DARREN-SAN'S FAVORITE AREA...
...AND I GOT PLENTY OF PICTURES OF THE FAMOUS HAMPSTEAD NEIGHBORHOOD, POLICE STATIONS, AND HOSPITALS.
KASHA
BASHA (CLICK)
KASHA
I ALSO WENT TO THE BRITISH MUSEUM, NATURAL HISTORY MUSEUM, AND EVEN A CASINO—IN SHORT, I HAD NEARLY ALL I COULD HANDLE OF LONDON.

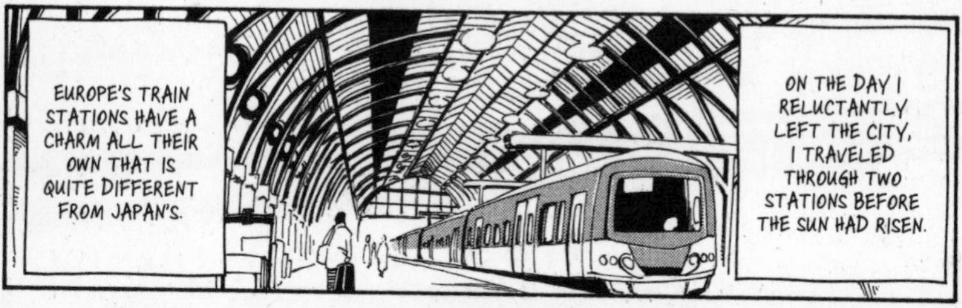
ON THE DAY I RELUCTANTLY LEFT THE CITY, I TRAVELED THROUGH TWO STATIONS BEFORE THE SUN HAD RISEN.
EUROPE'S TRAIN STATIONS HAVE A CHARM ALL THEIR OWN THAT IS QUITE DIFFERENT FROM JAPAN'S.

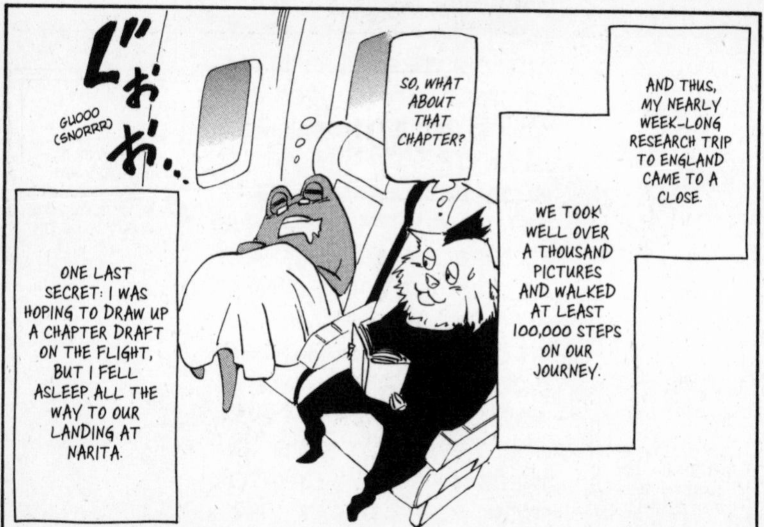
AND THUS, MY NEARLY WEEK-LONG RESEARCH TRIP TO ENGLAND CAME TO A CLOSE.
WE TOOK WELL OVER A THOUSAND PICTURES AND WALKED AT LEAST 100,000 STEPS ON OUR JOURNEY.
SO, WHAT ABOUT THAT CHAPTER?
GUOOO (SNORRR)
ONE LAST SECRET: I WAS HOPING TO DRAW UP A CHAPTER DRAFT ON THE FLIGHT, BUT I FELL ASLEEP ALL THE WAY TO OUR LANDING AT NARITA.

The End

MESSAGE FROM
TAKAHIRO ARAI

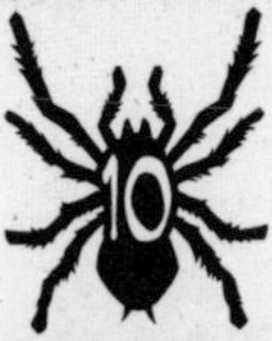
10

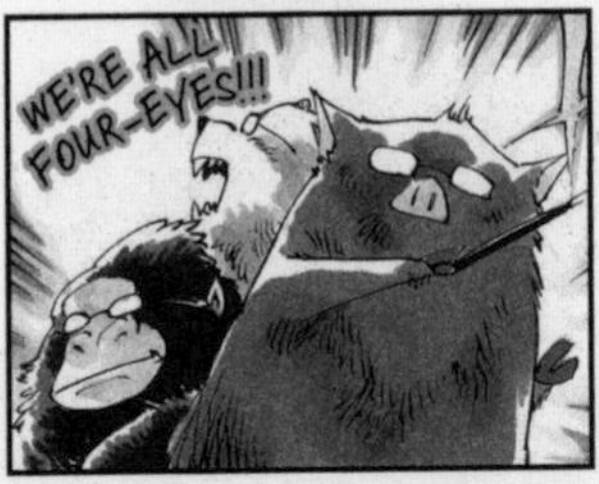
WE'RE ALL FOUR-EYES!!!

I HAVE ENDLESS GRATITUDE FOR THE STAFF THAT PUTS TOGETHER SUCH INCREDIBLE WORK, WEEK IN AND WEEK OUT. A-KUN HAS BEEN THE BACKBONE OF MY OPERATION FROM THE VERY START, WITH HIS VERSATILITY IN ALL MATTERS FROM SCREENTONES TO BACKGROUNDS. T-KUN, THE NEW GUY, WHOSE EXCELLENT MANNERS AND WILL TO SUCCEED CONTINUE TO IMPROVE HIS GAME. AND MY BROTHER, JUNYA, WHOSE IMAGINATION HAS HELPED TO CRAFT THE LOOK OF THE *CIRQUE DU FREAK* MANGA WORLD BETTER THAN I EVER COULD. WHAT YOU SEE ON THESE PAGES IS CRAFTED FROM THE SWEAT AND BLOOD OF THESE THREE FINE GENTLEMEN.

CIRQUE DU FREAK

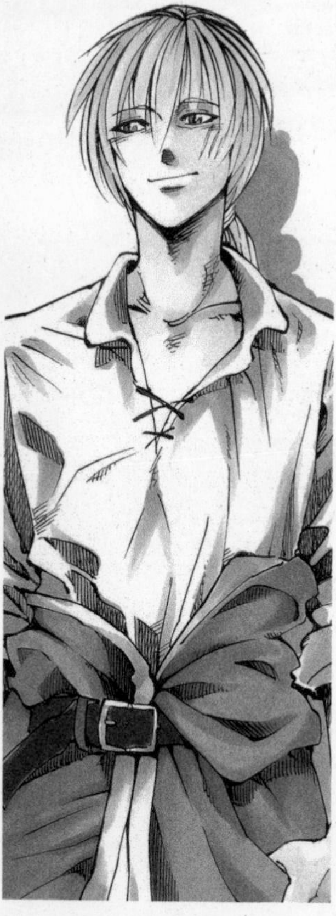

CIRQUE DU FREAK ⑩

DARREN SHAN
TAKAHIRO ARAI

Translation: Stephen Paul　　•　　Lettering: AndWorld Design
Art Direction: Hitoshi SHIRAYAMA
Original Cover Design: Shigeru ANZAI + Bay Bridge Studio

DARREN SHAN Vol. 10 © 2008 by Darren Shan, Takahiro ARAI. All
rights reserved. Original Japanese edition published in Japan in 2008
by Shogakukan Inc., Tokyo. Artworks reproduction rights in U.S.A. and
Canada arranged with Shogakukan Inc. through Tuttle-Mori Agency,
Inc., Tokyo.

English translation © 2011 Darren Shan

Yen Press
Hachette Book Group
237 Park Avenue, New York, NY 10017

www.HachetteBookGroup.com
www.YenPress.com

Yen Press is an imprint of Hachette Book Group, Inc. The Yen Press
name and logo are trademarks of Hachette Book Group, Inc.

First Yen Press Edition: July 2011

ISBN: 978-0-316-17607-1

10 9 8 7 6 5 4 3 2 1

BVG

Printed in the United States of America